THE MARTHA ODYSSEY

The Martha Odyssey

by **Bonny Gable**

The Martha Odyssey
Copyright © 2024 by Bonny Gable

All rights reserved. This book or any portion thereof may not be reproduced or used in any manner whatsoever without the express written permission of the publisher, except for the use of brief quotations in a book review.

Printed in the United States of America

Luminare Press
442 Charnelton St.
Eugene, OR 97401
www.luminarepress.com

LCCN: 2023923021
ISBN: 979-8-88679-446-5

*For my grandmother, who inspired my love for music
And for Bill, my soulmate and loving cheerleader*

PRELUDE

Fermata

May 28, 1931

"You're not dead."

The words cascade from my lips in a whisper. Fifteen years vanish in an instant as sweeping visions unfold in my consciousness. Two creatures aloft on rushing wind, sailing through tall grasses, trees that sing, crystal snowdrifts, and finally a cold black night. Cutting through darkness, arms clasped tightly, clinging to a life saved only by letting go. The press of lips with the urgency of an unknown fate that lies in the beyond. That beyond is now, this moment.

I'm sitting on an old iron bench along one of the serpentine paths that curl through the soft green lawn of Martha Washington College. I'm here to say goodbye to the old girl as she sings her swan song. Soon her doors will close on a thousand echoes of girls who frolicked in her halls, entrusting their hopes and dreams to her promise.

I was such a girl once. The dreams I brought through the Martha's doors for nurture seem naïve given the reality that eventually ensued. They were fantasies I'd invented. I wonder now whether anyone can truly imagine what lies beyond an unopened door.

Would they open it if they could?

The wild kaleidoscope of my days spent here is still spinning in my mind. I rise from the bench wondering if the person discovering me here is real or an apparition.

"No, Beatrice. I'm not dead."

Sonata

A Cappella

September 2, 1915

"Here's another lost soul."

A voice from behind startled me from my daydream. I turned to see a severe-looking lady in a chambray dress grasping the handle of a door I'd not heard swing open. Standing on the sprawling front veranda of Preston Hall, I had been awestruck by the lush green lawn dotted with manicured shrubbery that lay below it. At the lawn's center, a frothy plume sprang up from a dazzling octagonal fountain while an ornate iron fence neatly defined the perimeter, keeping all the grandeur neatly tucked within the campus of Martha Washington College. Beyond the fence, I had gazed up and down Main Street, a wide avenue appearing to stretch for miles and lined with grand houses or fancy shops. Even the imposing Abingdon Town Hall sat directly across from the campus. Nothing was familiar to me in this corner of southwestern Virginia, but I would need to call it home, for now.

"Ma'am?" My sputtered reply confirmed her assessment of me.

Thrusting an impatient hand toward the interior, she ushered me inside a wide vestibule, where I peered out over a sea of hats. My ungainly height stood me a good six to eight inches above the other girls, placing my gaze on their toppings of felt, feathers, and bows. Weaving my way through the chattering flock, I came to rest beside a magnificent grandfather clock that must have been a good nine feet tall. Comforted by a face I had to actually look up to see, I perched myself there. As the eldest child in a large family, I'd learned to create my own solitude in the midst of chaos. My thoughts drifted as I admired the craftsmanship of the fine clock.

"Good to see a like-minded soul at last," a voice chirped from below. I looked down into a pair of sparkling green eyes set above a dimpled grin.

"Excuse me?"

"Chopin. My favorite," said the grin, pointing to the sheet music peeping from the leather satchel slung over my shoulder.

"You're a pianist, too?"

"I wish. No, just an admirer. I'm here to study Expression, so I can give Mary Pickford and Theda Bara some competition when I get to New York."

I was trying to pretend to know who Theda Bara was when the tinkling of a bell turned everyone's attention to a large portal in the far corner.

"Girls, girls! Please follow me into the East Parlor." A distinguished-looking woman in a black taffeta dress had taken charge of the gaggle of wide-eyed girls, ushering us along as if conducting a cattle drive. "We have refreshments laid out for you there, which I'm sure will be welcome after your long journeys."

I had thought the vestibule sumptuous, but in no way could it rival the grandeur of the East Parlor. The walls were covered in brilliant emerald damask and lined along the bottom with a rich walnut wood paneling, which I later learned was called wainscoting. Silky drapes framed windows that seemed as tall as the sky. The ceiling was covered in decorative pressed tin with a huge crystal chandelier hanging from its center. I was a bit breathless.

"My, but you're gawking." A luscious green eye winked up at me. "It's a lot to take in, but there's no reason we shouldn't feel right at home. Girls with sense enough to love Chopin deserve pretty things."

Already seated around the magnificent room was a scattering of young women, smartly dressed in colorful afternoon dresses. We new arrivals created a dreary contrast in drab traveling outfits, our uniform of initiation into our new existence. We sipped tea and nibbled cookies, feeling the eyes of these women upon us: appraising, studying, sizing us up with practiced skill. Perhaps the lady in black really was conducting a cattle drive. Just then she appeared again, brandishing her tinkling bell.

"Good afternoon, ladies. I am Mrs. Long, wife of your college president, Dr. Samuel D. Long. I preside here as First Lady of Martha Washington College and also Headmistress. On behalf of our faculty, I welcome you all to our fine institute for young women. Our purpose is illustrated in the eloquent words of Colonel John Arthur Campbell, president of our founding Board of Trustees: 'As the county in which we reside is named after our illustrious General George Washington, so shall this school for women be graced with the name of his esteemed wife, whose domestic virtues made her a perfect model of female excellence.' We strive to mold all our young ladies to that model." Mrs. Long gestured above the fireplace mantle, directing our eyes to a large portrait of Martha Washington.

I wasn't sure I wished to be "molded" to anyone's model, no matter how excellent. I had come with a single purpose: to make my place in a world beyond my tiny hometown tucked into the Appalachian Mountains. And music was my ticket. It would lead me into a far more fascinating existence I knew was out there waiting for me. But while Mrs. Long prattled on at length, regaling us with the history of the school in an obviously well-worn speech, I assessed the young women around me. Despite my ambition and determination, I felt anxious, unsure of my place among so many strange young ladies. I'd been told they hailed from places much grander than mine. Not only large cities in Virginia such as Lynchburg, Roanoke, and our great capitol, Richmond, but also nearby states like North Carolina, Tennessee, and Kentucky. Some came from as far away as Texas, Louisiana, Mississippi, and Arkansas. My mind raced with questions: What were they like? What did they study here? and most of all, How would I fit in?

"Martha girls are strong because there is strength in numbers." Mrs. Long seemed to be on a new tack and I refocused on her words. "Each of you will thrive with the guidance and help of a selected young lady who has trod the path before you. Senior girls, please show your cards."

My eyes were instantly drawn to a silk-clad girl sitting directly across from me. A captivating smile bloomed on her lovely face, framed by hair the color of shimmering corn silk. To my surprise, the girl held a card emblazoned with "Beatrice Earle Damron" rendered in a bold calligraphy. As instructed, I obediently traversed the thick Persian carpet to sit beside my assigned "mother."

"Good afternoon, Beatrice. I'm Varina Armstrong. Welcome to the Martha."

I found myself looking into a pair of startlingly blue eyes. Her smile was warm, but the magnetic intrigue expressed in her face seemed to be mixed with the slightest bit of cool calculation. Most likely I imagined it, prompted by anxiety. I towered a good head and a half above her, but her regal pose on the settee left me feeling as if I had drunk Alice's Wonderland shrinking potion.

"Thank you?" I managed in little more than a raspy whisper.

"Why, yes, you may," she laughed, although not unkindly. Still, I shrank even more until she gently took my hand. "You don't know it, but you've struck Martha gold." I finally managed the expected smile. "Although, this is a new experience for me, too. I've never mothered a girl from 'Clintwood' before." Did the name of my hometown have a slight curdling effect on her tongue? My anxiety was working overtime. "Where exactly is that?"

"It's in Virginia, about fifty miles or so northwest of Abingdon. In Dickenson County."

"A mountain girl then! How delightful."

"I . . . suppose it could be," I replied, evoking another soft laugh from her.

"We'll just have to make sure it is."

Finding it difficult to relax under her steady gaze, I wondered if any of the delight would be mine. Although too well-mannered to allow her face to reveal her thoughts, I was seized with doubt that she considered me proper Martha material. I was silent, but longed to tell her, "No matter. I'll only be here for a year." Surely, I could be tolerated for that long.

"Now girls, please return to the vestibule, where my assistant, Rena, will distribute room keys. Your luggage has been ported to your doors." Mrs. Long had resumed her command of the room. "And as you settle into your new home, remember: there is no prouder undertaking than to become a true Martha Girl!"

WITH THREE SISTERS, I HAD NEVER HAD A ROOM OF MY OWN. Eager to see my new living quarters, I waited impatiently for my turn at the room assignment station.

"Beatrice E. Damron, room sixty," Rena barked as she slapped a key on the table in front of me. I picked it up and waited for further instructions, but she was silent.

"Which building is it in?"

"Ha! Think a freshman's gonna live in one of the fancy new buildings, do you? Up these stairs here, all the way to the top." She resumed her work and I turned to go. "And good luck keepin' warm this winter," she added with a delighted hoot, taking me down a peg further.

Later I learned the depth of my faux pas. Freshmen were confined to rooms in Preston Hall, the college's oldest structure, built in 1832. Litchfield Hall to the west and Mariah Cooper Hall to the east, built only two and three years earlier, contained brand new sleeping apartments reserved for upperclassmen only. I shouldered my music satchel and began the climb up several long, curving stairways to my room on the third floor. A childhood spent roaming hills, climbing trees, and riding horses had left me more fit than most of my comrades. I swept past several huffing and puffing girls, finally arriving at room number sixty. I was coaxing my key into the stubborn door lock when a high-pitched squeal erupted to my right.

"Oh my god, we're next-door neighbors!" Green eyes sparkled even larger than before from a head of bouncing amber curls rushing toward me. "We never got a chance to introduce each other. I'm Ruby Pearl Atkins."

"Beatrice Damron. But everyone calls me Bea."

"Oh, like honey bee. That's sweet. Sweet as honey," she winked. I didn't know quite what to say to that, so I uttered a soft laugh.

"Ruby Pearl is a pretty name."

"Yeah, my mom loves jewelry. But you can just call me Ruby. Until I get famous, that is. Then I'm going to drop the 'Atkins' and be known as 'Ruby Pearl,' star of stage and screen."

"Sounds like a great plan."

"Well, I'll let you get settled in. But come see me before dinner. I'm so glad we're neighbors!" She took off to her room in lilting skips, reminding me of a frolicking baby goat.

After another minute of twisting and turning the key, the lock finally released its hold and with relief I pushed open the door. I took only a couple of steps into my new abode when I heard a loud click from above. Instantly a swift vertical wind made a terrible swooshing sound as a sudden violent storm rained down upon my head, stifling my scream. Utterly stunned, I instinctively gasped for air. I looked down at my clothes, certain they were drenched, but everything was dry. Just as I realized that I could breathe, footsteps thundered behind me.

"I heard you scream, what's—" Ruby stopped short in my doorway, followed by two or three other girls straining to peer in.

Bewildered in a sea of calico, I faced them, speechless. A huge pile of knotted fabric swatches surrounded my feet. Torn scraps draped my shoulders and clung to my hat. One random strip hung limply over my forehead at a ridiculous angle. The girls behind Ruby began to giggle.

"Don't you girls have luggage to unpack?" Ruby barked as she shooed them away. She stepped into my room and shut the door in their faces.

I let myself be led to the bed, where I sat numbly as Ruby peeled away the stray scraps. She climbed on my trunk to disengage the makeshift release mechanism that had been triggered by the door, along with the cardboard box that had been painstakingly stuffed with the calico bomb. Then she deftly cleared the floor of the remaining detritus of my humiliation.

"Hey, I bet they select only a really special girl for a distinctive welcome like this," Ruby spoke a little too brightly as she worked. When the box was full, she tossed it into the hallway and out of my sight, then came to sit beside me. "It's like an initiation, you know? A big honor! If this doesn't make you a true 'Martha Girl,' I don't know what would."

She smiled and took my hand, and I couldn't help but smile back at my feisty little rescuer. "Thank you, Ruby. I'm glad we're neighbors, too."

Dinner that evening was an elaborate affair. The dining hall was as formally appointed as the parlor, if not quite as sumptuous. Filled with round tables clad in white linen cloths with fresh flowers at their centers, it felt more like a royal banquet than ordinary dinner on a Thursday evening. I longed for Ruby's company, but we were required to sit with our assigned "mother" for this first meal.

"There you are, Beatrice," Varina beckoned from across the room. Her voice came from a table situated in the corner between two large windows, where she sat flanked by two girls on each side. I had changed into my best Sunday frock, but gazing at the five dresses of fine linen and silk made me feel terribly plain. As I reached the table, she chirped her welcome. "We're so glad you're finally here!"

"Yes," another girl added, "we were worried you might have drowned or something."

Her choice of words made me internally flinch, but I returned her smile and involuntarily reached for my water glass. The other girls exchanged not-so-furtive glances. I had not yet learned that it was improper to make a move before the hostess, but Varina graciously ignored their reaction.

"I'd say you've not had a chance to meet anyone outside of your freshman group. This is Ethel St. John and Laura Mae Lewis, and to my left, Bessie Durham and Miriam Tuttle." We exchanged polite hellos, although, strangely, it felt more like facing a judge and jury. "I've mothered each one of them, so they've all had the benefit of my tutelage." The girls exchanged huge smiles among themselves, clearly proud to have shared this privilege.

"You're so lucky, Beatrice," cooed Laura Mae. "Yes, so lucky"; "Couldn't have been better," the others chimed their assent while Varina beamed.

"Varina grew up in Richmond and she knows absolutely everything about anything," Bessie added as the fawning continued unchecked. A waiter brought a tray of plated salads and began to place one in front of each of us. No one made a move to begin eating so I quietly waited.

"I understand you're here to study music, Beatrice. Piano, is that right?" Varina queried, though I sensed she already knew quite a bit about me.

"Yes, that's right."

"You two have the same major, Varina! You've never mothered another pianist before," Miriam interjected with excessive zeal. Turning to me, she added, "Varina is excellent, Beatrice. A master. Wait until you hear her play."

"I look forward to it."

"You won't have to wait long," offered Ethel. "Professor Zeisberg is holding a master class first thing tomorrow morning. All the music students will perform, even freshmen. That is," she added with a dubious smile, "if you have something prepared."

"I do, actually. Mrs. Counts taught me to always be ready for any opportunity to play." I wanted to quell any notion that performing for a master class would rattle me.

"Mrs. Counts?"

"My piano teacher. From back home."

"Mrs. Counts," Ethel repeated. "What an adorable name for a music teacher." She tilted her head with a faint smile, failing to mask the sarcasm gleaming in her eyes.

"I imagine Beatrice is prepared for all eventualities," Varina smiled at me as she flipped open her napkin with flare and placed it on her lap. I saw this was the signal for the rest of us to do the same. "And where is 'back home' again?" She kindly steered the conversation in a new direction. "I seem to recall you telling me it's somewhere in the Virginia mountains?"

"Clintwood. It's a town in Dickenson County."

This elicited blank stares from the other girls, but Varina had picked up her fork so we all could proceed with eating. The munching of lettuce filled the silence for a few moments, then Varina circled back to the earlier line of conversation.

"Performance opportunities here are mostly these master classes, along with semester recitals. Most music-making takes place in practice rooms, where we hone our skills in private."

"I'll be playing some of the time in the voice studio. I'm required to accompany some of the voice students for their lessons."

Varina's eyebrows shot up in surprise, her single moment of lost composure.

"Required? Why would you be 'required' to do that?"

"To help pay my tuition."

For a moment everyone was speechless, but Ethel was quick to find her voice.

"So, you'll provide a service in exchange for reduced tuition. In other words, you'll be 'working'?"

I looked around the table. The expression on everyone's face told me none of them had ever endured such a burden.

"Yes. But I'm quite used to it. I've played for church services for years, and accompanied singers for school programs." They all exchanged uncomfortable glances. "It helps keep the fingers nimble," I added, wiggling my digits in the air. My lame attempt at humor was met with nervous laughter and polite smiles, plus a not-quite-disguised pitying look from Varina. My hands sank to my lap and my eyes locked onto a single lettuce leaf floating in dressing. Thankfully, the next course was served and their interest in me vanished along with the salad plates. I ate the remainder of the meal in silence, listening to the idle chatter of my so-called betters.

Fantaisie-Impromptu

The following morning, I stood in the doorway of the Litchfield Hall auditorium, gazing at the stage on the opposite end. On its left side, a polished oak podium awaited speeches from the faculty members seated behind it in a tight cluster. In its right corner sat a double rank pipe organ, its shimmering brass pipes forming a crested backdrop that nearly touched the ceiling. But best of all, at its center stood an exquisite rare jewel: a seven-foot Steinway grand piano. I had never seen, let alone touched one. Mrs. Counts was unable to afford one for herself but had raved about playing them at Oberlin Conservatory. They had resonance like no other piano and were considered among the very best in the world. I was imagining my fingers running over its silky ivory keys when a printed bulletin thrust into my hand forced me to pull my eyes away.

At the very top of the bulletin was listed Professor Francis Josef Zeisberg, director of the Conservatory of Music, graduate of Royal Pedagogical Seminary in Habelschwerdt, Germany. His credentials were impressive: he'd mastered piano, violin, organ, and viola, and was a noted composer with published pieces for piano, voice, and organ. I contemplated what an honor, and a challenge, it must be to study under this accomplished man from Europe. Next listed was George Hudson Moore, assistant director of the conservatory and instructor of piano, organ, and harmony, followed by Charles Park, instructor of piano and harmony. Both were graduates of the College of Music in Cincinnati, Ohio. As a freshman, I would be assigned to one of them for my piano lessons.

Listed as director of the School of Vocal Music was Miss Sadie Le Grande, graduate of Women's College of Richmond, Virginia, with additional study under numerous experts in New York City and even Munich, Germany. This is who I would be working for, a very demanding instructor, so I'd heard. Hopefully, she'd find my playing satisfactory.

I took a seat several rows back, not wanting to appear too anxious. But any apprehension about performing for all these new people was far outweighed by the chance to run my fingers over those superb Steinway keys. I spotted Varina sitting in the first row chatting with Ethel and Bessie, who I'd learned were voice majors. It was obvious they resented the prospect of a student accompanist, and I dreaded their first lessons. Luckily, Mr. Moore or Mr. Park would accompany singers for master class. A sudden hush came over the hall as Professor Zeisberg took the podium.

"Velcome, young ladies, to our first master class of the 1915–16 academic year." He was an imposing figure, tall and broad shouldered, with a thick shock of black hair and a silver-laced beard. Heavy black brows hooded his piercing dark eyes. Eyes that looked as if they might be alternately gentle and intimidating. He spoke with a comfortable authority befitting his splendid reputation. "I look forward to cultivating promising new talent, as vell as helping many who have vorked hard in years past to put a crowning touch on deir labors. So, let us begin. Who vould like to step forward as first performer?"

A collective holding of breath was felt throughout the room, but only for a few moments.

"I would be delighted to play," came a voice from the front and Varina Armstrong marched forward. I had to admire her pluck as I watched her command the stage like she apparently commanded the energy wherever she went. She settled her sheet music on the rack above the keyboard as Bessie dutifully placed herself at the ready to turn pages. Launching into Liszt's "La Campanella" with gusto, she relished delivering the rapid runs, trills, and extreme leaps that traveled the entire length of the keyboard. It was a flashy piece that arrested rapt attention from everyone in the room, apparently her aim. She was excellent and everything her doting devotees had said she was.

When she brought the piece to a resounding end that prompted exuberant applause, it was plain to see she was the darling of this musical cadre. But before she left the stage, she fixed a smiling gaze directly on me for a long moment. It seemed to be her message that I was fortunate to have such a musical mother to navigate me through this year. Then again, I wondered if it was a decree of what I would have to accomplish if I were to survive.

Bessie volunteered to go next and remained on stage to sing a selection from Schubert lieder in a sweet if somewhat frail soprano. No doubt much of her lesson time would be consumed with breath support exercises, all the easier for me. She was the academic dean's daughter, so I imagined none of her professors dealt too harshly with her. What a pity if her potential was really left to languish like that. But her cherub-faced prettiness would garner her a rich husband and a prominent place in a church choir as soloist. Probably the exact career to which she aspired.

Next was a quite good organ performance of a Bach prelude and fugue, followed by more pianists interspersed with several singers, concluding with Ethel's tedious rendition of an aria by Puccini. As the lone freshman piano student, I felt it only proper to let all the others go before me. Then, after a torturous hour of itching to get my hands on that magnificent piano, I finally had my turn.

I was halfway to the Steinway when I realized my sheet music was still lying in my seat. I didn't need it, so I kept walking, thrilled to finally be taking my place at the grand instrument. "Lead with your best," I could hear Mrs. Counts say as I placed my fingers on the keys for Chopin's "Fantaisie-Impromptu," also my favorite. I took a deep breath and began the opening chords and arpeggios.

But I quickly grew alarmed when they didn't have their usual power. My fingers felt as if they were tapping tiny bricks. And worse, when my foot pressed the soft pedal to play the treble runs, I felt the entire keyboard jump and actually shift under my fingers. I stopped short in a panic, my hands hovering over the keys. Later I would recall Mrs. Counts telling me about the soft pedal on a grand piano, actually called the una corda pedal. It caused the hammer rail inside the piano to shift to the right, allowing the hammers to strike one less string than the usual three. That shift not only softened the sound, it changed its tone and color. In my excitement to finally play a Steinway grand, I had totally forgotten this explanation, but nothing could have prepared me for the way this felt under my fingers. The entire action of the keyboard was completely different from any I had ever played. Stiffer, more robust. More demanding. A far cry from cheap anonymous uprights with loose rattling keys.

I shook off my alarm and began again, commanding the extra strength into my fingers that had lain dormant playing lesser instruments. Soon I had the keyboard's stout action under control and I began to soar in my usual fashion. Eventually I became so absorbed in the music, my awareness of everything else fell away. When I'd concluded the piece, I sat still for a long moment letting the final strains echo in my head.

Unexpected enthusiastic applause erupted and snapped me out of my trance. I had never liked taking bows—they seemed to spoil the beauty of the performing experience—but I forced myself to stand and bend at the waist. A couple of students in the middle rows stood as they clapped, which seemed strange, but they had beaming smiles on their faces and I gave them a nod. As I returned to my seat, Professor Moore walked to the podium.

"Thank you, students, for these inaugural performances of our new academic year. But as we have a special announcement to make today, we are foregoing critiques." Mr. Moore paused as relieved mutterings scattered through the audience. "A fond patron of Martha Washington College, and of music, has seen fit to sponsor an unprecedented educational opportunity for two deserving students. With this unique sponsorship, one piano student and one voice student will be granted the means to further their musical training beyond the Martha's doors. We are grateful for this patronage, so to ensure we make the Martha proud, care will be taken to determine the recipients of this good fortune. In the spring we will hold a musical competition, open to any Martha music student in good standing. The two winners will be awarded a full scholarship to study music at the Peabody Conservatory of Music in Baltimore, Maryland."

Instantly the auditorium was alive with excited chatter. Faculty seated onstage looked on, beaming like proud parents. The ecstatic buzz continued until a hand shot up from the front row.

"Professor Moore," Varina called out, sounding oddly alarmed. "When you said 'any student in good standing,' surely you meant upperclassmen?"

"No, actually, the competition is open to any music student in good standing, from freshman on up. The conservatory's aim is to produce professional musicians; they're looking for talent, skill, and aptitude suitable for that path, regardless of class rank."

"Well, then who will adjudicate this competition? How will you ensure that the judging is impartial?"

"The conservatory will send two of their own faculty from Baltimore to adjudicate. I assure you their decision will be fair and unbiased. To any who wish to enter this competition, our faculty here at Martha Washington extend our very best wishes." Mr. Moore left the podium, signaling the end of the class.

Oblivious to the rustle of exiting students, I sat very still with my private thoughts. With such an award I wouldn't have to settle for the lone year of education my father had begrudgingly granted me. And the possibility to extend my schooling through my own efforts made the prospect even more glorious. But entering this competition would be a gargantuan undertaking. The rivalry for such an extraordinary opportunity would be fierce and I was just a freshman from a small mountain town that no one had even heard of.

The whispers and murmurs became a full roar as we filed out of Litchfield Hall. I was at the door about to make my escape when someone grabbed my elbow. I turned to see the two girls who had given me a standing ovation.

"Sorry to startle you, but we didn't want you to get away without telling you how much we enjoyed your performance. I'm Saluda French and this is Hazel Newberry."

"Oh, hello. And, uh, thank you." Dumbstruck, I stared at their smiling faces, then remembered their impressive performances. "I enjoyed your singing, too. Both of you. Beautiful voices."

"You're so kind. You're new here—Beatrice, right? And I understand you'll be our accompanist. What a treat that will be, Hazel!"

"We were a bit worried when we heard a student accompanist would handle the lessons," Hazel confessed. "But now those fears are completely laid to rest."

"Of course," Saluda concurred. "I've never heard such a glorious interpretation of that Chopin work. And totally from memory, too! Your first Martha master class was a triumph."

"After a rather rough start, poor dear." Varina had suddenly appeared at my side. "Thank goodness adrenaline kicked in and you managed to survive after all."

"She did much more than survive, Varina."

"Come now, Saluda, you singers are so forgiving. Bea understands that as her mother, I'm responsible for keeping her on her toes. But of course, voice majors aren't held to such high standards, so I understand your being so soft."

Saluda bristled, her eyes like daggers. "One lesson under Miss Le Grande's grueling demands would have you begging for mercy. And hobble that sharp tongue."

"I'm sure all the standards here are very high," I interjected before tempers got out of hand. "But Varina's right about my rough start. It was my first time playing such an upscale piano, and it threw me off."

"Well, of course," Varina soothed. "Those of us who grew up with Steinways wouldn't have that problem. I'm sure you'll get used to it with enough practice."

The Martha Odyssey

"Well, you've got a Steinway now, Beatrice, and it didn't take you long to get used to it." Saluda patted my arm. "When the scholarship competition rolls around this spring, you'll prove you're master of it."

"Oh, I'm not ready for anything so grand," I said quickly, almost afraid they had read my thoughts. And surely Varina would be a contender, which created further awkwardness.

"Nonsense, you're as ready as anyone here. Besides—"

"No! No, really. It's . . . not for me." There was a moment of uncomfortable silence with Saluda looking bewildered; Varina remained neutral. "I appreciate the compliment, but . . . I just need to focus on my studies. But I look forward to working with you and Hazel in your voice lessons. And cheering you on in the vocal scholarship contest." We all exchanged smiles, so I hoped things were smoothed over. "You, too, Varina. For piano."

"Well," Varina replied evenly, "as a senior pianist I suppose it's my duty to enter. I'll just have to give it my best and see what happens." Varina looped her arm through mine. "Let's take a look at what's offered for lunch, shall we, Beatrice? Have a good afternoon, ladies," she nodded, leading me off to the dining hall.

THE EXCITEMENT HAD LEFT ME WITH NO APPETITE—HIGHLY unusual for me—so I made excuses about needing to write some letters and headed back to my room. Depositing my music on the desk, I plopped heavily on the bed, the events of the morning churning inside my mind. I felt restless, in need of air and exercise. Even more, I needed respite from the swirling sea of females that constantly surrounded me. Some solitude and time to savor my heady experience with the Steinway was in order.

I changed into a plain cotton shirtwaist and a drab split skirt, gratefully leaving the corset behind. I didn't know why I had to bother with one anyway, with nothing to hold in and not much to hold up. After swapping out my shoes for sturdy walking boots, I grabbed my straw hat and departed the stuffy room. I managed to escape unnoticed through a service entrance at the back of the ground floor. A narrow wooden walkway stretched to a graveled area flanked on either side by the same lush green as the front lawn of the college. Veering off into the grass at my left, I took one of the many stone serpentine paths that wound through the eight acres of college grounds. Walking into the east side of campus where it was shaded by a good number of trees, I began to breathe a bit easier.

Near the edge of the grounds, the path curled back in the direction of the front lawn. But just beyond it stood a thick cluster of tall white pines. Reminding me so much of the forests back home, I was drawn from the path into this cool inviting haven. Branches knit together into a fragrant canopy worked their enchantment on me, and soon the crunch of pine needles beneath my feet set up a hypnotic rhythm as I left the Martha campus behind.

There was no path here, so I meandered at will through this welcome bit of wilderness. I was no stranger to traversing the woods, being the daughter of a timber cruiser. Papa claimed it was strictly men's work, but sometimes he needed an extra hand on a local job and took me along. I'd help cordon off plots of trees and copy numbers for his calculations while he wielded his magical measuring tools. But mainly I loved the chance to roam the forests.

I hadn't traipsed all that far when up ahead I noticed brighter daylight seeping into the thicket. Heading for the light, I came to a clearing with a wooden post-and-rail fence. It encased a round enclosure joined at the far end to a large barn. The barn's wide lower sections jutted out beyond the fence on either side, and a narrow gable-roofed top section towered above the middle. To its left was a small building of raw wood resting on a four-foot stone foundation, with a stone chimney climbing above its tin roof at one end. Beyond it sat an open shed; a shiny black buggy and a large green wagon rested underneath.

Stepping up onto the lowest fence rung, I saw the barn's massive sliding doors standing wide open. I tried to peer inside when suddenly a thunderous pounding erupted from within. Out of the doorway burst a tornado of shimmering black, snorting and flying toward me with the power of a locomotive. I clung fast to the fence post, mesmerized by the most beautiful horse I had ever seen. It swerved to its right and continued the spirited gallop in a graceful loop, interspersing joyful leaps and bucks along the way. Momentarily appeased, it stopped short, giving me a better look. The gelding proudly raised his sculpted head and with pricked ears turned his wide eyes toward me. The snowy white blaze streaking his face was framed by a glossy black mane, and the shimmer of his coat made him appear clothed in black satin.

"Quite the magnificent creature, aren't you? And just so keen to show it off." He listened to my voice, ears twitching, then tossed his head up and down. I laughed, and as if to challenge my insolence he took off at a prancing trot. He circled clockwise, turned and cantered counterclockwise, then with a spritely kick of his back hooves the rascally beast took off, disappearing back into the barn.

I lingered for a minute thinking of Nutmeg, my own beloved sorrel mare and such a pet she came trotting straight to me when I called her name. We'd spent many blissful hours rambling through the fields and apple orchards back home. I missed her already, but this unexpected discovery of equine presence nearby helped me return to the Martha a little less homesick.

Buzz, buzz, buzz. I was faintly aware of the sound as I dozed in the breeze from the open window by my bed. My sleepless first night, the excitements of the day, and my walk in the woods made me captive to slumber and reluctant to lift my heavy eyelids. Then a soft thudding sound crept into my ears.

"Buzz, buzz, bees are a-buzz. Hey in there, open the door!" I blinked as I recognized Ruby's voice, then padded my bare feet across the room to let her in.

"There you are, the rare and exotic Honey Bea—I knew you existed!" Ruby sauntered in and made herself at home. "I've been looking for you all over."

"I've been right here, just catching a few winks."

"Where were you at lunch? You were the talk of the dining hall!"

"Me? Why?"

"Your performance this morning, of course. All the music girls were raving on and on. How you made the piano roar, that they'd never heard a freshman play like that. They said you could rival Mr. Moore, whoever he is."

"He's the organ master here, and I'm certainly not his rival."

"They also said you could play circles around Varina Armstrong, a *senior* piano student. Isn't she the one they assigned as your mother?"

"Yes, and she's an exceptional pianist. I in no way played circles around her."

"But they said you didn't even use sheet music, so you bested her there."

"Well, it doesn't take me long to memorize something. And she was probably playing a piece fairly new to her."

"Oh, pooh! Are you always so diplomatic? When that competition rolls around this spring, we'll see who outplays who. Just think—attending conservatory in Baltimore! That's even closer to New York City, so when you finish there, I'll come up and we'll head off north to—"

"Whoa, whoa, Ruby, not so fast. I'm sure you'll get to New York one day, but things are different for me."

"Different how? If you're half as good as everyone says you are, you can't keep talent like that hidden away in the hills. You have to put it out into the big wide world, and this competition is your ticket."

It was uncanny how Ruby sensed my dreams were as big as hers. We both were from small Virginia towns, she from Galax seventy miles straight east from Abingdon and hardly bigger than Clintwood. But neither town was big enough to contain our ambition.

"Well, I'm just a freshman."

"But that doesn't matter, everyone said—"

"I know, I know; it's open to all levels. It's just . . . I think it's best left to the upperclassmen." Ruby opened her mouth to protest, but my raised hand gently stopped her.

"Well, there's always next year," she reluctantly conceded, allowing only a brief moment of quiet before returning to her natural exuberance. "Well, I have to go change, but I'll be back. Don't you dare stand me up for dinner!"

Dear little Ruby. I'd only known her for a day, but she showered me with the affection of a faithful puppy and was already my best friend.

Syncopation

Saturday morning dawned early after a short night. I had lain awake for a good part of the last two nights, hearing every creak and moan of the nearly one hundred-year-old building that cradled me. I'd also heard the passing of the train on tracks that lay a mere one hundred yards from the back of the campus. Midnight and four a.m., I already knew its schedule by heart. But I found the deep-toned hoot of its whistle and chugging rhythm of its wheels strangely comforting rather than intrusive.

I stared at the candle on my bedside table, already burned halfway down. Open flames were not allowed in our rooms, but my intense fear of the dark emboldened me to ignore the rules. I hoped the secret stash of candles I'd smuggled in would last until Christmas break. If confiscated, their absence would punish me more severely than any reprimand. When a hint of sunlight teased the curtains, I opened the window and extinguished the flame, sending the smoke curling out into the morning air. Looking over the campus lawn, I thought of the pine grove and what lay beyond it. I eased the window shut and quietly dressed.

While my Martha sisters blissfully snored in their beds, I silently crept down the hall. Despite my height and gangly limbs, I had a knack for moving about undetected. After descending all three flights of stairs and reaching the service entrance, I felt a small panic when I encountered a crew of cleaners reporting for early weekend duty. But my plain wardrobe allowed me to blend in and weave right through them unnoticed.

The Martha Odyssey

The morning air was shockingly crisp, casting off the fog of my sleepless night. Inside my skirt pocket, the apple I had saved from dinner bounced against my leg as I crossed the lawn and stepped into the pines. When I reached the corral fence the sun had just cleared the horizon, casting a brilliant glow on the barn. The doors to the corral were again wide open, but doors at the opposite end of the barn were shut, creating a long dark cavern that beckoned me. Seeing no one, I carefully climbed over the fence.

Inside the cavern was a long row of horse stalls on either side of a long corridor. I breathed in the familiar smell: sweet hay mingled with sawdust and musty manure. A scent my classmates would find repugnant but which was perfume to me. The happy crunching of grain devoured by strong teeth rattled the air, coupled with soft burring as the horses cleared their nostrils. I slowly walked through, stopping to peer in at each stall. The collection of mounts included a small dun mare, a pair of bay driving ponies, a blue roan gelding, a pair of gray draft horses, and a buckskin mare. Then in the last stall on the left, beside the buckskin, I saw him. His head was raised over the stall door, gazing so calmly he had obviously finished his meal long before the others. His dazzling white blaze stood out in the dim light, emphasizing eyes shining like polished orbs of coal.

With silent footsteps I approached, gently offering the apple from my pocket. He pricked his ears and breathed out a slow but wary snort. I stood unwavering, knowing patience as well as food was the key. Sure enough, he couldn't resist and dropped his head to sniff the succulent fruit. His lips tentatively pecked at it before his massive teeth chomped the apple in two. His head nodded gleefully as he chewed, juice flying in all directions. When the second half of the apple was gone, I ventured a stroke to his muzzle, which he graciously allowed. Eventually I was stroking his beautiful white face, daydreaming what Nutmeg might think of him.

"I see you've met the Czar." I gasped and swung around toward a deep voice coming from the other end of the stables. The bright morning sunlight silhouetted a tall man in the open doorway, his face obscured in shadow. Caught there uninvited, I froze.

"I'm sorry," I blurted when I could finally breathe. The man said nothing but began to slowly walk toward me, his silent approach more menacing than if he'd shouted. I began to back away. "I . . . I didn't think anyone was here. I just . . ." A little yelp escaped my throat as I collided with the set of massive stable doors, shut tight at that end. The man kept coming, no break in his stride. My eyes locked longingly onto the wide-open doors at the opposite end, all sorts of thoughts racing through my mind. My long legs made me a fast runner and I tried to calculate how to zip past him. Suddenly he came to a halt at the black horse's stall. Without a word he took the halter and began to lovingly stroke the horse's sleek neck, his caresses rewarded with a soft nicker.

Awestruck, I watched the pair of them. The man's hair was as glossy black as the horse's, snaking down his back in a single long thick braid. His broad shoulders, muscular arms and strong hands had the horse's solid yet graceful movement. His skin was a ruddy bronze tone, as if he spent a lot of time in the sun. They both seemed to possess an intoxicating power.

"Magic is at work here." The man directed his gaze at me. "Czar Alexander has irresistible charm."

A new bolt of alarm singed my throat at the sound of his voice so close. But he made no move toward me, and I realized he was talking about the horse. I swallowed hard and answered, "Yes. He . . . he does."

He turned back to the horse, running a sturdy hand down the horse's face. "But I just call him 'Xander.' To keep his arrogance in check."

He said nothing more, and suddenly I became conscious that I was in a barn alone with a man. Nothing unusual to someone who grew up on a farm; however, this was a complete stranger. But a man this gentle with a horse was bound to be gentle with a woman. Besides, I was as tall as he was.

"I saw him out in the corral on my walk yesterday," I ventured cautiously. "He was rather full of himself, putting on quite a show."

The man nodded with a knowing smile. I took a chance and spoke again.

"I just wanted to see him again. To find out—"

"So, you've seen him. It's best you not come again."

"But I—"

"This is no place for a *girl*."

I bristled at this unwelcome retort, but his tone was dead serious. I opened my mouth to protest when he turned to level his eyes at me.

"No one comes here, except on business. You have no business here."

His expression made it clear I had no choice but to leave. Taking one final glimpse of Xander, I walked down the long corridor of the barn. The other horses watched curiously and I longed to touch each one as I passed, but didn't dare.

Once out in the sunlight I discovered I was shaking, whether from humiliation or anger I wasn't sure. I took off across the corral at a run, scrambled over the fence and kept running into the pine grove. Eventually I slowed to a heavy-footed walk, my thoughts turning to all those lovely horses. But the mental picture was ruined by the stern face and harsh words of the man who'd discovered me there. I stalked back towards the Martha, fuming at the turn of events. And the farther I got from the stables the more determined I became to return.

The following morning was Sunday, which meant mandatory attendance at church. Mrs. Long had lectured, "The name of Martha Washington College is synonymous with education and culture in the fear of God," so, in addition to our academic duties, we were expected to worship and be well-versed in the Bible. Fifty-five years earlier the school had been instituted by the Holston Conference of the Methodist Church, and all students attended the

Abingdon Methodist Episcopal Church located a mere block down the street. Mrs. Long brooked no excuses—save broken bones or bedridden illness—for our failing to reach that destination. As was custom for mothers to do, Varina had promised to escort me and said to meet her on the front veranda at a quarter to ten. Thankfully I had finally been able to sleep the night before and felt rested and fresh. I was just stretching out from under the covers when I heard a sharp rapping on my door.

"Bea, are you alright?" came Ruby's frantic voice from the other side. Puzzled, I hurried to open the door. Ruby gasped to see me in my nightgown. "Were you still asleep? You've already missed breakfast and you're about to miss church!"

"I've got plenty of time. It's only eight-thirty."

"And we have to meet our mothers on the porch at a quarter to nine."

"But church doesn't start until ten."

"No, it starts at nine! Here, I'll help you. You can make it, but just barely."

In a sudden flurry of tossed gown, wrangled chemise and drawers (there was no time for a corset), a random dress and hairbrush, Ruby and I worked furiously to get me dressed. I was incredulous at this turn of events, certain Varina had said to meet at a quarter to ten. She even wrote the time on a postcard so I wouldn't forget. I spied the card on my nightstand and verified the script, but didn't take time to share it with Ruby.

Making an awful ruckus, we raced down the stairs and bolted through the front doors, coming to an abrupt stop on the porch. Varina stood there alone, her watch in her hand.

"Oh, Beatrice, finally!" Varina gasped in relief.

"I'm sorry, but your card says—"

"It's ten minutes to nine, but if we walk briskly, we'll just make it," she assured us, pocketing her watch. "Ruby, Myrtle said she'd be mortified if she were late, so I volunteered to escort you both."

All we could do was trudge down the street on either side of a resolute Varina. I felt terrible making Ruby miss her own mother, especially on our very first Sunday. And I wanted to defend myself about the wrong meeting time written on the card, but we were in such a rush it seemed awkward to press the issue just then. Finally, we reached the church doors where Mrs. Long stood as sentinel. The bells in the tower above began to clang, underscoring the admonishing scowl on her face.

"Varina, in all your years at Martha Washington, I've never known you to be late to church."

"I'm terribly sorry, Mrs. Long. But motherly duty calls." She ruefully glanced at me, then Ruby.

I wanted to hang my head, but since I was quite a bit taller than Mrs. Long that would hide nothing. I simply stood as stiffly as possible, hoping she wouldn't detect the absence of a corset. Mr. Moore had already begun the organ prelude, so we took the proffered bulletin and hurried to our seats. To my mortification, all seniors were seated directly behind the faculty's front pews, which meant we had to parade down the aisle before the entire congregation. What an auspicious beginning to my new religious life at the Martha.

We remained paired with our mothers for the entire morning, so after church I still had to endure an excruciating brunch with Varina and her gaggle of chattering acolytes. The meal ended without me having the opportunity, or the courage really, to confront her about giving me the wrong meeting time, so I decided to let it pass. In the hallway I hung back, ostensibly looking at portraits on the wall, wanting to catch up with Ruby and make amends for spoiling her morning. But she saw me first, came up from behind and playfully poked me in the back.

"Fascinated by all these old mugs, are you?" she teased. "They actually do seem exciting after this notoriously boring brunch."

"Ruby, I'm so sorry for making you late. I've felt terrible all morning for getting you in trouble with your mother."

"Oh, don't worry about it. I just told Myrtle that we both overslept."

"But you didn't have to say that when it was only me."

"I'm sure it's no more than she's ever done. Besides, I'm not going to rat you out to those snooty seniors, mothers or not."

I considered telling her about the postcard, but the damage was done and Ruby had taken the fall for me; that information would only spoil her kind gesture. "Thank you, Ruby. You're a true friend and I'm forever in your debt."

"And I know just how you can repay me." She grabbed my arm and marched me away, not stopping until we reached the Student Parlor. She parked me firmly on the stool before an elderly upright piano. "I've been hearing all this wonderful talk so now I want to hear the real thing. Play me some Chopin, Honey Bea."

My face broke into its first smile of the day. Ruby deserved the best, so I began with another favorite, Chopin's "Aeolian Harp" etude. She stretched out on the settee, feet propped on the armrest, as its melody sang out over rippling arpeggios and cleansed away the disconcerting events of the morning. By the final chord we were both breathing easier.

"That was gorgeous, Bea! You're *every bit* as good as everyone says. Play me another. Something fun this time." I played the first few minutes of the Scherzo in E Major as Ruby leaned toward the keyboard, watching my fingers tap out the whimsical tunes. When I stopped, she whistled and clapped. "That's the spirit! Now—play something I can dance to."

I began the B-flat Major Mazurka from opus 7. Ruby flitted around the room with abandon, arms floating and flapping at whim. Caught up in her energy, I was pattering the keys at a lively pace when I heard laughter from across the room. Ruby now had an audience, driving her to even wilder antics.

"Bravo, bravo!" Saluda and Hazel shouted and applauded when we'd finished.

The Martha Odyssey

"Delighted to entertain you," Ruby purred in mock diffidence with a sweeping bow.

"We heard you playing, Beatrice, and couldn't stay away," said Saluda. "Then Hazel had the best idea."

"I ran back to my room to get this." Hazel held up a new Irving Berlin songbook. "Miss Le Grande doesn't know about this—she would never allow it! But we wondered if you could play for us to sing some of these now. It is our day off, after all."

"I adore Irving Berlin!" Ruby cried. "Oh, yes, Bea, please, please, pretty please?"

"Well, I guess what Miss Le Grande doesn't know won't hurt any of us," I said, taking the book. To squeals of delight, I took their requests one by one. Saluda's favorite was "I Love a Piano," which became an instant favorite of mine. Hazel wanted the grand and popular "Alexander's Ragtime Band," reminding me of the Scott Joplin I loved to play for fun. They rendered these popular songs with the same rich and lovely voices I'd heard in their classical lessons, but Ruby's resounding lilt surprised me. She took on the hilarious "That Hula Hula" and had us all rolling in laughter.

"Now we have to sing a song just for Bea," Ruby declared after we'd caught our breath. "It's not in this book, but it's perfect." With spontaneous aplomb she chirped, "Be my little baby bumble bee..."

"Oh, my sisters tease me with that one all the time." I picked up Ruby's key and leapt into the accompaniment. Ruby kept the lead, with Saluda and Hazel answering, "buzz around, buzz around, keep a buzzin' round" and all the other charmingly silly responses. Finally, even I joined in, all of us belting, "Honey, keep a-buzzin' please, I've got a dozen cousin bees, But I want you to be my baby bumble bee!" for a grand finish. I missed my sisters.

"You know, Bea—now we know to call you 'Bea'—you really belong in the Euterpean Society," said Saluda.

"Ooh, yes!" Hazel squealed. "Mother is a charter member of the Euterpean Music Club in Fort Worth. It's one of the oldest music clubs in Texas. She was thrilled to learn they have one here."

"Ours is a literary society," Saluda continued, "so we hold debates, mostly with our rival club, the Washingtonians, but there's always a musical component to the events. To our way of thinking, the most important component."

"Oh, Bea, you'd be perfect! I don't think a freshman has ever been inducted, but with your talent it would be a shame to waste a year waiting for you to become an upperclassman."

I, of course, would never be an upperclassman, but I didn't dare let my face betray me. "It sounds wonderful, but I guess I'll just have to be patient," I replied. What else could I do?

Maestro

As I was about to dive into my first full week of classes on Monday morning, I received a notice that caused my mouth to go dry and my palms to sweat: I was to report to Mrs. Long's office directly after breakfast. Had she found out about my visits to the stables? Would I be sent home before classes even began? In the dining hall I barely nibbled my biscuit, waiting for the breakfast hour to end. Finally, it came time to march down the long hallway and, with my heart in my throat, stand before my headmistress.

"Miss Damron, the conservatory has come to a new decision. You have been removed from Mr. Park's roster." I hung my head in shame as my pulse thumped loudly in my ears and the room began to spin. What would I do? Where would I go? I couldn't return home and face my family, my father, Mrs. Counts! I felt my body sway. By heroic effort I held myself erect, only vaguely aware of Mrs. Long's voice, sounding muffled as if it was coming from inside a barrel. Suddenly there was a loud bark, "Well, does it?" I looked at her stupidly and squeaked, "What?" Heaving a deep sigh, she replied, "Your piano lessons with Professor Zeisberg, Wednesdays at eleven. I trust that suits your schedule?"

Thus, I had been saved from damnation and thrust into an accelerated program of study all in one fell swoop. My relief at not being expelled almost overshadowed my elation at the opportunity to learn from Professor Zeisberg. But the higher intensity lessons would demand a lot more of me. Accompaniment duties, classes, studying, and now extra practicing would consume all of my waking hours. I simply had to step up my pace.

The remainder of the week proved as busy as I'd predicted, and by Friday morning I was happy to begin my last day of it. Leaving my room for breakfast, I nearly tripped on an envelope poking out from under my door. I grabbed it to hurriedly read on my way down the hall, then stopped short when I pulled out a heavy card with an embossed seal and engraved text.

> *The Euterpean Literary Society*
> *of Martha Washington College*
> *requests your presence at a Rush Tea Party*
> *Friday, September 10, 1915,*
> *at Seven O'Clock in the Evening*
> *East Parlor and Society Hall*
> *Varina Armstrong, President • Ethel St. John, Vice President*
> *Saluda French, Secretary*

Thinking surely this was a mistaken delivery I flipped over the envelope, but on the front in a pristine calligraphy read "Beatrice Earle Damron." My next thought was that it was some kind of joke, another prank. Slipping the missive into my pocket, I continued on to the dining hall.

Varina was president, so, as my mother, had she made an exception for me? I didn't get the impression she would, since from all indications she had a strong penchant for following rules. And Ethel would never challenge Varina. That left Saluda, although I doubted the secretary had any influence over the president. I would have to proceed carefully to avoid possibly falling prey to another humiliation. What a minefield college life could be. Trying to navigate the social ins and outs in a world for which I had no experience was mystifying.

But an unexpected clue presented itself that afternoon. My last accompanist duty was for Hazel's voice lesson, and she entered the studio looking at me with twinkling eyes and a suppressed grin. After stealing impish glances at me all through the lesson, she collected her music to leave and with a wink said, "See you tonight, and don't be late!" before popping out the door.

I could never resist a dare, or the pull of curiosity, so I found myself walking into the East Parlor that evening promptly at seven. The room was already crowded with a plethora of young ladies clad in stylish tea gowns. As I owned none, I had to make do with my Sunday best again. I felt uncomfortably out of place, but no one came forward to escort me out. I recognized a few singers I had accompanied that week and some girls from the dining hall, but I really didn't know anyone.

"Bea!" Saluda called from across the room, a life preserver tossed into the confounding sea. Waving wildly, she summoned me to join her and Hazel at the refreshment table.

"Am I really supposed to be here?" I whispered as she foisted a teacup and cookie on me.

"You received an embossed invitation, did you not? So of course you are. One simply doesn't say 'no' to the Euterpeans." She and Hazel sported wicked grins. "Besides, it would be a grave sin to waste a whole year of music-making with an exquisite music-maker right here under our noses. And the Martha wants its good Methodist girls to avoid sinning at all costs, isn't that right, Hazel?"

"Absolutely. Having you here is keeping us on the straight and narrow. Why, Bea, you're a soul saver!" Their laughter was oddly reassuring.

"Well, it's good to hear everyone having a good time," a voice suddenly lilted from behind me. I turned and came face to face with Varina. "Beatrice, I see you've wandered into our private little meeting. Did you lose your way to the library?"

"Bea's not lost, Varina," Saluda came to my rescue. "She's here by invitation, just like everyone else."

"Oh. Are you sure? I don't recall any freshmen on the list."

"She showed me her invitation today in my voice lesson," offered Hazel, "just checking to see if she needed to bring anything. I told her 'Just yourself,' and so here she is."

I had feared a confrontation such as this and brought along the invitation just in case. I handed it to Varina, who perused it in perplexed silence. Certain she would declare this a mistake and quietly send me away, I was surprised to see her face break into a bright smile. "How nice of you to join us, Beatrice. So. Now I have someone I need to introduce you to. If you ladies will excuse us?" Taking my arm, she ushered me out of the protective sphere of Saluda and Hazel. She deftly maneuvered us through the maze of chattering students until I found myself standing before Ethel St. John.

"Ethel, it looks as though we have an unexpected hopeful at this evening's rush," Varina said too brightly. Ethel flashed a questioning look at Varina, who smiled a silent signal that I was here to stay.

"Ah, yes. Beatrice," answered a peeved Ethel. "She was my accompanist at this week's voice lesson."

"That's right. I'd forgotten that Beatrice is a working girl." Varina turned to give me a solicitous smile. "Ethel is one of our vetting officers. She'll be getting more acquainted with you this evening, with a few brief questions. Well, I must move on, but I'm leaving you in good hands." I watched Varina vanish into the crowd, then turned to Ethel, who had no smile for me, solicitous or otherwise.

"So, as a pianist, tell me about your training. Your teachers before you came to Martha Washington College."

"I studied with Mrs. Virginia Counts, in Clintwood."

"And?"

"And . . ." I struggled for what to say next. "I started taking lessons when I was five years old. And kept them up until I came here."

"This Mrs. Counts, she was your *only* piano teacher for all those years?"

"Yes. She was the only one in our town. And for all of Dickenson County."

"I see. So, you never traveled anywhere outside of Clintwood for lessons?"

"No. Only my father traveled, for his work. Otherwise, with my mother taking care of six children, we pretty much stayed put. I'm the oldest, so I had to help."

"I see. But your father traveled; what does he do?"

"He's a timber cruiser. He works large forested areas, so that takes him on some journeys. At home he tends our farm, and my grandfather's orchards and vineyard. He grows all kinds of apples, cherries, grapes. He even tried peaches one time." I knew I was rambling, but Ethel's dogged scrutiny was unnerving.

"Damron is a name I've never heard of before. Are all your people from Clintwood?"

"Well, my father was born on our farm, which he later inherited. It lies right on the edge of Clintwood and connects to my grandfather's farm, where my mother grew up. My great-grandfather planted the orchards on that farm. So, family as far back as I know lived somewhere in Dickenson County. After my father began working in timber, he built our house just inside the town limits. A bigger one, for the large family. My granddad lives with us too." Again, I sputtered a jumble of information, but Ethel listened with infinite equanimity.

"And your mother's people?"

I hesitated. Mama had never known her own mother, who died when she was just a baby. And Granddad never spoke of her, or of his own parents. Mother's family was mostly a mystery.

"Ah, it's just my mother and her father, my granddad." I smiled to fill the silence. Ethel raised her eyebrows and gazed at me for a few moments, then pressed on.

"What about attending concerts? Did you ever hear any professional concert pianists play?"

"Sometimes a musician traveling through would give a recital at the Methodist church."

"So, you never heard any of the greats? Hofmann, Paderewski,

Rubinstein? I would be surprised if they ever stopped in Dickenson County."

"Not in a concert, but Mrs. Counts kept a huge record collection for her Victrola. I would often stay after a lesson to listen to them. So, I've heard recordings of Josef Hofmann and Artur Rubinstein."

"Ah, well that's something. This Mrs. Counts, where did she get her musical training?"

"Oberlin Conservatory of Music in Ohio. Graduated when she was only twenty. Then did concert tours for a couple of years, playing cities all over the Northeast. When her husband inherited a business from his uncle, they moved to Clintwood. Then she performed in cities all over the South, until a terrible train wreck put an end to it. She was lucky to survive, but it crushed her right hand and leg."

"What a tragedy. Career destroyed and trapped in a small town the rest of her life."

I'd been told that Mrs. Counts was devastated after the accident, falling into a terrible depression and leaving the piano untouched for years. Then four-year-old me came along, hammering the keys of church pianos at every opportunity until eventually someone told my mother to take me to Mrs. Counts's home to play for her. Evidently, I awoke something in her because she agreed to teach me. Gradually, she took on other students until she'd fostered a whole passel of young musicians all over the county.

"Oh, she still performs," I jumped to Mrs. Counts' defense. Actually, she was terrified to board a train ever again, but I was determined she not be reduced to pity. "In towns nearby. She plays all of Zichy's repertoire for left hand. And his transcriptions of Bach, Chopin, Liszt. And Schubert. They're quite amazing. I even learned the orchestra transcription for his Concerto for Left Hand to perform with her. She's a marvelous pianist. An inspiration. She's the reason I'm here."

A small smile finally breached Ethel's lips, but failed to emerge in her eyes. I stood awkwardly with my cup of cold tea and half-eaten cookie, wondering if the next move was supposed to be mine.

"This has been a most interesting discussion, Beatrice," she said at last. "I've enjoyed getting to know you. The society will be selecting accepted pledges in the next week, so someone will be in touch soon about our decision."

It became obvious I was dismissed, so with a nod of thanks, and internal relief, I slipped away. This "rush" was supposedly a getting acquainted party, but it certainly felt more like an interrogation. I hadn't been questioned that thoroughly when I'd applied to enroll in the college. Apparently, the Euterpean Literary Society considered their membership enrollment terribly serious business. And though many girls likely coveted the chance to be among their numbers, I had no intention of holding my breath awaiting their highly important decision.

Aria and Recitative

At last, it was Saturday morning again. I awoke at the first ray of sun streaming through my curtains, anxious for my first chance in a week to go on my secret walk. I sat up recalling Monday morning's scare in Mrs. Long's office and contemplated the risk of visiting the stables again. But it was the first place I'd felt at home since arriving in this new and often perplexing collegiate world, and the sawdust, horse's hair, and saddle leather were calling my name. I banished further thoughts of risk and jumped into my walking clothes, filling my pockets with carrots pilfered from the kitchen produce boxes. It wasn't my nature to steal, so I made up for it by refusing the salad at dinner. I couldn't present myself to the Czar empty-handed.

When I reached the corral fence, there was no sign of the man but the stable doors were slightly open. Carefully I climbed over, ventured across the circle of battered earth, and slipped through the crack. Inside the shadowy interior I breathed in pungent smells that charmed my nose, but I had the distinct feeling of being watched. In a wary survey of my surroundings, I spied two tiny glowing spheres in the midst of a wispy golden cloud. I sucked in a quick breath when the cloud began to rise and sprouted two tiny horns. I blinked, adjusting to the dimness, to find a large orange cat staring straight at me from the top of a stall door. I released the breath, feeling foolish; all barns had at least one mouser to protect the sacks of grain from pillage. Remaining still, I listened to the sounds of crunching until convinced I was the only human present.

Quietly I strolled the row of stalls, stopping at each to break off a piece of carrot for its tenant. Although sated with oats and hay, not a one refused the sweet treat. I'd saved the biggest chunk of carrot for Xander, hoping to be rewarded with a nuzzle or a whicker for my gift. But my heart sank when I reached his stall and found myself staring into silent black emptiness. A strange ringing noise turned my head.

The high-pitched metallic "Clank! Clank!" clamored an uneven percussion from somewhere outside the barn. One of the massive doors at Xander's end of the stables stood open, revealing a second, larger corral. Slipping through the doorway, I followed the clanging sounds to my left and passed through the nearby corral gate. I then faced the front of the little plank house with the stone foundation and chimney that stood beside the stables. Its wide double doors were standing completely open, revealing a blazing fire in a sooty brick hearth. On the dirt floor beside it stood a worn tree stump with an anvil perched on top, its unyielding bulk bearing the brunt of merciless pounding on a horseshoe. Wielding the heavy hammer that delivered the blows was the man who had introduced me to Xander. His head was bound in a red bandanna and he wore a heavy leather apron, his only armor against the fierce heat and flying sparks. With measured and practiced strikes he tamed the hot iron into the unique curve of the hoof for which it was intended: the Czar Alexander, tied to a post nearby eagerly awaiting his new footwear.

Relieved to find Xander safe and well, I decided not to risk discovery and another harsh banishment. I slipped back into the barn, quietly opened Xander's stall door and deposited the fat carrot into his feed box. I smiled, visualizing his noisy delight at finding an unexpected reward for having his feet worked on. Even the dignity of an emperor would be cast aside when a tasty delicacy presented itself.

Hiking back to the Martha, I pondered what I'd just seen. I had assumed the man was the stable owner and felt a bit sheepish about trespassing. But stable owners didn't shoe their own mounts, they hired out the job to traveling farriers. So, this man was merely a blacksmith working in a forge the stable owner had built on the premises. He took care of the horses' feet but didn't have exclusive access to them—or the right to keep me away. I began to plan my next visit.

I MADE IT UP TO MY ROOM UNDETECTED, ALTHOUGH BY THEN I'd missed breakfast. To distract myself from my growling innards until lunch, I took a long bath to quash any lingering barn residue before the special event that evening. At five o'clock, Miss Le Grande was giving her faculty recital, with a special banquet afterwards for music students. This would be my most formal affair yet, and by the time my hair had dried that afternoon, it was obvious it needed special treatment beyond my meager skills. Ruby had been pestering me to try some new hairstyles, and I gratefully consented to let her apply her talents.

At a quarter to five, Ruby and I entered the auditorium in Litchfield Hall. I spied seats on the aisle near the middle, delighted to discover they were right in front of Saluda and Hazel.

"Bea, you look stunning!" Hazel gushed as Ruby and I seated ourselves.

"I love your hair like that," added Saluda.

"It pays to have a next-door neighbor who's an artist with a comb and pins." Ruby beamed at my compliment, but she deserved it. She'd even supplied a silk flower to place above my right ear. Lucky for me, it matched my one formal dress.

The four of us enjoyed an animated chat, Saluda asking if I had enjoyed the rush party and what happened after Varina led me away. I simply said I'd had a fun discussion with some senior members, hoping she wouldn't detect my fib. I could see Varina seated near the front on the aisle, with Ethel and the rest of their coterie spread out along the row beside her. A large bouquet of red roses rested on her lap as she held court, not only with her friends but several guests from the town as well. She seemed to know everyone.

"I see your mother over there, Bea," said Ruby. "I wonder who gave her those roses? They must have cost a fortune."

"Oh, they weren't given to her," replied Saluda, "she bought them for Miss Le Grande."

"Really? That seems extravagant."

"She's Varina's rave. Has been since her freshman year."

Ruby and I looked at each other, completely puzzled. Hazel picked up the cue.

"A rave. You know, a smash, a crush. Leave it to Varina to fall in love with the prettiest, most popular teacher here."

"She's always fawning over her," added Saluda, "secretly sending her little things, like an apple or a bunch of daisies. But for a big *public* event she splurges. It's a way to show off; not everyone is rich enough to afford roses."

I recalled that more than once last week some token or other had been left on Miss Le Grande's desk in the voice studio. She would usually just comment, "Oh, isn't that lovely," and set it aside. I hadn't paid it any mind, but could they all have been from Varina? Or did a lot of girls rave for the glamorous singer? If so, I imagined Varina wouldn't appreciate the competition. Thus, the expensive roses.

Suddenly the crowd broke into admiring applause as the celebrated vocalist crossed the stage to stand in the crook of the magnificent Steinway grand piano. From the jeweled headband sparkling across her glorious Gibson Girl upsweep to the train of the beaded silk gown curling around her satin shoes, Miss Sadie Le Grande was a stunning sight to behold. With a brilliant smile to the adoring crowd and a nod to Mr. Moore at the keyboard, her long-anticipated performance began. For the next hour and a half, we were captivated by strains of Schubert, Massenet, and Saint-Saëns rendered in a style that seemed to be Miss Le Grande's alone. Superb showmanship paired with her strikingly rich contralto voice left us all mesmerized.

The banquet that followed proved just as spectacular: a lavish feast laid out in the two parlors of the east wing of Preston Hall. With my plate shamelessly loaded with ham, turkey, and all the trimmings, I settled in with Hazel and Saluda at a small table next to a row of huge potted palms backed by a Chinese silk screen. We joked that it felt like dining in an exotic forest, but a little privacy was nice as we chatted and gorged ourselves on much better fare than the dining hall normally served on a Saturday night. After guzzling several glasses of iced tea with dinner, then coffee with dessert, the girls became desperate to visit the lavatory. I sat alone finishing my pecan pie, when gradually I became aware of chatter from the other side of the screen.

"Honestly, I don't know how you kept a straight face," someone was giggling.

"Well, I had a dreary chore to do, and I couldn't let the silly country bumpkin sidetrack me." I thought I recognized that voice and it stirred my curiosity. "But really, it was laughable. I mean, she grew up on a farm. She's had *one* piano teacher for her entire life, some crippled lady with only one hand! It's clear she's never set foot outside of—what was it, Dickensville?—until she came here."

I froze, my forkful of pie hanging in midair. Those remarks were about me, and the voice could only belong to Ethel St. John.

"And she's only ever heard a concert pianist play on a gramophone record? I can't imagine!" came a new disembodied voice.

"There's no way that sham education prepared her for admittance to the Euterpeans," Ethel scoffed. "I mean, really, learning piano from a one-handed teacher?" Barely stifled giggles accompanied agreements from everyone at her table. "Of course, maybe the Washingtonians will have her. Considering their slipshod standards, she's about their speed." A burst of uproarious laughter followed that I thought would end the conversation. But Ethel had more arrows to sling.

"However, the worst of it is her family. No one of any worth—she comes from dirt farmers! It's all her ancestors have ever done. At least on her father's side. The mother's side is even more appalling." Ethel paused for dramatic effect, prompting a chorus of gasps and demands to continue. "She has no earthly idea where her mother came from. Had nothing to say about it at all. Well, that can mean only one thing." Another dramatic pause, filled with comments from the others of "Scandal?" "Criminal activity?" "Illegitimate?" "Bad investments?"

"Who knows? Whatever it is, the bloodlines have been irreparably damaged."

By now, intense heat was rising from my neck and burning my cheeks. Breathing fire, I marched down the hedge of potted plants and rounded the Chinese screen to confront Ethel head on. But a familiar face stopped me in my tracks: at the head of the table sat Varina, directly in my line of sight. Her chatter halted mid-sentence and our eyes locked, my face betraying I'd heard everything.

I, too, was momentarily stunned. Ethel had spewed her cruelty without a word of protest from Varina. I was slaughtered like a lamb as she sat idle and watched. Changing the direction of my wrath, I stepped toward her when suddenly Miss Le Grande swept up to her side.

"Varina, darling, I want to thank you again for the lovely roses."

After a moment to recover, Varina found her tongue. "You are certainly most welcome, Miss Le Grande, and most deserving. Your performance was a true triumph."

The other girls chirped their effusive agreement and the fawning went on and on. Miss Le Grande relished it, of course, but drank it in with gracious politesse. Decorum dictated I stand aside, stifling my frustration. Suddenly she called my name.

"Beatrice! I didn't see you there, dear. Come over here and join us." I could hardly refuse my hostess and reluctantly obeyed. "Beatrice has been absolutely indispensable to me this past week. Her accompaniment skills have been utterly vital to our lessons, haven't they, girls?"

The singers at the table all murmured their assent, albeit in a much less enthusiastic chorus than before. Ethel was silent, visibly annoyed, but tendered a fabricated smile. Miss Le Grande turned to me.

"I knew once I heard you play in master class that we were going to make a good team."

"Thank you, ma'am," I managed, conscious of all eyes on me. "I'm glad you're pleased with my work."

"Didn't she play just marvelously, girls? Varina, I know you recognized her proficiency right away, too. Isn't it wonderful to get in fresh talent that will make the Martha proud?"

"Yes. Of course," came Varina's too-eager response.

"And her talent could be put to excellent use in the Euterpean Literary Society. A new asset to their musical performances. Varina, I'm sure you agree."

Varina squirmed as she glanced around at the others. "Well, that would, of course, be wonderful, but, um . . . I'm afraid we've already selected this year's pledges. And reached our quota. So—"

"Oh nonsense, dear, quotas can always be stretched."

"But we really are at capacity. Besides, Beatrice is only a freshman."

"Exceptions can be made, especially for such a talent," Miss Le Grande smiled warmly at me and patted my arm. Varina bristled. Did she agree with Ethel's assessment, or was she jealous of her long-standing crush's attentions to me?

"Well, I—"

"I won't have time for clubs," I blurted. "I'll be too busy preparing for the Peabody Conservatory scholarship competition." Everyone's head snapped toward me.

"Beatrice, that's wonderful!" Miss Le Grande beamed. "But you must make time for both. The Euterpean performances will be good practice for the competition; it'll be perfect. Well, now that's settled, I must move on to the other guests. You ladies have a wonderful evening!" Blowing a kiss, she floated away to the next table.

All eyes riveted on me. Varina sat in shocked silence while Ethel turned apoplectic, but there was nothing to be done. Miss Le Grande had unwittingly laid the trap and they were snared.

"It looks like we'll be adding another name to the pledge list, Varina." I turned to see Saluda leaning in the doorway a few feet away, sporting an innocent smile. Ethel shot her a vicious glare and violently jumped from the table, clattering dishes and silverware punctuating her sudden lunge.

"Ethel!" Varina snatched her arm and held fast, then steadily addressed us all. "It's been quite an exciting evening, and I think we're all tired. Perhaps we should return to our rooms?" She cast me an unreadable look as she firmly led Ethel out of the parlor, her obedient entourage trailing in their wake.

IN ONE BIZARRE TRIANGULATED CONFRONTATION, I'D BECOME an official Euterpean Society pledge and declared myself a competitor for the Peabody scholarship. No one was more surprised than me. My freshman existence as I had known it was irrevocably altered, plus I was now at odds with my so-called Martha mother. Varina's behavior had left me baffled and uncomfortable, so I simply avoided her for the next several days.

Late in the afternoon on Tuesday, I took refuge on the back lawn with a book, settling on a bench nestled into some holly bushes where I thought I was hidden away. I was fully absorbed in my reading when an unmistakable silky voice floated to my ear.

"How are you, Beatrice?" I raised my head but remained silent. "I see you've discovered my old secret hiding spot."

"I'm not hiding." I wouldn't have her think I was slinking around like a timid mouse.

"Of course not." She lithely lowered herself to the bench, forcing me to scooch and make room. "I came here a lot during my freshman year, too. Whenever I needed solitude." Silence hung in the air between us for several long moments. "You and I are a pair, you know. Perfectly matched soulmates."

"Oh?" I fixed her with an incredulous stare. "How so?"

"We come from vastly different backgrounds, but in spirit we're exactly alike. We both want to accomplish great things, be the best at what we do, fight for what we want, to make—"

"Like you fought for me against Ethel." The sarcasm was a new taste on my tongue. "You sat there while she said terrible things about me, and my family, my teacher, tearing us to shreds, and you did nothing! Except join in the giggling."

"Oh, no, Beatrice. I didn't, truly. You must believe me." She took my hand, but I jerked it back, wrapping my arms tightly around my book. "I was simply exercising silence to avoid trouble. Just waiting for Ethel to blow off steam, knowing it would play itself out."

"At my expense."

She breathed a soft sigh. "And that wasn't fair. I'm sorry."

I couldn't look at her; I wasn't ready to believe her.

"Look, I'm in a difficult position, as leaders always are. Trying to placate egos, tend to everyone's needs, balance loyalties. Sometimes it might appear I'm doing one thing, when I'm actually doing another."

We both watched a squirrel with a too-large walnut in its mouth scamper up the side of a tree, determined to hustle the prize all the way home to its nest.

"The world is a harsh place, Beatrice, and people say harsh things. But you have to learn to ignore it, to rise above it."

"So, it's that simple?"

"Yes. It actually is, and I'll help you learn how. Why, you're destined to be my best protégé yet."

I'd grown up in a large family where someone was always making a mistake. Mama taught us to repent and make amends, forgive and move on. Without her to turn to, I needed to trust her wisdom. Despite Varina's "soulmate" theory, ours seemed an improbable partnership, but I supposed it was worth it to try again. Still, a formidable obstacle now lay between us.

"And the music scholarship competition?" I ventured.

There was a tense moment of silence, as if Varina's optimistic bubble was about to burst. Then she lifted her chin with a whimsical smile.

"It's the Fates, you know, challenging us. Pairing us together, then inserting a contest. So, we simply challenge them back. We'll both strive to be the best musicians we can be and force the Fates to decide the winner." Before I could respond, she'd patted my arm and departed, leaving me to watch her lofty flaxen curls sail away on her highly held head.

Pizzicato

As dawn broke on Saturday morning, I was already making my way through the pines. Munching bread and cheese I'd secreted away from the dining hall, I fortified myself for a confrontation with the man at the stables. When I arrived, the stable doors were again slightly opened, so I brushed the crumbs from my hands, boldly grabbed the handle of the left door and shoved. It rumbled open along its rail, unleashing a huge rattling roar. I did the same with the righthand door and peered down the center of the huge maw I'd created. Standing in the open doorway at the opposite end was the man. He held a pitchfork handle-tip to the ground with its tines pointing up, giving the impression of the devil himself.

"You," he called in his deep baritone.

"Yes, *me*." I struggled to keep my voice even.

"I told you to stay away." An intimidating severity weighted his words, but I took a deep breath and pushed on.

"Are all these horses yours?"

His eyes locked with mine in an unrelenting stare.

"As good as," he finally answered.

"But they're not, are they?" I ventured a few steps into the barn. "You're just a caretaker, and a farrier. A mere blacksmith." I felt badly putting it like that; smithing was grueling work. Still, I had to make my case. I chanced a few more steps. "So, you have no right to keep me away."

His face darkened, his penetrating stare almost palpable.

"Why do you want to come?"

"I care for horses, too."

He said nothing and began to walk toward me. The spikey thorns of the pitchfork drew my eyes like a magnet and I struggled to hold his gaze. I felt blood pulsing in my ears when he came to a halt in front of me.

"Then show me."

I flinched only slightly as he thrust the pitchfork in my direction, then nodded for me to take it from him. The flood of relief at not being skewered renewed my courage and I grabbed the handle firmly.

"I've been mucking stalls since I was three years old. A little manure doesn't scare me."

He nodded to my right. "The stalls on this side are waiting for you." I turned to see that the first two stalls housed the massive gray draft horses, whose volume of manure was sure to be enormous. A twinkle of amusement radiated from his eyes and his lips curved slightly upward. I ignored him and set to work.

With rolled up sleeves and loosened shirt buttons, I tackled the overnight deposits with firm plunges of the pitchfork. When the mess was cleared, I commandeered the nearest wheelbarrow to haul the refuse to an outside compost heap. I then raked clean straw from the stall's corners into the middle, gathered fresh straw from new bales, and scattered it over the entire floor. I would force him to admit I worked as well as any man.

My steam was running low as I approached the last stall, but I perked up instantly when I swung the door open. I blinked dumbfounded at what looked like my own Nutmeg, somehow transported from home. The shiny red-brown coat, white stockings, white lacing in the mane, and thin white stripe down the face were all there. But this was a sorrel gelding, not a mare. He was gentle to the point of friendly, letting me stroke his soft muzzle and sleek neck. This charming discovery erased the drudgery of the work, and before I knew it, I was finished.

The new sorrel gelding's stall was directly across from Xander's, where the man stood watching me. Neither of us had spoken since I took up his challenge, and we regarded each other from opposite sides of the barn. As casually as possible, I brushed the dirt from my hands and lowered my sleeves. My split skirt had to be filthy, but I didn't dare touch it. When I was once again buttoned, I crossed my arms and we looked each other directly in the eye.

"You show a lot of pluck. And strength. For a girl."

His remark vexed me, but I didn't waver.

"I've done the work of a man." His response was a silent stare. "So, I belong here, just like any man." Several long moments passed and I thought I'd won.

"Still, you should stay away."

"What? Why? I love these horses same as—"

"Because you have no business here!" His shout silenced me, but underneath his stern look I sensed pain. "Now go away." He turned and stomped away, heading for the gate to the forge.

"Well, I won't!" I shouted after him, but he kept walking.

I refused to let him spoil my victory and fished in my pocket for a piece of carrot. When I handed it to the sorrel gelding, he gladly accepted and bounced his head with delight while he chewed. I laughed, giving his forelock a tousle before moving down the row of stalls to give out treats, coming up the other side to end at Xander's stall. "Sorry I don't have extra to give you today. You have to share with your new mate over there." As I held his halter, I sensed a new presence, then glanced toward the open doorway to see the man there watching us.

"You're as stubborn as you are strong," he said, but without malice.

"I consider that a compliment." I turned back to watch Xander enjoy his treat. "Also, there's something else you should know about me: I'm not from this town."

I waited while he digested this, patiently stroking Xander's head for as long as it took.

"This place is deserted on Saturday mornings. So, if you must, come then. But tell no one."

"It's a deal."

I turned and thrust my hand forward to shake on it. He hesitated, then took a step forward to accept. Just then a small shape came whizzing past my feet toward him, sprang up to his belt buckle and scrambled onto his shoulder. It was the orange tabby cat, staring at me with a self-satisfied smirk from its high perch. I was embarrassed to have startled, but it had shot out of nowhere with astonishing speed.

"Ah, Wesa," the man murmured to the cat. "You've come out of hiding now all the work is done." The man scratched the feline's head and it closed its eyes in bliss.

"I'd forgotten you had a barn cat."

"He's been with me two years, now. An excellent mouser."

"Hello again, Wesa. An unusual name for a cat."

"Not really. It's Cherokee for 'cat.'"

The man walked to a stack of straw bales. He gently leaned so the cat could climb off, his long black braid falling over the broad shoulder that had so tenderly cradled it.

"I need to be getting back," I said, suddenly aware how late it might be.

"Thank you for your work. Well done."

I nodded and headed for the back doorway, then swung back around.

"I'm Beatrice, by the way." He looked at me for a moment.

"Jonah," he replied. I offered an awkward smile and went on my way.

I should have recognized early on that Jonah was Cherokee. My granddad seemed to know that Indian tribe quite well and had told stories about them all through my childhood. But only to me, calling them our "secret stories." He said with so many children in the house, I needed something just for me, and I loved him for that. And now a secret story was part of my college adventure.

Bonny Gable

THE PROMISE OF WEEKLY VISITS TO THE STABLES HELPED ME endure the demanding academic schedule, even if I remained unsure of my place in the Martha social landscape. When everyone learned that Professor Zeisberg had selected me, a freshman, as one of his piano pupils, it had caused quite a stir. Apparently, that had never happened before. His lessons were grueling, but having the benefit of his training for the scholarship competition was well worth the extra intensity. I needed to sharpen every arrow in my quiver, so instead of card games and gossip in the evenings, I secluded myself in one of the deserted practice rooms, working to coax some magic from the ivories.

On one such evening, I was fully immersed in the difficult passages of a Brahms sonata when I sensed some strange overtones. I thought it must be vibrations in the old Story and Clark upright I was playing, since all pianos relegated to the practice rooms were a bit past their prime. I continued to play on, but when pausing to change to another section of the piece I heard the unmistakable strains of music that were not emanating from my piano. Someone else was taking advantage of the isolated joys of evening practice. I kept quiet and listened, then realized the music wasn't coming from a piano but from a string instrument. I hadn't known there were any string players at the college. None had played at master class and my professors had never mentioned any. But the sound was undoubtedly coming from a violin.

Curious, I stepped into the hallway, where I heard the plaintive tones ringing more clearly, though still at a distance. The player was quite skilled, their solid tone resonating an ethereal quality. I gingerly crept down the hall, stopping to press my ear to each door, but the music wasn't coming from any of the practice rooms. Was the player using a classroom? Or brave enough to breach protocol and practice in one of the parlors? If my piano playing was a hindrance—I could become a bit boisterous when working out a problem—maybe they'd taken refuge in some secluded spot. I decided it was best to leave them alone.

But the memory of that elusive music stayed with me for the next several days. I asked around in all my music classes about a violin student, but no one was sure if there were any. I even asked Ruby if she had a friend who played.

"Fat chance!" she laughed. "But, hey, do you think I might have a secret admirer who's practicing to serenade me?" Her big green eyes took on a dopey, dreamy look.

"I think that kind of thing only happens in one of your melodramas."

"Or in a fancy Italian restaurant, like they have in New York City. They even have ones where the waiters sing opera to you while you eat."

"Ruby, you read too many magazines."

That night in the practice room I heard the violin again. The same melody as before, rich and sorrowful, echoing from a distance. I checked all the practice rooms and then ventured into the classrooms, but no one was there. Except for me, the entire building was completely empty, yet the music played on. It had to be someone playing in their dormitory room, which wasn't allowed either. But if their neighbors didn't mind, they might get away with it. Whoever it was, they were bound to play at the next master class, where I could finally meet them face to face.

SATURDAY HAD BECOME MY FAVORITE DAY OF THE WEEK, AND I arrived at the stables anxious to hand out my stolen treats: a pocketful of apples. But stolen was a bit too harsh; I'd actually saved one from lunch each day and cut them in half. I planned to slip the one extra half to the new sorrel gelding as a welcoming gift.

Fully expecting to muck stalls again, I was surprised to see the gelding's stall already clean. As I handed out apples down the row, I saw the others on that side were clean as well. I crossed to the opposite side to slip a treat to the dun mare when an odd noise turned my head. Jonah came bounding down the corridor pushing an empty wheelbarrow, his long loping strides making its lone front wheel rattle comically on the uneven turf before halting in front of me.

"Good morning, Beatrice."

"Good morning, Jonah." I seized the handles of the wheelbarrow.

"The other side is finished, so the draft horses are taken care of." A small smile creased one cheek as he handed me a pitchfork.

"Thank you." I kept a straight face, determined to hide my immense gratitude.

"But I'll still do Xander's stall. He doesn't take to women." The remark plus his matter-of-fact tone instantly raised my ire.

"He takes to my apples and carrots very well!"

"I know he likes your tasty gifts, and that's all well and good when he's confined. But he's very high-strung, and somewhere in his history he's had a bad experience. I can't risk it."

I wanted to say more but reluctantly acquiesced. This relationship was new, and there was no point in rocking the boat. Not just yet, anyway.

I started on the dun mare's stall, working out my frustrations with vigorous thrusts of the pitchfork. After only a few minutes, my palms began to smart a bit. I was annoyed to think I'd gone soft in just four weeks away from the farm, but the blisters from my work the week before were still forming calluses. The only way to toughen up again was to soldier on.

Jonah finished Xander's stall and disappeared, leaving the stable quiet except for the scraping of my pitchfork. Curious, I stretched up to look out the small window at the back of the stall, since the blacksmith forge was visible on that side. Its doors were flung open, but no sounds rang out and no smoke curled from its chimney. Was he avoiding me? I knew from experience that when men didn't want to discuss something with a woman, they simply walked away. Or maybe he wanted to show he trusted me, by not hovering while I worked. It was a good sign and played into the proposal I had planned.

When he finally came back, I expected him to examine the stalls I'd cleaned, but instead he went directly into the tack room. I heard him shuffling harnesses and bridles and went to stand in the doorway. He was aloof to my presence, but I plowed ahead with my opening argument.

"Remember I told you I've been cleaning up after horses since I was three?"

"I do."

"Well, I've been riding horses since before I could walk."

"Impressive." He didn't look my way, just continued his busyness.

"And in all that time I've never come across a horse I couldn't handle."

"And how much time would that be?"

"Eighteen years."

He turned and studied me for a long moment. His question was a sly way to find out my age, and I wondered about his. His body was ripe with youthful strength, but his bronzed weathered face carried a careworn look. It was difficult to say, but I discerned he was ten years or more my senior. Suddenly he lifted a long leather lead from its peg and handed it to me.

"Go pick a mount."

Tamping down my delight, I grabbed it and headed toward the stalls.

"Except for Xander," he quickly interjected.

I was so thrilled I didn't argue. Besides, I instantly knew my choice.

"This one, the new gelding."

"Copper."

"That's his name?"

"Copper Penny, to be exact. He shone like a brand-new penny when he dropped from his dam. And he's not new here."

"But I saw him for the first time last week. Where was he before that?"

"At what was supposed to be his new home. A rich fellow from down in Bristol bought him as a surprise birthday present for his daughter, so he could teach her to ride. But she didn't want him. Prefers to gad about in a buggy or a motor car to show off a pretty dress."

I couldn't fathom turning away such a magnificent gift. When I walked him out to the front corral, the sunlight played on his rosy coat that still glistened like a new penny. Jonah gently bridled the horse without a single struggle, handed me the reins, then went to lean against the corral fence. With no saddle in sight, I was instantly wise to his challenge: I would have to ride bareback to prove my claim of experience. I'd ridden bareback countless times, but it had been several weeks since I'd been on a horse at all.

Without a word, I led Copper to the center of the corral. He was only slightly taller than Nutmeg, who was fifteen hands high, and mounting him from the ground would make a much better impression on Jonah. I gathered the reins at the horse's withers and grabbed a good fistful of mane. Stepping back to face his rear, I gave a good skip on my right foot and then sprang forward on my left to propel my right leg up and over Copper's back. Immediately pulling myself upright, I said a silent prayer of thanks that not only had I made it up, I also had not sailed completely over the other side. Long gangly legs came in handy but could also betray you.

Firmly seated, I gently squeezed my thighs and we began our short jaunt around the corral. After once around at a walk I urged Copper into a gentle trot, the gait that can often unseat a bareback rider. But not me. When I pressed for a canter, we both relished the faster speed. The breeze we created cooled the sweat from my face and whipped through my hair. After a few rounds, we crossed the center and circled several times in the opposite direction. When I felt I'd proved myself to Jonah, I pulled the horse to a halt right in front of him. I remained mounted as I looked him in the eye, enjoying my chance to tower over him for a bit, and waited.

"I was right," he said calmly.

"Oh?"

"You have a lot of pluck and strength. For a girl."

"I have pluck and strength, period!" I exploded. "And skill with horses. And I'm not a girl, I'm a woman. Old enough to go off to college and make my own way." I hadn't meant to reveal I was a student. All he had to do to be rid of me now was report me to the school authorities.

"Up the hill there at Stonewall?"

I didn't answer. I'd never given much thought to the other female institute situated next door to the Martha, shrouded as it was by tall pines like the ones I navigated to the stables. Stonewall Jackson College also educated women, but it regimented its charges much like the Confederate general it was named for. Occasional glimpses were caught of girls in stiff gray military-style uniforms, marching in straight-as-an-arrow lines to class or to services at their founding church, Sinking Spring Presbyterian. The school was the Martha's neighbor, but the two could not be more different. I was actually amused that Jonah would think I was a student there.

I swung my leg over Copper's neck and dismounted, then took the reins to walk him around the corral. He hadn't been ridden long but still needed some cooling off, and frankly, so did I. When we finally returned to his stall, I saw a bucket with a brush, curry comb, mane comb, and a soft cloth Jonah had left there. Did he think I wouldn't know those things were needed, or was he being helpful? I didn't dwell on it, just went to work brushing Copper's coat and rubbing him down. He closed his eyes, savoring the comforting motions of my hands, movements that calmed me as well. After tucking him back into his stall, I stood a bit longer, stroking his face and neck.

"Everyone has secrets." I popped my head around to find Jonah standing in the doorway of the tack room. "Yours is safe with me."

Trying to conceal my relief, I only nodded, then gave Copper one last pat on the neck.

"He's all cleaned up now." Then after an awkward pause, "I'd best be on my way, then." I walked toward the back doorway.

"And Beatrice . . ." I turned to face him. "You've made the most of your eighteen years. It shouldn't go to waste."

Contrapuntal

Graduating from mucking stalls to riding horseback buoyed me through the busy week that followed, which ended in a Friday master class. The prospect of discovering the violinist had filled me with excited anticipation, tempered by concern about playing for the entire department for the first time since I'd declared my intent to enter the scholarship competition.

My fellow music students and I entered Litchfield Hall, greeting each other with smiles: some friendly, some nervous, some merely polite. Everyone was beginning to sense where they stood in this group, and what they might have to do to shift their position. This jostling for status was foreign to me, but I understood it came with the territory of venturing into the world of a professional musician. Even the world of training to be one.

The order of performances would be from seniors to freshmen, so I settled in to listen while stealing looks around the auditorium. I hoped to see someone with a violin case, perhaps a brand-new student, starting the semester late for some reason. But no violins had played by the time the freshmen were to perform, and my heart sank. All the music students in my year were either pianists or singers, none harboring a secreted violin case under their chair. When it came my time to perform, my thoughts turned back to the competition. But once my fingers began communing with the keys, I managed to escape into the music as usual and block out both concerns for a while. When class ended, I mustered up the courage to pursue my search again.

The Martha Odyssey

"Excuse me, Professor Zeisberg? Um, sir . . . may I ask a question?" I'd never before approached him, only obediently attended my piano lessons where I hung on his every word. His sheer size, as well as his booming voice and thick German accent, were still a bit intimidating.

"Ah, Beatrice. You haf more questions about your Brahms? I see you vorked on the passages we discussed."

"Thank you. No, it's not about the Brahms. I wanted to ask, is there any student here taking violin lessons?"

"Violin? Vonderful instrument. I vould love to teach it, but at the moment there are no students here who vish to play."

"Oh. Well, um, have you, by any chance, been playing one here lately? In the evenings?"

"No, not for many veeks. I have a beautiful Mittenvald my father gave to me vhen I left for America, but it has been sent avay for repairs."

"Oh. I see."

"Vhen it is returned I play for sure. Almost efery day. Maybe you vould like to learn?"

"Uh, well. I never thought of it. Maybe?"

"Goot! I must go now. I see you in your lesson next veek."

"Yes. Thank you, professor."

I watched him walk out of the auditorium, my face clouded in a frown. Suddenly Varina was at my side.

"Why the glum face, Beatrice? I hope Zeisberg wasn't lecturing you. I thought you played magnificently."

"Oh. No. I was just asking a question."

"Well, good. Come on, then, let's cheer you up with some lunch." She took my arm and pointed toward the doors.

"I'm not really hungry."

"Well, you will be by the time we get there. Besides, I hear they have apple cake for dessert. Didn't you tell me you love anything made with apples?"

Even my usual colossal appetite didn't overpower a nagging uneasiness.

"Varina, you've been at this school for over three years now, and you must know everyone here. Is there anybody, student or teacher, except Zeisberg, who plays the violin?"

"Oh, what a surprising question. Well, let's see... there was one student my freshman year, but she transferred two years later. So, since then, no. Why do you ask?"

"Oh, just curious." We began walking toward the dining hall in silence, then I stopped on the steps. "But what about this year's freshmen? There might be some you haven't met, and maybe one of them plays?" I felt like a pestering child, but Varina gave me an indulgent smile.

"Why don't I help you ask around?" she offered. "I'll get the freshmen roster from Mrs. Long's office, then you take names starting with A through L, and I'll take the rest."

I was surprised that Varina was so patient with what surely must seem like a petty interest of mine. But it would take the entire weekend to make all those inquiries, so I readily accepted her offer.

Most freshmen girls slept late on Saturdays, rendering them unavailable for questioning, so the following morning found me headed back toward my clandestine indulgence. Despite my pique at Jonah's stubbornness, he'd redeemed himself by saying my experience shouldn't go to waste. Anyway, no matter how much he got under my skin, I couldn't stay away. I would just have to trust him to keep my secret.

As I approached the corral fence, bright metallic sounds pierced the air, signaling Jonah at work in the forge. I crept into the barn and strolled among the stalls, enjoying a rhythmic symphony of contentment as the horses crunched their grains. Chunks of carrot bulged in my pockets, waiting to serve as dessert. I felt a kindred spirit with creatures taking pleasure in nourishment, as I was certainly fond of food myself.

I heard a stirring in the one empty stall and leaned over its door. Wesa sat very erect with his head cocked and ears pointing forward, eyes focused intently on the old dusty straw. I heard a soft rustle, then quick as a lightning strike, his paw scooped up a small field mouse to toss into the air. Landing with a soft thud, it took a moment to catch its breath before scrambling to its tiny feet to amble away. But Wesa deftly batted the poor creature, first one way, then another, and finally backwards toward himself. For several moments he watched it for signs of struggle. When satisfied it had succumbed, he clamped it between his teeth and triumphantly trotted to a corner to enjoy his meal. I did not feel a kindred spirit with this method of dining.

While the horses finished breakfast, I ventured out to the forge. A roaring fire blazed in the pit as Jonah held up a peculiar-looking tangle of metal and intently studied it with an appraising eye. He placed it back in the fire briefly before applying meticulous hammer blows to alter its shape. He was as absorbed in his work as I could become in my music. When his hammering stopped, he again scrutinized every detail. Suddenly he plunged the metal into a bucket of water, sending up a profuse sizzle. After pulling it out, he turned the dripping piece over and over in his hands, a satisfied smile spreading over his face.

"That's a funny-looking horseshoe." A test to see if he thought I was really that ignorant about blacksmithing. Fortunately, he didn't take the bait.

"This is part of a special order." He tossed aside his bulky gloves and held up the most unusual andiron I'd ever seen. He handed it to me, the metal still warm. It felt plenty hefty but also alive as I ran my fingers along its surfaces, alternately smooth and prickly. A triangle of elaborate scrollwork with curled tips formed a sturdy base with a single acanthus leaf on top. From the leaf sprang up a gently curving stem that ended in a finely sculpted dragon's head. I was in awe how its lines and swirls gave an otherwise bulky implement a delicate and dramatic shape. There was no doubt I was holding a work of art.

"And this came from a simple lump of metal."

"And the fire and the hammer." His eyes glistened at the new creation in my hands.

"How do you know how to shape it?"

"The flames kindle it to a hot red glow, and I just listen to the metal. Then work until it becomes the shape it's meant to be." He'd neatly hung his apron and bandanna on nearby pegs. I handed back the andiron, which he lovingly laid on a wooden work table to finish cooling. I was fascinated by his smithing but anxious to get to work, hoping for another ride.

"Which stalls should I do today?"

"Which stalls would you like to do?" He walked past me, heading back inside the stables. I caught up and fell in step beside him.

"You're giving me a choice?"

"Let's say I'm curious. Which would you choose?" He was teasing, but I played along.

"It certainly wouldn't be the draft horse stalls, so I would take the opposite side. Including Xander." He gave me a look, but let the remark pass.

"Actually, you don't have to choose. They're all done." He ignored my surprise and simply walked into the barn and opened the tack room. "Copper's saddle is the last one on the right. His bridle is just above it." Without a word I moved quickly before he changed his mind. He watched me tack up the horse to make sure I did it properly, but I didn't care.

"Keep to the corrals," he called as I took off to put Copper through his paces.

ON MONDAY MORNING I WAS STILL HOLDING TO ONE LAST HOPE of finding the mysterious violinist. At breakfast I finally located the last freshman on the roster, only to discover she didn't play any instrument, let alone a violin. The long hours of quizzing had come to nothing. No violinist existed at the Martha at all, and I was forced to concede that what I'd heard wasn't real. I stoically returned to my seat, oblivious to the chatter of my tablemates and wondering what this revelation meant for me. Was adjusting to a new environment too stressful? The rigors of a college curriculum overwhelming? Anxiety over the competition manifesting itself in a bizarre way? I stared at the muffin on my plate, as if it would suddenly speak and provide the answers. I feebly plucked it up and took a bite, then another and another, forcing nourishment into myself to fortify my resolve: I would not let a little setback knock me off course.

Still, when evening came, I couldn't bring myself to enter a practice room alone. For the next few days, I casually roamed the practice hallway between classes on the chance someone had ditched their time slot, leaving a room empty and filled with comforting daylight. I snitched a random half-hour a couple of times, but it was hardly enough. I worried about the consequences of curtailing my practice time so severely.

On Thursday I was momentarily distracted by the Euterpean Society meeting for new pledges immediately following dinner. I was still dubious about this venture. Just like my assignment to Professor Zeisberg for piano lessons, the exception made for my class rank had caused a stir and raised the stakes for me. On the other hand, more chances to perform could only help my chances in the competition. I did my best to stay positive.

The glamour of the rush party in the East Parlor had been exchanged for the drab utilitarian decor of a seldom-used classroom, imposing a sober, no-nonsense atmosphere on the gathering. I slipped through the crush of girls at the doorway and weaved my way to a seat in the corner. I recognized only Bessie and a few other voice students, and of course Varina. Evidently it was only the president and sophomore pledges plus me, the lone freshman.

"Welcome, pledges," Varina called out over the chatting group, prompting everyone to settle. "You are all privileged to be here tonight because you've been properly vetted and recommended by our officers. I congratulate you on your good fortune."

She gave a brief history of the Euterpean Literary Society and outlined the rules, duties, and expectations for members. She also described events for the coming year, some of which would entail visits to Emory and Henry College, a school for men just ten miles away. This sent the room atwitter. I imagined the chance to primp and preen for a male audience sent a thrill through most of them, but to me the thought of matching wits with the male intellect, and the male ego, was the most appetizing.

"However, before participation in any of these events," Varina went on to say, "each pledge will go through a rigorous initiation process. You become a Euterpean only after your worthiness has been proven." She ordered us to meet again the following evening at midnight on the rear porch of Mariah Cooper Hall. We were told to dress all in black and, under threat of losing our pledging privilege, sworn to secrecy. With trepidation churning in my gut, I reluctantly raised my right hand.

But the meeting and its distraction ended and I could no longer put off my piano practice. I slowly made my way to the practice hallway, where two of the rooms were occupied already: one with a pianist and the other a voice student. Relieved to have company, I played my warm-up scales, actually reveling in the cacophony created by the Bach partita in one room and strains of a Puccini aria in the one opposite. But soon the voice was silent, and by the time I finished my exercises, I heard the Bach player exit her room and leave the hall. I sighed and dove into my new assignment: a Liszt rhapsody that posed a thorny challenge requiring all my efforts to conquer. Although I knew better, I gave in to the natural desire to amuse myself with the fun sections first instead of tackling the most difficult passages.

My fingers were happily racing over the keys in typical Liszt fashion when I thought I heard it. I stopped abruptly, ears perked, but all was quiet. I gave my shoulders a good shake and began to play again, but after only a minute or so the sound crept back. That undeniable lush tone of a violin. I thought my mind was playing tricks, punishing me for having fun rather than tending to hard work. I switched to the first difficult passage of the piece, certain my concentration would overpower any imaginary sounds wanting to interrupt me. Still, the violin melody sounded with even more intensity than before. Persistently I played on, but the stringed instrument in the distance insisted with its mournful melody in ghoulish counterpoint to the rhapsody that was desperately unfurling under my fingers. I bore down on that poor piano, playing faster and harder, pounding the keys with fury until at last I leapt from the stool, grabbed my music, and ran from the room. I didn't stop until I was safely in the middle of the lawn outside, where I dropped to my knees gasping for breath.

"Bea. Bea!" Ruby came running from a cluster of bushes where she and a couple of other drama students were sneaking cigarettes. She knelt down in the grass beside me. "What in the world happened? What's wrong?"

"It's nothing," I lied, panting and trying to calm my racing heart.

"You look like you've seen a ghost!"

"Oh, Ruby," I put on a good face and struggled to speak between breaths. "Your imagination . . . it's . . . going to serve you well one day."

"Well, if you didn't see a ghost, you're a better actress than I am."

"No. No!" I insisted. "I just got a little short of breath, that's all. It's dusty in the practice rooms. I started coughing."

"Hmm, just dust, huh? Well, that's boring."

"Yes, well. Some of us like boring just fine."

"If you say so. Okay, up you go. Let's get you back to your room."

I was grateful for Ruby's exuberant chatter; it actually had a soothing effect on me. I let it lull me into a stupor until finally, at light bell, we were forced to say good-night. After she returned to her room, I lit two of my candles. For hours I lay in bed staring at them, begging sleep to come.

Nocturne

Plodding through the next day was pure drudgery on my scant four hours of fitful slumber. Thank goodness there was no master class that Friday or I would have made a royal mess of it. But I did have the Euterpean initiation that evening, which would rob me of even more sleep. As much as possible throughout the day I kept Ruby by my side, the constant patter of her voice a distracting comfort. Playing cards in my room that evening, she spied my black outfit laid out on a chair and teased, "Geez, Bea, where's the funeral?" I made up a story about reorganizing my armoire, and she simply rolled her eyes.

At light bell I bid her good night, then set my alarm clock for eleven thirty and placed it under my pillow. I lit a candle and tried to nap, but only nervously stared at the flame. When the muffled alarm sounded, I shut it off and slipped into my black skirt and jacket, plus the huge black scarf all pledges had been provided. I wrapped mine completely over my head and neck, then added black gloves. The morbid ensemble was intended to prevent our discovery, but thankfully it would also fend off the autumn cold.

I snuffed the candle and slipped something extra into my jacket pocket, to be kept secret. I was not about to go into the dark night without my flashlight. My sisters knew about my paralyzing fear of the dark and had pooled their meager coins together to buy it for me as a going-away present. "Just for emergencies," they said, knowing batteries were expensive. Fully dressed and armed, I stealthily slipped from my dorm room to the outside unnoticed.

Still, I was alarmed by the pitch-black darkness engulfing the back lawns and fought off an urge to pull out the flashlight.

Finally, I reached the rear porch of Mariah Cooper Hall, where Varina stood with a lantern, its dim sliver of light a tiny relief. She was flanked by two established Euterpeans: Ethel, of course, but also Ruby's mother, Myrtle Latham. I didn't know many of the pledges, but it was a comfort to be in the company of other warm bodies. After everyone had arrived, Varina stepped forward.

"We're going to take a little walk off the campus grounds. We'll be traveling some secluded back streets, sometimes in separate groups of three, so stay with your leader. I will head the front group, Myrtle the center, and Ethel the rear." Varina took off, sure of her steps even in the dark, with the three nearest girls queued closely behind. Not wanting to jostle with the others, I took my spot in the last group, which unfortunately left me with Ethel.

We left the Martha's back lawn, traveled west past a lumber yard, then crossed a wide, dusty street. We slipped behind several buildings whose rear lawns were dotted with shielding trees, then squeezed between two of them to cross Main Street at a stretch bare of streetlights. From there a narrow side street took us to Plumb Alley, which was little more than a dirt path but ran the length of the town in a straight line (thus its name) between Main and Valley streets. It was lined only with livery stables and outbuildings at the rear of homes that faced those major streets, and it served as utility access as well as a secluded path for us. We turned left and kept walking for several blocks.

At the end of Plumb Alley, we turned right to walk half a block up Russell Road, stopping at a large iron gate to our left. Varina stood before the gate and gathered us around her. Bunching into a tight huddle, we tried to muster warmth from each other and share the meager glow of her lamp.

"Incipient Euterpeans," Varina intoned, her tongue chipping at consonants like an icepick. "You will celebrate great literature and music, created by great people departed from this earth. By keeping their creations alive, you honor these dead poets and masters and prove the importance of remembering those who have lived before us. Ladies, we now enter the realm of the dead."

Myrtle pushed open the gate, a massive barrier of tall black spindles topped with sharp spikes and shaped into a gothic dome. Its forbidding presence loomed above us, conjuring the feeling that each spike was pricking at my heart as we followed Varina inside. Sprawled before us, pale flat stones jutted up from the ground like broken teeth. Halting beside one, Varina's lantern provided just enough illumination to see that it was inscribed: a name, a line of text, some numbers. It was a tombstone. They were all tombstones. We were in a graveyard.

Varina didn't linger here but led us on to a strange-looking mound of grassy earth, taller than any of us and overgrown with creeping strands of ivy. Built into one side was another iron gate, a small replica of the one at the graveyard's entrance. I shuddered to think what lay beyond this lesser grid of spikes.

"This is the most impressive grave in Sinking Spring Cemetery. It is the resting place of John Henry Martin, who passed on a mere sixteen years ago. As you can see, the gate to this grave faces directly down Valley Street. Mr. Martin was proud of the many properties he'd built there and wanted to be buried standing up so he could keep an eye on them in the hereafter." Pondering this creepy notion, we pledges turned to look down Valley Street, though we saw nothing in the pitch black.

"Each of these graves has a story, and we mustn't forget them. Their stories remind us that our journey on Earth is limited. We have to find our purpose and nurture it."

Varina worked up a full-blown sermon as she continued a litany of the dead buried there: pioneers and farmers; noted citizens of Abingdon and Washington County; soldiers of the Civil War and those who had tended their wounds, including young ladies from our very own Martha Washington College who stayed to work as nurses when the school converted to a field hospital. I marveled

The Martha Odyssey

at the history contained in the turf of the cemetery's eleven acres, but chilled thinking how many bodies rested beneath our feet. I was wondering how much longer we would stand in the cold when Ethel began handing each of us a large sheet of paper. It felt sturdy and thick, curling at the edges much like butcher's paper. Myrtle followed her, giving out thick Conte crayons. I was puzzled to think what we might do with these in such utter blackness.

"Now we come to your initiation task," said Varina, as she held her lantern before a nearby gravestone. Myrtle held one of the paper sheets against its front while Ethel applied several swift strokes with a crayon. Ghostly letters and numbers appeared on the paper, a perfect replica of the tombstone's engraving.

"Each of you will be taken to a grave of a woman who died in her youth," Varina directed. "You will do a grave rubbing of her headstone to take back to your room. Every day for the next three weeks you will look at it and ponder your mortality. Consider what that young woman might have done had she lived, and compose a short essay of her imagined life story. At the induction ceremony, you will read your story as your rubbing is burned."

Aided by extra lanterns Myrtle and Ethel were now allowed to light, we were led to our selected graves. No one spoke as we held the paper in place for one another, and I couldn't decide if the silence was calming or simply enhanced the spooky atmosphere. When each of us had finished our grisly task, we huddled together again while Varina examined each rubbing with her lantern. She halted before me, holding the light on my rubbing for a long moment. Mine had been a simple grave marker bearing a single word, "Beth," with the birth and death dates. I didn't think it was in any way remarkable, but Varina took it from me and held it up for everyone to see.

"The soul in this grave was especially brave. One of our Martha girls, who came to a particularly sad end. During the Civil War, the winter of 1863 to be exact, a severely wounded Union captain was captured as a spy and carried to the Martha through a secret underground cave system the Confederates used to smuggle ammunition. John Stoves was his name. He was secreted up to a room on the third floor of Preston Hall and placed into Beth's charge. She had a kind heart and nursed Captain Stoves faithfully—so faithfully that they soon fell in love. But despite her devoted care, the young captain's condition worsened, and soon he knew the end was near. 'Play something, Beth' he whispered. 'I'm going.' As she had done on many a night to soothe him, she took up her violin. With tears in her eyes, she played him a sweet Southern melody as he breathed his last."

A new chill trickled up my spine. I told myself to not be silly and tried to shake it off.

"When a Confederate soldier entered the room to take him, she stopped him in his tracks. With a mixture of sorrow and pride she said, 'Sir, he has been pardoned by an officer higher than General Lee. Captain Stoves . . . my John . . . is dead.' She fell immediately into mourning, and died just a few weeks later. Supposedly of typhoid fever, but some say of a broken heart."

Varina solemnly handed the rubbing back to me, her woeful tale causing an even more somber mood to descend upon us. Finally, Ethel broke the silence by asking Varina which room the captain had died in.

"Why, I believe it was room sixty."

The number landed on my ears like a flaming arrow. My paper slipped from my hands as I began to hyperventilate and tremble all over. The girl beside me grabbed my arm, but I broke her grip and backed away. Needing to be far away from that place, I turned to run but instantly stumbled over a tombstone. Ignoring my throbbing shin, I got up to sprint away when a strong hand grasped my arm.

"Beatrice, what's wrong?" Varina whispered and pulled me close. She was surprisingly strong; her firm grip and the lantern's light momentarily settled me. In between shuddering breaths, I answered.

"Room sixty. Preston Hall. That's my dorm room."

Varina gave a sympathetic sigh and pulled me into a hug. After giving me a few moments to calm down, she turned to the group.

"It's time for us to return to the Martha. Fall into your groups as you did before." Looping her arm through mine she whispered, "You will walk up front by my side."

It felt foolish to be escorted like that, but I didn't refuse. Ethel handed me the rubbing I'd dropped with what seemed to be a smug, somewhat sinister smile on her face. But it was dark, and I was still shaken; I could have misread her. I was glad to be leaving that place behind and longed to light a comforting candle by my safe warm bed.

MY EYES OPEN ON A DIAPHANOUS RIPPLE IN THE AIR NEAR MY *window. The sight should alarm me, yet I feel strangely drawn to it. I creep across the floor, the wooden boards warm under my bare feet. At the window a soft breeze billows the curtains against my face as I look out over the lawn, vividly illuminated by preternatural moonlight. A smile blooms on my face as I gaze at the sight below: Xander, standing tall, proudly surveying his kingdom, his silky midnight-black coat glistening in the moonglow. Suddenly he looks up and says, "Come." It's perfectly natural that he speaks. "It's too far," I answer, but I take a seat on the windowsill. "Come," he says again. He's so enticing I can't help but reach for him, and I find myself floating gently downward until I come to rest on his back. I fit there perfectly! I close my eyes, lean my head on his neck, and wrap my arms around him. I feel as if we are one creature. His muscles flex as he carries me forward, gently and smoothly, like gliding through water. Gradually he builds up speed and I sit up to relish the ride, which soon becomes a roaring gallop. The campus is forgotten as we race through a field of tall grass, the wind blowing fiercely and splaying my hair across my face. But I don't care because Xander is leading and I trust his path. His stride changes as we begin to trudge up a hill. Eventually we enter a tangle of trees. Here it's cool among fragrant evergreens, where I'm lost but don't feel lost. Suddenly the trees disappear, replaced by rocks. First small ones, then larger ones, and ones taller than me all scattered and jutting from the ground in a wild, haphazard maze. I slip off Xander's back to give him a rest and he nibbles the tender grass growing between the rocks. For a long while I admire the stunning view through the moonlit clouds. A breeze begins to blow, chilling the air around me. I turn back to Xander, but he's gone; he's slipped away into the outcropping of rocks. I search for him, hunting among the jagged stones, turning every which way in the chaotic maze. The wind is stronger now, and colder. I run through the maze, but the more frantic my search, the faster the wind blows, whipping around the rocks, howling and whining. I try in vain to call Xander's name above the roar. Suddenly the whining becomes the high-pitched twang of a violin, seizing me to a sudden halt. This can't be! But it plays on and on, every stroke of bow across strings an assault on my ears. I have to find Xander, so I run faster and faster, dodging rocks left and right, the macabre tune screeching at every turn, building its deafening crescendo until—*

Jolting upright, I gasped for air. I jerked toward the candle by my bed, my rapid breathing quenching the flame. Desperately I grabbed up a match and willed my trembling fingers to relight it. Then, pulling the covers up around my chin, I wept.

Cantabile

The next morning, the sun was quite high by the time I woke. I'd missed breakfast but had no appetite. Climbing out of bed, I stretched my stiff muscles, full of kinks from the night's tensions. Anxious for bright daylight and fresh air, I hurriedly dressed in my barn clothes.

Approaching the rear of the stables, I heard a strange voice inside and ducked quickly behind the edge of the open doorway. Peering in, I saw Jonah hitching the draft horses to the green wagon while another man sat high above him on the wagon's seat. He was holding the harness reins and talking at length about the "lovely jaunt" he was taking his family on, a picnic at a place called Shallow Ford. He seemed to think he was granting an unusually generous gesture, bragging about the magnificent spread they were going to enjoy. Jonah listened as the man jabbered on, and I witnessed a tedious but necessary part of his job. When the wagon was finally ready, Jonah slid open the front stable doors to let the man exit through a front corral gate. I waited to enter until the last squeak and rattle of the wheels faded into the distance.

Walking toward Copper's stall, I spied Xander across the corridor. A strange chord of apprehension struck me as a horrid flashback from my dream zipped through my head. But I'd never been anxious around a horse, and I wouldn't let crazy mind games change that. I crossed to Copper's stall, where he gently nudged me as I scratched his forelock, letting me linger with my head bent over his. I was so lost in my melancholy I failed to hear Jonah's approach.

"Your friend has missed you."

My head popped up, and for a moment I didn't know if he was talking about himself or the horse. I quickly decided he meant Copper.

"I've missed him, too," I said, but didn't look Jonah's way.

"He knows he's special to you, since you chose him to ride over the others."

"It was easy. He looks so much like Nutmeg. My own horse, from back home."

"Where is home?"

"Clintwood. It's in Virginia, but a long way away." Jonah waited while I scratched at Copper's ears. "And now I'm supposed to make the Martha my home. But it isn't working out too well." I paused my ear-scratching, realizing I'd revealed my school. I wondered if it mattered anymore.

"Come with me," he said, and began walking without waiting for me. I followed him into the open tack room, where an old stall door balanced over two barrels created a makeshift table. It was laden with bridles, harnesses, and a couple of saddles, with a three-legged stool sitting beside it on the floor. Jonah grabbed an apple crate and set it on the opposite side. "Come sit," he said, patting the upturned crate. I sullenly accepted his invitation while he seated himself on the stool. "Nothing lifts the spirits like the smell of clean leather." He handed me a cloth and opened the pots of saddle soap and linseed oil on the table. He said no more, and I was grateful he trusted me to know what to do.

I took up the nearest bridle and began cleaning it. The pungent aroma of the soap infusing the leather prickled my nostrils, and the repetitive rubbing motions began to sooth my tense muscles. We toiled in comfortable silence, the work inducing a kind of meditative trance. By the time I'd finished my second bridle and tackled a saddle, my nerves had calmed. I regretted Jonah seeing me gloomy.

"You must wonder why I'm so glum."

"I don't need to know. Unless you need to tell."

I swirled my cloth in the soap, then gave a few vigorous strokes to the saddle before I spoke again.

"I came to the Martha to study music." Jonah nodded but didn't look up from his work. "And there's a lot riding on my success." I spilled my quagmire: that Mrs. Counts had such high hopes for me; that my father, who didn't believe in college for females, insisted I succeed at the one year he'd given me or my younger sisters would never get the chance; and then there was the scholarship competition, both wonderful and daunting. "I don't want to disappoint anyone. So, I work hard. At my classes, my piano lessons, and the . . ." I paused, buffing vigorously at the leather while I thought what to say next.

"Do you enjoy playing the piano?" Jonah spurred me on.

"Oh, yes. I love it. I started as a small child, as soon as I could climb up on the piano bench at church. I'd pick out melodies I'd heard, and make up some, too. At home I'd complain, 'My fingers are itching,' and beg someone to take me to the church to play. Until my granddad finally bought a used upright for our home." I bore down on the saddle with my cloth. "But practicing piano at the college is not the same. Not the same at all." The dark cloud crept over me again and held my tongue.

"How is it different?" Jonah gently prodded.

After a deep breath my story tumbled out. "I've been hearing sounds. Sounds that aren't there." Jonah listened, eyes intent on his polishing cloth, while I described hearing the violin music over the last couple of weeks. When I finished, he kept silently working. I worried he must think me deranged and wouldn't want an unhinged lunatic handling any of the horses.

"You are a musician too full of music," he said finally, laying aside a bridle gleaming with the fresh sheen of linseed oil. He picked up a buggy harness and continued cleaning, as if his simple statement explained my dilemma.

"What do you mean?"

He gave the long leather strips several strokes with his cloth. "A honeysuckle vine creeps around the limbs of a tree until it's so entangled it becomes a part of the tree. When a leaf falls into a brook, it's swept into the power of the rushing water and travels for miles. A musician becomes entangled and empowered with sound." He looked up to see my brow furrowed in confusion. "It's the Cherokee belief about music. That it's sacred. It summons power from nature and spirits. This power frees the imagination and lets the mind soar in all dimensions. You become so full of music that your mind is hearing what your ears don't. It's nothing to be afraid of. It's a blessing."

He quietly reached for the other side of the harness and continued his saddle soap lathering. I wasn't sure I bought into what he'd said, but was glad he trusted me to hear an outpouring of Cherokee wisdom. It made it easier for me to trust him to hear my story's troubling complication.

"That may be, but there's more."

In a voice a bit shaky, I told him of the Civil War soldier dying in my room while a Martha girl played violin for him. Without breaking the flow of his cloth, he briefly raised his eyes to me.

"An interesting story, but is it true? Or is it a legend that creates notoriety for the college?" I thought back on the gravestone. Only the word "Beth" and the dates of her birth and death were carved on it, nothing else.

"I suppose it could be only a legend. A very sad one. Which of course makes it a gripping story."

"It's natural to want a story to explain something we don't understand. But sometimes a story is just a story. Even if this one's true, that doesn't mean it's connected to the music you believe you're hearing."

I considered telling him my dream, but decided I'd dished out enough craziness for one day and went back to my task. By the time everything was buffed to a brilliant sheen and hung back in place, I felt as restored as the tack. I thanked Jonah for including me in the task and turned to leave. As I neared the back doorway, he bellowed one more question.

"Have you ever been to the Meadows?"

It was a large expanse of rolling grassland that lay beyond the railroad tracks. He offered to take me on a ride there the following Saturday. I wanted to say yes so badly I could taste it, manure and all. But if a Martha Girl were caught riding out in the wild with a man, unchaperoned, it would be all over for her. Reluctantly I said that if I were a boy, I'd surely take him up on the offer, but sadly had to decline. At least he still trusted me with the horses.

Capriccio

Despite Jonah's reassuring counsel, I spent the entire next week avoiding the practice rooms altogether. My only time at the piano was when I accompanied voice students or played popular songs and ragtime in the parlor with my pals. My less-than-stellar lesson with Professor Zeisberg on Wednesday proved that signs of neglect were starting to show. That bode poorly for the competition as well as my grade point average. This couldn't go on. I had no choice but to return to the practice rooms, but I desperately needed daylight to have the courage to enter them.

Every Friday morning, the music conservatory office posted a new practice room time slot sheet for the following week. Freshmen signed up last and not before eleven o'clock, so with a voice lesson to accompany at that time, I usually had last pick of all. But that Friday Miss Le Grande ended the lesson early, which sent me racing with fingers crossed to view the sheet. To my consternation, I found very few daytime slots left, forcing me to choose odd hours worked in around my classes. It would mean a lot of running back and forth across campus and shifting study time to evenings, but there was no other solution. I would just have to manage.

"There's something for you in the tack room." Jonah greeted me without ceremony the next morning. Thinking there was more leather to clean, I was surprised to open the door and see no table set up, nor pots of soap and polish. But on the nearest wall pegs that usually held bridles, I noticed some odd items and lifted them off one by one: a man's work shirt, gray with a half placket of buttons in front; a man's wool vest; a newsboy cap and a pair of trousers with galluses buttoned to the waist. I quickly closed the door and changed, tucking my hair snugly up under the cap. Giddy as Cinderella, I stepped from the tack room.

"Christmas came early this year!"

"Who are you?" Jonah asked with a deadpan face.

"Well . . ." I paused to muster my best baritone. "Benjamin."

"That's who I thought you were." He tried to be serious but I saw mischief in his eyes.

I broke out of the corral on Copper's back with a sense of freedom I hadn't known since arriving in Abingdon. We followed Jonah and Xander over the railroad tracks, through the trees and toward the open fields with a shared sense of anticipation. The further we rode from the stables, the more I felt like a new person. Which, for the time being, I was.

It was a gorgeous October day, a perfect mixture of crisp air and warm sun. That sweet spot of long-awaited relief from sweltering temperatures without the chill of oncoming winter. The horses kept up a brisk trot as we approached the gate to the Meadows. Jonah opened it deftly while still astride, and once inside, I followed as he kept Xander to a mild lope across the field. I longed for more speed, but this wasn't my horse so I deferred to Jonah's lead. But several minutes into our ride I got my wish. He finally put Xander into a lively canter that Copper only too willingly matched. The fields seemed to go on for miles as we navigated gentle peaks and valleys of grassy earth. When we reached the fence on the far side, we slowed to a trot and turned to travel along the fence rails. The horses settled into an easy walk, snorting and shaking their heads in exhilarated pleasure.

"I don't know who enjoyed that more, Copper or me," I said, a bit breathless.

"Xander's not complaining either."

We rode in silence for a while. I savored the absence of confining walls.

"There's nothing better than this. On horseback, out in a grassy field. I finally feel . . . like I'm home."

Jonah smiled, his eyes gazing toward the horizon.

"Where is home for you?" I ventured, hoping to unlock some of his mystery. "Or has this town always been your home?"

"No. But it should have been." He said no more, but his enigmatic reply intrigued me.

"It should have been?" I prompted.

Long moments passed before he spoke.

"Centuries ago, the Cherokees' home was in the East, in the Appalachian Mountains. Some clans lived in this very region. Then European settlers came, encroached more and more on tribal lands. The Cherokee had no choice but to fight to keep it. In lots of bloody battles. One was near where we're riding now, a bare century and a half ago. The Battle of Black's Fort."

I recalled Varina's lecture that awful night at Sinking Spring Cemetery. The very first grave ever put there was for a man who had been killed by a Cherokee.

"The Cherokee were forced to stand up for what was rightfully theirs. Still, a lot of folks don't see it that way. They have strong ties to their own history. And long memories."

He fell silent again. But if this wasn't his home I wondered where he came from.

"Where were you born?"

"Far away from here. Out west, in what's now the state of Oklahoma."

"Indian Territory?"

He nodded. "But it was a miracle I was ever born at all."

I stared at the side of his face, prompting him to explain.

"My grandfather crossed the country from the east as a papoose on his mother's back. Part of "Nunna daul Tsuny—the trail where they cried."

My high school history class touched briefly on the Trail of Tears, but Granddad told me horrid details. Cherokee forced to leave their tribal lands and march over a thousand miles to a special territory in the west. The grueling journey was mostly on foot, ravaging the tribe by disease, cold and hunger. It killed thousands.

"My grandfather very well might have died, but my great-grandmother was determined he would live. She gave most of her meager food rations to her baby. When she died, my grandfather was given to a woman whose child didn't make it. He became her son and a part of her clan. Grew up, married, and had children—one of them my father."

"Your great-grandmother was a saint."

"Except for her sacrifice, I wouldn't be here."

I still wondered how he came to Abingdon. And if he was all alone.

"It must be hard, living so far away from family."

"But I don't, really. Here I'm with my ancestors, and my own flesh and blood."

I was puzzling over this surprising statement when suddenly he turned Xander to the left and launched him into a canter, Copper following on his heels. Jonah had granted enough self-disclosure for one day. I would have to wait for more.

The following week was an adventure in time management as I struggled to adjust to my new unconventional practice schedule. It kept me zigzagging all over campus, and skipped lunches put grumbles in my belly. Ruby overheard a particularly raucous growl during literature class one afternoon, prompting Miss Lewis to call us down for giggling. When Ruby learned about my bizarre schedule, she began sneaking me sandwiches so I wouldn't starve.

By Saturday morning I was in need of diversion more than ever. But to my dismay, I awoke early to see the sun climbing toward a ceiling of grayish clouds that threatened to curtail a riding excursion. Keeping my fingers crossed all the way to the stables, I was overjoyed to see both Xander and Copper tacked up when I arrived. Jonah was confident that with an early start we could beat the wet weather, so I hurried into my "Benjamin" clothes and we took off. This time, after crossing the railroad tracks, we veered farther left and rode into a wide-open field. There were no fences here and we were free to wander unencumbered.

It was still only mid-October, but the cloud cover created a nip in the air, making the horses frisky and itching to break into a jubilant gallop. Jonah looked at me with a silent question, I nodded my assent, and we gave them their heads. They ran as if racing a train, their powerful muscles propelling them forward at breakneck speed. It felt as though they could take flight at any moment.

When they'd had their fill, we pulled them back to a trot, settling their excitement. Eventually we slowed to a walk so we could all catch our breath.

"Now that's what I call a real ride," I declared.

"I'm glad you survived."

"You had doubts?"

"Of course not." His eyes looked straight ahead, but I saw the sly grin.

We rode in silence for a while, enjoying the good view of the countryside from a slightly higher elevation. My mind wandered back to Jonah's story about his family origins. I'd puzzled all week about how he got from Oklahoma to Virginia, and especially what he meant by "Here I'm with my ancestors and my own flesh and blood." But I feared a direct question would silence him, so tried a different tactic.

"Where did you learn blacksmithing?" He took several moments to answer.

"From another blacksmith."

"Okay. Another blacksmith *where*? In your home village?" I waited patiently.

"Pennsylvania." Silently he rode on.

"And why there and not Oklahoma?" I persisted, my look indicating I was determined to hear more.

"The Carlisle Industrial Indian School," he said finally. "When I was twelve years old, their officials came to our village, rounded up all children who were of age, and put us on a train to Pennsylvania."

It took me a moment to absorb the shock of that scenario. "That's a really long distance from your parents."

"That was the whole point. To make us forget our people, our language, our religion.

"But . . . why?"

"To remake us into *white* Americans. They claimed to be saving us, and to do that they needed to kill what was Indian in us. So, everything we'd known from birth was forbidden. And not just Cherokee, but children from Apache, Cree, Sioux, Chippewa, Lakota. More tribes than I can remember. The first thing they did was change our name. They lined us up in a classroom facing a blackboard with a long list of English names. By turns we were handed a stick and told to point to a name, which from then on would be our only name."

"So that's when you became Jonah?"

"That's when I outsmarted them. I'd already learned some English at the mission school near our village. My Cherokee name is Equoni Yona, River Bear, or just Yona for short. Jonah is the English version, so I pointed to that name."

"Clever."

"But it was really hard for students with no English. They doled out harsh punishment to anyone caught speaking their native tongue."

My heart hurt trying to imagine coming to a new place to live where you didn't understand anything said, and forbidden to even speak.

"Next, they took our clothes and gave us a white man's uniform. Then cut our hair. To us long hair stands for strength, a sign of our dignity. And for some, like the Lakota, cutting it is a symbol of mourning. So, after their hair was cut off, they wailed for hours."

I looked at Jonah's long black braid tumbling down his back. The thought of a child crying while his hair lay on the floor was heartbreaking.

"We were forced to stand in lines and march everywhere—to class, meals, our bunkhouses—just like a regiment of soldiers. So many rules you couldn't possibly learn them all, but if you broke one you were whacked just the same. Or sent to the 'guard house' for confinement. I became very familiar with the interior of that Revolutionary war relic." He paused with a frown on his face. I didn't know how to respond. "I learned the basics of blacksmithing at Carlisle, but it was not a happy place for me."

We'd come to a small lake, fed by a stream flowing below the knoll we'd been riding on. We stopped and dismounted, letting the horses take a small drink. I felt guilty that my prying questions had stirred bad memories, and tried to steer the conversation in a new direction.

"So, you became a blacksmith when you finished school?"

His gruff laugh surprised me.

"In a way, yes. But fortunately, I didn't finish school."

"Fortunately?"

"The school had an 'outing' program, where students were sent away to work during summer break. There my luck changed. I was assigned to a local farmer who was also a blacksmith. Actually, an artisan. He believed that just because something was useful didn't mean it couldn't be beautiful. He taught me special techniques."

We pulled the horses' muzzles from the water so they wouldn't overdrink, then let them nibble on patches of green grass still growing near the water's edge.

"He wasn't like anyone at the school. He was a good man, kind. His wife, too. From the start they treated me like a son. Working there was like being in a family again." Jonah went quiet; we watched the horses graze. "At the end of my second summer there, I returned to school to find a letter waiting for me. Sent from my home village, three months earlier, telling me my parents had died.

The Martha Odyssey

No one had brought me the letter and I was so angry. I hadn't gone home to help bury them, wasn't there to pray over them, or . . ." Jonah's face grew dark and I wanted to kick myself.

"I was furious with hatred for the school and tried to run away. Jumped the train and rode a freight car for twenty miles, but they caught me and brought me back. Did another stint in the guard house. After that I stopped talking. The only thing that kept me going was the thought of the blacksmith's farm in summer. I worried they would give me a new assignment, as another punishment. But Mr. Schumacher, the farmer, asked for me by name so I got to go back. And that summer everything changed." I was relieved to see Jonah's face soften.

"The Schumachers were appalled to hear what had happened and vowed to end my misery at Carlisle. They fixed it so I could stay on with them. Later they inherited the property here in Abingdon. Getting older, they thought winters would be milder in the south, so they sold their Pennsylvania farm and moved here." Jonah pulled Xander's reins back over his neck and promptly mounted, signaling the end of his story. I quickly followed suit, but he turned to me before launching our mounts into a brisk canter toward the stable.

"So, to answer your question: the school wasn't finished with me, but I was finished with the school."

Agitato

The exhilaration of that fabulous ride carried over into the following week, giving me renewed energy for the erratic movements of my new schedule. Flying from one agenda item to the next with a singular vision—like a buggy horse with blinders—I was in mid-flurry early one afternoon when the sound of my name jostled me from my workaholic zone.

"Beatrice! Beatrice Damron!" Varina shouted across the front veranda of Preston Hall. She trotted over to where I'd abruptly come to a halt. "For a moment I thought you were a mirage. Aside from church services on Sundays, I've hardly seen you. How are you?"

"Oh. Well, um, fine. You know. Really busy, with school." My rambling reply only perplexed her more.

"Obviously, something's keeping you terribly occupied. I just don't want my motherly duties to go slack." She offered a questioning smile and I squirmed under the amiable scrutiny.

"I'm fine. Really. I've been taking piano practice during the day, lately. Working it in between classes. It keeps me on the run a bit."

"I see. Well, don't overdo it. Be sure to make time for rest."

"I will."

"And a little fun, too." She winked and patted my shoulder before moving on into the hall. Her words caught me off guard, and for a shocking moment I wondered if she knew about my excursions to the stables. But I quickly decided that was absurd and put it out of my mind. I had too much to do to before sundown.

But when sundown came, I had one last task to attend to. One I dreaded, yet could deny no longer. The gravestone rubbing sat tucked behind my armoire, unseen by my eyes since that night at the cemetery. Thinking about the soul it represented still gave me the shivers. I had absolutely no desire to compose her story, let alone ponder my own life and what I might leave behind. I was too busy trying to create a life for myself in the first place. But the Euterpean Society induction ceremony was coming up that very Saturday evening and I was running out of time. I was sitting on my bed pondering the dismal assignment when a fortuitous knock at my door pulled me from the edges of despair.

"Don't hide away in here, Honey Bea." Ruby pushed the door open and waltzed into the room. The knock was now only a formality, actually more of a joke between us since we treated both rooms as our own. When I looked up, I had a sudden epiphany. I gazed at her as if a brilliant halo surrounded her entire body.

"What?" She giggled with a bemused smile.

"Ruby, you are a gift from the heavens above."

"Well, tell me something I don't already know." She struck a series of perfectly executed Delsarte moves, landing in a magazine-ready pose on my vanity chair.

"How about putting that magnificent dramatic flair of yours to good use for a friend?"

"My dramatic flair is always available, especially for you, dear one. How may I be of service?"

I retrieved the rubbing paper from its hiding place and handed it to her.

"Where did you get this?"

"You know what it is?"

"Of course, I do. It's a gravestone rubbing."

"You never cease to surprise me, Ruby. I'd never heard of them before I was forced to make one." I broke my vow of silence and told her about the initiation at the cemetery, and how I was charged with writing a story of this person's missed life. Instead of being repulsed, like me, Ruby was openly intrigued. She sat enthralled as I related the tragic tale of the girl nursing the dying soldier during the Civil War. I feared she might make a connection with my recent interest in violin players, but the romance of the lovers dying only weeks apart consumed her attention. She jumped from her chair and immediately began spinning a new tale as she paced the room, each plot point punctuated with dramatic movement, gestures, and facial expressions. It was Theatre of Ruby at its finest.

When her performance concluded, I gave her the most thunderous round of applause I could manage by myself. She took a wide bow, then sat fanning herself with one of my music folios and coached me as I jotted down notes for the story. I kept thanking her over and over, but she only protested, claiming it was the most fun she'd had all week. That night I slept like a log, relieved to have that onerous task off my plate.

On Friday morning I arranged with Miss Le Grande to arrive late to the eleven o'clock voice lesson, hoping to have first dibs at some better time slots on the practice schedule. At first look I couldn't believe what I saw, so scanned the entire schedule again. To my horror, I discovered all the daytime hours were taken. I stared at the sheet as the grid of tiny boxes beside the evening hours formed a net trapping me like a helpless rabbit. I was paralyzed with fear but simply could not ignore my need to practice; there was too much at stake. My trembling fingers struggled to grip the pencil, and with shaky marks I claimed my evening hours.

The rest of that day was spent in a kind of trance. How could all the daytime hours have disappeared so suddenly? I'd examined the initials in those time slots, but they didn't match names of anyone I knew so I couldn't even try to make a trade. Not that I had anything to bargain with anyway. When evening came, I felt exhausted from stress as well as work, so I begged off the usual card games and gossip in favor of turning in early. As I set out my bedside candle for the night, I saw that my supply was dwindling fast. I went to sleep contemplating how to procure more to see me through until I returned home for Christmas.

I CAN SEE IT, JUST AT THE END OF THE ROAD I'M WALKING ON. Only I'm not walking but riding in a wagon with no horse in front of it. Noiselessly it floats along, and I can see everything for miles around. Soon I see my house, my home. I'm home for Christmas! But the grass in the yard is green, petunias are blooming, and the maple trees are full of green leaves. My littlest sister Jenny sees me and comes bounding down the porch steps, takes my hand and leads me through the front door that opens on its own. My other sisters wave at me from the parlor. Lillian pokes her head out from underneath a tower of pillows piled high on the floor. Why would Mama allow her to do such a thing? Gladys sits on top of my upright piano, swinging her legs. She should get down from there before she breaks it. Jenny points toward the dining room where Nutmeg stands at the table eating apples off the turkey platter. "Doesn't that make Mama angry?" I say, but all three sisters just laugh. Darkness begins to grow inside the house, and suddenly it's night, and the four of us are walking through the hallways. I carry a single candle. They take me up the stairs and through all the rooms, but every time I turn a corner one of them vanishes. I'm left alone and the candle is burning down fast. I search for my sisters, in and out of doors leading in and out of rooms, on and on like this until I don't recognize any of the rooms; they are in my house but they are not of my house. I call my sisters' names and strain to listen for their voices. I hear a faint sound from above and know it's Jenny. She doesn't answer me but she's crying, the same high-pitched wail she made as a baby in the cradle. I have to find her. "I'm coming!" I call and race for the stairs that lead up to the attic. It takes forever to reach them while the wailing gets more and more frantic. I abandon the candle and scramble up the stairs. When I summit the top step, I tumble onto the attic floor in the pitch-black dark. Instead of Jenny's wail, I hear a violin bow *drawing back and forth along the strings, an eerie imitation of a baby's cry. I clasp my hands over my ears, but the horrific squealing only becomes stronger. Blindly, I race across the floor to escape the sound, but the violin fills the entire space. In wild, looping circles I run, crashing into boxes and trunks, hands still clapped firmly over my ears. Then the faintest glow of light appears from a window at the rear of the attic. I run toward the light, faster and faster, the wail of the violin tight on my heels, driving me to madness and I jump—*

With a thud I landed on the floor by my bed. My candle was burned out completely, the room illuminated only by a muted moonglow through the window. In a panic, I felt my way to the box of candles hidden underneath my armoire. I desperately wanted to light two, but felt I couldn't spare another. With covers wound tightly around me, I sat staring at the single flame and waited for the relief of sunrise.

At daybreak I wrote a letter to Lillian asking her to please send a money order to purchase more candles. A phone call would have been faster, but I couldn't afford the fee or risk anyone overhearing my request. It left Lillian the problem of getting the money in the first place, but she was clever and resourceful.

I dropped my letter in the post box outside Mrs. Long's office on my way to the dining hall. The horrors of the nightmare had robbed my appetite, but then the passing of those early wakeful hours left me weak and empty. I'd learned that more than bread and cheese were needed to sustain me on Saturday mornings, so I forced myself to eat a full breakfast before heading out to the stables.

Jonah was still cleaning stalls, and without a word I pitched in, extra anxious to get out into the open spaces and shake off my worries. It was the last Saturday in October, sunny but decidedly cooler, and one of the last clear days before cold breezes and drizzle would signal the onslaught of winter. The horses loved it, feeling keener than ever to race the chilly wind. This time I didn't wait for

Jonah's signal and launched Copper into a full gallop as soon as we reached the field. Xander naturally followed, but for once Copper kept the lead. I imagine Jonah held him back, somehow sensing that a wild ride of abandon was what I needed. And he was right.

I let the gallop go on a bit farther than on our last ride before pulling Copper back to a trot. Jonah directed us to a worn path leading into a grove of trees and we followed this trace among the oaks, sugar maples, and hickories at a relaxed walk. Most leaves had fallen and scattered, pressed into the earth in a mosaic of yellows, greens, and golds, with occasional splashes of bright orange or scarlet. A patchwork quilt like the one Lillian and I shared at home. The thought turned my mood somber despite the boisterous ride, leaving me disinclined to talk. Instead, I focused on the shuffle of the horses' hooves, the scurry of a rabbit bounding over the forest floor, the cawing of a crow that lulled me into a dreamlike state.

"Do you hear them?" Jonah's voice startled me.

"Who?" I blurted, looking around for people nearby. I was certain my disguise had failed and I was finally caught.

"No one to worry about," Jonah chuckled. "It's just the forest spirits. They're speaking."

"Oh." I breathed, relieved we were still alone. "I've never thought about the forest *having* spirits."

"Everything in nature has an intelligent spirit, just like us. Sometimes they're very talkative." He looked over at me with a whimsical grin.

I thought back on my childhood. Even at an early age I'd spent hours wandering through wild, wooded thickets.

"Actually, I think I've always been able to feel them."

"I'm sure you have."

"Do you think they mind us treading on their territory?"

"It's not their territory. But it's not ours, either. Everyone has equal claim."

We rode on, the silence punctuated only with the quiet burr of the horses' occasional snorting.

"Do you think these spirits ever speak in dreams?"

"Sure. Dreams are a gift of the spirits."

I pondered this notion, fighting the dread threatening to slither back into the pit of my stomach. Soon I felt Jonah's eyes on me, sensing my discomfort.

"Do you hear how these forest sounds work together?" he ventured.

I pushed the black thoughts from my mind and took several long moments to listen.

"It's sort of like a good piece of music," I said. "Where the harmony works really well."

"Well put. What you hear is balance. A relationship in balance is peaceful. But when balance is disturbed, there's trouble."

"It's easy to feel balanced in the woods, on a horse. It's my natural habitat. But elsewhere, lately . . . it's . . ." He waited patiently, but I didn't know how to go on.

"We're not truly separate from anything," he offered gently. "Maintaining balance—with nature, other people, even ourselves—keeps fear from getting the better of us. So, when fear creeps in, remember the 'forest music.' The sound of balance."

I wasn't sure it could be as simple as that, but I appreciated Jonah's effort to soothe me with Cherokee philosophies. We soon came to the end of the trace and turned our mounts toward home. By then I was in a much better frame of mind, pestering him with light banter all the way back to the stables.

Operetta

After a long and thankfully uneventful Saturday afternoon nap, I luckily found the bathroom deserted. I leisurely scrubbed myself into a presentable state worthy of the Euterpean Literary Society induction ceremony that evening. We were expected to look well-groomed but also serious, so I donned my best skirt and white organdy blouse with the ruffled collar. Not too fancy, but neither too plain. I brushed my hair, tied it into a sensible knot in the back, and trotted off to supper.

"Wow, look at the serious scholar," Ruby teased when I sat down at her table.

"You know what tonight is."

"Yes, I do—your big dramatic debut! They're gonna love your story."

"They'll love *your* story."

"Nonsense, I just gave you a little boost. But I do wish I could come and perform it."

"You and me, both. I'd much rather watch you than read it out loud myself."

"Then you'll have to imagine me acting it out. You'll be inspired!"

I tried to retain that thought as I walked into the meeting room with my notebook tucked under my arm. The entire group was in attendance, and I was comforted to see the friendly faces of Saluda and Hazel in the crowd. I took my place in the front row with the other new girls just as Varina called the meeting to order. Ethel then read the history of the Euterpean Literary Society at the Martha and I was intrigued to learn it had begun in 1873 as the Sappho Literary Society. Miss Lewis had been lecturing on ancient Greek poets in literature class. I'd learned Sappho was not only a rare female poet but also most likely enamored of other women, and that the term "lesbian" was derived from Lesbos, the Greek island where Sappho was born. This literary society had labored under her name for twenty years, changing its name to Euterpean only after the rival Washingtonian Literary Society was formed. Had there been more to this practice of "raving" than anyone knew? Both in and out of class, my eyes were opened to new and strange things all the time, so I had to wonder.

Soon we moved on to the society pledge. Varina laboriously read line by line as we repeated after her, promising to uphold its guiding principles lest we lose our privileges. Leading a life of accomplishment was a major emphasis in the pledge, addressed in the form of our stories about the departed souls of young women deemed not as fortunate as we. Each pledge had to stand, display her gravestone rubbing to the group before placing it on a nearby desk, then take the dais to read her story aloud. As the only freshman pledge, I would read last and sat thanking Ruby for saving my hide. But I was anxious to be rid of that rubbing, so when my turn finally came, I gladly stepped forward.

"Beth continued in her role as a nurse throughout the Civil War, working tirelessly to heal and comfort countless soldiers who languished in pain so far from their homes. She not only attended their physical wounds and illnesses, but she also soothed their souls with her exquisite violin music. Each time she played, tears welled in her eyes as it conjured the memory of her beloved Captain Stoves, whom she had been unable to save. She quelled their loneliness, as well as her own, by sitting at the soldiers' bedsides, reading to them or engaging them in distracting conversation, just as she had for her lover. When the fighting ended and the Martha was once again restored to its former glory as a women's institute of higher learning, she resumed her studies with renewed fervor, devoting herself to earning the highest marks and perfecting her violin technique.

"By the time she graduated in 1868, she was the finest violinist in the state of Virginia. Many a symphony orchestra vied for her services, but she could not be enticed by their offers of prestige and lavish salaries. Beth had ideas of her own. She wanted people to experience music as they never had before, and to make classical music accessible to people in all walks of life. She combined elements of classical music with music of the people—tavern songs, folk ballads, music hall tunes—and created a whole new genre, which eventually became known as 'The Beth.'

"She was a musician way ahead of her time, using brisk tempos and unique rhythms that were the precursors for the jazz and ragtime music to come. She even composed original pieces to add to these adaptations of popular music. Armed with this arsenal of new musical offerings, she produced performances that soon became wildly popular. She and her violin always took center stage with a chorus of lady violinists behind her. Decked out in the most dazzling costumes, the wild gyrations of their bows as they twirled and swiveled their hips created a spectacle unmatched anywhere. Her productions were so successful she began to branch out.

"Teaming up with dancers and actresses, she created her very own 'dramatic orchestra,' with her violin always leading the way. It was an instant sensation. No one had seen anything like it. They played to sold-out houses in New York City for months and months before going on tour to play the finest concert halls all over America. She was then invited to take her group to Europe, where she met with even greater success. While on tour there, she met Etienne Dubois, the only man who could ever be a match for her dear Captain Stoves, and fell madly in love. Following a torrid affair, they decided to make their union permanent and married in Paris during the 1889 Paris Exposition in a gorgeous outdoor ceremony beneath the Eiffel Tower. Etienne, an accomplished artist, continued to tour with her and created beautiful paintings in every city in which she performed.

"They both loved Europe so much they decided to reside there permanently after Beth retired from performing. Settling in Italy, they built a quaint villa in a lush Tuscany vineyard where their many friends visited often and staged dances and dramatic scenarios on the piazza for their own entertainment. Etienne made beautiful paintings here, not only of the lush countryside but also nudes of their friends. These were the best of his collection and fetched handsome prices. But they lived quite comfortably on the wealth amassed from the success of Beth's musical productions, so all proceeds from the paintings were poured into generous donations to Martha Washington College. Beth made history as a pioneer in musical entertainment, and her innovations in musical performance remain an unsurpassed gift to the world."

I closed my notebook and returned to my seat to a mixture of enthusiastic and merely polite applause. Compared to the noble tales spun by my fellow pledges, who obviously opted to play it safe, Ruby's concoction was quite a departure. However, the sputtering giggles from the pledges in the front row proved it served to break the tedium of the evening's procedure. I had no idea what the officers or other members thought of my story. But I had completed the assignment and it would just have to do.

Varina proceeded to carry the stack of grave rubbings outside for the ceremonial burning and we silently followed. We marched to the end of the serpentine brick path that stretched to a secluded spot far beyond the edge of Litchfield Hall. There Ethel struck a match to the tombstone replicas, now withered and dry as the bones that lay in the earth beneath their matching facades. I watched the papers go up in flames and imagined the spirit that haunted me disappearing into the smoke for good, rendering me finally finished with my violin visitor.

Having been duly inducted, we were led back into Preston Hall to join Halloween festivities already underway in the parlors and society hall. Our school colors of black and gold fit the occasion well, with streamers in those hues draping across ceilings and cascading down walls. Evergreen boughs were strategically placed, as were carved jack-o'-lanterns. Images of witches and skeletons hung garishly in the windows, backlit by the outdoor veranda lanterns. The only other sources of light were the shrouded table lamps and dozens of candles casting an eerie glow on the entire scene. The actual holiday wasn't until the next day, but apparently celebrating a ghoulish holiday on a Sunday was too unladylike for a True Martha Girl. How fitting it was to have burned the grave rubbings and exorcise our ghosts on the eve of All Hallows' Eve.

I spied Ruby by the punch bowl, decked out in a Cleopatra costume she had devised out of remnants from the drama storage closet and deftly applied makeup. She caught my eye and waved me over. "Don't you love what they've done with the place?" she asked with her trademark wink, a bizarre gesture given the heavy kohl painted on her eyelids. "There's everything you can imagine to remind folks of spooks." I nodded and took a large gulp from the cup she handed me, anxious to soothe my smoke-parched throat. I grimaced at the sickeningly sweet liquid.

"I know," Ruby sighed in sympathy. "It needs a good shot of whiskey to mellow it out." We both stifled grins. "It's a good thing I brought along my 'perfume bottle,'" she winked, reaching into the pocket of her glamourous robe and stealthily scanning the room.

"Ruby!" Wide-eyed, I leaned in with my best stage whisper, "You wouldn't!" She gazed at me with devil-may-care insouciance, then threw back her head in a boisterous laugh.

"I'm just teasing. I'm not lucky enough to have any. But the look on your face was priceless!" Her infectious laugh forced me into a giggle. "Hey, let me show you what's over in the society hall." Ruby grabbed my hand and dragged me like a puppy on a leash. I polished off my punch and deposited the cup on a table, almost missing the edge.

In a corner of the adjoining hall was a bizarre-looking makeshift tent. The front drapes were pinned back, revealing a low table swathed in dark red brocade with tassels and scattered with tea candles. A shaded floor lamp provided the only other illumination. Seated at the table was an exotic-looking older woman in a brilliant blue satin head scarf, its long sash hanging over one shoulder. The circlet of gold resting on the scarf ended in a single emerald dangling on her forehead. Her billowy white blouse was cinched at the waist with a black corset, and her voluminous red skirts blended seamlessly with the table covering. An art easel held a sign stating "Madame Esmeralda" at the top and "Step Inside—Learn Your Future" at the bottom. A large open eye with flames for eyelashes graced its center.

"Isn't this just dilly?" Ruby was beaming. "Well, go on. See what's in store for you."

I gingerly edged closer, and was about to turn back when a voice from within called out in a florid Hungarian accent.

"Come! Come, my child. Madame Esmeralda will read your future and tell you your destiny." Flamboyant gestures of her arms caused her copious bangle bracelets to rhythmically jingle and ping, transforming her into a human tambourine. Ruby's not so gentle nudge sent me stumbling forward, so I crouched down and slithered into the fortune teller's den.

"Very good, my darling. Take your seat before me."

Only a large plump cushion sat before the low table. I felt like a newborn giraffe as I struggled to buckle my legs beneath me and plop down on it. Madame Esmeralda immediately thrust her arms out to the sides, closed her eyes and took in deep breaths.

"I am breathing in your essence. I detect a warm breeze but also a cool wind. A creature strong and capable, but also reticent. Dutiful and compliant but also tricky and cunning."

My stomach did a little flip. Did she somehow know my comings and goings? But even looking past the garish costume and discounting the phony accent, I didn't identify her as anyone from the college.

"Now, give me your hands." She turned them this way and that, the rings on each of her fingers sparkling in the candlelight. Finally, she held one hand palm up and traced its surface with her index finger. "You have traveled a great distance," she intoned to dramatic effect. "Far from your home. But you have a greater distance yet to go." Well, that wasn't such a big leap. Most of us were from somewhere else and hoped to go to new places after college.

"You have many friends. Many, many . . ." She furrowed her brow, which didn't surprise me; I was far from popular. "Oh! Many animals! Many animals are your friends." A wild guess, or a trace of lingering barn scent? I was still skeptical but pleased with the comment.

"And . . . aha! A young man is coming into your life. He will pursue you, but you will not give your affections so easily. You must find a way to release your heart." My skepticism held fast. What college girl doesn't want to hear that prediction?

"But there is something more." She pulled my hand close to the lamplight, forcing me to stretch and brace myself on the table. "Ah, most unusual . . . you will make another journey. A secret journey. Alone, through darkness and danger. Difficult! But leading to salvation." She held my gaze with her unblinking eyes, solemnly pressing my hands together for a long moment before releasing them. She said no more, so I awkwardly pushed myself off the cushion, untangling the heel of my shoe from my skirt hem as I stood. "Thank you. Madame," I croaked and made my exit. I hustled across the room, anxious to put distance between myself and that tent. In an instant Ruby was by my side all atwitter.

"Wasn't that fun? What did she say? What's the big future for my Honey Bea?"

"Well, first she said—"

"Never mind, I was eavesdropping."

"Oh. Then, don't you think most of that was rather predictable?"

"Maybe. But still, she puts on a good show. After all, she's had lots of experience."

"You know her?"

"No, but they say she performed theatre for years and years. Right across the street, in what they still affectionately call the 'Opera House,' inside the town hall! Can you imagine?"

We had migrated back to the refreshment table, where Ruby plucked two large cookies from a plate and handed me one. It was in the shape of a cat, coated in black icing with two yellow dollops for eyes. It looked rather menacing, but suddenly I felt ravenous and took a large bite. If it was some kind of omen, then I would destroy it with my teeth.

Toccata

Monday ushered in a new week of academics and, now that I was an official Euterpean, my first of their regular Monday evening meetings. Scheduled directly after was my first evening practice-room session in over three weeks, and I found it difficult to quell my apprehension. At least the meeting provided a distraction as well as a small delay.

"Good evening, and welcome, new Euterpeans." Varina was all smiles as she faced the gathering. "We are proud to count you as sisters and to announce that we now boast a society forty-four members strong." In the front row Myrtle and Ethel led an enthusiastic round of applause. "Considering our recent ceremony, our meeting will be short, but we have another exciting announcement." She held up an ornately embossed sheet of parchment with text in a fancy script and read aloud:

> *The Hermesian Literary Society*
> *Of*
> *Emory and Henry College*
> *Requests the honour of your presence*
> *At their*
> *Autumn Debate*
> *Saturday afternoon, November thirteenth*
> *Nineteen hundred and fifteen*
> *Emory, Virginia*

The room was instantly abuzz with excited chatter and squeals, as apparently the invitation was issued quite a bit earlier in the year than usual.

"This is our first off-campus invitation of the year, and the chance to match wits with the men over in Emory is always a thrilling challenge. So tonight, we'll carefully organize our debate team and plan our presentations."

As a novice, I was surprised to be asked to perform on the piano but welcomed the opportunity. While listing my performance-ready pieces to Varina, I took care to avoid indicating any preference, but I was secretly pleased when she settled on a favorite, Chopin's "Heroic Polonaise." Once given my assignment and released from the meeting, I was forced to finally make the dreaded trek to the practice hall.

Walking the long corridor flanking the row of tiny rooms seemed an interminable journey before I reached my assigned one at its end. I stood before the door for a long moment before slowly opening it, then silently blessed the person before me who had left the light switched on. Settling on the stool, I began my warmup with a tentative Hanon finger exercise, one ear on alert for any wayward sound from afar. I repeated the exercise in various keys, eventually increasing the volume as I became more at ease. However, nothing aside from singing voices and pianos accompanied my initial labors. Grateful for the immediate need to tackle the polonaise, I spread out my sheet music and began. This beloved piece was a solace to my nerves and when I finished, I dove right into the rest of my repertoire. Playing one piece after the other in quick succession, allowing no silence, my courage held fast, and before I knew it two hours had passed. Two hours of pure piano bliss, completely devoid of string music.

As the week wore on and each uneventful evening of practice made me braver, I eventually forgot to listen for the violin. Perhaps the burning of Beth's grave rubbing had purged malignant subconscious thoughts and my mind had been cleansed. Maybe I'd kept the forest music close and was returned to a state of proper balance, like Jonah had explained.

By Thursday I began to look longingly at Rena whenever she delivered the mail post. I knew it was too soon for Lillian to have received my letter, let alone gather funds and post a money order. But I was already cutting my candles in half to stretch my supply and needed to replenish it before much longer. The Euterpean challenge with the Hermesians was little more than a week away and good sleep was imperative. Besides my solo, I was to accompany Ethel showing off her vocal prowess in German lieder. I didn't mind playing for her lessons, where Miss Le Grande kept her ego in check. But rehearsing for the Euterpean event was done entirely on our own, and Ethel was quite bossy and unnecessarily fussy about her accompaniment. As a lowly freshman I could only grit my teeth and silently comply.

That evening I was eager to take refuge in my own music. I now looked forward to retiring to the practice room in the evenings, happy to once again appreciate the solitude of the tiny enclosed chamber and the shadow of nightfall enveloping me with music. I shut myself away and settled in for a long industrious session. Cavorting with chords, arpeggios, and lyrical lines, it didn't take long to give myself over to the enchantment of the sounds. I was totally absorbed in my productive trance when suddenly a discordant melody intruded. I jerked my fingers off the keys as if they'd suddenly become hot coals. My throat clenched as I waited, but there was only silence. I shook my head in hopes that I hadn't heard it and tentatively resumed playing.

My fingers trembled and faltered, but I determinedly pressed on. I ignored the dynamic markings in the score, allowing the volume to build unnaturally; mezzo forte became forte, then fortissimo, then fortississimo in my desperate attempt to block out anything other than pure piano sound. Still the unwelcome tune crept back in and overpowered my efforts. In horror I listened to the errant overtone: the unmistakable singing of violin strings. I clapped my hands over my assaulted ears but knew, undeniably, that I had heard it. Visions flashed before my mind's eye: Beth's tombstone in the dark cemetery, the grave rubbing on brittle butcher paper destroyed in flames, the smoke that was supposed to carry this curse away. Violently knocking over the piano stool, I scooped my sheet music into a ragged jumble and forced my wobbling legs to race away from those haunting strings.

Ruby opens my door and giggles. "Come on, Honey Bea!" She takes my hand and pulls me through the door. But instead of stepping into the hallway, we're outside on a grassy lawn. We start skipping over the grass, eventually stopping at a huge picnic table laden with all kinds of food: bowls of fruit, fried chicken, cakes and pies, a plate of Mama's homemade rolls. We eat and eat and eat, though I don't ever feel full. Ruby pulls me away from the table and we float over the lawn into the pine trees. We zip in and out of the trees, then suddenly I can't see her anywhere. I'm still floating through the trees when I come to a clearing at a large brick courtyard. There's Ruby, glittering in a dress decorated in beads and tiny jewels. She parades back and forth, showing it off. Then she's dancing with a man with a small black mustache wearing a beret cocked on the side of his head. He twirls her around and around, until suddenly she's naked. I try to shout "Ruby!" but she just laughs at me. The man sits on a wicker chair, smiling and watching her twirl, and she doesn't care at all. She wanders into a garden and begins to pick flowers, but the flowers aren't flowers, they're cats' heads. She places the heads in a basket where they twitch their whiskers and blink their eyes at me. Ruby pets them and they love her. They begin to mew, softly at first but then louder. They want their bodies and they're telling me to find them. I search the flower garden, through rows of peonies, under every rose bush and every shrub. I keep walking and searching until there is no more garden, but I still hear them mewing, their cries coming more rapidly and urgently now. The sound makes me cry, too, and I come to a large pile of sticks that suddenly catches on fire. I back away from the flames, but the mewing becomes faster, a cacophony of piercing high-pitched wails that wrenches at my heart. Smoke billows up from the flames and the wailing is coming out of it, more and more shrill until I hear a gruesome violin glissando soaring up and up and—

My eyes jerked open, wet with tears that had soaked my pillow. In a panic I sat up to see my half candle spent, but relieved to see the first light of dawn peer through my window. At least I didn't have to struggle alone through more darkness. But my bed felt uneasy, and I rose to face a long, arduous day.

It was a master class Friday and I was due to perform the Rachmaninoff Prelude in B-flat Major from opus 23. It was a majestic piece I was eager to conquer, but with its relentless sextuplet and triplet chords and runs, the most difficult work I'd ever attempted. Professor Zeisberg had raised the bar for me, insisting that without the challenge of more demanding pieces, I would never grow. But remnants of my bizarre dream lingered in my head, and getting into a proper frame of mind to perform was the more problematic challenge.

Nervously I tried to ready myself, unbraiding my hair, brushing it vigorously, then trying to arrange it in one of Ruby's fashionable knots. But the mirror revealed only a hopeless mess, prompting me to fling the hairbrush across the room. I put on my drabbest dress to suit my miserable mood and searched for my shoes, which I'd frantically flung off after reaching the safety of my room the night before. Crawling on hands and knees, I stretched underneath my bed to retrieve them. When a sharp rapping on my door startled me, I conked my head on the iron bedframe. "Hold on!" Wincing in pain, I extracted myself from the bed's dusty underbelly as Ruby casually flung the door open. Not expecting to find me splay-legged on the floor rubbing my aching head, with hair sprouting in all directions like a deranged halo, she popped out her usual effervescent greeting.

"Come on, Honey Bea!"

Those words and the sight of her startled me more than her knock on the door. I felt mortified recalling how she'd been portrayed in my awful dream. How could I conjure such risqué images? It was even more proof I was losing my grip. Fortunately, Ruby only saw humor in my predicament and came to my rescue.

"Beatrice Earle Damron, have I not taught you better than this?" she teased with a sparkling laugh and pulled me off the floor. "Take a seat and let me work my magic. Where's your hairbrush? We'll have to be quick or all the waffles will be gone."

With the help of a good friend and a good breakfast, I was in better spirits by the time I sat in Litchfield Hall, sheet music in my lap, gazing up at the Steinway. I had always looked forward to my chance to play it, and today was no different; no matter what, I would relish my time at that keyboard. Suddenly I felt the swish of a skirt on my thigh.

"I see you have the Rachmaninoff for us today," Varina breathed in my ear as she seated herself next to me. Seniors never sat with underclassmen, especially freshmen, so this was a first. I supposed that now as a fellow Euterpean as well as my mother, she felt she should lend her presence to me on certain occasions. I would have felt more comfortable with Saluda or Hazel, but tried not to let her intimidate me.

"Yes," I answered dutifully. "It's still very new to me. Quite a handful, but I can learn lot from it. And, besides, I love it." Why was I yammering on like this? Varina smiled sweetly at me and I squirmed in my seat.

I thought I would have time to calm down, but the performance order was announced and I was first on the roster. After sitting on the piano bench, I hesitated a moment, then, though I didn't normally do so, placed my sheet music on the rack above the keyboard. The pages were a crutch, but I simply hadn't spent enough time with the piece to feel totally confident and thought I shouldn't chance it without them.

It was a good thing I didn't. I played the first page well enough, though without my usual aplomb. I continued with the second, and then the third, when I began to feel my memory falter. About to panic, I quickly reached up to flip the page and find my place; a rather deft move but not without consequences to the bass line. I recovered and pressed on for two more pages, which were not exactly stellar but uneventful. On the next page the same thing happened with my memory and again I scrambled with the pages to find my footing. I played on, making a mess of the sextuplets and failing the dynamics, desperate to just hang on. Finally, I reached the closing passages, rendered more feebly than the magnificent piece warranted, but at least the nerve-wracking performance was finished.

After returning to my seat, I sat completely numb. I'd made a royal mess of it, and kept my eyes glued to my notebook while I dutifully recorded my critiques from Mr. Moore and Mr. Park. Professor Zeisberg was disconcertingly silent, his one comment, "If you need a page turner, arrange one before you sit down to play," somehow more mortifying than the critiques of the butchered Rachmaninoff. Varina placed her hand over mine and gave it a sympathetic squeeze. I couldn't look at her, either.

As I listened to the other music students, I pondered what on earth could be wrong with me. I was grateful when a couple of organ students took their turns, the sonorous emissions reverberating from the pipes allowing me to mentally escape. Then it was Varina's turn to take the stage, and I noticed she left her sheet music behind in her seat. She calmly placed her fingers on the keys and launched into the third movement of Beethoven's "Les Adieux" sonata, also an extremely challenging piece. But Varina seemed entirely at home with it. Unencumbered with pages, she simply communed with the instrument and sailed through the piece. In total command of its harmonies and trills, she blithely hammered chords with fervor and executed its copious sixteenth-note runs like child's play, concluding with a thrilling flourish. It was stunning, and everyone in the room knew it.

When class was dismissed, I wanted to quit the auditorium immediately but was caught in the crush of students descending upon Varina to offer praise. She did her best to remain reserved, but I couldn't help feeling she was inwardly gloating. Visions of the music competition danced before me, and I knew this was only a precursor to what lay ahead. Her thirst for winning was even stronger than I had imagined. I would have to double down on my efforts to have any hope of defeating her. But I had to defeat my demons first.

I finally broke away and headed for the auditorium doors, my escape hindered by the bottleneck of chattering females just outside. It gave Varina the opportunity to catch up with me.

"Beatrice, can't you wait for your tired old mother?" came her mock admonishment.

"Oh. Well, I saw you were busy. Great job with the Beethoven today. It was stunning." I knew she expected a compliment, which she honestly deserved.

"How sweet of you to say that."

We finally made our way into the hallway to retrieve our coats. I thought she would depart my company in favor of her usual colleagues, but she kept by my side. "I wish I could return the favor, but we both know you were off your game today." Nothing tops off public humiliation quite like hearing the unvarnished truth. I walked on without comment. "Beatrice, I know something must be troubling you. But no one can help if you don't talk about it."

"I'm just tired, that's all."

"I'm sure you've been tired before, and still played well. It has to be more than that."

She looped her arm in mine as we descended the front steps, then guided me across the lawn to a bench under a large oak tree. Its scarlet and russet leaves composed a canopy that sheltered us in diffused light. Patiently she sat waiting for me to spill my guts. She knew how powerful silence can be, how palpable its force. And, like a pot about to boil over, I eventually lifted the lid to let out some steam.

"I've been having dreams." A gross understatement, but it was a start. She nodded sympathetically and I explained how the dreams morphed into horrible nightmares that robbed me of sleep. Of course, being robbed of my sanity was the greater fear, but I didn't want to tell her about hearing the violin in the practice room. I only said the nightmares always ended with me hearing a violin, a grotesque, horrible piercing sound that violently woke me. She studied me for several long moments, expecting me to say more.

"That's terrible, Beatrice. No wonder you're tired and frazzled."

"I've never told anyone. But I admit, it does feel better to say it out loud."

"But that doesn't fix your problem. These dreams have to stop."

"I have no idea how to make that happen."

A light breeze whisked by and we silently watched dry leaves dance over the grass.

"Well, I do." She met my puzzled look by taking my hand firmly in hers. "Meet me tomorrow night, an hour after light bell, in the attic of Mariah Cooper Hall." I continued to stare with furrowed brows. "Just trust me. If you want to put an end to this misery, meet me tomorrow night. Now, we both have to get to class or risk losing precious free time working off demerits."

Misterioso

Saturday night found me alone in my room anxiously awaiting the clang of the light bell. Ever since leaving Varina's side, worries about her mysterious "cure" had plagued me. Thankfully, a freshman excursion to White Top Mountain had consumed the day and provided a distraction (though I'd chafed at missing my visit to the stables). A train filled with chattering girls had taken us up the mountain, the second highest in Virginia, to the depot at a clearing just below its top. In the distance we viewed Mount Rogers, the highest peak in the state, where no train traveled at all. We laid out blankets for a picnic where we could admire the majestic vista. Later we tramped the grounds, spotting the occasional red-tailed hawk, red-breasted nuthatch, or Eastern bluebird that made its home where nature was allowed to thrive nearly untouched.

The bell finally sounded and I watched my clock, anticipating the mysterious meeting with a mixture of hope and dread. After forty-five minutes had passed, I began creeping with practiced silent steps through the hallways. Skulking farther and farther from my room, I searched the darkness for what was affectionately known as the "tunnel," a narrow fifty-foot passageway that connected the second floors of Preston and Mariah Cooper. My fingers skimmed the walls until I finally felt the curve of the tunnel opening, then discreetly trained my flashlight beam on the two steps leading into the passage. Steps I'd heard caused many a tripping fall for girls attempting to rush through just as the light bell thrust them into darkness.

As I traversed the long corridor, the faraway street lamps cast a shroud of eerie light through its windows. I was nearing the end when a sudden clatter followed by a skittering at my feet ricocheted down the length of the tunnel. I stifled a yelp and chaotically shined my light in all directions, desperate to see what had joined me in this creepy passageway. But only linoleum tile and plaster revealed itself.

Gathering what was left of my wits, I proceeded through a doorway. It led into a wide hallway with a staircase to one side, which I climbed to the third floor. Reaching a similar hallway, my light searched until it landed on an obscure narrow staircase in the far corner leading to the attic. I tiptoed up to its landing, coming face to face with a closed door. Taking a deep breath, I placed my shaky hand on the knob and tentatively gave it a turn. To my relief, a subtle light emanated from inside as the door slowly parted from its frame. It swung open wide, revealing the glow of a candle illuminating Varina's face from across a round table.

"Put away your torch, Beatrice, and come join us." A quick survey of the scene revealed four other girls standing around the room. Myrtle, Ethel, and Bessie—the core of her usual entourage of comrades and minions—plus one other girl I didn't recognize. Each held a candle and gazed at me, their solemn expressions unnerving in the ghostly luminescence. I was considering a hasty retreat when Varina's silky commanding voice beckoned us all. "Take a seat, ladies." In unison, all four candles floated toward the table, then joined Varina's in a circle at the center. The girls took seats on either side of her with a lone chair sitting empty, directly in Varina's line of sight.

"What is this?" I managed to squeak.

"We've come to help you, Beatrice." The honey in Varina's tone only added to the eeriness of the setting. "We're going to make your dreams go away."

"But I told you that in confidence."

"An undertaking like this requires many hands."

"Just what are we undertaking? And how will it help?"

"We're going to call upon the source of your dreams and ask her to cease. More hands multiply our strength."

"It's a séance, Beatrice!" A half-whispered squeal from Bessie, unable to contain her excitement.

"Quiet, child!" Varina spat, refusing to be upstaged by a silly underling.

"A séance?" I was incredulous. "But I've never—"

"It's the only way," Varina decreed, keeping tight rein on the situation. "The violin you hear in your dreams is an indicator of what—or who—is causing them. We have to make contact if you want them to stop." She clearly meant Beth, the Civil War nurse whose patient died in my room. I had feared the same all along. It's what struck such panic in me each time I'd heard the music, awake or in a dream. I shook my head, my mouth gaping wide.

"There's nothing to fear," Myrtle interjected. "Lots of famous people conducted séances. Queen Victoria held them at Buckingham Palace, to ask the dead prince for political advice. They've even been held in the White House. Mary Todd Lincoln used them to contact her dead son, Willie. President Lincoln attended some of them, too."

"Myrtle is our finest student of history, with an impeccable memory for facts on all kinds of topics," purred Varina with a nod to Myrtle, a reward for obediently following her script. "Now, Beatrice, you can remain miserable, or . . ." With both hands she made a grand gesture toward the lone empty chair.

I didn't like this, not one bit. But that frightful journey in the dark would have been for nothing if I didn't stay. The faces around the table gazed at me expectantly as candle flames made flickering shadows dance on their pale cheeks. Reluctantly I sat down, pocketing my superfluous flashlight.

Everyone opened their hands wide and placed them on the table, palms down with smallest fingers touching. I followed suit and we created a macabre daisy chain that echoed the circle of candles. When they all closed their eyes, I resisted; but a firm nod from Varina signaled I was not allowed to abstain. Comforted by the thought that at least I wasn't alone, I gave in to darkness. Soon Varina began a slow, rhythmic breathing, each successive breath deeper and broader, preparing to intone her call.

"In the shroud of darkness here,
we have made a pathway clear
for restless spirits to tread this night,
by way of candles burning bright."

More deep breathing followed, reverberating in the otherwise silent room. Despite the presence of others, I struggled against my phobia. Tilting back my head, I slitted my eyes and took a peek around the table. Everyone's eyes were sealed as if in fervent prayer. I took relief in Varina's next command.

"All eyes on the candle flames. Lead the spirits toward the light."

Obediently we complied, all staring at the tiny blazes as if harnessed with blinders. We were watching the wicks wither into the melting wax when suddenly the flames began to bend and falter. Oddly, a breeze had begun to stir in the small room.

"Beth," Varina intoned. "Beth, can you hear me?"

The flames whipped back and forth, threatening to disappear. I willed them to stay alive, shivering in the cool air swirling around us.

"If you can hear me, give us a sign."

Two knocking sounds rang out in the darkness. I sucked in a tight breath and held it.

"Are you here with us? In this room?"

Everyone was silent. Again, two knocking sounds, louder this time. The candle flames suddenly stilled, their yellow peaks reaching for the heavens.

"What do you want, Beth? Why does your music play in the world of our dreamer?"

Varina began to sway from side to side, her eyes darting wildly in all directions. A low guttural moan rose from her throat, sounding mournful rather than scary. She closed her eyes as her head lolled in circles. Suddenly she threw her head back and her body gave a tremendous shudder.

"John!" The name escaped her lips in a high-pitched tinny voice, nothing like her usual rich, silky alto. "John. My captain. He's so far away." Varina began to sway again as the voice murmured on, "So far away, far away, far away . . ." uttering these two words in a strange undulating melodic loop. The unrelenting repetition was getting unbearable when a sudden piercing shout broke the maddening chant. "My captain!" We all jumped and Bessie yelped. "He is not at peace, lying with the Confederates. They are not his people. He is mine. Join our earthen beds. Bring his to mine. Then we will sleep, together. Forever."

Varina's swaying had turned into thrashing. She gripped the table edge as her shoulders thrust violently in erratic waves and her breathing grew more and more rapid. Suddenly she lunged forward, flinging her arms onto the table and heaving a huge exhalation that snuffed out three of the candles. The smoke curled into the air, its acrid scent filling our nostrils as we sat frozen, waiting for what came next. Slowly Varina opened her eyes and lifted her head. She looked at the candles and sat upright, looking around at all of us.

"Have I been sleeping?" Varina asked in a confused whisper but in her own voice.

"Far from it," answered Ethel. "Apparently, you roused the dead from sleep."

"You did it, Varina," Myrtle breathed in admiration. "You made contact."

"Yes!" "It was spectacular!" Bessie and the other girl cried at once.

"Was it Beth?" Varina ventured. The others nodded and spewed forth a jumble of affirmative replies; Bessie was overcome with tears. "What did she say?"

"She's very restless," Myrtle explained. "And so is her lover, this Captain John who died under her care. She said he's not at peace, lying with the Confederates."

"But what does that mean?"

"I think he must be buried in the grave for Unknown Confederate Soldiers at this cemetery. But Captain Stoves was a Union officer. 'They are not his people' were her words."

"Yes," breathed Bessie, "then she said, 'He is mine.' Isn't that the most romantic thing?" Her huge smile was met with impatient, stoic stares.

"She did say she wanted them to sleep together," Ethel smirked.

"She didn't mean *that*," Myrtle retorted. "She just wants them to rest together for eternity. 'Join our earthen beds,' she said. 'Bring his to mine.'"

"What an odd request," Varina mused.

"Maybe, but I think I know what to do. We can't go digging in the Confederate grave, there's no way to know which bones belong to Captain Stoves. But we can scrape some dirt off the top of the grave, take it to Beth's grave and mix it in with the soil there."

"Yes. Then they would share a grave and be happy, together. She'd no longer search for him, and no longer play her violin trying to find him." Varina smiled and turned her gaze in my direction. "Beatrice, now you know your task."

"Me?" I gulped; my throat was suddenly dry.

"Yes. It has to be you. She comes into your dreams, you're the only one who can fix this."

I gazed at the meager glow of the two remaining candles as they all fixed me with expectant stares. The last thing I wanted was another trip to the cemetery. Tampering with graves was disrespectful, besides against the law. It would require the cover of darkness, which meant another long nighttime trek. The notion was unsavory as well as risky, and I wanted no part of it.

"No."

"But Beatrice, you—"

"I'm sorry, but I can't." I abruptly stood and Varina reacted as if I'd thrown cold water in her face. "I came to this meeting, you offered your help, and I thank you for your efforts. But no." I swung the door open to leave but was halted by Varina's voice.

"Oh, Beatrice..." For a moment she let my name dangle in the cold attic air, then, "Sweet dreams."

FORTUNATELY, EXHAUSTION BLESSED ME WITH DREAMLESS slumber for what was left of the night. As Sunday morning's light began to pierce my curtains, I lay in bed replaying the evening's scenario in my mind. I didn't believe in the séance, and I refused to be sucked into Varina's penchant for drama and Bessie's exuberance for sensational romance. Logical explanations could be found for everything that had happened: the knocking a tapping heel on the wooden floor, the breeze a ceiling fan with a rigged string controlling the pull chain, and the spooky atmosphere conjured by the late hour, the darkness, the solemn faces in the candlelight. And I was primed for it all after my ordeal of getting there in the dark.

The night's expedition had been of no help to my dilemma, and I found it difficult to concentrate during church. My Bible professor, Mr. Rector, delivered the sermon and I really should've been taking notes but sat idle. Instead of singing the words of the hymns, I focused on their accompaniment, analyzing harmonic structure. When it all finally ended and we were leaving, I took a detour to the ladies' room on the second floor. As I turned onto the landing of the stairs, I came face to face with Varina.

"Good morning, Beatrice."

"Morning." I was curt but had no energy for pleasantries. I looked past her to indicate my desire to move on.

"I worried about you all night long," she ventured. "Were you able to sleep well?"

"I'm fine. I slept just fine." Only half of that was true and she sensed it.

"I wish you would reconsider. You know, the plan we discussed," she spoke with practiced discretion while a couple of girls descended the stairs beside us.

"It's out of the question. I'll handle this my own way."

The Martha Odyssey

"But I don't think—"

"I said I'm not interested." My agitation gave me away, but I didn't want to discuss it. "Now, if you'll excuse me, I really need the ladies' room."

"Very well, then." I could feel her watching me as I trotted up the stairs and escaped down the hallway.

I stayed extra minutes in the lavatory to make sure Varina was long gone. When I finally emerged, the hallway was deserted so I took some time to explore. I'd never been on this floor and natural curiosity led me to peek into the rooms lining the corridor. Most appeared to be Sunday School rooms, each particular age level revealed in the drawings and decorations on the walls. One was obviously a nursery with its cribs, high chair, and oodles of toys. The largest one at the end of the hall, to my surprise, hosted a rather fine baby grand piano. There were also bookshelves with hymnals and large folios, and chairs set up in rows. I looked longingly at the baby grand.

"Did'ja forgit somethin'?" The voice swung me into an abrupt about face. There stood a pale meager-looking woman, not quite five feet tall, in a plain dark dress and white bib apron. With a mop in one hand and a bucket in the other, she looked up at me with patient innocence.

"Uh, ah, no. I was just, uh, admiring the piano."

"Oh. Thought ya was a choir member, what come back fer your purse or hat." She pronounced it "quar," but I knew what she meant. Many elderly members of the tiny churches in the hollers of Dickenson County referred to their choirs the same way.

"No. I'm just a student, from across the street. So, this is the choir room?"

"Yup. Wensdey nites and Sundey mornins. Just sits here the rest o' the week. I still clean it, though. Ever week, on Mondey. But I comes in on Sundeys sometimes, when I hav'ta keep my grandbaby on a Mondey."

"Oh. Well, I'll get out of your way, then." I smiled at her and turned back for one more hungry look at the piano.

"You play?"

"Ah, why, yes. A little."

"Well, if folks ain't singin' in here, an' I ain't cleanin' then come on an' play it, anytime ya want."

"Really?"

"Just sits here gatherin' dust. You could hep me shoo the dust bunnies away." She cackled at her own joke, and my face broke out into a broad smile at my good fortune.

"Well, thank you. I'd love to. And I'll be sure to scare them off real good."

I said goodbye and left before she might change her mind. I knew it really wasn't hers to offer, but if anyone asked, I could truthfully say I was given permission to play the choir room piano. Feeling lighter than air as I bounded down the stairs and out onto the street, I all but skipped back to the Martha.

Polonaise

Trudging back and forth from the Martha to the church put a squeeze on my time and energy over the next week, but it was well worth it. And when an unfortunate music student fell ill midweek, I picked up some extra daytime practice hours on campus. By Saturday morning I finally felt prepared to meet the Hermesian Literary Society at Emory and Henry College. I was excited about performing but frustrated to have another week away from my furry friends. To ensure they didn't forget me, I snuck in a quick trip to the stables to hand out apples and carrots. I then took care to clean away any barn aroma before marching off with the others to catch the train.

I was excited and curious to be heading to another new destination. But when we disembarked at the Emory depot, I was surprised at the rather desolate surroundings. The Abingdon depot sat in the midst of a bustling town full of shops and businesses, the streets alive with buggies, wagons, and motor cars. Emory was a mere village, with a tiny post office and bungalow-sized depot flanking the lonely tracks. Soon we were approached by an older gentleman in brown tweeds accompanied by two young men. The older man introduced himself as Mr. L. W. Crawford, English professor and faculty advisor, but he was immediately eclipsed when the tallest of the young men boldly stepped forward.

"Charles Edgar Sloan, senior, and president of the Hermesians." A dashing figure in a sleek black wool overcoat and gray silk muffler, he tipped his black Homburg hat with a broad smile. He turned toward the other young man wearing a gray tweed coat much like his professor's. "And this is Walter Lee Harrison, junior, our esteemed vice president." A vast constellation of female eyes took them in hungrily, twittering and murmuring until Mrs. Long, there to chaperone, gave them a stern look. "Now, ladies, if you will please walk this way." The men escorted us across the tracks and onto a road through a stand of trees where the college campus opened up before us. Here the surroundings were far from desolate.

Lush grassy grounds sprawled in all directions, still a rather rich green even in the autumn chill. To our right Mr. Crawford pointed to the college's beloved Duck Pond, where a flock of mallards paddled and a pair of beautiful white swans sailed across the water like two elegant snowy chariots. From this vantage point, we saw the entire campus rested on a terrain of gentle hills rather than the flat ground that bore the Martha. Small but stately faculty homes dotted the landscape, along with larger buildings for classes and students. On the highest knoll stood a long brick building sporting a large shiny dome, the college's brand-new observatory. We were then led up a hill to Byars Hall, the site of the afternoon's event. It was an impressive building, fronted with a robust rounded tower that spanned the structure's two-and-a-half stories and was topped by a conical roof that appeared to pierce the clouds. I felt as though we were entering a medieval castle.

On the top floor we entered Hermesian Hall, a room as impressive as the building's façade. Tall narrow windows with half-moon tops allowed slices of the afternoon sun into the room, lending it a warm, expectant glow. I followed Saluda into one of the rows of heavy wooden chairs. Their slightly concave seats, artistically carved backs, and gently sloping arms hugged you firmly, giving you no choice but to sit up straight and feel important. At the front, a raised platform with two square areas jutting out left and right was sectioned off by oak balustrades joined to hefty square newels topped with thick round finials.

"I'll give it to these boys, they sure know how to decorate a room," Saluda said, watching me gaze at the wall beyond the balustrades. Three grand wooden arches built into the wall hosted three murals, each depicting a human figure in colorful flowing robes. Across the top of each arch was red lettering that I guessed was Greek. These framed murals were the most striking feature of the room.

"They're beautiful paintings," I agreed. "And I see they've honored us with their artwork." The painting on the right depicted a lovely black-haired lady swathed in a blue robe that unfurled in small tendrils all around her. It was undeniably the muse Euterpe, playing her long slender double flute.

"Yes. But, of course, Hermes, the messenger god, gets top billing."

I stared at the figure in the center arch, swathed in a loose green robe that barely covered his privates. Wings sprouted from his helmet and his feet, and also from a strange-looking stick held in his hand.

"Are those snakes wrapped around his stick?"

"Yes, two snakes. Copulating," Saluda answered with a wink. Warmth crept into my cheeks, although it shouldn't have. I'd seen plenty of that growing up on a farm. "It's okay," she laughed, "it's just your run-of-the-mill Greek herald's staff."

"And I think the painting on the left is Erato?"

"Correct. Young men can't resist a sassy red robe and giant lyre. Plus, they would never neglect the muse of erotic poetry."

"You've taken Greek with Dr. Long, haven't you? What's it say along the top?"

"My Greek pronunciation is horrible, but in English it says, 'Wealth, the wealth of the soul, alone is true.' Hmm. A rather high-minded sentiment for boys who revel in sex poems." We burst out laughing, but just then Charles Sloan came striding to the front of the room.

After greeting everyone, he began the afternoon's presentations by graciously inviting the Euterpeans to present first. That meant we heard Myrtle's tedious essay on the American Revolutionary War which, while meticulously accurate, didn't get the event off to the most scintillating start. Next came a serious-looking Hermesian who read an original poem he called "Ode to Venus" which, ironically, was rather dry and not at all erotic. It could've been much improved with some of Ruby's colorful idioms.

Eventually, things picked up with a debate regarding America's entry into the present war in Europe. Varina took the side of President Woodrow Wilson, who believed America should remain neutral. Walter Harrison favored Teddy Roosevelt's position that we retaliate against the Germans for sinking the British ship *Lusitania* and killing more than a hundred of its American passengers. Both sides made compelling arguments, but I had my own reasons to lean toward Varina's. My brother Jim would be tempted to enlist, and even my father might volunteer, both chilling thoughts that I didn't want to entertain. The debate concluded to vigorous applause, alerting me it was time to accompany Ethel's vocal selections. I was worried that German lieder directly following that discussion might cause discomfort, but Ethel would not be denied. "These songs were composed long before the war," she announced before singing, "so we can still appreciate German artistic creativity."

Next, another Hermesian gave a persuasive speech advocating the inclusion of Oscar Wilde's literature in the English curriculum. It was actually a much spicier presentation than the poem about Venus. Then finally, it was my turn and for the next little while I didn't have to think about anything but the Chopin harmonies, trills, and runs emerging from my fingers. After the final chord, I was a little reluctant to take my bow and leave the keyboard behind.

The closing presentation of the day was the long-awaited debate on women's suffrage, with Charles Sloan opposing the amendment and my good friend Saluda audaciously taking up its cause. If Charles had thought his opponent was going to be a pushover, he was soon proven horribly wrong. Saluda answered his every challenge with irrefutable counterarguments that clearly surprised him. Her final argument became a rousing inspirational speech that had us on our feet for a standing ovation. At least on the Euterpean side of the room.

The Martha Odyssey

With effort we quieted ourselves long enough for Mr. Crawford to thank us for coming and direct everyone to the dining hall for a reception. There we found two large tables decked with centerpieces of fall leaves and squashes, each laden with food and a punch bowl. All the excitement had made me quite hungry, but I tried not to make a pig of myself as I sampled the offerings on every tray.

"That was a fantastic rendition of Chopin's 'Heroic Polonaise.'" Startled, I turned abruptly to see the president of the Hermesians grinning at me over the rim of his punch cup. When I didn't speak, he thrust out his hand. "Charles Sloan. It was a pleasure to hear a fresh take on an old masterwork."

After some precarious juggling to try to free up my hand, I awkwardly placed my cup on the table's edge. "Thank you."

"It's also good to meet new talent. You must be in your second year at Martha Washington."

"Actually, no. I'm a freshman." This, too, felt awkward.

"A freshman? In the Euterpeans! That's a first. I say, you've done very well for yourself, then."

"Well, I—"

"Charles! I've been searching all over for you," Varina crooned as she appeared suddenly at my elbow. "That was quite the boisterous contest between you and my secretary. I didn't know you were so adamantly opposed to women expressing their desires at the polls."

"Oh, I have a lot of experience with women expressing their desires." The words slid from his lips smooth as silk. Varina smiled her most winning smile, but he cast her an inscrutable look. "I just think the polls are an unsuitable place for them to do so."

"And I just think our lady proved you wrong. You'll be surprised how soon we'll get there."

"Well, I'm surprised right now by this new gem you've brought us today." He turned to smile at me. "I was going to scold you for hiding her, but she tells me it's her first year at Martha." I blushed under his admiring gaze. Varina's smile vanished.

"Well . . ." she stammered only briefly, "we thought we'd experiment. Offer to let a totally green student learn from experienced Euterpeans. With the aim to nurture fresh talent."

"A fresh rosebud, on the verge of a beautiful bloom." He spoke to Varina but leveled captivating hazel eyes on me. I'd never been compared to a flower before. It was a bit thrilling. "I congratulate you, Varina. Well done." Varina's brows lowered and her eyes flitted between Charles and me.

"Yes, but let me tell you about our plans for the spring debate." She thrust her arm through his, instantly steering him away.

"So nice to meet you, Beatrice," he smiled over his shoulder as Varina commandeered him into the crowd.

I watched him walk away, a little stunned. Then I felt foolish and decided some fresh cold air would bring me back to my senses. I turned to make a swift dash toward the front door, promptly crashing into a large silver tray of finger sandwiches. The tray went instantly airborne, a flash of sunlight glinting off the silver like a lightning bolt before it struck the floor with the clang of a giant cymbal. The poor chap who'd been porting it slid to the floor in a hopeless effort to seize the capsized vessel, but sandwiches sailed in all directions as it wobbled in thunderous circles before finally coming to rest on the hard linoleum floor. A dreadful silence hung in the room as every eye turned in our direction, but my horrified eyes were latched to his prone figure.

"I am so, so sorry," I choked out my pathetic apology. "Are you hurt?"

His white shirt, black vest, and now lopsided bow tie were speckled with parsley, olives, and bits of pimento cheese. But kind eyes looked up at me from behind spectacles thrown askew and obscured by a lock of light brown hair wagging over his forehead.

"I'm fine, miss," he said with a meek smile. He deftly pulled himself to standing, the parsley and olives falling to the floor like raindrops. "Are you okay?" he had the grace to ask.

Before I could answer, a man in a short black coat with large brass buttons brusquely pushed between us. "What the devil did you do, oaf?" he muttered testily in the young man's face. "Go get a broom and clean this up, pronto!" Turning to the crowd he raised a cheery voice. "We apologize for the inconvenience, everyone. Please carry on. We'll be out of your way shortly." I turned back to speak to the young man, but he had disappeared into the kitchen.

Staring into my plate, I stood perfectly still lest I cause another food disaster. Within moments Hazel was by my side, kindly leading me to where Saluda was having a lively discussion with Walter, the young man who had debated Varina. Thankfully, they weren't discussing the war, only exchanging jokes and opinions about movies they'd seen. I let their chatter wash over me, but it was hard to quash my remorse as I stole surreptitious glances at the unfortunate young man cleaning up my mess.

Eventually the refreshments were whittled to crumbs and we embarked on a walk around the campus. I enjoyed trudging along the gently rolling hills of the estate, but my mind kept drifting back to the young man with the tray. Finally, I made an excuse about leaving my bag at the reception and made my way back to the dining hall. Instead of entering the front doors, I searched the sides and back until I found the service entrance. I was considering slipping through the door when the young man emerged toting a package of garbage. I flattened myself against the brick wall as he trotted toward the bin, whistling all the way, the apron he now wore flapping in the light breeze. He clanged the lid shut and turned back toward the door, stopping short when he saw me.

"Oh! I didn't expect to see anyone back here. Did you get lost from the tour?"

"No, I, uh, actually . . . I came looking for you."

"Me?"

"Yes. I wanted to apologize, properly, for crashing into you like that, with the tray."

"Oh. Well, thanks, but really, it's all right. Just an accident."

"But I got you into trouble with your boss."

"Henry?" He gave a short laugh. "I mean, of course, Mr. Phelps. Don't worry about him, he just thinks everything has to be fancy. Too fancy, if you ask me."

"Oh, it wasn't too fancy. Uh . . . I mean . . . it was just right. Everything was wonderful. Delicious, too."

"Well, glad to hear it. Like I tell him, people just want to eat and have a good time."

"I hope he's not too angry with you."

"Ah, he won't fire me, I'm on work study. Besides, I'm his best worker."

"Oh. You're a student." I smiled then. "That's like me. I have a job at Martha Washington."

"Wow. I didn't think any of the Martha girls had to work."

"I wouldn't be there if I didn't help pay for it. But I don't mind." He smiled at me, but in such a different way than Charles had. "What do you study?"

"Mathematics. I love numbers, my head's full of them all the time."

"It's the same for me with music."

"Was that you on the piano today? Or did you sing?"

"Piano. You don't want to hear me sing!"

"Me either!" We both laughed. My embarrassing moment with this young man had been banished.

"Well, I'd better get back to my group before they think I've fallen into the Duck Pond."

"It was sure nice of you to come find me. Your mama raised you right."

"Thank you."

"Your mama give you a name?"

"Oh, yes. Beatrice. Beatrice Damron."

"Nice to meet you, Beatrice, I'm—" he stepped forward thrusting out his hand, then remembered he'd just been handling garbage. "Whoa, that was a close one!" He laughed at himself. "B.C. White here."

The Martha Odyssey

"B.C. That's your name?"

"Yeah. Well, Blaine Chester, actually, but I like just B.C."

"Oh, okay. Nice to meet you, B.C." Unable to shake hands, we simply exchanged smiles, which seemed to come easily to him. "Well. I'd best not be late."

"Have a good trip back to Abingdon."

"Thank you." I started toward the side of the building, then turned back and called, "Have fun with those numbers in your head."

"Always do."

Glissando

I had hopes that Monday morning's mail would finally bring my long-awaited request from Lillian. I ate a quick breakfast, then on my way to class made a detour to Mrs. Long's office. On a table just outside the office door, Rena organized the incoming mail for distribution, and if you got there early you could pick up your own before she went on her rounds. But I rounded the corner only to see an empty table, forcing me to wait until after lunch.

The drudgery of the morning was not without its highlights, however. Several girls congratulated me on my performance at Emory and Henry, then in Hazel's voice lesson she bragged on me to Miss Le Grande. Compliments were nice, but mostly I was relieved to be in good form again thanks to clandestine practice at the church.

Lunch came and went, but no mail for me. With a disappointed sigh I shrugged on my coat and headed out to my secret practice room. Just as I approached the sidewalk that led down the street toward the church, I suddenly heard my name. I turned to see Varina trotting to catch up with me.

"I haven't had a chance to speak to you since the reception on Saturday."

I'd been in the proximity of Varina several times since then—on the train home, in the dining hall, at church. Yet somehow, she'd "missed" me, always busily engaged in seemingly urgent conversation with others. Why was she bothering to seek me out now?

"I was pretty tired after all the excitement. I've been mostly laying low."

"Yes, that unfortunate crash with the sandwich tray. You must have been mortified!"

That wasn't the excitement I was referring to; there was much more to the day than that. She'd neither congratulated nor comforted me, and now only saw fit to remind me of my worst moment.

"Well, I apologized to the poor fellow. He was very kind about it."

"Yes, aren't all the Emory men just the finest? Even their workmen."

"Oh, this young man is a student, too."

"Is he?" She raised her eyebrows. "I guess you two have something in common, then." She smiled, but I decided to ignore the remark.

"Did you need something?"

"I just wondered where you were going, in the middle of the school day."

"I . . . left my Bible over at the church after yesterday's service. Thought I'd run over after lunch to get it." I was a wicked sinner, lying about both church and the Bible.

"But, it's Monday. The church will be locked."

I hesitated but felt forced to explain. "The cleaner will be there. She can let me in."

"I see. I didn't know you were privy to the cleaning schedule." She gave a light laugh.

"That's the way it usually works, at most churches. Cleaners on Mondays." I remained silent while we shared an awkward moment.

"Well, I won't keep you, then. Onward to your Bible, and I must get to class."

I walked on toward the church, keeping a slow pace to appear unperturbed. Still, it felt as though Varina were watching me the entire way.

Tuesday passed with no post for me and only three candles left. Even slicing them in half, I wouldn't be able to get through another week. Wednesday morning's mail also disappointed, leaving me troubled and without an appetite. I barely picked at my lunch, made one more check at Mrs. Long's office, but ultimately trudged empty-handed to accompany my next voice lesson. After an endless hour of Ethel's pompous warbling, I was relieved to head for the door as soon as I was dismissed. Flinging it open, I was startled to see Rena standing there, a large box in her arms.

"Postman just brought this in. Got left behind from the mornin's delivery. Miz Long said to hunt ya down. There's a letter for ya, too." She plopped both package and letter into my arms, nodded, and took off. I stood staring in disbelief at my unexpected largesse.

"Thank you!" I called down the hall. She only threw up her hand in brusque acknowledgment, her relentless tromping gait never breaking stride. Immediately I secreted away to my room with my prize. Settling on the bed, I quickly untied the string and tore away the heavy brown paper. Inside were several small packages and tins, with a sheet of folded note paper on top.

Dear Bea,
I hope this box has reached you in a timely manner, and that its contents have survived their journey intact. I know you were expecting something else altogether, but I put the idea into Mama's head that you would like some tidbits from home so that I could follow through on your request without raising questions. I hope you like what we've sent, particularly a special buried treasure that is wrapped up snug! Everyone sends their love, especially me. I miss you lots!
Your devoted sister,
Lillian

Unwrapping the packages set my heart ticking with gratitude and homesickness. From Gladys was a handstitched plaid handkerchief; she knew I detested dainty, lacey ones. Little Jenny had decorated a card with pressed zinnias from Mama's garden. Even Bascom had wrapped a slender cylinder of wood with a slanted hole whittled near one end and a note: "To whistle at the boys walking by on the street!" The tins were filled with tastes from Mama's kitchen: oatmeal cookies, biscuits made with sweet potato, and chocolate fudge—a rare treat she only made at Christmas. Jim had packed a dozen apples from our orchard: three each of Winesap, Golden Delicious, Stayman and Jonathan. They were nestled on top of a green woolen blanket pinned with a note from Granddad: "For cold nights." It was his way of sending me a warm hug. Not surprising, there was nothing from Papa, still stubborn in his opposition to my leaving home for college.

I was thrilled with each thoughtful gift, but I started to panic when I found no money order in the box. Spying the letter I'd carelessly tossed on my night table, I swept it up to tear open. But the address was not written in Lillian's distinctive backhand with curly loops and flourishes. It was in a very staid script in a heavy black ink. I was stunned to read the return address: "Charles E. Sloan, Emory & Henry College, Emory, Virginia." Why in the world was an Emory student, president of the Hermesian Literary Society no less, writing a letter to me? I'd never received a letter from any boy, let alone one I'd only met once.

I dropped the envelope like a hot potato and rummaged on my bed for Lillian's note from the top of the box. Searching her words over and over, it suddenly jumped out at me: ". . . particularly a special buried treasure that is wrapped up snug!" I pulled out the blanket and unfurled it, discovering a box which I popped open with relish. There before my delighted eyes were candles, dozens of them in all their waxy, white gorgeousness. I held them to my nose, breathing in the pungent tallow that spoke safety and comfort. "Thank you, Lillian!" I shouted, not caring who might hear me, before I closed the box and tucked it underneath my armoire.

That evening I invited Ruby, Saluda, and Hazel to my room, thrilled to finally play host with a box from home like so many other girls. They raved over Mama's baking, Saluda declaring that blending sweet potato into a bread was sheer genius. Hazel was amazed that the apples were grown right in my home soil. "You mean, all your life you could just pick one off a tree anytime you wanted?" I told her yes, in autumn when the fruit was ripe; otherwise, it meant quite a tummy ache. We munched and gossiped for the good part of an hour before I was ready to share my other bit of news.

"I got something else in the mail today, and I don't know what to make of it." I pulled Charles's letter from under the book where I'd hidden it. At the sight of an unopened letter, Ruby snatched it from my hand with unbridled curiosity.

"It's from Emory & Henry College!"

"Emory?" Saluda and Hazel chimed together.

"'Charles E. Sloan,' it says." Ruby cast a sly glance in my direction. "Why, Bea, a swell from the college up the tracks is all sweet on you."

"And he's the president of the Hermesian Society," Hazel informed Ruby. "You must have made quite an impression on him, Bea."

They were making my cheeks turn redder than the Winesap apple I'd just eaten. "I'll bet it's just a thank-you note, for playing piano at the debate. Or a congratulations, something like that."

"Lots of us performed that day, but no one else got a letter from Emory," Saluda said with a wink, which deepened my blush.

"No more speculation—open it!" Ruby thrust the letter at me, her huge emerald eyes shimmering in anticipation. I slit the envelope with the apple carving knife and began reading.

"Dear Beatrice, I hope this note finds you well and having a good week back at the Martha. It was delightful to have you as a participant in our autumn Literary Society event on Saturday. I must say you played the Chopin beautifully. Hermesian Hall is a hallowed space for us and we were honored to have you perform there."

"You see, just a thank-you letter." I folded it and reached for the envelope.

"Wait!" Ruby cried. "That can't be all, you didn't even read a closing."

"Well, it's—"

"Bea Damron, give me that letter!" Ruby plucked it from me and read aloud.

"It was also an honor to speak with you afterwards, however briefly. I would like an opportunity to extend our conversation. Might I call on you at your campus sometime soon? I am free most weekends. Please answer back and let me know when would be most convenient for a visit. I look forward to hearing from you. Kind regards, Charles Sloan."

Ruby let out a long, low whistle while fanning herself with the page. "Bea, the fellow is positively *on fire* for you." Saluda and Hazel added whoops of agreement, all three exploding in animated chatter.

"Will you all stop it," I protested through my suppressed smile.

"You're going to answer him, aren't you? You have to write him back," Ruby insisted.

"I don't know." Now it was their turn to protest. "But I'll give it serious thought." They agreed to let that promise satisfy them. For the moment.

THURSDAYS I HAD MY HEAVIEST SCHEDULE, SO THE FLURRY OF activity the next day was a blessing; it kept my mind off Charles's flattering but puzzling letter. My history with boys was limited to brothers and schoolmates, so I wasn't accustomed to this type of attention. I could always best the boys at Clintwood High in any subject and they saw me as a freak obsessed with the piano. So, they left me alone.

When I headed to the church that evening, I traveled a new route that wound around the east edge of campus. I couldn't risk another sighting by Varina or anyone else as I slipped away to my covert rehearsal space. All was quiet as I slid through the side door, up the stairs to the choir room and settled on the bench before the baby grand. After scales and Hanon exercises, I dived into the fresh challenge Professor Zeisberg had issued: yet another Rachmaninoff, "Moment Musicaux, Opus 16 Number 4." It proved quite a workout for my brain and my fingers, so afterwards I decided to treat myself by playing the Chopin polonaise. Just once, I promised, since it conjured that nice feeling of Charles's compliment.

My fingers had gamboled along the keyboard for several minutes when suddenly an uneasy feeling gripped my gut. Immediately

I lifted my fingers from the keys, surprised to feel disturbed playing one of my favorites. After a few moments I continued on, but soon a discordance crept into the music. I stopped again, only to hear the reverberating of strings inside the piano bed. Distracting thoughts of Charles must have caused me to bungle it so I began again, playing on with more intense fervor. But just when I had built the tempo and volume to a frenetic state, my music was utterly eclipsed by the intruding dissonance: the unmistakable sound of a violin.

I sat there paralyzed. Its melancholy tune sawed on and on, soaring among high notes then dipping low into a bass line that pierced me and chilled me to the bone. I grabbed my music folio and ran from the room, down the hall, down the stairs, not daring to shut off any lights as I went. The side door slammed shut behind me as I raced for the street and its well-lit lamp posts. Entering the campus, I forced myself to slow to a walk and fortunately made it inside Preston Hall and up to my room without being unduly noticed. I immediately turned on all the lights, lit one of my new candles for good measure, and paced the floor in an effort to calm myself. When light bell sounded, I lit a second candle so a flame could burn on either side of my bed. But it would be a long, long time before sleep would visit me.

Running, running, slowly I'm running uphill, a deep river current impeding my forward movement. In the distance lampposts blossom with dusty glow, and it takes all my strength to run toward them. As I crest the hill, the lampposts get shorter and shorter, their electric lights turning to flames, the flames joining together in one huge blaze that sends up a cloud of billowing smoke. I fly up into the smoke. It swirls me inside its cloud, but I fight through it, thrashing and clawing and coughing. It vanishes and I'm kneeling on gray prickly grass where my gravestone rubbing lies before me. The wind sweeps up the paper and it quivers and ripples in the air, then becomes fluid. A filmy white cloth like a window drape, only it's a long flowing gown with a head of long silver hair emerging from the neckline. The wind becomes stronger. It whips the hair from the face, revealing two dark holes instead of eyes, empty and unseeing. A large gaping hole is its mouth, from which echo the sound of vibrating violin strings. The gown sways back and forth in rhythm with the peculiar music that grows softer and softer until it is a whisper of words. I strain to hear them take shape, the same words uttered over and over in a beseeching chant, becoming stronger with each repetition. "Captain. Come to my bed." I scream a soundless scream as I scramble backwards and collide with a crooked oak tree. Up and up I climb as the voice pleads, "Captain, come . . ."

I awoke clawing at the wall behind the headboard. My mouth was open wide, my scream halted by the grip of my constricted throat. I crumbled into a heap on my pillow, gulping for air. I stared at the still-burning candles, thankful the twin flames had not abandoned me.

As soon as it was daylight I dressed and left for breakfast. I arrived before my friends and sat alone, sipping tea to soothe my throat. Soon Varina and her tribe came bustling in and took a table on the far side. I involuntarily gave a slight shudder at the sight of her but took one last gulp of tea, squared my shoulders, and crossed the room.

"Good morning, Varina; Myrtle, Ethel, Bessie," I made an effort to look them all in the eye.

"Good morning, Beatrice," Varina smiled up at me; the others murmured a simple "Morning." "I see you're up and at 'em early. Busy day ahead?" I found her cheerfulness annoying.

"Yes. Well, but first I wanted to ask you something." I paused, searching for the right words; they all stared expectantly. "It's about what you talked about, before." Even though no one was nearby, I lowered my voice. "That night, at the . . . séance." Glances rapidly leapt around the table.

"The 'ritual' we discussed?" Thankfully Varina's tone was also discreet.

"Yes. I've decided it would be best, after all." Although I was obviously ill at ease, I didn't intend to confess the latest dream. Varina didn't question me and I was grateful.

"A wise choice. We'll do it tonight, won't we girls." The others were taken aback but knew better than to contradict their queen. "It's too bad Laura Mae isn't here this morning; these theatrical types aren't early risers. Well, too bad, we'll proceed without her. Meet at midnight on the back porch of Mariah Cooper. And wear all black, like before." Having duly issued her orders, she took my hand. "No need to fret any longer, Beatrice. Your troubles will soon be over for good."

Descant

The tall iron gate of Sinking Spring Cemetery tendered an ominous greeting at the end of our silent trudge through the cold night. I felt again inside my pocket for my secreted flashlight, an amulet against the murky dark. Varina swung the gate open and beckoned us inside, the faint glow of her lantern our only guide as we followed her sure steps into a far corner of the cemetery. Here a short iron fence surrounded a large rectangular plot where unknown Confederate soldiers had been laid to rest. Varina led us through its small gate and we formed a circle at about a dozen paces in. It felt strange to think of all the bones lying beneath our feet, with not so much as a small marker anywhere to give any soul some meager remembrance.

With a nod from Varina, Ethel handed me the spade she'd toted with her. Grasping the handle and stem, I pricked the earth with the point of the blade and placed my foot firmly on its top. Cold November temperatures had rendered the ground quite solid, but there'd been no frost yet to harden it into impenetrable brick. I thrust the blade into the soil, willing my muscles to overpower the tremulous feeling inside my gut. A clod of soil loosened that I set aside and poked with the spade. Repeating the process twice more, I collected a sufficient heap of crumbled dirt to shovel onto a cloth Bessie laid out on the ground. I tied up the cloth, then hoisted my funereal bundle to bear on to Beth's grave.

With every step of that long walk, I felt more beleaguered by the load. The physical weight tugging my arm was minor, but the emotional burden weighed on me with the heft of an enormous boulder. At last, we reached the spot where the lonely pale stone rose from the ground, the feeble marker of a once-vibrant soul. A pitiful remembrance for a girl snatched from life so young, especially one so kind and caring. No wonder her spirit was unsettled; the injustice of it was too cruel. Probably she didn't want to haunt me any more than I wanted to be visited by her; she was just troubled. I was sad for what had befallen her, but desperate to put an end to her music and thus my dreams.

I again took up the spade and roughened the grave's surface until it was minced enough to accept the dirt from my improvised pouch. After untying the knots, I poured out the fresh earth from the Confederate grave, then used my fingers to sift and knead the soils together. I was so preoccupied with my task I hardly registered the bitter cold seeping into my knuckles. When the soils were thoroughly mixed, I rose to my feet and silently prayed: "Beth, may you now truly rest in peace with your captain." No one spoke, their heads lowered out of respect for the moment.

I was quietly brushing the dirt from my hands when a strange sound broke the silence. Stopping to listen, I heard it again, a voice in the distance. It sounded like singing, but I couldn't make out any words. I looked at the others, but everyone still had their heads bowed. I thought it must be the wind, since I felt a breeze whisking dry leaves from the jagged branches of the graveyard trees. Bending down, I retrieved the spade, and when I rose again a glimmer of white emerged within my direct line of sight. It appeared to be a tall monument, one I hadn't noticed before. Then it began to move. It seemed to float as if on water, coming in our direction. Paralyzed, I watched it slowly shorten the distance between us. It was a girl in a long white gown, silvery tresses wafting around her alabaster face. An unnatural song, spawned from deep within her throat, pealed its macabre tune. The same tune I'd heard so many times: the melody of the violin. I screamed and furiously scuttled backwards away from the grave, losing my footing in the scramble. Varina and Myrtle gripped my arms just as I was about to fall.

"Beatrice, what's wrong?" Varina cried, trying to steady me.

"Don't you see?!"

"See what?"

"Over there!"

"Where?"

I watched all the others as they looked about the darkened cemetery, then looked back to me with puzzled faces. No one saw what I saw. No one heard what I heard.

A wild panic seized me and I jerked my arms free. I dashed for the cemetery gate and flung it open, letting it bang shut behind me with a horrible clang that reverberated into the night. Straight ahead I ran with unearthly speed, my footsteps thundering beneath me in rhythm with my pounding heart. I was headed down Valley Street and would need to turn to the right at some point in order to reach the Martha. Unaware of the distance I'd traveled, I made a blind turn onto the street I thought led to the college. I ran faster in this new direction, frantically searching in the pale street light for the green spheres of manicured shrubbery that lined the front lawn of the Martha. When they failed to come into view, I sensed something was odd. To my right, a stone wall rose up from the street, buttressing a low hill with pines on top. I was on the far side of Stonewall Jackson College, having missed the Martha completely! But I pressed on, racing towards a place where I always felt safe.

I didn't break stride until I reached the corral fence. Clutching the top rail to catch my breath, I cursed myself—until that moment I had forgotten all about my flashlight. Fishing it from my pocket, I flicked on its shallow beam, grateful for the meager relief from darkness. I climbed the fence and crossed to the stable doors, which, of course, were securely locked with a heavy chain looped through the handles. But above my head the much smaller door to the hayloft was only latched. It would have to do.

The construction of the stable doors was typical: each sturdy slab attached to a raised frame and middle crossbar, with a set of crisscrossed planks above and below it. The design gave the doors strength but also provided a climbing surface if one was nimble enough. Pocketing my flashlight, I reached through my legs to grasp the back hem of my skirt, pulled it forward and up, then firmly tucked it into my waistband. With one foot on the lower crisscross of the left door, I grasped its frame and hoisted myself up. Grabbing the top of the upper crisscross next, one more well-placed foothold on the crossbar let me reach for the lintel encasing the rail on which the doors slid back and forth. In this manner I scaled myself upward, like a clumsy spider creeping up a rocky wall.

The lintel was fairly deep and I gripped it with both hands, pushing with my feet to reach the edge of the sloping hayloft roof. I then pulled myself up to sit on the lintel. From this perch the barn's bead and board exterior provided handholds I could use to scoot myself to the hayloft door, only to discover the slide bolt latch so rusted it wouldn't budge. But the triumph of my climb was too hard-won to be thwarted by a little corrosion. My fingers ached with cold, but I willed them to grasp the gritty curved handle and pry it from its weather-beaten tentacles. I wrangled hard and persistently, but my precarious perch limited movement. Tears of frustration welled up in my eyes at the futility of my efforts, but in exasperation I gave one final heroic tug. To my surprise, it magically broke loose. The bolt slid raggedly but released the latch, prompting a joyful laugh as I swung the door open.

I wasted no time crawling inside to a pile of sweet-smelling hay. I lay there stretching muscles that had worked harder in one night than they had all week, rubbing and blowing on my cold stiff fingers to get the blood flowing again. After pulling the door shut, I trained the flashlight beam around the loft. It came to rest on Wesa, who petulantly raised his head in my direction. Once certain I'd received the full effect of his sullen stare, he stretched his mouth into a huge yawn and nestled his head back into the straw.

"If you'll excuse me, sir, I think I'll find more pleasant company below."

Keeping my light on the loft floor to avoid falling into the hay chute, I navigated to the ladder at the opposite end. I pocketed my light for the descent, but the soft low nicker coming from Copper's stall was all I needed to find him. I let him sniff me and he immediately pushed his velvety muzzle into my neck. All my tensions broke away as I hugged him and stroked his neck, bringing on a deluge of tears. The ever-patient Copper stood perfectly still while I emptied myself of the anxiety and fears that had consumed me for the past weeks.

When I'd recovered enough to breath normally, I retrieved a couple of saddle blankets from the tack room and joined Copper in his stall. As if he'd known I would be calling that night, he'd made no mess in the straw. I folded one blanket into a roll for my head and pulled the other over me, flipped the flashlight on, and then positioned it in the straw. I knew my eyes would not shut that night, but I was content to lie staring at a soft glowing circle on the wall, willing its batteries to last until daybreak.

I wondered how long I'd been riding in the wagon. It seemed like forever. It was covering some rough terrain because the bumping of the wheels was jostling me something terrible. In the distance I heard someone calling my name. I hunkered down tighter, trying to still the jostling. But the wagon was getting closer because my name was getting louder.

"Beatrice? Beatrice?"

I opened my eyes, then squinted in the dim light. I was looking into Jonah's face.

"What are you doing here?" he asked. I pulled myself up on my elbows to look around, then remembered. But the stall was empty except for Jonah and me.

"Where's Copper?" I shot up off the floor.

"He's just outside, he's fine. But are you?"

I stood there dusty and bedraggled, still groggy from the late night. I began to sway and Jonah took my arm.

"You're cold," he said and picked up the blanket from the straw. Wrapping it around my shoulders, he ushered me out of the barn and into the blacksmith shop. He lit the fire in the forge and pumped the bellows until a fierce glow blossomed. He placed a wooden box beside it and ordered me to sit there until he returned. Grateful for the warmth, I simply basked in the fire's heat, barely noticing when he came back with a paper sack and earthenware jug. From the shelves lining the wall, he took a small canister and a tin coffee pot. After tossing dark granules into the pot and pouring in water from the jug, he placed a small grate over the fire and set the coffee pot on top.

From the paper sack he brought out something square wrapped in a checkered napkin. "You need this," he said, placing it on my lap before turning to retrieve two mugs. I pulled back the corners of the napkin to find a sandwich made with thick slices of dark bread. It looked delicious, but I realized it was Jonah's lunch.

"No, I can't. It's too much," I protested and refolded the napkin. Without a word Jonah retrieved the sandwich and placed it on his workbench. He took a froe, held it over the flame for a few seconds, then thrust it into the sandwich to cleave it in two. Handing me one of the halves, he issued an irrefutable order, "Eat," and stared until I obediently took a bite. Donning a work glove, he lifted the coffee pot from the grate to pour steaming black liquid into the mugs. The sandwich tasted heavenly, made of a succulent ham smothered in butter on a bread that had an earthy sweet flavor. I suddenly felt ravenous and didn't have to be coaxed into taking more bites. I washed them down with sips of coffee, strong and somewhat bitter, but blissfully hot.

"I've never seen bread this dark before," I said before polishing off the last bite.

"Pumpernickel. Made from rye. My adopted mother taught me how to make it. The Schumachers were German."

"They *were* German?"

"They've passed on. Influenza and pneumonia. About four years ago."

"Oh. I'm sorry." Then dawn broke in my head. "But wait. 'Adopted mother?'... So that means..."

Jonah nodded and poured more coffee while I sat feeling like a dolt. I'd blithely assumed he was the caretaker, a "mere" blacksmith, when all the while he was the owner of it all. And too polite to correct me.

"But let's talk about you. For a college girl to sleep in a barn rather than her own soft bed, there must've been a very good reason."

I took another large gulp of the strong coffee, then told my entire miserable story: the ghostly violin music, the recurring nightmares, the horrifying ordeal at the cemetery, and my terrified escape. Jonah listened intently, sipping his own brew without a word until I concluded with my discouraged admission.

"Something's wrong with me. There's no way out of this and nothing I can do but go home." Utterly spent, I dissolved into tears all over again. Most men are disconcerted when a woman cries, but Jonah was calm and steady, waiting for my sobbing to subside.

"Do you remember, when we were riding a few weeks ago, the forest music?" I wiped my face on my sleeves and nodded. "Your balance has been disturbed."

"Oh, I'm unbalanced alright. That's what I'm telling you, I'm insane!"

"No, you're not. But you need to regain balance within yourself."

"How?" I fought back more tears.

"Remember, it has to do with how we're closely intertwined with nature. If you trust me, I can share an old Cherokee custom, a ritual for warding off bad dreams."

I sat staring at the fire. The disastrous cemetery ritual had been my last hope, but it hadn't helped at all. It had only made my nightmares appear to come to life. The last thing I wanted was to go back to Clintwood in disgrace, disappointing everyone who'd put their faith in me. And even if I left here, would the dreams stop or would I take them with me?

"Alright. I trust you."

Before I knew it, we were riding out toward the open field. Jonah had added a rugged jacket to my Benjamin ensemble, but he had told me to fold up my skirt and blouse and tie them to my saddle. He'd tied a rolled-up blanket and a small sack full of something to his own saddle. As promised, I asked no questions.

As we cantered through the field, our only illumination was diffused predawn light, and I wondered how Jonah was able to navigate. We were headed in the direction of the small lake we'd seen on our last ride, then veered off in the direction of the stream feeding into it. When we reached the tall oak tree that stood beside the stream, we stopped and dismounted.

"We're going to use the rushing water of this stream for a purification ceremony. It's called Anadawosgvi, or 'Going to Water,' and it's for cleansing the spirit. We should have fasted before, but of course, we didn't know we were going to do this. We've made it here before sunrise, though, so I'm sure we'll be forgiven. I chose this particular spot so we can look to the east and face upstream."

Jonah took the rolled blanket and sack from his saddle and told me to untie my extra clothes. Walking to the side of the oak closest to the stream, he dropped the sack on the ground, grasped two corners of the blanket and unfurled it. He then flipped it behind him and held it with outstretched arms, resembling a massive eagle about to take flight.

"You have to plunge yourself in the water. Seven times. So, remove your boots and stockings, and keep them off, then change into your school clothing. That way your boy clothing will stay dry for the ride back. I'll turn around now, to give you privacy."

I did as I was told, clenching my teeth against the cold morning air. Jonah kept talking, which helped distract me from the fact that

The Martha Odyssey

I was undressing in the presence of a man.

"Water is very important in Cherokee tradition. They see it as a living being, and they call a river 'Yunwi Gunahita,' 'The Long Man.' With his head in the mountains and his feet in the sea, he's a pathway to another world; he speaks and answers prayers. Another reason I picked this spot is because it has the personality of a sacred place. Medicine men say animals can recognize one, and I've seen lots of animals and birds come here to drink. Plus, there's the ancient tree, and the smooth rocks the Great Spirit has been polishing for centuries."

When I was changed, I tapped Jonah's shoulder. He dropped the blanket and ushered me to the edge of the stream.

"This ritual should be done by a medicine man," he told me. "But since I still remember how my father was taught long ago, it's okay for me to do it."

He instructed me to stand with my feet just touching the water. Its icy currents rippled over my toes in a chilling rush, a foretaste of the seven frigid submersions yet to come. Placing himself behind me, he told me to look into the distance. He uttered a Cherokee prayer softly under his breath. The words were indiscernible, not that I would have understood them. Later he explained that medicine men did this so that others would not steal their prayers. He wanted to be authentic.

He completed the prayer and simply said, "Now." I stepped into the middle of the stream and lowered myself flat until the water rushed over my entire body. The cold was shocking, but not as shocking as what I'd already been through. I raised my torso and knees long enough to catch my breath, then immediately plunged myself again. I recalled my childhood swims in Big Sandy River and knew that holding back only prolonged the sting of the cold. When I rose for the seventh time, I was grateful to see Jonah's extended arms ready to help me up and out of the stream.

I quickly began to wring out my hair as he led me back to the blanket. He shook out several rubdown cloths from the sack on the ground before again forming his blanket wall and dutifully turning his back. Working quickly, I removed my drenched shirtwaist. Then impulsively I decided to also take off my camisole so I could dry off thoroughly before pulling on the shirt. I did the same with my skirt and drawers before stepping into the trousers. It was quite daring of me, but the wet undergarments would only soak through my dry clothes, making for a miserable ride back to the barn. And, I reasoned, if I trusted Jonah to take me through this ritual, I could trust him to not turn around.

When I was dressed, we repacked our things onto the horses and headed out on the return trip. I held my shirtwaist in one hand and the reins in the other, and Jonah did the same with my skirt, the wind drying them on the ride back. My undergarments had gone into the sack with the rubdown cloths, so I had insisted on tying it to my saddle. Back at the stable, Jonah fired up the forge again, shutting me up in there to finish drying my things. When they were thoroughly baked, I changed again and took my Benjamin outfit back to the tack room. I found Jonah there, puttering around aimlessly.

"I don't know how to thank you," I said softly. We glanced at each other awkwardly, neither of us knowing quite how to look at one another.

"No need. It's the Great Spirit's blessing, not mine." He stared down at the leather reins he was shuffling in his hands.

"Well. I'd better get back to the Martha."

He looked up briefly. "Of course," then returned focus to the reins. I walked away, stopping to say goodbye to Copper.

"Beatrice," he called, stepping out of the tack room. "I think this must be yours." He thrust my flashlight into my hand, its light spent from its long vigil the night before.

"Oh. Yes. It is mine. Thank you." I started turning to leave.

"And Beatrice," he held onto the flashlight for another moment. "Remember: pluck and strength—that's who you are."

Pathétique

The sun was climbing the sky as I returned to the Martha. But the hour was still early and other girls were either at breakfast or sleeping in, so I avoided meeting anyone on the stairs. After a quick stop at my room for a fresh outfit, I scooted off to the bathroom for a hot soak in the tub and a good shampoo.

I lay blissfully engulfed in the soapy water, letting my thoughts drift. What would Pastor Stewart back home think of what I'd just done? I didn't see any great differences between what Cherokees believed and what Methodists believed, or any other Christians for that matter. The Cherokee religion seemed to be more closely knit with nature, which made sense to me. They saw the human world and spirit world as intimately connected, with the spirit world presiding over both. How was that different from Christians believing that God watches over us, over every creature on earth? Pastor Stewart might call it blasphemous to practice a Cherokee ritual, but I didn't feel that way at all. The Almighty God or the Great Spirit—it all seemed like the same thing to me. I shut my eyes and drifted into a light sleep. Suddenly a loud bang on the door intruded upon my solitude.

"Who's in there hoggin' the tub? There better still be some hot water!" I knew that voice.

"Ruby?"

"Bea?" The door popped opened and Ruby stuck her head inside, laughing.

"I thought you'd still be in bed. It is Saturday morning, you know," I said with a nervous laugh, trying to hide my fluster. She came in and shut the door with her backside, sliding to seat herself on the floor.

"Heck, no. I've been up since the crack of dawn. Miss Fakes had the entire cast over at Litchfield Hall for one last rehearsal before this afternoon." I'd completely forgotten about Ruby's play. My plans for an afternoon nap were instantly dashed, but there was no way I would miss her performance. "I didn't see you at breakfast, though, so *you* were the sleepyhead today," she added in a mock admonishment. Of course, with Ruby's habit of sleeping in, she wasn't aware that I was scarcely in the dining hall on Saturday mornings. But I played along and took my scolding; it was a good cover for my absence.

"Guilty as charged. Just hand me a towel, then, and I'll free up the tub."

It took the next couple of hours for us to dry and coif our hair, and by then it was time for lunch. Entering the dining hall, I held my head high as if nothing was amiss, but dreaded seeing Varina and the other girls just the same. Looking around for a table, I inadvertently spied her, already seated with her bevy of minions and searching the room with worried eyes. I pretended not to see her, but in my peripheral vision detected her relief at seeing me. It did my heart good to know she'd been worried. I didn't fear them snitching on me, since they would only incriminate themselves if they did. So, at tables on opposite sides of the hall, we all busied ourselves eating lunch as if nothing unusual had happened at all. We then marched over to Litchfield Hall to see a drama on its stage, one that could not possibly match the intensity of the drama played out in our little lives over the last twenty-four hours.

RUBY WAS WONDERFUL. I'D NEVER SEEN "A MIDSUMMER NIGHT'S Dream" but couldn't imagine a more perfect Hermia. "Though she be but little, she is fierce" was Ruby all over, and she dazzled the audience with her energy and wit. Even so, after giving her hugs and lavish praise afterward, I was relieved when she departed for the cast party. I took the opportunity to grab a quick supper and go to bed early. I slept like a rock.

However, pulling myself together the following morning proved a Herculean task. I awoke to a throbbing headache, and when I finally sat up in bed it felt as though my muscles were screaming at me. But missing church was out of the question. I massaged my head for a few minutes before mechanically dressing myself, including the dreaded corset. I needed propping up via any method available to me, including a large mug of black coffee at breakfast to give my senses the kick they needed.

But it wasn't enough. The one block walk to the church exhausted my reserves, and by the time we stood to sing the second hymn I was feverish and sweating. The words on the page blurred and I began to sway. Saluda grabbed one arm and Ruby my other, our hymnals crashing to the floor and alerting Mrs. Long. One look at my lily-white face with beads of moisture freckling my forehead and she insisted I come with her immediately. I was surprised at the firmness of her grip as she propelled me from the sanctuary past rows of alarmed and curious eyes. I didn't remember much after that, only faintly aware of being tucked into a bed in the college infirmary.

The remainder of that day and the next were a blur, a series of long, deep sleeps. Heat and cold raged a vicious contest to see who would claim me as their prize. I was seized by shaking chills, feeling I'd never be warm again despite layers of heavy blankets. These bouts were followed by a sweltering heat that prompted me to toss the covers away against someone's insistence that I lay still while they applied a cool wet cloth to my head. Occasionally I was roused to sip water or broth.

By Tuesday morning, I was finally fully awake and able to sit up, propped with an extra pillow. Mrs. Adams, the infirmary nurse, brought me a small meal of oatmeal, toast, and hot tea, and I was actually hungry for the first time in days. But as I chewed the toast, I realized something amazing: in all the time I'd slept, I hadn't had a single dream. Was I cured? Even if I was physically ailing, the thought that my nightmares could be gone for good promised a speedy recovery.

After Nurse Adams took my tray, praising my tiny accomplishment, I lay back on my pillows and took notice of my surroundings. There were four iron-framed cots, a braided wool rug warming the wooden floorboards, and three windows with pale blue curtains tied back to let in sunlight. Two cots on the opposite wall were neatly made up with crisp white sheets and a blue wool blanket. The cot next to mine sat empty, but its rumpled sheets and skewed blanket indicated a recent occupant. Someone would come along soon to strip it, so I shut my eyes and sank down into my covers to block out the noise.

In the next minute I heard footsteps, although they were uneven shuffling sounds rather than the purposeful marcato of a nurse. Next came the complaint of cot springs under a sudden load and the rustle of sheets as someone tucked into them. My curiosity won out over the need for solitude and I rolled over to face the other cot. I saw the profile of a pale face and long hair splayed over the pillow in a mousy brown tangle. Something about the girl was familiar, so I propped myself on one elbow for a better view. I felt sure I'd seen her, and only recently.

"Good morning," I ventured tentatively.

"I suppose so, if there are any good mornings in here." Her voice sounded scratchy. I kept staring, feeling I should know her.

"When did you come in?"

"Saturday night. Or maybe it was early Sunday morning. It was the middle of the night."

"Sunday morning for me, in the middle of church. I barely remember it."

She turned toward me and her face became fully visible. Her

pasty skin emphasized the shadows encircling her eyes. But even in her sick pallor, after studying her for a few moments, I remembered.

"I know now. Where I've seen you," I said. She raised slightly to look closely at me, her eyes widening while her forehead creased into a frown. "You were in the play. With Ruby Atkins. Saturday afternoon."

Her frown relaxed and she settled back onto her pillow.

"Yes, I was."

"You played Ruby's chum. Helena, right?"

"Right."

We both rested for a minute. I was surprised how exhausting talking could be when you hadn't done it for a few days.

"I'm Beatrice, by the way. But everyone calls me Bea."

She nodded. I raised on my elbow again and looked at her expectantly.

"Laura Mae," she finally reciprocated. The name sounded vaguely familiar.

"I feel like I've met you, even before Saturday's play." I wracked my memory, but couldn't think of where else I would know her from.

"I don't think so," she replied in a small scratchy voice, then rolled over on her other side.

I thought she might be in pain or already tired, so I didn't tax her with more conversation. Laura Mae. I tossed the name around in my head, but nothing helpful presented itself. I felt a little tired myself and we both dozed off.

BUT YOUTH CAN BE AMAZINGLY RESILIENT, AND BY THE END OF the day we had both perked up quite a bit. Between brief naps, Nurse Adams had us up and moving about, and sitting in chairs for meals. After lunch, we were tucked back into bed by a student nurse assisting that day, who said we'd been prescribed a spoonful of tonic twice a day. She held up a little blue bottle and measured out some of its contents, then leveled the spoon at Laura Mae.

"Stop!" Nurse Adams bounded over and snatched the blue bottle from the student nurse's hand. "What did I tell you about double-checking labels? This clearly says 'Ipecac Syrup.' To *induce vomiting*." She thrust the bottle at the girl's face on each offending word. "And just when we got them eating solid food. Pay attention, girl!" I felt sorry for her, trembling and face turning beet red. Her angry supervisor stomped to the medicine cabinet for the tonic, then stood watching like a hawk as the young nurse gave us the correct medicine.

"That's better," Nurse Adams barked, then turned to us. "If this tonic works like I think it will, one more day of confinement should do before you two are back on your feet." Thanksgiving would be the day after that, so we were thrilled to know we'd be sprung free for the holiday.

The tonic evidently worked, because the chatter between us steadily increased. I learned that she, too, was from a small town, Pontotoc in Mississippi—which, though in the flatlands, sounded a lot like Clintwood—and had also felt timid and out of place when she first arrived at the Martha. I told her how much my music helped me, how I could lose myself in it and take little respites from social pressures. She felt the same way about the theatre. Once she stepped onstage and escaped into a character, her shyness disappeared and she felt as brave as a conqueror.

Nurse Adams noticed our renewed liveliness and called for Mrs. Long to bring us our books and assignments. I actually welcomed some mental stimulation since I missed the piano something fierce. I had been going through my pieces in my head whenever I dozed, but it was a poor substitute for the feel of the keys underneath my fingers. We settled into our studies, but after a while I noticed Laura Mae scribbling all over a sheet of paper. Seeing me crane my neck in curiosity she offered, "Oh, this is something else I do to escape." She turned the paper to show a stunning drawing of a dog with its head jutting forward, a front paw lifted and its feathery tail stretched out level behind. "This is Demetrius, one of my Irish Setters. I have his brother, too. Lysander."

Her love of dogs matched my love of horses, and we talked at length about our favorite companions (omitting the ones belonging to Jonah, of course). "Describe Nutmeg for me," she said, and as I talked her pencil frolicked over a fresh page. A few moments after I'd gone quiet, she handed me the paper. I was stunned to see my childhood horse looking back at me with her soft dark eyes. The likeness was incredible, but Laura Mae only shrugged shyly when I praised her. We both missed our pets terribly, and I felt bad that she had no substitutes like I had for Nutmeg.

Nurse Adams sternly reminded us that we were still recovering and should devote any energy reserves to our studies. We dutifully quieted and returned to our assignments. But as we studied, I occasionally felt Laura Mae's eyes on me, lingering there intently. This didn't particularly make me uncomfortable, but I detected a certain sadness or unease about her, making me wonder what was on her mind. I decided it was best to pretend I hadn't noticed. If she needed to talk about something, I hoped she now regarded me as friend enough to confide in me.

After lunch on Wednesday, Nurse Adams handed out some correspondence that had been delivered for us. She'd been holding it, she said, until we had regained sufficient strength, not wanting to expose us to undue excitement. More likely, Mrs. Long told her not to distract us from our assignments. We hungrily tore into the envelopes.

"It's from Ruby," I said, smiling down at the careless scrawl on the page.

"Yours, too?" Laura Mae looked up at me, surprised.

"Yes, she's my best friend. Our rooms are next door to each other, and we just hit it off from the first day. To be honest, I don't know how I would've survived those early days here without her."

"She has that effect on people. So sweet and helpful. And a remarkable actress."

Both our notes conveyed Ruby's lament of how unfair it was that illness had struck us down, that she missed us terribly and sent wishes for a speedy recovery. To Laura Mae, she sent compliments on her play performance, and said she couldn't wait to have her back to study scenes with. To me, she sent word that I'd had a visitor on Sunday afternoon, and that part I just had to read out loud.

"And not just any visitor, but one Charles Sloan of Emory and Henry College! Bea, it was the most romantic thing, how sad and disappointed he was to hear you were ill and confined to the infirmary. Then I painted the most evocative picture of you, lying frail in the throes of fever in your sheer nightgown with flowing hair curling about your shoulders. It was thrilling to see how he pined for you, like a lost puppy! He declared that as soon as he got back from his holiday at home in Richmond, he would make a return visit and looked forward to seeing you in rosy good health once again." I was certain she'd lavishly embellished the scenario, but Laura Mae and I got a good laugh out of it.

IT FELT WONDERFUL TO WAKE UP IN MY OWN BED THURSDAY morning, and I knew immediately what I was thankful for: nights of dreamless sleep! I was actually feeling at peace and believed that even when dreams returned to my nights, they wouldn't be the haunting variety that had plagued me for weeks.

I was so stuffed from the magnificent turkey dinner we'd been served the previous evening that I wasn't in the mood for breakfast. Instead, I dressed and headed straight down to the Student Parlor, closed the door, and seated myself before the upright piano. It had been a full week since I'd played and it felt like coming home. We had the entire day free of classes and I thought I just might spend it all right in that spot. I played through my most familiar repertoire first, as a reward for surviving my ordeal and to get my musical juices flowing again. I thought back to what Laura Mae said about transforming herself into a character and stepping into another world where courage came easily. It was the same for me with music, and if I closed my eyes, I could even see—

"Boo!"

I yelped as two sharp pricks into my ribs made me bolt and nearly fall off the stool. I swung around wide-eyed to come face to face with Ruby, who instantly shrieked with laughter.

"Ruby, you rascal!" I gasped, but couldn't suppress my own laughter. "My brother used to do the same thing!"

A large gilt-framed mirror hung on the wall over our piano back home. Bascom would try to evade it by crawling on his knees all the way from the front hall, through the parlor doorway and across the carpet to sneak up behind me while I played. But I had a sixth sense about mischievous siblings and always caught him just before he could poke me in the back—except for one time! I was too engrossed in the music and failed to hear the faint scraping of his knees on the rug, and he got me. He rolled onto his back in laughter and never let me hear the end of that one.

"And I'll *never* tell him about this," I added as our giggles subsided. She'd come to fetch me for lunch and babbled all the way there about a package she'd received from home.

"It arrived yesterday," Ruby pouted, "but Mrs. Long put it in the kitchen cold storage, 'So as not to distract you from dining with your Martha sisters on Wednesday,' said her note tucked under my door this morning." I snickered at her excellent imitation of our headmistress. "Well, I'm distracted now, but I can't pick it up until the lunch shift ends at two o'clock."

Opening it in Ruby's room later was like Christmas morning. "Mama must have felt so bad about me not getting to come home, she really overdid it with this goodie box." And she wasn't kidding. I'd never seen such an array of delectable treats: country ham, sausages galore, and even fried chicken; three loaves of homemade bread, two jars of pickles, a lemon pound cake, a tin of caramel fudge, two jars of preserves—strawberry and blueberry—and a paper sack of roasted chestnuts. "No turkey leftovers for us!" Ruby declared. "We'll have a picnic in my room tonight and dine in style."

Ruby also included my friend Hazel (Saluda was traveling) and a friend from drama class. But with enough food to feed a small army, I asked if we could invite Laura Mae as well. I'd noticed her sitting alone in the dining hall at lunch, looking a bit lost during the holiday. She was surprised when I showed up at her door, but she smiled and accepted gladly. With Hazel in attendance, she wasn't the only junior fraternizing with freshmen, and we all settled in comfortably for a fine feast. My usual voracious appetite had returned in full force and I sampled everything.

But stuffing our mouths didn't prevent lively conversation. We gossiped about teachers, boys and romance, and life beyond our years at the Martha. Everyone shared their ambitious plans while I nibbled nervously on my second slice of cake, hoping no one would ask me. But Hazel mentioned the music scholarship competition and Ruby wouldn't let me off the hook. So, in the midst of a stupor from heavy eating, the late hour and easy comradery, my defenses fell away and I divulged my circumstances. "If I don't win, I'll be going back home after just one year. My father's orders." Everyone was quiet for a long moment, no doubt thanking their lucky stars they had more understanding fathers. Then Ruby broke the tension, declaring it impossible that I would lose because she'd already written my acceptance speech. She hopped on a chair and performed it with outrageous dramatic flair, our laughter helping us segue into cleaning up and scooting back to our rooms before light bell.

I was last to leave, but just after I'd flopped on my bed and kicked off my shoes, there was a timid knock at my door. Thinking it was Ruby with a last tidbit of gossip that couldn't wait until morning, I was surprised to open the door to Laura Mae.

"Oh." I stood looking at her curiously.

"Bea. Yes, uh . . . I'm sorry to disturb you. I . . ."

"No, it's fine. I'm still up."

"Oh, good. I . . . um, well, I . . . I just wanted to thank you. For inviting me. Tonight."

"Well, sure. I mean, you're welcome. There was plenty of food, and you and I both know Ruby. It was only natural for you to be there." I wanted to avoid saying I'd noticed her loneliness.

She looked into my eyes with a slightly pained expression. I wasn't sure what to say next, but then she sighed and tendered a small smile.

"Well. It was nice of you. Of both of you. To have me. Thank you, again." She abruptly turned and walked away.

"Good night," I called after her. She halted midstep and turned back.

"Good night, Bea." She held my gaze for a moment and then rushed down the hallway, her hurried steps clattering on the wooden treads as she descended the staircase.

Falsetto

When Friday morning came, too early, it was back to full academic grind for lowly underclassmen. But with most senior voice students still gone for the holiday, I was relieved of accompaniment duties for the afternoon. With the luxury of extra time, I put in some extra piano practice and then scampered back to my room for a nap. I lay watching the sun animate the colors of my patchwork quilt as I wiggled my toes beneath it, lulling myself into a deep sleep.

Too soon a muffled thumping intruded into my slumber. As I groggily raised my head, it grew to a precise knocking in an urgent rhythm that couldn't be ignored. I slogged across the room to again find Laura Mae on the other side of my door. She had the same pained look on her face from the night before.

"Bea, I have to talk to you." She walked straight into the room without hesitation. "Please close the door." A strange turn of events, but, curious, I obeyed. Embarrassed by my rumpled bed covers, I sat down on them and gestured for Laura Mae to take my vanity chair.

"I couldn't sleep at all last night," she began. "I'd come back to your room, you know, after the party in Ruby's. I was going to talk to you then. But . . ." Nervously wringing her hands, she jumped from the chair and started pacing the room.

"What is it?" She was pitifully distraught.

"I feel so guilty. I'd been feeling guilty already, but . . . after hearing your story, about your schooling and your father, how you need so much to win the competition, I just . . ."

"What are you talking about?" She took a few more paces and stopped.

"That night. In the cemetery. You saw a girl, in a white gown. She was singing. If you can call it singing. Making strange singing-like sounds..."

I blanched at the memory. "How do you know about that?"

Laura Mae looked at me. "It was me." Her face crumpled into a mask of remorse. "And I'm so sorry." She was crying now, uncontrollably, coughing out words with each miserable sob. "I didn't want to scare you, Bea, I didn't. It's just... Varina convinced me it was the only way to rid you of your dreams. But when I saw your face. Saw you run away, terrified... And then you got so sick." She sank to the floor, dissolving into a flood of tears.

It became clear to me then. A picture in my mind of my first day at the Martha. A group of girls in fine silk dresses, sitting around a dining table. Then a darker picture. Another table, a circle of candles, the same girls with the same queen bee at the center. The séance. Laura Mae had been at both those tables. I stared at the wretched puddle on my floor, and it didn't match up. I couldn't reconcile the girl I'd gotten to know in the infirmary with a girl who would carry out such a foolish and gruesome plan.

"I shouldn't have listened to her." Laura Mae had cried herself out and could breathe again. "I should've known it was wrong. But she's had such a hold on me, ever since she was my mother freshman year. I can't believe it now, but I actually adored her. I was this timid mouse from the swamps of Mississippi. Did I tell you the other girls used to call me 'catfish'? And she was so sophisticated, with her fine clothes and her fancy talk. She just took people in hand, and didn't let anybody make fun of me. Taught me to be a lady, or so I thought. But really, she just intimidates people for her own good. She doesn't care who she has to step on to forge her own path."

We were both silent for a long while. I was seething inside, but when I looked at Laura Mae, I only felt pity and disappointment. It was a mean trick and she'd been complicit, but at least she'd repented. She'd had the guts to tell me the truth, to let me know I wasn't crazy, seeing ghosts.

"You got sick, too," I said softly and helped her off the floor. Gently lifting her chin, I looked into regretful eyes. "I'd be lying if I said I wasn't angry. But you did the right thing in the end. And I appreciate that."

She nodded, silently for fear she'd break into tears again, and slowly walked to the door. She turned the knob, but suddenly I stepped forward and placed my hand on her shoulder to hold her there a bit longer. I had one more burning question that sorely needed an answer.

I STOOD ALONE, STARING AT THE COLUMN OF SUNLIGHT BLAZING into my room, mesmerized by the dust motes churning in an aimless dance inside. Slowly the shock gripping me gave way to an anger that burned brighter than the sun. It bubbled up inside me, prompting me to grab the nearest object and hurl it with all my might. No sooner had my heavy literature book slammed against the wall with a booming thud, than I'd swooped up my shoes from the floor and flung them one by one at the armoire. Next came my brush and comb followed by my hairpin box, bursting open to spray pins in all directions. Like a madwoman I worked through the stack of my remaining books, aiming at each wall by turns. My poetry book hurtled towards the door just as it began to open, nearly smacking Ruby in the face.

"Bea! What on earth are you doing in here?" We exchanged a brief startled stare before I began pacing in wild loops and Ruby shut the door behind her. "It looks like you declared war on your room. And the room lost."

"Do you know why I got sick?" I fumed. "And why Laura Mae got sick? At almost exactly the same time?"

"Ah, you two shared a toothbrush?" Ruby shrugged, trying to soothe my fury with subtle humor. I stopped pacing and opened my mouth to tell her, but closed it. I opened it again, then returned to pacing.

"It's probably better you don't know. But somebody's going to pay!"

I flung open my door and stomped down the hall and down a flight of stairs. I headed straight for the tunnel to Mariah Cooper Hall, not caring who saw me. Varina's room was somewhere on the first floor, so I bounded down the staircase and began knocking on doors. My rapping grew more frantic with each unanswered door, until finally around the first corner one flew open at the hand of a highly perturbed girl dressed only in her underwear. I ignored her rude greeting.

"I'm looking for Varina Armstrong."

"Well, you're looking in the wrong place," she retorted. "Her room is that last one, end of the hall. Number one fourteen."

I didn't see fit to thank her and simply headed toward Varina's door.

"But you're still out of luck," she called after me. "She went down to Bristol to holiday with a friend. Won't be back 'til Saturday night." With a satisfied smirk, she retreated into her room, slamming the door as a parting shot.

To prevent giving this impertinent girl any satisfaction, I marched back around the corner and up the hall, waiting until I'd reached the bottom of the staircase to stomp my foot and scream in frustration.

"A real bitch, huh?" I looked up to see Ruby crouched against the banister halfway down the stairs.

"Ruby! What are you doing here?"

"I needed a front-row seat to whatever this is that has you so riled." I climbed the stairs to plop down beside her.

"I'm so angry I'd forgotten about the 'senior privilege' of leaving campus for Thanksgiving. I have to see Varina, and in her room, but I have to wait 'til tomorrow night!"

"You said 'somebody's going to pay.' Who's the somebody? And how will they pay?"

I looked at Ruby, head cocked and crystal green eyes brimming with curiosity like a perky young spaniel. She was a good friend whom I'd always been able to count on, no matter what. I had nothing to lose—and most likely a whole lot to gain—by taking her into my confidence. But not on the stairs where we might be overheard.

"Let's go back to my room first."

"Wait!" Ruby reached behind her. "You shouldn't be traipsing about in your stocking feet." I laughed as she handed me my shoes, not too worse for wear after their collision with the armoire.

Safely secluded in my room, I laid out my story in all its horrendous details. I didn't, however, share my experiences with Jonah and the horses. I trusted Ruby, of course, but needed to keep that part of my world to myself. She listened intently to my tale, interjecting responses that alternated between sympathetic and outraged. But all the while, I sensed little wheels turning in her clever head. Sure enough, by the time my hair-raising recital was over, she had developed a plan of action. She would tell it to me only if I promised to let her help.

Crescendo

Ruby looked adorable. Although pretty as a picture and utterly feminine, she'd made herself into an absolutely darling young boy.

"It's easy to see why they let you tag along. Who could say no to that face?"

Ruby rolled her eyes and fastened her galluses while I tugged on my split skirt and old cotton shirtwaist I wore to the stables. "Stop gawking and go get that broom from the cleaning closet." She was once again donning the disguise from phase one of her plan, accomplished that morning. With purloined clothing from the expression department costume storage—plaid shirt, knee britches and socks, a tweed newsboy cap—Ruby had joined a cleaning crew hired to do a special spit and polish scrubbing of Mariah Cooper Hall. Ruby had heard about the crew because of Myrtle's complaining. "I'm the only senior who didn't go away for the holiday," Ruby had parroted, "and now all Mariah Cooper residents have to get up early on Saturday and sit in the dining hall for the entire morning." She could even mimic Myrtle's sour face perfectly.

Ruby had made a point to help clean room one fourteen, then deliberately dawdled to ensure she was left behind to finish up. She then placed a coil of thick rope—also lifted from the stage props and concealed beneath her shirt—on the floor and firmly tied one end to the radiator beneath the window. She knotted the other end of the rope and fastened a long length of twine just above the large knot. Carefully unlocking the double-hung window, she threaded the twine over the sill and down the brick exterior until it nearly reached the ground. She then eased the window back down and left its latch unlocked before quietly exiting.

Now having successfully taken a surreptitious detour to the gymnasium on our supposed way to the Saturday evening meal, we were well into phase two. Luckily, the late November sun set early, and darkness fell fast just when everyone was busy in the noisy dining hall. Walking from the gymnasium toward the rear of Mariah Cooper in the heavy dusk, I had a strange sense of déjà vu. Only a week earlier I'd traversed the darkness and crawled into a window where I wasn't supposed to be. But executing this plan was the only way to set things right. I felt amazingly calm because I also felt totally justified.

When we reached the spot just below Varina's window, we took one last look around to make sure we were alone. Then, since I was taller, I raised the broom and placed the tip of its handle underneath the horizontal top of the lower window's frame. I gave a hard push, but the rounded tip slid sideways and the broom clattered to the ground. My frustrated grunt was accompanied by a couple of choice expletives from Ruby. We flattened ourselves against the brick until we were certain we hadn't been heard, then tried again. I aimed for a corner of the window's frame instead and applied slow but firm pressure. To our relief, the window steadily slid upwards and I managed to open it enough to pull through the rope.

We began tugging on the twine, holding our breath until we saw the knot of the heavy rope peep over the window sill. Ruby whispered, "Yes!" and I let out a sigh as we kept up the steady pull. The knot of the rope was about half way down the brick when the twine suddenly cascaded onto my head. I looked dumbly at Ruby, then we both gazed up at the rope knot lightly swinging in a tantalizing circle above us. "It must've worked itself loose when it slid over the radiator," I whispered. "Give me a leg up." Ruby shot me an incredulous look since I was a head and a half taller than she. But despite her petite stature she was strong as an ox, and I explained that it was just like mounting a horse. I would do a little hop and propel myself up with my own force, and she would mostly serve as a balancing device. "Just use your thighs to bear the weight."

It took three tries before I reached high enough to grab the knot, but when I did, I pulled with all my might and toppled to the ground on my rear end. Ruby's hands flew up to her mouth, whether in concern or to cover a laugh I wasn't sure, but I gave her a thumbs up that I was okay. Within minutes, we'd scaled the brick wall and climbed inside Varina's room. After a quick breather, I untied the rope and sent it flying to the ground, shut and latched the window, then closed the drapes. With no visible trace of our entry and everyone in the dining hall, I felt safe enough turning on the bedside lamp.

"Okay, Ruby, lead the way. Show me how a good 'room stacking' is done."

She grinned and rubbed her hands together like a dastardly villain in one of her beloved thriller films. We tackled the bed first, tearing off the fancy satin coverlet and half a dozen lacy pillows and scattering them around the room. Then, grabbing the metal frame at the foot of the bed, we raised it up to lean the entire bed against the wall. We scooted the dressing table across the room and braced it against the leaning bed. There were chairs plus a footstool that we arranged one on top of the other in a higgledy-piggledy tower beside the armoire. Two "Martha" pennants hung from the crown molding on a long length of ribbon, arranged among several others from men's colleges where Varina no doubt had admirers. We ripped them down and draped them over the bed in a haphazard manner. Flopping down on the throw rugs to catch our breath, we realized we needed to roll those up to stash somewhere. Ruby decided that leaving them poking up through the metal posts of the bedframe had the most dramatic flair.

"Now for the really scrumptious part!" Ruby chuckled. With one deft motion, she swooped the dresser scarf off the vanity table, along with Varina's fine accoutrements so prettily arranged on top.

Brushes and powder puffs took flight along with small boxes that burst open, sending hairpins and jewelry soaring before landing at random on the floor. She opened drawers and pulled out stockings, camisoles and other unmentionables, tossing them in the air like confetti. She directed me to start on the armoire, but I was drawn to the wardrobe steamer trunk standing in the corner and draped with a shawl. Brushing away its covering, I snapped apart the metal buckles, then tried the latch at the center. It did not budge, even after several mighty tugs that nearly cut my fingertips. Ruby was now busy tying knots in Varina's underthings while I rummaged through the mess on the floor for a box, a purse, or anything that might contain a key.

"Bea, I've got this. Pull out stuff from the armoire. We're getting short on time."

I ignored her and continued my rummaging, even underneath the table. No luck, so I crawled to the armoire and started on its bottom drawers. Blouses and more underwear, but I pulled them out in the ridiculous hope a key might be tucked inside the boning of a corset. Several mangled piles blossomed on the floor as I tossed each item aside, then felt the corners of emptied drawers for traces of a false bottom. Nothing. Ruby was now tying knots in the spoils from these drawers, so I opened the doors of the armoire to relieve Varina's dresses from their hangers. Most were of fragile silk, organdy, or crepe de chine and I merrily flung them out into the room to wherever gravity saw fit to land them. In the midst of this effort, we suddenly heard a train whistle in the distance.

"Rats! Okay, Bea, that's our signal. Let's go."

"We can't go before you've done something with these fine dresses. What kind of room stacker are you, anyway?"

I needed more time, and thankfully Ruby couldn't resist the challenge of corrupting them, then arranging them in bizarre poses around the room. While she was absorbed in her high jinks, I rifled through the pockets of Varina's practical skirts and jackets. My nimble fingers swept every one, my heart sinking a little each time they came out empty. Irritated at my futile efforts,

I scooped out all the remaining garments onto the floor, revealing a long woolen coat hanging on a peg at the back. I grabbed it and immediately poked into its many pockets. Still nothing.

"Well, that's it for sure," said Ruby as she placed the final dress in an obscene pose across the vanity table mirror. "We need to go."

Out of utter frustration, I sank heavily to the floor clutching the disappointing coat. Its skirt fanned out in front of me, landing on the wooden floor with a muffled clink. With new fervor I reached for the hem of the coat and pressed my fingers along its edge. I kept pressing frantically until at last, at the edge of the kick pleat, I was rewarded. Flipping the hem over to expose the inside lining, I bit the threads with my teeth and pulled until the satin ripped away from the wool. Out fell a shiny brass key.

"This is it!" I was ecstatic. Ruby wasn't enthused.

"But Bea, there's no time." She rushed to the door and released the inside lock. "The depot's less than two blocks away, we need to get out of here."

"Not until I've opened that trunk."

"We've done plenty of damage without it."

But I was already across the room, my trembling hands on the trunk's lock. I inserted the key and gave a quick turn, surprised how easily the latch came undone. I swung the trunk open and what I saw inside made my heart stop. I quickly pushed it closed.

"Ruby, you should go."

"We *both* need to go."

"I still have business here, but you don't need to be mixed up in it."

"I'm already mixed up in it, and I'm not leaving without you. Look, Varina's going to be here any minute!"

"Yes, and I need to see her. Face to face."

"Look, you wanted to make her pay, and we've done that. Now let's—"

The door swung open as the overhead light clicked on, finding us staring into Varina's stunned face. She glared at me, then Ruby, looking her up and down, then turned her attention back to me.

"What can possibly be the meaning of this," Varina growled through clenched teeth, seething that her private sanctuary had been violated. And in a such a magnificent manner.

"I might ask you a few questions instead." I stood tall and looked her right in the eye. "Like, what is the meaning of a fake séance? If you'll pardon the redundancy. And what is the meaning of a fake ritual in a cemetery at night, where a girl is forced to parade in a thin nightgown in the bitter cold, and another girl is frightened out of her wits? Where they both become deathly ill and have to spend a week in the infirmary. Where—"

"I had to rid you of those horrible dreams," Varina cut in. "I had to make you visualize them, come face to face with them. Otherwise, they would haunt you endlessly. I did you a favor." She'd returned to her usual haughtiness; I hankered to smack it right out of her.

"A favor, you say?" I slowly walked over to the trunk and flung it open, enjoying the widening of Varina's eyes. "You call this a favor?" I reached inside and extracted a leather violin case. A gasp erupted from Ruby, the only one in the room surprised by my revelation.

"Yes, Ruby. This is the one thing I didn't tell you. I asked Laura Mae why she sang that particular melody in the cemetery that night. She said Varina taught it to her. Varina played it on the piano for her, then told her to sing it in a macabre style, like a witch from "Macbeth." And how did Varina know the melody? Because she composed it. And played it on a violin. Whenever I was practicing piano." By then I had taken the violin from its case and held it out toward Varina. "Would you like to give us an encore?"

Varina stared at the instrument as her jaw tightened, her faint eyebrows knotted into a scowl and her chest heaved with indignant breaths.

"I won't stand for this! I won't! I'll report you to Mrs. Long for breaking in. And vandalizing, both of you. You'll be on your way home by this time tomorrow."

"And wouldn't you just love that. Your competition for the music scholarship neatly removed." I slowly walked forward until I was within inches of her self-righteous upturned chin. "There's one little problem with that notion. We can do some reporting of our own." Varina blanched, then trembled with rage realizing the implications of what I'd just said.

"Get out! Get out of my room, now!" She screamed in my face but I refused to flinch. She instinctively turned toward her dressing table for ammunition, but it was no longer in its place. Momentarily flustered, she frantically scanned the scattered detritus, then grabbed a pile of knotted stockings and heaved them toward me. She proceeded to grab whatever items were within reach and hurled them at me and then Ruby by turns. I'd never seen her out of control and it was fascinating. To shield Ruby from the unmerciful volleys, I grabbed her arm and pulled her out the door. But I dashed back inside once more.

"Here, you'll need this for your next haunting." I propped the violin against the wall and slammed the door shut, barely escaping the lethal thwack of Varina's hairbrush.

I didn't know if I'd done myself any favors by the underhanded caper Ruby and I had just pulled off. By exposing Varina, I could very well have signed my expulsion notice. But it felt good to uncover the truth. And, I reasoned, if it turned out that I could remain at the Martha, at least I'd leveled the playing field.

Concerto

Divertimento

DECEMBER 1, 1915

A monumental sea change shaped my days following that risky escapade in Varina's room. I'd been freed to move forward unimpeded by disturbing sounds or strange dreams, and my outlook shifted to a positive shade of hopeful. I had also learned exactly who my true friends were. The betrayal by someone I was supposed to be able to trust astonished me, at first feeling as if I'd lost my anchor and been set adrift all alone. But you can't lose something you never had, and Varina had never been my ally in the first place.

Of course, my exposure of her treachery prompted her to gather her flock around her even tighter. I wondered if her cohorts had known about her tricks with the violin. Probably not. No matter how tight a rein she had on them, I doubted Varina truly trusted them not to break like Laura Mae did (thankfully), although she'd paid a price. After I'd seen her sitting alone several times, in the dining hall or at church, it was clear Varina had completely ostracized her. Finally, I simply sat down next to her, and without a word we became friends.

I told her about Varina and the violin; I felt she was owed that much. She felt badly for not suspecting it, because she'd known Varina had played violin when she was younger, back home in Richmond. Varina had also fallen in love with the cello player in her string quartet. When he'd jilted her, she locked up her violin and vowed never to touch it again. I listened to this story, incredulous at the thought of a beau jilting Varina. She was incredibly beautiful after all, and charming when she wanted to be. But I'd also witnessed her wrath when things didn't go her way. So, complete abandonment of the instrument followed by using it for an evil deed actually fit her profile. But Laura Mae took no pleasure in sharing this story with me. As a matter of fact, she was rather wistful and appeared almost heartbroken. It made me wonder if Varina had once been not only her mother, but also her rave.

But friendships and estrangements aside, there were still three more weeks of academic demands before we could leave for Christmas break. I'd been concerned about lost practice time due to my infirmary confinement, but the absence of worry in the practice rooms made my time there much more productive. I played with renewed fervor and abandon.

With only a few Saturdays left until Christmas, I savored every minute of my secret excursions to the stables. Riding Copper was as thrilling as ever, but ever since the water ceremony, a strange electricity had crept between Jonah and me. Neither of us knew quite what to do with it, so we tried focusing our attention on the horses and other matters. He was pleased my bad dreams had vanished, although I kept my discovery of the culprit violinist to myself. I wanted him to believe he had provided the cure. There'd been power in that water ritual, power that bound us together in a way I was at a loss to describe. I just knew it made my insides tingle whenever I was near him.

Curiously, this feeling lingered even when I wasn't at the stables. It was puzzling, but rather delightfully annoying the way it would pop up when I least expected it. Ruby caught me smiling sometimes and teased me unmercifully, although unaware of the true source of my dreaminess. I allowed her to make her assertions, since it provided me with a good cover.

She thought it was due to my visitor the Sunday following Thanksgiving. True to his word, Charles Sloan had made the trek from Emory and asked to call on me in the East Parlor. I'd forgotten all about his letter, so I was astonished and unprepared when he turned up. But Ruby was elated and dying to lay eyes on him, and she insisted on coming with me to greet him. I'd hoped she would remain with us, but after sizing him up, she claimed a drama club meeting and tossed me a wicked wink as she departed.

I was momentarily unsettled, but thankfully Charles was a skilled conversationalist. After we'd exhausted our common ground—the Hermesian/Euterpean event of a few weeks before—he talked at length about his studies and plans after graduation. I learned he enjoyed music and sang in the men's glee club at Emory and Henry. He sat at a gentlemanly distance on the settee, although his eyes held me in an unrelenting gaze that I found a little uncomfortable. But then he wanted to hear about my piano repertoire and I was surprised how easily I opened up. Our conversation was intellectually stimulating, but I felt the dynamic between us went no further than that.

Certain he'd found me rather dry and dull, it was a total surprise when he asked to call again. For lack of any good reason not to, I agreed. Ruby was thrilled to hear it and let her imagination run wild with romantic scenarios starring Charles and me. But I listened patiently, since indulging such talk made her happy and let me keep my secret.

WITH THE CALENDAR PAGE FLIPPED TO DECEMBER, CHRISTMAS preparations began to augment already busy schedules, but in the nicest way. Almost every day, a fresh batch of pine branches or garlands were brought inside to tuck along windows and mantles or drape on the sweeping staircase banister. The fragrance tickled my nose every time I walked through the foyer or parlors, which I tried to do as much as possible just to enjoy the scent.

The best part was the magnificent evergreen tree installed in the East Parlor. Here the Young Women's Christian Association of the

Martha would host its annual Christmas tree program on the Friday before we left for break. In this lovely tradition, the community nurse collected names of needy children, and every student chose a boy or girl to play "big sister" to for the evening. We were to purchase or make gifts to fill a stocking for our chosen child, then when all the children gathered for carol singing and games, we would present their stocking from "Santa." I chose a six-year-old boy, William, hoping to relive the days when my own brothers were small and innocent.

When Charles made his second visit the next Sunday, I was secretly glad to have the parlors looking so festive. The evergreen aroma lacing the air added a new energy to the atmosphere and put me in a talkative mood. I told him about William and the stocking I was preparing, then rambled on about seeing my family soon and what Christmas was like at home. I stopped suddenly, worried I had monopolized the conversation. He was gazing at me with a twinkle in his eye, then quietly asked me to the annual Christmas dance at Emory and Henry College. I was rendered speechless, but he chuckled and repeated his invitation for Saturday the eighteenth of December. "I won't take no for an answer," he smiled, and so it was settled. When later I told Ruby, she became ecstatic.

"Oh my God, the eighteenth of December! Do you know what else is happening on the eighteenth of December?"

I had no clue.

"Gosh, Bea, how could you not have heard? One of Martha's own is getting married, to the president of the United States, no less!"

"What?"

"It's all Miss Fakes wants to talk about. Edith Bolling, well, now Edith Bolling Galt—she got married before but now she's a widow—is engaged to Woodrow Wilson. But she used to be a student here, at Martha Washington College, and now she's going to marry the president! On December eighteenth, the same day you'll go to the big dance with Charles! Isn't that a scream?"

I didn't quite see a romantic connection the way Ruby did, but it was entertaining to see her so overjoyed. For the entire next week, she spent our every spare minute together discussing what I would wear or experimenting with a new hair style for me. The only garment I owned considered even remotely formal was the one good dress I wore for recitals. Ruby looked it over and declared, "I'll be your fairy godmother and transform it into something magnificent just in time for the ball." She began to create a new design for my modest frock, toying with ribbon, lace, and other notions, I imagined pilfered once again from costume storage.

On Friday came another surprise: an unexpected package in the mail. As Rena plopped it in my hands, my heart skipped a beat when I read the postmark: "Emory, Virginia." I quickly tucked it under my music books to secret up to my room, where I set it on my desk to stare at for a good ten minutes. Accepting a dance invitation from Charles was one thing, but it was far too early to accept a gift. I would see him for certain on Sunday, when his Emory glee club joined the Martha choir to sing a Christmas cantata at the Abingdon Methodist Episcopal Church; I could simply hand it back to him then. I composed a speech in my head: "Thank you, it was a lovely gesture, but I couldn't possibly." But my curiosity got the better of me. Tearing away the string and paper, I opened the box, then burst out laughing. I turned its colorful contents out on the desktop: two red pencils, a box of crayons, a small toy top, a small book titled *Doggie's Doings* and shaped like a dog, two lollipops, and two candy canes. There was a note inside: "For your little William, with best wishes for a Merry Christmas. Yours truly, Charles Sloan." He'd guessed I couldn't resist generosity directed toward a child, and he was right.

I greeted him with an open smile at the postcantata reception that Sunday and immediately thanked him for his kindness to William.

"Oh, it hasn't been all that long since I was a wee tike at Christmas," he chuckled. "I just put together some of my favorite things from back then." When he grinned, I noticed the charming dimple in his cheek. I began to regard him in a new light.

"The Christmas tree program is this coming Friday, and I can't wait to see his little face."

"Wonderful. Then be sure to rest up for our big event the next day." He winked, but thankfully before my cheeks turned rosy, his friends called him away to return to Emory. "Until next Saturday, then," he waved over his shoulder and disappeared through the door.

———

DESPITE RUBY'S RIBBING THAT I WAS ABSOLUTELY MOONY-EYED for Charles, he was easily pushed from my mind as I plowed into the next week of academics. But my resolute engine of industry abruptly stalled late Tuesday afternoon when another mysterious package arrived. This one had a large return address printed in bold block letters: "The H. P. King Company, Department Store, Bristol, Tennessee." Curious eyes and excited murmurs trailed me as I hauled the huge box up to my room. I'd only heard stories about the magnificent mercantile on State Street in Bristol, a twin city where the state line between Virginia and Tennessee ran right down the middle of town. It sold the finest merchandise in the region, and the few well-to-do ladies from church would make the journey from Clintwood to shop, then parade in their fine outfits on Easter Sunday. But I'd never set foot inside it and couldn't imagine how this package found its way to me.

Reverently I placed the box on my bed and for a moment simply admired it. Then carefully relieving it of its fasteners and lifting the lid, I gingerly brushed aside the gleaming white tissue paper. My eyes were greeted by a swath of deep red velvet graced with dazzling beads that glistened even in the muted afternoon light. The stunning color and sparkle reminded me of the large ruby stone in Mrs. Counts's wedding ring. When I gently lifted the beaded velvet from its tissue bed, a billowing cloud of chiffon followed beneath it, falling to the floor at my feet. Holding the gown against my shoulders, I slowly turned toward my vanity mirror. I was staring dumbfounded when Ruby came bounding into my room.

The Martha Odyssey

"Hey, Bea I heard—Ah! . . ." For once even Ruby was struck dumb. But only for a moment. "That is the most gorgeous gown I've ever seen! It was in your big box?"

Still staring in the mirror, I mutely nodded.

"But when did you go shopping? And why didn't you take me with you?"

"That's just it, I didn't. I don't know how this came to me."

Ruby rummaged in the box and retrieved a card from the tissue. "Well, this solves the mystery: 'Can't wait to twirl you around the dance floor on Saturday. Yours truly, Charles.' Oh, my goodness, Bea, you've hit the jackpot!"

"No! I can't keep it. I can't accept a gift like this, I hardly know him."

"You do so know him; he's been visiting you for weeks now. And besides, you've already accepted a gift from him."

"But that's not for me, it's for a little boy's Christmas stocking."

"Which *you* are putting together. So, it's still a gift and you accepted and you're going to accept this one."

"But you've worked so hard on my own dress, and it's turning out beautiful—"

"Oh, fiddlesticks, you can wear that anytime! You're wearing this dress, and that's final. Ooh, and I know just how to do your hair. Let me get my magazine to show you."

Ruby was out the door in a flash and I knew I'd lost the battle. Looking back at my reflection, I had to admit the rich crimson color complemented my dark chestnut hair and deep brown eyes, making them vividly alive rather than the murky pools I'd always judged them to be. Even if I felt out of my element, Ruby could have her fun dressing me up like a doll. It was only for one evening.

Minuet and Trio

Finally, it was Friday, leaving us with only holiday festivities and packing for the journey home. The Christmas tree program was a huge success and little William was overjoyed with all the goodies in his stocking. Charles had indeed known what would strike his fancy, although I added practical items like socks and mittens with the bonus Miss Le Grande had paid me.

When the Saturday morning sun woke me, I felt both excited and despondent. Happy it was my day to visit the stables, but sad it would be my last trip until I returned in January. I hurried my steps through the cold December morning, loaded down with apple treats plus a small beribboned parcel tucked inside my wool jacket. Jonah hadn't said much about it being Christmastime, except that his adopted parents had been Lutheran and he had celebrated Christmas with them in the past. I couldn't quite tell how he regarded the season now, but hated to think he might be on his own for the holiday.

As I approached the corral fence, I caught a whiff of coal smoke and spied a thin greenish-gray cloud snaking up from the forge chimney. I entered the stable to hand out treats and say goodbye to my four-legged friends. I'd even saved Wesa a bit of ham, the closest thing to mouse meat I could manage. Copper's treat was given last so I could linger and give him one last grooming before I left. Vigorously stroking his coat with a body brush, I talked softly to him with such concentration that I was startled to discover Jonah watching me. My gasp was met with a grin so guileless that I had to laugh at myself.

"Sorry," he said. "I just enjoy watching you two together." I stopped laughing, but couldn't drop the smile from my face. We held each other's gaze for several moments, his eyes warm and comforting. Finally, I pointed to the heavy gray objects in his hands.

"You started hammering early this morning."

"Yes, an urgent order." He held up a set of candleholders in the most unique shape I'd ever seen. "No doubt a Christmas present someone forgot to buy."

He handed them to me and I turned them over and over in my hands. One was taller than the other but each had been shaped into a delicate bow with broad twists in the middle of the stem. As they curved up to cradle the candle cup, they were joined at one point in their bend, each balanced on a half-circle base to make them completely stable as a set.

"They're beautiful. Whoever finds them under their tree is very lucky." I handed them back and Jonah stored them in the tack room. I finished up with Copper, tucked him back into his stall, and threw my arms around his neck for a final goodbye hug. When I pulled away, I once again found Jonah standing beside me.

"The candleholders are not the only thing I've been working on. Close your eyes and hold out your hands." I was surprised but did as I was told. Jonah placed a smooth warm object in my cupped hands. "Keep your eyes closed and bring your hands up to your nose." When I did, I breathed in a pungent, earthy but sweet fragrance that permeated my nostrils and throat. The aroma was not unfamiliar, but I couldn't quite name it. "Now look."

I opened my eyes to see a small figure of a horse. It was carved from reddish-brown wood, slightly marbled with ivory streaks. The detail was uncanny: tiny eyes and nostrils with perky little ears made its face come alive, tiny grooves in the mane and tail gave a flow to the hair, and its tiny hooves were perfectly rounded. After studying it with wonder, a thrilled whisper escaped my lips.

"It's Copper!"

"I thought you might like something to remember him by over the holidays."

I was so touched and overcome I nearly cried. "It's amazing. The most beautiful gift I've ever received."

"I made it from *atsina tlugv*, a cedar tree. In Cherokee tradition, cedar wood holds powerful protective spirits. Carry it with you, and they will protect you."

I looked into his eyes again. "Thank you." He answered with a bashful smile. I was so taken with his gift, I almost forgot the parcel hidden in my coat.

"I have something for you, too." Jonah seemed as surprised at my package as I'd been a few minutes before. He slowly undid the wrappings and stared at my gift. In the quiet I began to worry I'd made a mistake, then a huge smile sprang to his face. He carried it directly to Xander's stall, where the horse sniffed it and softly snorted. Jonah laughed, holding up the framed pen and ink drawing of Xander's proud head with ears perked, nostrils flared, and eyes blazing bright.

"I'll never forget the impression he made on me the first time I saw him," I said, "so I asked an artist friend to capture that image." I was grateful for Laura Mae's amazing talent.

"Well, Xander, you have been immortalized in a work of art. You'd better live up to this honor." Jonah gave him a couple of loving slaps on the neck. "Thank you, Beatrice. This will hang in a special place where I can enjoy it every day."

I was so happy he liked it, but still saddened to think he might be alone for the holidays. With his parents gone I wasn't sure if he still observed any traditions, or went to church.

"What will you do? On Christmas day, that is?"

He looked pensive for a long moment, then smiled at me. "Oh, there's a family down in Bristol that always invites me for Christmas dinner." He didn't elaborate further, and I felt it would be prying to ask anything more.

The Martha Odyssey

"I suppose I need to get back. There's a lot of packing for my trip home tomorrow." I looked down at the wooden horse in my hand, thinking how much I would miss Copper. And Jonah.

"I guess we'll see you after the new year, then. Sometime in January?" His eyes searched mine; he wanted to know a date.

"Yes. I get back January thirteenth. A lucky day! And I'll come here the first Saturday after I get back." I could tell that promise pleased him. "So, I won't say 'good-bye.'"

"Of course."

I gazed at him for a moment longer before walking to the back barn doors. Before leaving I turned back, pleased to find him standing in the same place, watching me leave.

"Merry Christmas, Jonah!"

"Merry Christmas, Beatrice."

Trekking back to the Martha, I realized I'd forgotten all about the dance that night. But I didn't want to think about it just then. I wanted to dwell on the sweet exchange I'd just had with Jonah. I clutched the cedar horse to my chest, right up against my heart.

Ruby had been working her magic on me all week and that evening got to witness the fruits of her labors. She'd begged and borrowed from all her friends to find me proper accessories, then taught me how to wear them as well as manage myself in the fancy new evening gown. I wasn't accustomed to a floor-length dress, much less a train that felt like a puppy nipping at my heels. I kept looking behind me, but Ruby ruthlessly coached me to hold my head high and look forward. She made me practice walking, negotiating stairs, and dancing. She was an indispensable marvel; without her, I would have floundered for sure.

I entered the banquet hall at Emory and Henry College determined to act like the sophisticated lady Ruby had created, but I was instantly dazzled by the totally unexpected scene. Whoever had festooned the hall had taken their cue from the blankets of snow that engulfed our landscape in winter. The holiday decorations were all white, and every garland or centerpiece as well as the giant Christmas tree was laden with a fluffy white substance that mimicked snow. Candlelight in tandem with twinkling electric lights made the entire room glisten like icicles in the sun. The wintery setting relaxed me; it made pretending to be a fictional character in a storybook rather easy after all.

"Welcome to our little soiree." Suddenly Charles was at my side. I had no idea what he meant, but I plastered a smile on my face. "I have to say, you look stunning tonight."

"Oh! Well, thank you. I mean, thank you so much for the dress." I looked down at it awkwardly, then darted my eyes around the room. The magical snowscape wasn't helping my nerves as much as I thought it would. "You really didn't need to do that."

"But of course, I did. I had to know what color flowers to get you." With a smile and a wink, he produced a corsage he'd been holding behind his back. It was a bundle of red rosebuds tied with red velvet ribbon, a perfect match to the velvet of my gown. I gazed at it, speechless, as Charles produced a long hatpin from his pocket and brought the corsage to my left shoulder.

"I'll take care of that!" We both popped our heads around to see Mrs. Long striding toward us. In true chaperone fashion, she would prevent any male hands slipping inside a girl's garment. The other Martha girls stood nearby with their dates, dutifully awaiting Mrs. Long's assistance with their flowers. Saluda was there, invited by Walter Harris, whom she'd met at the Hermesian debate. Her presence had provided me comfort on the awkward train ride we'd endured with Ethel, Bessie, and their eternal queen, Varina. The three of them, wrapped in elegant brocade fur-trimmed evening coats, chatted a little too gaily among themselves and cast occasional disdaining glances at Saluda and me in our plain black woolen coats. But once we'd shed our wraps at the entrance to the banquet hall, I caught Varina staring at me in what appeared to be disbelief tinged with envy. Ruby had indeed worked a miracle

The Martha Odyssey

if I'd earned any kind of admiration from my worthy adversary.

With corsages pinned firmly into place, Mrs. Long released us to our dates and Charles led me onto the dance floor. Passing by Varina and her date was unavoidable, and she glared at me with contempt. I didn't know why she cared so much, since she herself was dressed beautifully and her date was also a handsome Hermesian. Surely, she'd learned about Charles's visits to me at the Martha and shouldn't have been surprised. Of course, she also knew my meager wardrobe couldn't have included the extravagant gown or accessories I wore. Her stare made me feel like a kept woman.

But I had more important things to concentrate on and congratulated myself after making it through the first dance with no smashed toes or ripped hemlines. I was silently thankful for those tedious deportment classes freshmen were forced to attend, and for Ruby making me practice in the actual dress.

"Let's go have our photograph made while it's still early," Charles said and led me off to a far corner of the room. A full-size sleigh was sitting at an angle with a placard that read, "Dashing through the snow, in a one-horse open sleigh" in front of it. "Of course, we won't get very far with no horse, but it'll make a great picture." Charles grinned broadly and I realized that was my cue to laugh at his joke. The photographer was busy with another couple, so we stood aside and waited. In a few moments a voice bellowed from behind.

"Charles! Old buddy, how are you tonight." We turned to see Varina and her date taking their place in line for a photograph.

"Vincent, old man, I'm just great." The two men exchanged salutations complete with raucous faux punches and backslapping despite their formal attire. Meanwhile, Varina and I exchanged obligatory polite greetings. Suddenly Charles placed his arm around my shoulders.

"Do you all like my choice of American Beauty?"

Vincent chuckled awkwardly, Varina subtly rolled her eyes and I was momentarily alarmed. But then Charles lightly touched my shoulder.

"The roses. They're American Beauties. The color of your gown, Beatrice. I knew when you were all decked out like this you'd stand out like a jewel in this snow."

The others politely laughed while my warming cheeks completed my crimson ensemble. I glanced down at the roses, their stifling sweet aroma assaulting my nose. I thought of the tender fragrance of the cedar horse Jonah had given me that afternoon, and how much more it spoke to me than these obviously expensive and showy roses. Thankfully, the photographer called us up just then and it was socially permissible to walk away.

Not only was I embarrassed, but also a bit perturbed. Varina had already made me feel cheap, and now Charles had made me feel like a show pony. I was beginning to seriously doubt the wisdom of accepting his dress, and maybe even his invitation to the dance. Luckily, Saluda and Walter waved at us from across the hall as we exited the sleigh. I crossed directly to them without looking back at Charles, although he dutifully followed. He had too much money invested in me to abandon me, plus he and Walter were best buddies. I decided I just might make it through the evening if we stayed close to my good friend and his.

Soon we girls excused ourselves to the powder room, where we could chat easily without the fellas. I learned that at least Saluda was having a good time, that she liked Walter quite a lot. She told me her first attraction to him was how he went head-to-head with Varina at the debate. She loved how he'd made her sweat. Saluda was smart and well-grounded; it took more than a pretty face to catch her attention. I admired her for that.

Walking back down the hallway from the lavatory, we had to stop short when a waiter sprang out from the kitchen door lugging a large bowl of punch.

"Whoa!" he exclaimed as he halted. We all held our breath watching the frothy liquid slosh back and forth. Amazingly, it settled without a single drop escaping the crystal vessel. "That was a close one, ladies. Much obliged for your patience." He smiled and gingerly stepped back to let us pass.

"Wait," I said suddenly, studying his face. "I know you, don't I?" He took a moment to look at me properly, his eyes brightening with recognition.

"You're from Martha Washington, right?"

"Right! I'm Beatrice. Beatrice Damron. And you're . . . just B.C." His face instantly lit up.

"That's me! B.C. White." We stared at each other with silly grins on our faces. "You look really different from the first time I saw you."

"I guess I do," I laughed.

"But you look good! Really pretty. Tonight."

"Oh, well. Thank you. You know, it's Christmas and all." I looked over at Saluda, who was enjoying our little scene immensely. "Oh, gosh, where are my manners. This is my friend, Saluda. Saluda French. She's from Martha Washington, too."

"It's so nice to meet you, Just B.C.," she said in her typical easygoing manner to lighten the moment.

"Nice to meet you as well, Saluda." We all stood smiling for a moment. "Well, I'd better get this punch to the table. And let you ladies get back to your party."

Saluda and I swooped our hands towards the hall in mock formality to usher him ahead of us. He chuckled and gladly took the favor.

"Where did you meet that charming chap?" Saluda asked, holding me back for a moment. I reminded her of my embarrassing crash with his tray at the Hermesian reception the month before, then said I'd found him later to apologize.

"So, you literally 'swept him off his feet,'" Saluda teased me. "I thought only men did that to women, not the other way around."

"Well, I don't know about that, but I seem to have a special talent for clumsy moves in social situations."

"Oh, Bea. Your 'talent' is that you're totally unaware of just how attractive you are. Men find that utterly irresistible." She smiled and winked as she looped her arm into mine. "So please, don't ever change."

As we strolled back into the hall, I felt lucky to be on Saluda's arm. I'd never had a big sister; that had always been my role. I hadn't realized how much I needed one myself, but Saluda was that to me. Ruby, of course, was my bosom pal; but Saluda was someone I could look up to and use as a guide. If only she'd been paired with me as my Martha mother . . . But Granddad had always told me, "Thinking 'if only' never did anybody a lick o' good." He'd also said the only person you could count on was yourself. I wasn't convinced that was entirely true, but I'd learned it sure did pay to make smart choices about whom to trust.

Rhapsody

Intermezzo

January 13, 1916

A real winter snowscape greeted me as I made my way from the Abingdon train depot to the Martha with satchel and valise in tow. January clouds had dropped three inches of snow the night before and workmen were plying their shovels to create rudimentary paths on the sidewalks. Gray clouds gathering above promised more frozen precipitation, so I was glad to make it safely inside Preston Hall and up to the third floor before it began to fall. I unlocked my door to the sound of soft clanging, signaling the boilers were already running. I said a quick prayer of thanks, set down my luggage, and warmed my hands over the radiator.

My Christmas back at home had been the sweetest I'd ever known. Granddad picked me up from the train in Fremont, our chatter never ceasing as his familiar old wagon ferried us along the bumpy road into Clintwood. Anxious as I was to see my family, I cherished this time alone with him. He regaled me with all kinds of stories, making me feel like a little girl again.

As soon as I spotted our house in the distance, tears warmed my eyes. When I saw my sisters running to meet me before we even came to a stop, I no longer held them back. We held each other in a quadruple bear hug, little Jenny clinging like a crab to my thighs. I broke away when Mama came out, throwing my arms around her and holding on as if I might never let go. My brothers stood on the porch, uncharacteristically reverent. Jim greeted me with a quick hug, Bascom with a playful punch in the arm.

It was hard to believe that just the evening before, I'd been dressed in a velvet gown, sparkling feathered clip in my upswept hair, pearls at my throat, and satin gloves that reached past my elbows. That young lady was merely a character in a fiction of Charles's and Ruby's invention. I'd played my part well enough, but I was relieved to discard her and return to the real Bea. Of course, it made a good story for my sisters, who wanted to hear everything about my new adventure at the Martha. I shared as much as I thought prudent, making sure not to omit the parts about my hard work for the demanding academics and music conservatory requirements. They needn't think it was all fun and parties.

I kept my story of Charles to a minimum, simply saying I'd met him at the debate and he had invited me to the dance. I didn't share that his pursuit hadn't ended there like I'd hoped. Before we had left the dance, he had steered me toward the Christmas tree and, while Mrs. Long's back was turned, he quickly took my chin in his hand and stole a kiss. I pulled away in surprise and he grinned his signature grin, pointing to a bough of mistletoe hanging above us. All I could think was that it was my first kiss, and it had been with someone I hadn't chosen. He then pressed a small card with his home address into my hand, begging me to write to him over the Christmas break. I smiled stiffly and tucked it into my glove, which he apparently regarded as consent.

Charles wasn't the only one to surprise me before leaving the dance. In the commotion of retrieving coats at departure time, I became separated from Saluda and suddenly found Varina at my side. She kept her gaze straight ahead but directed her lowered voice to me. "You need to know you're only the latest in Charles's vast collection." I was startled Varina spoke to me at all, but I remained silent. "Every year, he looks over the new crop of freshmen girls, then picks one to toy with and display to his friends. But the novelty soon wears off, and he'll toss you aside like all the others." She pushed ahead of me to grab her lavish evening wrap, elaborately fan it over her shoulders and tuck herself into the frothy fur collar before stepping out into the cold night. If she'd only known how much her news secretly delighted me.

I later decided it was only polite to send him a Christmas card, like everyone did during the holidays; it wouldn't mean anything special. But just before New Year's Day, I received a letter from him. Gladys had collected the mail that day and ran shouting to my room, Jenny and Lillian rushing on her heels. They begged me to read it aloud, but I demurred. "It's private college girl stuff. I'll tell you when you're older." This was met with groans of protest as I shooed them away. I did, however, share it later with Lillian. I owed her a favor for the clever way she'd kept me in candles for the entire semester.

But Charles's letter had troubled me because it was a bit more than simple holiday greetings. He had shared a lot about his home and family, gone on at length about our time at the dance, and claimed he couldn't wait for his next visit. I hoped it was just holiday blues talking—that when he got back to his friends at Emory I would fade to a faint memory. I didn't want to lead him on, even if I did need a good cover for my real feelings directed elsewhere.

Every day over the Christmas break, I would secret myself away in some obscure place—the attic or the hayloft of the barn—and take out the cedar horse Jonah had given me. I would run my fingers over the smooth ripples rendered by Jonah's knife, then place it under my nose to breathe in the sweet cedar scent. I didn't share this with anyone at home, except Nutmeg. "Don't worry," I said as I brushed her after our rides. "No one could ever replace you. Copper's just taking care of me while I'm away." She rubbed her muzzle up and down my arm to remind me she took first place in my heart.

I lifted my hands from the radiator to pull back the window curtain and watch snowflakes pour from the sky. I had pondered chancing a quick trip to the stables as soon as I got back, but the nasty weather made it impossible. After the cheerless chore of unpacking, I crept down to the practice rooms to put in a couple of hours before dinner. The next day was the first Friday of the semester with its customary music master class. I wanted the faculty, as well as certain students, to see that I hadn't slacked off during the break.

The practice rooms were not yet properly heated, and my hands felt nearly frozen by the time I stopped for dinner. But chilled fingers were forgotten the moment I walked into the dining hall. Ruby flew at me and we hugged as tightly as I had hugged my sisters at home.

"Where have you been?" she squealed. "I was afraid you'd gotten stuck in this snow."

"Just getting in piano time before tomorrow."

"Better watch out, you'll get branded as a 'grind' if you're not careful."

She walked me to the table where Saluda and Hazel were seated and another glorious reunion ensued. I looked around the hall for Laura Mae.

"No one's seen her yet," offered Hazel. "Mississippi is a long way off, and she's not used to such vicious snowstorms. She may be waiting one out somewhere in Tennessee."

But the mystery came to light the next morning when Rena surprised me with a letter at mail call. I took it with an ounce of dread, thinking it was from Charles, but I ripped it open quickly when I saw the Mississippi postmark.

Dear Bea,
I hope this letter finds you well and that you had a joyous Christmas at home with your family. I was very happy to be back home with family I'd missed so dearly. And of course, Demetrius and Lysander! However, my health is not what it ought to be. I've had recurring problems with my lungs ever since the illness that put me in the Martha infirmary. Although the silver lining to that experience was that I got to

know you, I'm afraid I'm having a battle getting completely cured. My parents insist I stay here in Mississippi where it's warmer during the winter months, so I will not be returning to the Martha this semester. I will sorely miss you and all my drama friends—please say hello to Ruby for me!—but I hope to be fit and well next fall so that I can come back and be with you all once again.

Your true friend,
Laura Mae

A tiny gray cloud settled over me. It was so unjust how the poor girl had been abused for another's gain. I hoped when Varina heard of this she would feel good and guilty, but I doubted she had that capacity. As for me, I had no hope for ever seeing Laura Mae again, since one way or the other I wouldn't be here the next year. It was so unfair.

SATURDAY MORNING DAWNED THROUGH HAZY GRAY CLOUDS, although the sparse daylight was brightened by the blanket of white still covering the ground. The January sunrise came nearly two hours later than when I'd made my first journeys to the stables, so my window of safe time was much slimmer. There were also snow drifts to negotiate, but I had anticipated them and brought back a pair of stovepipe boots Granddad had abandoned. Two pairs of wool socks made them fit perfectly, and I could stuff the bottom of my split skirt into the tops once out of sight of the campus. My heavy coat, woolen muffler, and cap Mama had knitted me for Christmas, plus old leather work gloves, completed my ensemble. Not only was I buffered against the cold, I was conveniently unrecognizable.

As I trudged through the pines, I fingered the cedar horse hidden deep in my coat pocket, anticipating seeing Jonah's face. Bobbing against my back was an improvised sack made from an old scarf, filled with treats for the horses. I was ruminating on how to divvy them up as I approached the back stable door, but halted when I heard men's voices talking in hushed tones. Tucking myself behind the door's edge, I peered in to see Jonah and another man standing outside a stall at the opposite end. At the man's feet was a large black leather bag: the unmistakable vestige of a veterinarian. I tensed at the sight of it and strained to hear what they were saying.

"Thanks for coming, Doc. Just sorry it was the middle of the night."

"That's quite all right, Jonah. No stopping Mother Nature."

The man gave Jonah a gentle pat on the back, gathered up his bag, and trudged wearily out the front stable door. I closed my eyes and pressed my forehead against the doorframe. My joyful reunion with the horses and Jonah was tainted by dread of what had brought the veterinarian. When I heard the engine of the vet's motor car sputter I stepped inside the door and slowly crept down the corridor toward where Jonah stood looking out the front door.

"Jonah?" The fear in my voice made it breathy and small.

"Beatrice," he said softly when he turned. "You're back." He looked dazed and I thought he must have forgotten I was coming. Four weeks was a long time. Long enough for someone to fade from your thoughts. Although he'd never left mine.

"Yes." I managed a weak smile. "But what have I come back to? I saw the vet. Has something—"

"Oh!" He shook his head and crossed to me, surprising me by taking my hands in his. "No. Nothing bad, anyway. Come look." He smiled and led me to the spare stall next to Copper's. When I peered over the door, my panic instantly dissolved.

I was looking at a horse I'd never seen before, its head bent toward a tiny creature standing precariously in the straw. The creature blinked up at me with shiny black eyes planted in a slender, snowy white face that tapered to a soft pink muzzle. Atop the face, a shock of stubby black mane sprouted between perky white ears flopping in all directions. Its mother lovingly licked its neck and back, scrubbing the fuzzy coat that sported large splashes of bright white and coal black. I had seen many a newborn foal, but none as adorable as this baby looking like a freshly minted stuffed toy. A happy tear slid down my cheek watching it wobble on spindly legs and take in the new, strange world it had been thrust into.

"A dandy new filly," Jonah nodded at the little pinto. "And a miracle. Almost didn't make it, but Doc Gilmer got here just in time."

Looking more closely at the mare, I saw she was a rather pitiful sight: far too thin with a dull sandy coat ruffled with dry crusty patches. The contrast was startling and I wondered how such a poorly looking animal could produce such a perfect little marvel.

"Yes," I breathed. "A 'Miracle.' That's what we should call her." Jonah nodded his agreement. "When did you get this mare?"

"Doc Gilmer, the vet, brought her in just a few days ago, right before the big snow hit."

"I'm sorry I missed her arrival."

"You would've been even sadder to see her then: head hanging low, coat matted with dried mud, dehydrated as well as malnourished."

"Surely this isn't the vet's horse."

"No, he rescued her from a mismanaged farm out in the county. The old owner died back in December and it's not clear who inherited it, but the fella hired to run it was nothing but a lazy drunk. His care for the animals was hit and miss, and he was too stupid to realize this mare was in foal. I've fed her well since she got here, but she's still weak. Had a hard time delivering."

"How awful. But thank goodness the little filly seems perfect."

"Doc says nature will favor new growth. What nourishment she got went to the foal."

"And now she'll have her own. You'll nurse her back to health, and I'll help." I was instantly afraid I'd overstepped and looked at him sheepishly, but he only grinned.

"Of course."

Jonah turned back to the mare and his tone changed.

"Still—and I don't dare say this to anyone in town—but, I'd like to horsewhip the fellow responsible for this." His eyes had a look of utter contempt that I'd never seen before. I didn't doubt that if he discovered the culprit, he would hunt him down and do just that. And I couldn't blame him.

There would be no ride that day. Jonah was exhausted from his sleepless night, even if he denied it. I ignored his protests and helped him muck stalls, then made him promise to go home to rest. As I trekked through the pines again, I wondered where Jonah lived. I imagined his house: his kitchen, his sitting room, his bedroom, with him crawling wearily into bed. I held tight to the wooden horse inside my pocket all the way back to the Martha.

SUNDAY MORNING DAWNED AS COLD AND GRAY AS THE DAYS before. Like my fellow Martha girls, I wished for a new snowfall that would allow a lazy linger in bed. But a peek through my window curtains was disappointing; our presence would be expected at morning church service, no exceptions. At least lunch afterwards was some consolation: a delicious beef stew with corn muffins, piping hot to warm us up after our walk in the cold. Saluda and Hazel showed Ruby and me the latest popular songbooks they'd received for Christmas and we all headed off to the parlor. My visits from Charles had usurped our special time for satisfying illicit musical tastes and I'd missed our Sunday afternoon romps. When late afternoon came, I didn't want it to end.

"Oh my God, this is so much fun," Ruby panted after performing a rousing impromptu dance to "Alabama Jubilee." "But Bea, I was certain we'd be interrupted by your usual tête-à-tête with Charles." Her raised eyebrows signed a silent question.

"No, not today," I replied evenly. "And probably not any other day. He's most likely lost interest." A flood of protests followed.

"Why would you say that, Bea? It's obvious he's absolutely smitten," Ruby insisted.

"Because Varina told me the truth about him."

"And just what was this great 'truth' Varina deigned to share with you?" Saluda asked with narrowed eyes.

"She said every year he picks a new 'freshie' girl, toys with her for a while, then tires of her. And it's fine, I've made my peace with it."

"Ha! So that's her story now?" Saluda and Hazel exchanged a knowing look. "Let us tell you the 'real' story." Saluda pulled me onto the middle of the sofa, where the story volleyed at me from both sides.

"Charles fell for Varina when they were both freshmen," Saluda began, "and they courted for two years."

"They were quite the handsome pair," Hazel interjected. "Turning heads at every dance or party."

"Then last year, Varina set her sights on another Emory and Henry student, someone richer and even more handsome, and she dropped Charles like a hot potato."

"Varina's new catch sported her around for a year, plying her with gifts and buying her fancy clothes."

"Then after his graduation his parents sent him on a luxury tour of Europe. And she hasn't heard a word from him since! Varina would love to have Charles back, but he's smarter than that."

"He's done with her. She tossed Charles aside but she can't stand to see anyone else with him."

"The only reason Charles didn't come today is because Emory students won't come back until this coming Friday, the twenty-first. Walter told me in his last letter. Didn't you correspond with Charles over the break?"

"Well, yes. But I guess I got the dates mixed up." It wasn't totally a lie, since I'd sent the Christmas card. But I'd never answered his letter, hoping my neglect would dampen his interest. I smiled and pretended I was glad to hear their news, but my stomach churned at the thought that Charles might still pursue me.

"There you go, Bea, everything's explained," said Ruby, exchanging a look with me. Neither of us was surprised to learn about another facet of Varina's treachery, but we wouldn't divulge our own recent history with the blonde vixen. "Oh, and when he visits next Sunday, you've got to invite him to our Valentine's Ball!" Ruby's eyes were suddenly aglow. "It's the only fun thing to look forward to this winter, and you simply must have your beau at your side."

All eyes fell on me expectantly. "Well . . . only if Saluda invites Walter."

"It's a deal," said Saluda. "And I'll insist he bring dates for Hazel and Ruby."

That promise elicited a shy smile from Hazel but a rousing shout of approval from Ruby. She immediately burst out with "Everybody's doin' it, doin' it, doin' it," coaxing us all to join in the Irving Berlin song as she swung us into an outrageous version of a Turkey Trot. Whoever Walter brought for Ruby would have one wild and crazy night he would never forget.

Etude

Monday morning came too soon, ushering in a full two weeks of exams, term paper presentations, and music juries that pushed all trivialities from my mind. The jury would serve as my final exam in piano, but I didn't really dread it so much. Even though it would be performed before the music faculty for a written critique and a grade, most of us found performing for our peers in a master class much more intimidating.

When my appointed time came, I sat down at the Steinway in Litchfield Hall, took calming breaths, and awaited my instructions. I would be given a major key and then play its scale, two-handed in three octaves, ascending and descending. I was expected to know its relative minor and play that in its natural, melodic, and harmonic forms. It was a sneaky way to assess not only technique but knowledge of theory, but I was glad for the chance to warm up. I hadn't touched the Steinway since mid-December and needed to refamiliarize myself with the action of its keyboard.

"E major," came Mr. Moore's command. Four sharps, an almost equal number of black and white keys. Trickier than one might think but not too formidable. To get my bearings, I took a slightly slower pace on the major scale, then increased speed as I played through the minor scales. By the time I launched into my jury piece, I felt more confident with the piano's stiff action. I'd chosen the Rachmaninoff B-flat Major Prelude from opus 23, intent on redeeming my botched performance when I'd first played it in master class. After its opening runs and chords, I began to relax into the piece and actually "listen" to the music, concentrating on phrasing and dynamics the way Professor Zeisberg was teaching me to do. It wasn't all about perfect technique, he said. I had to make the piano *sing*—to find its voice and let it soar.

I lifted my fingers from the keys after the final notes, the only sound lingering that of scratching pencils as professors scribbled their critiques. But as I left the stage, I thanked myself for all the times I'd run everyone out of the parlor at home so I could practice. I walked into the wing just as the stage door slammed shut, catching the edge of a blue gaberdine skirt that hadn't slipped away fast enough. I rushed forward to help release it and when the door reopened, I stood face to face with Varina. She'd been there the whole time, spying on my jury. We said nothing and she promptly shut the door in my face. It occurred to me her jury would be coming up soon if not directly after mine, so I stayed behind.

The wing space was tight, but I located the fake potted ferns used to decorate performances and tucked myself behind them. Two more juries went by, but my patience paid off when I finally glimpsed Varina at the Steinway. I hoped she suspected I was listening, although I doubted it would rattle her. Very much, anyway. She played her scales then began her jury piece, again the third movement of Beethoven's "Les Adieux" sonata. Apparently, she'd also put in extra hours over break because her performance was even more magnificent than before. I wouldn't get the benefit of the faculty's oral critique, so I couldn't know what they thought, but her determination was evident. Varina wanted to win. But not more than I did.

True to his word, Charles showed up to visit on Sunday. I kept it brief since Martha girls were in the midst of exams, but I also kept my promise and invited him to the Valentine's Ball. Walter had come to see Saluda, so she put in her request for dates for Hazel and Ruby. The following Sunday, two shy but spiffy-looking lads trailed Charles and Walter into the parlor, claiming the girls wouldn't want to ask young men sight unseen. I suspected it was the other way around, but once they laid eyes on Hazel and Ruby, they left thanking their lucky stars. Even if they really didn't deserve it.

The next morning, we greeted the last day of January as the first day of our new semester, complete with a Euterpean Literary Society meeting that very Monday evening. I learned our first event would be a debate with the Washingtonians on the twenty-fifth of February; then two weeks later, we would host the Hermesians in a debate here at the Martha. Varina proceeded to make assignments, which would be the same for both events. "That way, everyone will have a practice run before we face our cocky male opponents," she smirked. Her assignment list did not include me as a performer, only as an accompanist. Varina herself was to perform a piano solo, as well as debate. My snub wasn't a surprise, but she'd also excluded Saluda, as debater or singer, and Saluda wasn't having it. "As a senior and an officer, I'm telling you that not only will I debate, but Hazel will sing." Saluda was secretary and in charge of program printing, rendering Varina powerless to change it; she had no choice but to concede. I smiled broadly at Saluda, who in that moment was the high priestess of pluckiness.

MY FAVORITE EXTRACURRICULAR ACTIVITY WAS STILL MY secret one. Every Saturday, no matter the weather, was spent on Copper's back. I bundled up tightly against the biting cold, but the horses loved it, and I loved how it revved up their energy. When a fresh snowfall greeted us the first Saturday in February, they were even more eager than Jonah and me to race over the newly blanketed terrain. Effortlessly they carried us across the Meadows, leaping over frothy white drifts, our faces pelted with frosty crystals flying up from their churning hooves. Once they'd had their fill, we steered them into the wooded paths at the far end of the field.

They soon settled into an easy stroll once inside the sparkling canopy of ice-covered trees. It seemed like a mystical passage into a fairytale land, where everything was forever clean and white. The air was infused with mingled scents of fresh snow and evergreen, making my nose, throat, and my whole insides feel scrubbed clean as well. We rode for quite a while in the soothing quiet before Jonah stopped and pointed off to the right.

"See that cluster of evergreens over there?" Just beyond some oak and hickory trees, bare-branched this time of year, grew a scattering of shorter, bushy evergreens with pointy tops. Cedar trees. I reached into my pocket and pulled out the wooden horse.

"Did this have its beginnings over there?" He smiled at the sight of it. "I've done what you told me. This little steed goes everywhere with me."

"It must be doing its job. You look very well these days. At least what I can see of you in those piles of winter clothes."

"I assure you it is. What's under these clothes is in quite good shape."

"Yes, I remember."

I quickly looked away from him, my cheeks burning and not from frostbite. Had he caught a glimpse of me when I'd changed clothes that morning at the creek? But there it was again, that tingle in my stomach. Strangely, I found I actually didn't mind if he had. I caught myself smiling and pulled my muffler up tighter around my face. If he sensed my fluster, he was kind enough to not mention it. We urged the horses back into a walk and continued along the path.

"Legend says that when a Cherokee looks at a cedar tree, he's looking at his ancestor."

"You're descended from trees, then?" I flashed him a teasing look over my bulging muffler; his laughter put me back at ease. "So, what's this legend?"

"A long, long time ago, the first Cherokees living in the world thought they had a smart idea: to never have night. They prayed,

'Creator, make it daylight all the time.' Now, the Creator knew all things exist in twos—day and night, life and death, good and evil, feast and famine—but granted their wish anyway. Soon they had lots of problems: forests grew too thick, it was very hot, no one could sleep. So, they begged, 'Creator, make it night all the time.' But that caused problems as well: it was very cold, crops stopped growing, they couldn't see to hunt. They grew weak and hungry, and lots of people died. Then they cried, 'We've made a terrible mistake, please forgive us.' So, the Creator divided each day between light and darkness again. And for the people who died during the long days of night, a new tree was created as a resting place for their spirits."

"So, your ancestor is in this little piece of wood."

"So the legend says."

We rode in silence for a minute, but I saw my chance to ask a question that had been burning inside me.

"The cedar trees here. Are they the ancestors keeping you in Abingdon?"

"There are cedars in lots of places. Supposedly my ancestors could be in any of them." He was being evasive, but I couldn't resist probing further.

"When I asked why you stayed, you said, 'I'm here with my ancestors, and my own flesh and blood.'" He didn't say anything, and after a few moments I pressed on. "But spirits aren't flesh and blood." There was silence for a few more paces.

"This is probably a good place to turn around."

Without further comment, Jonah brought Xander's head around and headed us back toward the field at a trot. When we reached the open terrain, the horses traveled at an easy canter back through the snowy paths they'd plowed earlier.

At the stables, we busied ourselves with rubbing down our mounts, exchanging a few neutral comments about riding in the snow compared to grass and the like. I thought my inquiry was forgotten and was saying goodbye to the other horses when Jonah came and took my hand. Quietly he walked me over to sit on a stack of straw bales.

"I did say that to you, about my own flesh and blood. It's only fair that I explain."

Jonah, at one time, had had a wife. Several years after he had joined the Schumacher household, Mrs. Schumacher became a bit frail and hired a young girl to help with domestic chores. She was a stranger in the area, newly arrived from Philadelphia to live with relatives after her parents died. When Jonah helped her down from the wagon after her journey to the farm, their eyes locked. She turned out to be a very good fit for the job, and for Jonah.

"Her name was Azalia." He reached for the rawhide pouch at his waist and pulled out a worn union case. From the photograph inside appeared a heart-shaped face with rich dark skin glowing like chestnut wood polished with lemon oil. Full lips were slightly upturned at the corners, unable to suppress a smile dancing in black almond-shaped eyes. Even in worn sepia tone, they gazed at me with a dewy luminescence. Ebony hair swirled in a graceful upsweep, giving focus to an elegant cameo pinned at the center of her collar. "She was dressed for our wedding. Mother, Mrs. Schumacher, gave her that brooch."

Two years later, the family moved to Abingdon. They set up their new household, filled the stable with horses, and fired up the blacksmith shop again. Down in Bristol they found a Lutheran church, important to the Schumachers. Azalia, a city girl, was very different from other young ladies here and found it difficult to adapt socially. But she was content to stay close to home where Mrs. Schumacher, growing more and more feeble, needed her.

By the end of that first year, Mrs. Schumacher took ill with influenza and passed within a few days. Only a few months went by before an inconsolable Mr. Schumacher succumbed to pneumonia. The losses were difficult to bear for their tight-knit family. But the following spring, the clouds began to lift when Azalia told Jonah a baby was on the way. They became busy with new tasks: she making baby quilts and clothes, he building a cradle.

But when her time came to deliver, there was trouble. The child, a little boy, never drew breath. Azalia fell unconscious and passed away hours later.

"I had gone to fetch the doctor, again and again and again. Even went to his home and pounded on the door. Every time I was turned away. 'He's on another call,' they said." Jonah's voice grew bitter. "More likely, the birth of a 'griffe' was not a priority." He looked to the ground with a dark frown. "When he finally showed up at midnight, it was too late."

He named the baby boy Usdi Yona Asgitisdi, Baby Bear Dream. Wrapped in a tiny quilt Azalia had made, he was buried with his mother, both enclosed in a quilt from the marriage bed. They were placed directly in the earth in the backyard of Jonah's house, their heads facing west, their life force returning to nature. And just as he'd done for his parents buried there, he planted a blueberry bush beside their grave. With each summer harvest he felt their presence.

Jonah closed the case and tucked it back into his pouch. "That night I vowed to never need anyone in this town again." We sat in silence then, each deep in our own thoughts.

The tardiness of the doctor was very likely due to unavoidable circumstance. At least that's what I wanted to believe. But left inconsolable at the devastating loss, Jonah would never be convinced the delay wasn't deliberate. Finding no words to comfort such a tragedy, I simply reached out my arms and pulled him close. He returned my embrace, each of us leaning into the warmth.

MY WALK BACK TO THE MARTHA LEFT ME CHILLED TO THE BONE. I shed my barn clothes and headed to the dining hall for a cup of the hot chocolate they provided on mornings of a new snowfall. When I knocked on Ruby's door, I was met by a bleary-eyed, tangle-haired moppet just emerging from bed. She agreed hot chocolate was exactly what she needed after the night she'd had, so in an unexpected role-reversal I helped Ruby pull herself together.

At the late morning hour, the dining hall was deserted except for a rowdy bunch of girls from the basketball team sitting near the door. We filled our mugs and took a table in the far corner. Ruby took a long, careful sip of the steaming drink and moaned.

"I feel like I've been to China and back."

"What?"

"Didn't anyone ever tease you, when you were a kid, that if you dig in the dirt long enough you could dig a hole to China?"

"What are you talking about?"

She explained her exhaustion was the result of the previous night's escapade. With a play performance under her belt, she'd become eligible for the Melpomene Society, the dramatic sorority on campus, so with exams over, the initiation ritual ensued. She took a couple more fortifying sips, then launched into her tale.

"They took all the pledges outside to the back of Litchfield Hall, where all those thick, thorny bushes grow, and made us crawl through them. Even in a coat and gloves, I couldn't escape a few scratches." She pulled up her cuffs to display angry red streaks dotting her forearms.

"Ugh, that's awful."

"Oh, that was the easy part. Behind the bushes there's a cellar door nestled in the ground that apparently the school's forgotten about. The lock is rusted through, so it was easy to unlatch and lift open. Then we had to follow Nell Sexton—she's the sorority president—down into a hole along some crude rock stairs to a hard dirt floor. So, we're walking along behind Nell's one measly flashlight, and she tells us we're in a haunted tunnel that's been there since the Civil War. Her grandfather was a Confederate soldier and she overheard him talking about it. The Confederates used it to smuggle ammunition, but when some Union soldiers found out, they chased two Confederate soldiers and killed them inside the tunnel! To this day, their ghosts still linger there, trapped underground forever."

My eyes were huge dark pools by then, animating Ruby even more.

"So, by now our knees are knocking and our teeth are chattering, but we had to keep walking until Nell finally whispered, 'Halt!' We watched her step down more rough stairs until her light shone on a decrepit wooden door. It had a bulky wooden turn-button latch that she wrestled with until it finally slid upright. But just as soon as she pushed the door open, this loud barking roared out, and we all screamed until Nell shushed us. There were these small rooms with iron bars for walls, and dogs barking and snapping behind them. Nell tossed something through the bars and that shut them up. Then, one by one, we climbed down and found ourselves inside the old county jail! They only use it now to take in dogs that might be rabid, so that's why Nell brought a pouch of ham slices. It felt like we'd been walking for hours, but we were just in the bottom of the Town Hall, right across the street from the Martha."

She paused to take a long sip from her mug and I patted her hand. "Ruby. I knew you were brave, but this tops even our 'little adventure.'"

"Oh, that's not all. One of the cells was empty, and each of us had to take a turn being shut inside it. Then, to be let free, we had to improvise a scene, telling what horrendous crime we'd committed and then making a convincing plea as to why our lives should be spared. Nell and Evelyn Boyd, the vice president, played judge, jury, and jailer. And relished it a bit too much, in my opinion."

"I didn't know any other group on campus did hazing. Yours sounds as dreadful as mine was."

Ruby nodded, wiping some sticky chocolate from the bottom of her mug and licking it from her finger. "Of course, now in the light of day with my belly warmed up, I have to admit it was all rather clever. Except for that tunnel! It still makes me shudder just to think of it."

"You know, when Varina told that story in the cemetery, about Beth and Captain Stoves, she said he'd been carried by soldiers through an underground cave system and up a secret stairway into the Martha. This tunnel must be part of that system."

"Oh, gosh. It has to be." Then she started laughing. Softly at first, and then throwing her head back in a mildly maniacal guffaw.

"What?" I asked, bewildered.

"Well—you can't dig a hole to China, but apparently you can dig one to the county jail!"

Battaglia

I was impatient all week for the next Saturday morning. Hearing Jonah pour out the story of his tragedy, I felt drawn to him more than ever. The impending Valentine's Ball that evening nagged at me, but I banished it from my mind as I headed to the place I loved most.

Climbing over the fence, I heard the vibrant ring of hammer strikes and spotted smoke curling from the forge chimney. Hopefully, Jonah was creating art instead of just ordinary horseshoes. Inside the stable I greeted Copper first, as always, but next the new mama and baby Miracle. Under Jonah's meticulous care, the mare was recovering well: gaining weight and making good milk— proven by the filly's ever-growing spunkiness. Every visit, I spent time socializing Miracle, then exercising and grooming her mother. The luster was creeping back into the mare's coat, slowly revealing she was actually a Palomino. I dubbed her "Marigold" and vowed to revitalize that beautiful golden color.

I took her out to the back corral with the filly following close behind, leaping and kicking in pure joy at being outdoors. Marigold trotted in a circle on a loose lunge line, the playful antics of the little paint horse entertaining us both. Before long, Miracle bounded right up to me and let me ruffle her stubby mane. At four weeks old, she was totally calm with my touch, so introduction to a halter would come soon. Heading us all back into the stable, I stopped short just inside the doorway, unsure of what I was seeing in the dimmer light. I blinked, then squinted my eyes, because it appeared I was looking into the face of Charles Sloan.

"Beatrice?" Incredulous surprise flooded his face. "What are you doing with my horse?" The question was absolutely absurd and I remained frozen in place.

"What is your business here?" Jonah walked toward us from the front doorway, still wearing his red bandanna and leather apron. He carried a newly forged fireplace poker, still warm from the fire. Charles abruptly swung around to face him.

"Charles Sloan, here." He approached Jonah with a deliberate stride bordering on a swagger. "I've been searching for my horse and now I've found it. But your question," he wheeled back to face me, "is better put to you, Beatrice. What on earth is your business here?"

I was still dumbfounded at the sight of my two worlds colliding. Jonah ignored his question and fixed him with a hard stare.

"You haven't found your horse here."

"It's standing right in front of me. It was taken from my father's farm back in January. I'm the appointed overseer and have his inventory right here." He pulled a crumpled paper from his jacket pocket. "Here's the listing: one Palomino mare in foal. So, in fact, two horses were taken."

"Two horses nearly died. They live only because a merciful vet rescued them from the drunken farmhand you hired."

"I don't do farm work."

"You don't oversee, either. It's the middle of February and you're just now searching for them."

"I have college studies to attend to, something you'd know nothing about."

"I know the value of animals. If you don't care for them, you can't have them."

"Those two horses are mine!"

"They'll not be taken and mistreated!"

Jonah's angry voice thundered as he shook the fireplace poker in Charles's face. It had a basket twist handle at one end and tapered to a sharp point at the other, a thing of beauty but indeed lethal if wielded as a weapon. Jonah had said he felt like whipping the scoundrel who'd neglected the mare. I held my breath.

"Is that a threat?" Charles spoke in a venomous whisper. The men held each other in a tense silent stare for several dreadful moments.

"You'll be sorry," Charles spat at Jonah before turning to glare at me. I stared back, waiting for his tirade, but he only turned on his heel and stomped out the front doorway. Jonah and I said nothing as Charles cranked his automobile engine and sped away.

My mind was in a mad swirl. The discovery that I'd been consorting with a man responsible for cruelty to a horse shocked and repulsed me to my core. And the terrible confrontation between all three of us posed a whole set of other damning possibilities. While Jonah hadn't really posed a physical threat to Charles, poker in hand notwithstanding, Charles had clearly issued a verbal threat to Jonah. My stomach lurched at the thought of what Charles might do.

Jonah had good cause for keeping the horses, since Charles had clearly been negligent. But Charles's anger might send him straight to the authorities, thinking his wealth and social stature gave him power. What if he reported me as well? I wasn't doing anything illegal, but the authorities would feel obligated to tell the college I was at the stables alone with a man. On that point alone, I was stunned he hadn't lashed out at me more. Then it dawned on me that it was a point of pride: he was chagrined that his girl kept company with a stable manager, so he wouldn't dare admit to Jonah that I mattered to him.

"I'm sorry you had to see me angry." Jonah let the poker dangle at his side.

"You had every right to be."

"So, you know him?"

I was momentarily disconcerted. I thought of all the visits, the dance at Emory, the Valentine's Ball that evening. All parts of a world separate from my world with Jonah.

"He's . . . I met him at a school event. A debate at Emory and Henry College. He's a student there . . ." My voice trailed off; Jonah needn't hear more. And there was no more, not really.

"I don't think he'll be back."

I sincerely hoped Jonah was right.

RUBY TOOK MY ARM TO LEAD US DOWN THE STAIRCASE IN A grand procession as if we were being introduced to the queen of England. I couldn't suppress a giggle.

"Stop it, Bea. I'm showing off my handiwork."

Ruby had every reason to be proud. I had refused to allow Charles to buy me another dress, so she'd insisted on sprucing up my mundane wardrobe. She'd returned from Christmas break with several yards of a lovely chiffon and fashioned a delicate pleated bodice for my homespun recital dress. She then sewed handmade lace roses to the waist and neckline, transforming it into an exquisite evening frock. I tried to enjoy the moment and not think about facing Charles. Or wonder if he would even show up for me to have to face.

The dining hall had been wonderfully transformed for the Valentine's Ball. Miss Bremer's senior art class had festooned it with vivid red streamers, hearts, and cupids, as well as bouquets of red paper flowers. Standing in my all-white dress among that bounty of scarlet was a reverse of my presence at the Christmas dance at Emory; I nervously wondered if it was an omen. I toyed with a rose on my dress until Ruby admonished me to stop fidgeting. Just then, I spotted Charles entering with Walter and their two buddies for Ruby and Hazel. As we signed in our dates on Mrs. Long's register, Charles lavished the warmest of greetings on our headmistress, but had only a cold "hello" for me. We then led our guests into the sea of white dresses and Sunday-best dress suits.

That was the last I saw of Charles, up close anyway. Ruby, Hazel, and their dates kept me company until I insisted they go dance. I meandered about for a few minutes before taking refuge in one of the chairs against the wall. Soon Saluda and Walter spied me and came over to chat. By turns Ruby would come, then Hazel, and so on all evening, no one mentioning the obvious—that Charles had abandoned me. I kept politely declining the pity dances their dates offered, until finally Walter insisted.

He kept up a jovial conversation and I smiled gratefully—until I caught a glimpse of Charles, blithely dancing around the room in the arms of Varina Armstrong. I hadn't been surprised that he'd left me in the dust, but I was shocked to see where he had turned his attentions. When Walter caught me staring, he quickly declared he was dying of thirst and suggested we get some punch. Back at my chair, despite my protests, he and Saluda sat with me for the rest of the evening. Ruby and Hazel soon joined with their dates, who goaded Walter and Ruby into a storytelling contest. They kept us all in stitches, making it the most fun evening I'd had in a long while.

I felt a bit sheepish about everyone thinking I was crushed by Charles. Unaware that he'd only been a cover for my feelings for Jonah, they naturally viewed me in the role of wronged lover. But my only reaction to the matter was incredulity at his renewed alliance with Varina. I just hoped and prayed Charles wouldn't take any more revenge on me than that.

I DIDN'T SEE VARINA AGAIN UNTIL THE EUTERPEAN SOCIETY battle against the Washingtonian Society two weeks later. Her ambitious plan to have this event serve as practice for our March contest with the Hermesians had, in my opinion, been folly. Everyone was trying too hard, risking less than stellar showings when we faced the men at Emory and Henry. Myrtle had chosen an antiquated and irrelevant topic, claiming "Bismark had done more for Prussia than Victoria had for England." Her dry arguments and pedantic, tedious droning bored us to tears. Yet after only lukewarm arguments with few convincing justifications, she was declared triumphant and showered with thunderous applause, led by Varina and her cohorts. Then Ethel had insisted on performing Delibes's "The Indian Bell Song" from his opera *Lakme*, a piece that Miss Le Grande had warned her would not be ready to take public for years. To say it was butchered was kind, yet her performance, too, was met with the same unearned applause. She and Myrtle both sat utterly pleased with themselves.

The only two saving graces were Hazel's lovely performance of Debussy's "Beau soir," a sensible choice sung beautifully, and, I had to admit, Varina's performance of the Presto agitato movement of Beethoven's "Moonlight Sonata." It was a showy piano piece, displaying her abundance of technical dexterity more so than musicianship, but I'd never heard her play it before. She must have worked it up over Christmas break and saved it to pull out for dramatic effect. I had aspired to play it myself one day, and wondered if I could ask Dr. Ziesberg to assign it to me. Then I quickly admonished myself; my teacher was a much better judge of appropriate challenges. If I wasn't careful I, too, would fall prey to the trap of overeager ambition.

Bel Canto

The month of March roared in like the proverbial lion, with howling wind swirling freezing air in all directions. Its course could change on a whim, making every trek across campus an athletic feat. It whipped at our faces without a moment's warning, snatching hats away like invisible thieves on phantom horses. Most of us agreed a fresh snowfall was preferable. But with the threat of snowstorms nearly past, visiting artists would begin to arrive on campus, which caused its own whirlwind of activity indoors.

A great deal of excitement surrounded the impending arrival of a famous operatic soprano. Franceska Kaspar Lawson from Washington, DC, was to give a concert in our very own Litchfield Hall on Friday evening. An overly enthusiastic Miss Le Grande repeated Mrs. Lawson's long list of credentials and accomplishments to each one of her voice students until I could have recited the singer's biography in my sleep.

But there was a perk for me in all this. Professor Zeisberg and Mr. Moore were traveling that week to give their own performances, providing me extra free time to devote to competition practice. At our master class the Friday before, Varina had not played the flashy Beethoven piece she'd performed at our Euterpean event, which struck me as odd. If she was planning such a challenging piece for the competition, I thought she would perform it at every opportunity. Her avoiding it in master class made me wonder if Professor Zeisberg had assigned it to her after all, or if it was her own doing. If so, she was even more audacious than I gave her credit for.

That Varina harbored secrets was certainly no surprise, yet her overt behavior at times was baffling. She came to the voice studio expressly to ask if she could help with the concert, perhaps providing refreshments for the performers backstage. Miss Le Grande was flattered, and told her Mrs. Lawson preferred only water while performing, but she and Mr. Park would be delighted to partake. I wondered who she was trying to impress, then suddenly remembered the close proximity of Washington, DC, to Baltimore, Maryland—and the Peabody Conservatory of Music. Mrs. Lawson no doubt had colleagues there, ones that might be judging the scholarship competition.

The concert was splendid. From the moment Franceska Kaspar Lawson placed herself into the crook of the Steinway, you couldn't help but fall under her spell. With a demure but intense command of the stage, her crystalline voice soon filled the hall with French arias and songs by Rameau, Le Roux, Debussy, and Bizet. I was especially drawn to the aria from Bizet's opera *The Pearl Fishers*. It was about a love triangle and set on an island in the Far East, a place so remote and exotic I wondered if I'd ever have the chance to see it for myself. Her second set comprised Russian songs, and although I'd played Rachmaninoff and Rimsky-Korsakov piano pieces, I'd never heard the Russian language, spoken or sung. It was striking and robust. Then came German songs by Brahms and Eckert, so I was back in familiar territory from voice lessons I'd accompanied.

When the first half of the concert ended, Ruby and I stepped into the aisle to stretch our legs. We strolled the length of the hall and back several times, having an animated chat, me about the music and Ruby about the singer's stage presence and gorgeous gown. Suddenly Bessie appeared out of nowhere and tugged on my sleeve.

"Miss Le Grande wants to see you backstage." Bessie's eyes were like saucers.

"Me?" I wondered if I'd heard correctly. "Why?"

"I don't know, but you have to come right now!"

I suspected her sense of urgency was overblown, but with a bemused shrug to Ruby, I followed her into the stage wing. As I cleared the curtain, I caught sight of Varina and Ethel hovering near a table in the corner, presiding over a large tea urn surrounded by finger sandwiches. Ethel was frowning as she peered at something in the palm of her hand.

"What's this?"

"Give me that!" Varina hissed as she grabbed it from her like Wesa snatching up a mouse. "It's . . . a gourmet flavoring. For the tea. My mother sends it special from Richmond." She quickly stuffed it into her skirt pocket, but not before I'd gotten a good look at the small blue bottle. It looked familiar. However, the label had been only partially visible, the letters "I-P-E-" revealed before it disappeared. Varina abruptly turned from the table, her eyes instantly locking with mine in an astonishment she failed to disguise. At the same time Miss Le Grande appeared from the green room, marching directly toward me with swift deliberate steps.

"Beatrice, we've been beset with an unfortunate turn of events. Mr. Park has taken suddenly ill. Very violently ill."

A collective gasp came from the region of the tea table and Varina immediately stepped forward. "Oh, no. That's terrible! But poor Mrs. Lawson. She's come all this way."

"Yes, it would be a shame if she couldn't finish her program, so—"

"I'd be more than happy to serve as accompanist," Varina interrupted her with a honeyed voice. Miss Le Grande ignored her and looked straight at me.

"I called you back here, Beatrice, because with both Professor Zeisberg and Mr. Moore absent, I'm afraid we must press you into service tonight." I stared mutely at the sheaf of music she held out to me.

"But Miss Le Grande," Varina insisted, "I am the senior piano student after all, with several years of Professor Ziesberg's training under my belt."

"Playing as an accompanist is a special skill, Varina, and to my knowledge you've no experience with that. Now, Beatrice, the songs left on the program are pieces you've already played except for the Henschel and Russell. But they're fairly easy, so look them over for a few minutes and I'm sure you'll be fine."

She walked away to attend to Mrs. Lawson, leaving me to endure a vicious stare from a livid Varina. But I had no time to waste on her resentful wrath. While she and her minions cleared away the tea things with unnecessary clamor and made a noisy exit, I read through the pages intently, imagining my fingers on the keys. Miss Le Grande was right, the pieces new to me were easy, and I began to breathe calmly. By the time I heard the sound of her voice again, she was onstage announcing the change in accompanist. Mrs. Lawson was in place in the wing, ready for her entrance. She smiled at me warmly and winked, so like Ruby that it gave me that extra dose of courage I needed to follow her and take my seat on the piano bench.

Her first set of songs were by British and American composers, and, while not as beautiful as French or Russian, hearing my own language helped put me at ease. Then for the finale, and highlight, of the program she returned to French, Delibes' "The Indian Bell Song" from the opera *Lakme*. This was a particular delight for me, since familiarity with the accompaniment left me at ease to enjoy Mrs. Lawson's stunning voice. It lilted through the intricate melodies, executing the difficult leaps and high notes with the grace of a gazelle. But I also couldn't help indulging in a little schadenfreude (a new word I'd learned from Professor Zeisberg), imagining how mortified Ethel must be for everyone to hear how this aria should really be sung.

It was a glorious close to the concert that received roaring applause and a standing ovation for Mrs. Lawson. Still, she insisted I come forward and bow with her before leaving the stage, a gracious and generous gesture that I would never forget. Once backstage, she was also generous with her thanks.

"Beatrice, if you ever come to Washington, I insist you visit me. I have connections there if you'd like to pursue your music further." With a squeeze of my hand, she was swept away by Miss Le Grande to meet her adoring fans. In awe, I stood for a moment in the quiet of the stage wing, tucking her promise into my heart for safekeeping.

Making my way from the stage into the teeming crowd to find Ruby, I suddenly stopped short. The vision of a small blue bottle flashed in my mind, coupled with a spoon and crumpled bedsheets. "IPECAC" its label said, and then I knew. Mr. Park's illness was no accident; it was the result of Varina's "flavoring" for the tea. Although it shouldn't have, the revelation astonished me. It was a cold reminder that to get what she wanted, the depths to which Varina would stoop were limitless.

I STOOD RIGIDLY AT THE ENTRANCE TO SOCIETY HALL, USHER-ing guests and dreading the sight of Charles. It was Saturday afternoon, a week following the Lawson concert, and the Euterpeans were hosting the Hermesians from Emory and Henry promptly at four o'clock. A month had passed since the Valentine's Ball, and all that time I'd been anxiously wondering if Charles had reported seeing me at the stables. And if he'd shared that bit of news with Varina, although I couldn't fathom her keeping silent about something so incriminating. When it was time to begin and he hadn't crossed the threshold, my shoulders finally relaxed. But I puzzled over what could keep away the Hermesian's esteemed president.

As a return courtesy, we allowed the Hermesians to present first. They opened with "Batrakhomakhia" or "Battle of the Frogs and Mice," Homer's parody of the Iliad. The presenter's commentary was actually funnier than the bits he read from the comic poem, getting things off to a splendid start. Next, Varina took center stage, captivating everyone with the Presto agitato movement from Beethoven's "Moonlight Sonata." Her speed and accuracy left the Hermesians duly impressed, and she bowed deeply with a self-satisfied smile. An essay was read and more poetry recited before it was Myrtle's turn to debate Walter about Bismark and Queen Victoria. As expected, she was soundly tromped and Walter's buddies graced him with a vigorous round of applause. Since I was seated in the back row, I joined them.

Then it was time for me to play for Ethel. At rehearsal the week before, she had briskly removed my music for "The Indian Bell Song" and handed me music for a standard Schubert lied, struggling to maintain her dignity. But she made a quite decent showing with a song she'd actually mastered. More poetry, an essay, and one last debate followed before the program would close with Hazel's delightful aria. But when she finished and I rose to leave the piano bench, an accompanist from Emory slid past to take my place. Varina announced one more aria, by a Hermesian singer, and I was stunned to see none other than Charles Sloan striding forward. His arrival was extremely late, but his demeanor proclaimed he was not to be denied.

With a sharp nod to the pianist, he began, "Quanto e bella, quanto e cara," from Donizetti's *L'elisir d'amore*. An aria from an opera buffa—how utterly appropriate, or so I thought. *How beautiful she is, how expensive; the more I see her, the more I like her*, he crooned directly to Varina, who sat conveniently before him in the front row, basking in his shameless display of emoting. He had a rather good tenor voice but was mangling the Italian unmercifully. I wondered who else, besides our singers, would know the difference. Yet afterward Varina jumped up with effusive applause, giving everyone no choice but to join her in a standing ovation—a shame when other presentations were far more deserving. Charles and Varina made a good pair, all right; they both had an insatiable thirst for the spotlight.

SINCE WE ALSO HOSTED THE HERMESIANS FOR A LENGTHY dinner afterwards, the evening seemed interminable. By the time light bell rang, I was already gratefully snuggled deep under quilts, my heavy eyelids barely allowing a blurred gaze at my bedside candle flame. Like every Saturday, my day had begun before daybreak, at the stables with good physical labor that I loved.

I'd grown curious that Jonah always arrived before me. On a ride in the Meadows, he'd pointed out his house in the distance, isolated on the corner of a large vacant plot on Market Street near the railroad tracks. So, I knew he didn't live terribly close by. When I commented that morning that he must rise awfully early, he confessed that sometimes he slept in his forge. "In the cold months, it's actually easier to heat than my house. Plus . . . sometimes . . . I just don't like being alone there." He went quiet and I didn't ask anything more. Then he told me the dun mare had had a bad case of colic the day before. The vet had come and treated her, but he wanted to check on her at night for the next couple of days.

Ever since I'd learned of the tragedy of Jonah's wife and child, I'd kept my cards close to my chest concerning my feelings for him. I wasn't sure how long someone might grieve for such a loss and hadn't wanted to intrude upon a sad memory. That Jonah sometimes couldn't bear to be in his home suggested the hurt still ran deep. I wouldn't risk complicating our friendship, so as I drifted into sleep, I contented myself that for now I would simply keep him, and his horses, good company.

FUGUE

Furioso

March 12, 1916

My nose twitched. My eyelids fluttered and slowly lifted to nothing but blackness. My brow scrunched at a pungent smell. A faint whiff of a smokey tang. I sat up and reached for my candle, burned to a nub and long cold. But the aroma of smoke clung to the air, heavier than any candle could muster. Footsteps outside my door thumped a rapid bassline accompanied by random voices, pitched in the high range of panic. Suddenly a sharp clanging pierced the air, different from the other bells that called girls to classes, to dinner, to bedtime. The fire alarm was calling us, hopefully, to safety.

Gathering on the lawn in front of Preston Hall, we were a helter-skelter throng in various stages of undress. Some had tossed dressing gowns hastily over shoulders or grabbed quilts to serve as shawls, but some shivered in only thin flannel nightgowns. Although trained to keep shoes by our beds at night, many had dashed outside with bare feet. All were stunned into a terrified silence when the firetruck came racing onto Main Street, its clanging bell sounding a desperate, deafening alarm. It swiftly bypassed the Martha, breaking our silence with exclamations of confusion. We followed it with our eyes until it stopped well east of us at the horrifying sight next door. A raging blaze held Stonewall Jackson College under siege.

The roof had been completely burned away, allowing black smoke to billow up into the night sky. Yellow-orange flames performed a wild dance in the windows, devouring the timbers within. Firemen wielded heavy firehoses fat with water, aiming their sprays at a hungry fire that grew fiercer by the minute. The power of the spray was no match for the power of the inferno. Only small portions were extinguished while the flames beyond gained velocity. The firemen bravely fought on, despite the growing futility of their labors.

In the meantime, our matrons called us to attention and herded us back inside Preston Hall. Ordered to stay on the first floor, we spilled into the parlors and the society hall, huddled tightly together but thankful for the body heat. The Stonewall students had taken refuge with us and clung together in a tearful cluster. Mrs. Long took charge, aided by Martha senior girls. I caught glimpses of Varina; her white-blonde hair hanging loose over her dressing gown made her hard to miss. She was waltzing among the poor frightened girls, making a show of patting hands and cooing comforting words. But by the time Mrs. Long was pairing each Stonewall girl with a Martha girl who would take her in for the night, Varina had magically vanished.

Ruby and I found our charges hunched together in a corner, strangely apart from the others. One was a frail young girl named Anna, a boarding high schooler barely fifteen years old, with a tear-stained face and round troubled eyes. She hesitated to let go of her frightened classmate, her teeth biting into her lower lip as Ruby gently coaxed her forward. The girl she was so reluctant to leave was my charge, Mary, whose rather wild-looking eyes stared straight ahead. I introduced myself, but she didn't move or speak. I gently put my arm around her shoulder and guided her up the stairs to my room.

Her bony shoulders shuddered, with fright or the cold it wasn't clear. I dressed her in my thickest wool sweater and replaced her damp stockings with my boot socks. She still hadn't spoken, but I tucked her into my bed and laid on an extra blanket. I sat by the window with my head tilted toward the disaster that continued to unfold beyond it. The tiny street that separated Stonewall from our campus was filled with the detritus of the tragedy: odd pieces of furniture, trunks, bundles of clothing, all piled upon the pavement in a sad heap. Firemen fought the raging blaze for two more hours, but water pressure from their hoses proved too frail to furnish the deluge needed to quell the flames. When the water supply dwindled to a trickle, they were forced to concede defeat. Weary and dejected, they kept vigil until dawn, when at last the entire school lay in scorched ruins.

Miraculously, there were no fatalities. The only physical wounds were minor scratches or bruises, although the emotional trauma would linger for some time. When morning came, we were instructed to let our charges rest while we Martha girls were marched off to church, despite our own short night of sleep. Mrs. Long was adamant: "We must send up prayers of thanks to God for sparing these children from the inferno!" And she was right, of course. We all knew it could have just as easily been Martha girls scraping up the charred remains of our college existence, and we were humbled into gratitude and sympathy. The remainder of the day was spent tending the girls' immediate needs: coaxing them to eat, sorting out clothing and belongings, making plans for their lodging. I didn't mind my nursing duties; I rather liked having Mary with me. It was like having a little sister around again.

ON MONDAY WE ATTENDED CLASSES WHILE THE STONEWALL girls gathered in the Litchfield Hall auditorium for a full day of fire investigation interviews. I worried about Mary. I'd been able to coax a few words from her the day before but wondered if she'd speak at all to a fire marshal. By midafternoon I got my answer when I was called from class to sit with her during her interview. She looked up with visible relief when she saw me, and I held her hand while the officer proceeded with his questions: Were you in your room when the fire broke out? Sleeping? How did you learn there was a fire? How did you get out? To the first two questions, she replied a simple "yes" and then answered only "I don't remember" to the others, but at least she was talking.

When he asked if she'd seen a man inside the building, she went silent. He repeated the question, then looked at me and I gently squeezed her hand. But she was still quiet. He elaborated, telling her a man was seen leaving the premises after the fire truck arrived. "That Indian fellow, the blacksmith. You see him?" At this my blood ran cold, and I feared Mary would feel it in my hand.

She shook her head and whispered, "I don't remember." He asked her to speak up and she repeated the words louder, then repeated them over and over until I had to calm her down with a hug.

I looked at him with a silent plea to end the interview. With a heavy sigh he said, "It's okay, I'm going to bring the man in for questioning anyway."

I stood to lead Mary away when she abruptly cried out, "Wait!" startling both me and the officer. I sat while she continued.

"I did see him. But it was before the fire." The officer scribbled a quick note. "In the hallway. About midnight, I was walking to the lavatory. He came out of one of the bedrooms. He saw me and started coming toward me. I turned and ran, but he chased me. He ran up behind me and caught me around my shoulders, one hand grabbed my breast and the other pulled at my nightgown." She was sobbing with her face buried in her hands. The officer was scribbling furiously while my heart pounded, incredulous at what I was hearing. "Then I, I kicked his leg. Hard with my heel. And punched his stomach with my elbow. So, then I got away. And ran to my room. Slammed the door and pushed my trunk against it to keep him out." Mary sniffed and wiped her nose on her sleeve, then sat up perfectly straight. "Then I got into my bed and went to sleep."

I stared at her, totally baffled. Mary had hardly spoken a word in two days, then suddenly erupted with this story. And I knew it couldn't possibly be true. It was probably out of line for me to speak, but I couldn't help myself. "Earlier you indicated you didn't remember much, is it possible this was a dream?"

Mary didn't even glance at me but looked the officer right in the eye. "No."

The fire marshal returned her stare with a barely suppressed smile, then flipped his notebook closed. "You've been very helpful, Mary. Thank you for your time." Instantly, she shot up from her seat and out the door, leaving me to trail behind her. At the door I turned back to stare at the officer. Surely, he didn't believe such an outrageous story? But his thoughts were hidden behind the stoic mask of law enforcement.

I didn't see Mary after that. By the time I'd finished classes for the day, she had packed her scant belongings and been taken to the home of a family in town. By dinnertime on Tuesday, all of the Stonewall girls had been placed, most in private homes like Mary, with the remainder setting up in spare rooms at the Martha. Stonewall had already declared spring break, giving their students the remainder of the week plus a good two weeks more to recuperate, so many were already traveling home. When they returned, they would take classes in the Dagmar Hotel a couple of blocks east of us, proving that Stonewall Jackson College, like the famous Confederate general it was named for, was determined to stand against adversity.

IN THE PLETHORA OF STORIES SURROUNDING THE GREAT FIRE, I struggled to glean the truth from a rumor mill that churned without respite. But when Tuesday's dinner gossip included news that a wagon shed downhill from Stonewall had also burned, I abandoned caution and set out to see for myself. Fortunately, the sun had dipped below the horizon and it was nearly dark. After nearly colliding with the corral fence, I flipped on my flashlight and curved around to the forge, where I trained the beam beyond it to the edge of the property. A carpet of black rubble met my eyes where the shed should have stood. The green wooden wagon had disappeared into ash, and the charred skeleton of the buggy lay tilted in the debris like a ghoulish bird cage.

I studied the scene, feeling empty. Those vehicles would never again feel the pull of the lively bay horses or the tall majestic grays. I heard Jonah's slow heavy footsteps behind me. When he reached my side, I didn't hesitate to pull him into an embrace. I breathed in the scent of his hair, still laced with smoke but also horsehair and leather.

"Thank heavens you and the horses are okay."

"For the most part. I lost the little dun mare." I held him tighter. "Still, looking at the sight up the hill there, I think how it could've been worse."

I sighed heavily. "It's a shame the Stonewall fire had to find its way down here."

"It didn't." Confused, I stepped back to face him. "When I woke up in the forge, only the shed was on fire. I fought for a good hour to put it out, wrestling with the water hose against the wind. Then I saw the tree tops up the hill in flames, and beyond that the roof of Stonewall burning. I ran up there to help get people out."

"That was brave."

"Sometimes people don't wake up, they breathe in the smoke and die. So, I broke the glass in the basement door and ran up to the top floor first, closest to the fire. I opened doors, made sure they were awake." Mary's account to the fire marshal made me angry all over again.

"Still, it was a selfless act. Your own place could've erupted in flames again."

"It didn't take that long, really. Once the fire truck came and everyone was outside, I came back here. Nothing else had caught fire, but I'll have to pay Mr. Hutton for his buggy. I don't have insurance. He's already taken away his two buggy horses and their harness."

He walked closer to the shed's charred remains, shaking his head. "I haven't lit the forge fire in days, and nothing inside the shed could've combusted on its own." Hearing this, I wondered if someone had deliberately set fire to Jonah's shed, and if he suspected the same.

"The shed was fairly close to the street," I ventured. "People can be careless with their cigarettes."

"Maybe that was it. Some late-night walker, probably drunk, tossed one over the fence." We speculated no further, only stood together staring at the blackened remains of the shed. A simple vice coupled with carelessness; the damage was heartbreaking. But if it was arson, the damage was alarming.

Doloroso

The devastating fire had made for an exhausting weekend that lasted for several days. Finally, on Wednesday, things began to settle into some semblance of normal. Several Stonewall girls were lodged in our extra rooms, clinging to each other and sharing only the occasional shy smile until, one by one, most departed for their extended spring break. Martha girls were still busy with classes, looking forward to our own spring break, which would begin after the following week. I was hoping to catch up on practice, and sleep.

But that normalcy was shattered Thursday morning at breakfast. I joined a flock of girls gathered at Saluda's table, where she held a copy of the Abingdon Herald, a local newspaper. The headline jumped out at me like a fireworks explosion: "Local Blacksmith Arrested for Arson." The sentence beneath stated, "Jonah Schumacher suspected of setting fire to Stonewall Jackson College." I staggered backwards into a chair at the next table, grabbing it to barely save myself from a fall. Rushing from the dining hall, I blindly headed for the back service entrance at a near run. I nearly crashed into Rena rounding a corner with an armful of mail, her stern admonishment snapping me back to my senses. It was broad daylight, so I had to be smart about my movements. I retrieved my black jacket, a hat, and a book from my room, then casually walked out the front door. Taking a circuitous route, I inched my way around Mariah Cooper Hall and back across the rear campus until I came to the pines, crossing my fingers that I was undetected.

It was eerily quiet at the stables. The massive back doors were closed but unchained, and when I flung them open seven maned heads turned my way, flooding me with relief. Even Miracle's little muzzle poked up above the stall door. The front stable doors stood completely open and with a glimmer of hope I ran through them and around to the forge. But only a cold morning draft filled the empty space that should have been warmed by a bright fire in its hearth. My agonizing grief morphed into a terrible surge of anger, making me want to scream and throw things. Instead, I slammed the forge doors shut, fastening the latch as best I could, and ran back to the horses.

Working quickly, I filled the empty feed boxes and nearly dry water pails. Remembering the boy's clothing stashed in the tack room, I changed before clearing the worst of the muck from the stalls. After a good two hours, I was back into my school attire, pulling the stable doors shut in an attempt to make them appear locked. Then it was a mad dash back to campus to see what damage I may have inflicted by my absence.

I made it to my room undiscovered, cleaned up, and got to the voice studio in time for the third lesson of the day. Steeling myself for a tongue lashing from Miss Le Grande, I was astonished when she greeted me with a smile. Students for the first two lessons were on a class field trip, which she assumed I knew, so I played along. It seemed the turmoil of the fire had caused a juggling of agendas, and I breathed a prayer of thanks.

At lunch, I spied the newspaper abandoned on a tabletop and read the arrest story more thoroughly. "Following accounts of Mr. Schumacher being sighted at the fire and leaving the scene, a swift arrest was made Wednesday morning at the suspect's place of business." A photo accompanied the article: Jonah in handcuffs standing outside his forge with two deputies on either side giving him stern looks. They'd been so concerned about making this show that they hadn't bothered to lock up his property or make provisions for his horses. "Suspect will remain in custody pending arraignment." The cruelty and injustice ignited my anger all over again.

I began to spend every spare minute at the stables, feeding and cleaning stalls. I turned the horses out into the corrals two at a time for exercise, except for Xander, who I turned out alone. His pent-up energy was fierce, and he burned it up showing off like he did the first day I saw him. That seemed like ages ago, but brought a smile to my face. It also reminded me of Xander's portrait, hanging in Jonah's forge. Behind doors I could not lock. Before I left for the day, I took it from its place of pride on the wall facing Jonah's anvil. It would be a shame if anything went missing, but that item was truly irreplaceable.

Friday morning, I got up extra early, working through breakfast to tend the horses in order to make it back for master class. Sleepless, weak, and behind on practice, I made a poor showing with my new Beethoven piece, the third movement of the "Appassionata" sonata. The critiques were harsh, as I well deserved, and I humbly took my licks while wondering how I might make up the lost time at the keyboard. Varina was last to perform and played more splendidly than ever. She tossed a smirky smile my way as she returned to her seat, and I couldn't help but seethe in resentment. While most of us were taking in Stonewall girls and spending time helping out, Varina had somehow avoided that responsibility and kept to her normal schedule. But explaining that to the music faculty would have been regarded as whining, so there was nothing to do but endure.

By Saturday morning, as I scooped grain into feed boxes, I began to worry how long the present supply would last. Jonah had said he purchased it once each quarter, and the end of March was only two weeks away. I climbed into the loft to take a quick inventory of the hay supply, relieved to see enough there to last until first summer harvest.

I cut the string on a hay bale and tossed a section down the chute. It hit the dirt floor below with a soft thud, followed by a sharp cry of, "What the devil!" Momentarily stunned to learn I wasn't alone, I gathered myself and scrambled down the ladder. Before I reached the ground, the voice called out to me.

"Hey, sonny. I've got two horses here and I've come to fetch them." I knew that voice and it sent a shiver down my spine. Once my feet were planted on dirt, I turned to face its owner, who was furiously beating hay and dust from his hat. He still didn't recognize me, only sauntered directly toward Marigold's stall. In a flash I was standing in front of it.

"These horses aren't going anywhere." Turning to look directly at me, his face darkened.

"Beatrice. Well, well. I see you're still hanging around with criminals."

"The only criminal here is you."

"I beg to differ, and so does the court order I have right here in my pocket. The law clearly states those horses are mine and I've come to claim them."

I grabbed the pitchfork leaning against the next stall and held it in front of me.

"He can expose you for animal neglect!"

He glared at me with a crooked smile. "You know, in addition to taking my horses, that Indian guy threatened me with a weapon. So, horse theft and attempted assault piled onto arson adds up to a hefty list of crimes. And I'm not exposed for anything except ownership of those two horses in that stall."

He pulled a paper from his pocket and waved it in front of me. I couldn't risk causing more trouble for Jonah; I had no choice but to stand aside. After they'd been led away, I slumped to the ground in front of Marigold's stall and a flood of tears drenched my face. As all my pent-up tensions broke loose into a soft sobbing, I felt a soft nudge against my thigh. I looked up to see Wesa sitting beside me, staring forlornly into my eyes. "Poor fella. You miss him, too, don't you?" He answered me by curling up in my lap, keeping me warm as I wiped at an endless trickle of tears. We sat together in our misery, eventually falling into an uneasy doze.

"And who might you be?"

I was startled awake and found myself staring into another man's face. This one looked gentle and kind, although perplexed. Wesa sprang from my lap and scampered off as I clumsily attempted to rise. The man instinctively held out his hand to help me.

"I'm Beatrice," I said without thinking, then suddenly remembered I was still in boy's clothing. But my cap had fallen, leaving my hair tumbling around my shoulders. I didn't know what to do, so said nothing more.

"I'm Doc Gilmer, the veterinarian." Instantly awed to be in the presence of the man who had saved Miracle, I couldn't find my tongue. "Jonah told me he had a lad who worked for him sometimes. By the name of Benjamin. Would that happen to be you?" A warm grin spread across his face with a quick wink. I took a breath and nodded.

"I've been taking care of the horses ever since . . ."

"The terrible tragedies."

He'd been out of town for a week and had just heard about the fire and Jonah's arrest, so he came immediately to check on the horses. We walked through the stables and he looked in each stall. He was sad to hear the dun mare had died, more fallout from that terrible night. At Marigold's stall I told him about Charles: the court order, his threats of charging Jonah for theft and attempted assault. I couldn't hold my anger.

"It's not right! You, and Jonah, saved her and her foal. I can't stand the thought of them both back at his farm."

"Well, this 'document' he waved in your face was bogus, designed to intimidate. Even though he does own the horses. Or his father does, that is. But the local commonwealth's attorney is a friend of mine, so I figured if anybody came to his office squawking about them being here, I would just explain the severe neglect and dire need for my medical care."

Outraged by Charles's deceit, I was pacing the corridor while Doc watched with sympathy and bemused admiration.

"Now, don't fret. I was always going to return them anyway, once they both got healthy. *And* a decent caretaker was hired. I'll look into that first thing Monday morning." He stopped me and patted my shoulder in a fatherly gesture. "You've done a first-rate job, taking care of all this." I told him I hadn't minded at all, working it in around classes. And that surely the fire report would come in before Monday's arraignment, and Jonah would be released. He smiled indulgently. "I'm sure Jonah appreciates you, but we'll gather in some help." After an awkward pause, I told him it was amazing nothing had been stolen, since the entire property had been left unlocked. He left right then to go to Withers Hardware and buy new locks, promising me a set of keys. "You've certainly proved you can be trusted."

By the time Doc Gilmer returned, two more men had come, owners of the buckskin mare and the roan gelding. I'd shifted my voice to its lowest register, trying to prove convincing as a reliable caretaker, but they chose to move them to other stables. We'd lost seven horses in a matter of days. Despite the vibrant presence of Xander, Copper and the draft horses, the newly empty stalls lent a hollow and desolate atmosphere to the place.

I returned to campus, rushed through lunch, then hid away in a practice room for the remainder of the afternoon. More than needing to make up lost practice time, I longed for the consolation the piano always provided. Placing my callused fingers on the keys felt like coming home. I blocked out all the sadness that had unfolded beyond the thicket of pines bordering the Martha. For comfort, I indulged in a few of my Chopin favorites before tackling the Beethoven piece I'd made a mess of in the last master class. I gave all the troublesome sections a good thrashing out, not leaving the piece until I was absolutely confident of them all. I emerged only for supper, then slinked off to my room to fall exhausted into bed.

On Monday, Doc's son tended the horses in the morning, so my trip to the stables could wait until after classes. Doc would attend Jonah's arraignment, then come that afternoon with a report. It was nearly impossible to concentrate on schoolwork, my thoughts consumed with anticipation of news coming at five o'clock.

"Good afternoon, Beatrice." Doc ambled through the stable door, his posture and slow gait betraying a solemn mood.

"Hello, Doc." I stopped stroking Copper with the dandy brush and studied his face. "What happened today?"

He looked all around the barn before he spoke. "When you're finished with that fella, let's sit down together and I'll fill you in." Not a reassuring prelude, but I swiftly returned Copper to his stall and joined Doc on some straw bales.

He'd learned a proper caretaker was now employed at the Sloan farm where Marigold and Miracle were living but promised to still check on them as often as possible. He also assured me Charles had made no charges of horse theft or attempted assault against Jonah. However, the fire report was still outstanding, so the arson charge still stood. But there was an even bigger problem: Jonah was also charged with attempted rape.

"That's absurd!" I cried.

"I agree. I've known Jonah for years, ever since the Schumacher family moved here." Doc slowly shook his head. "It's absolutely unimaginable."

"But the newspaper said nothing about . . . that charge."

"They wouldn't print it. Considered too sordid for delicate lady readers." I silently scoffed at that, recalling Mary's unvarnished recitation to the fire marshal. Undoubtedly the reason Jonah was charged. "And aside from the accuser, apparently several girls reported seeing him in the building." Had Mary bribed them? Or were they sympathy accusations? "And to make matters worse, Stonewall faculty confirmed Jonah had been repairing the iron fence around the school, in close proximity to the girls. To their minds, that must have provoked 'temptation.'" The whole preposterous story was snowballing, creating a bad scene for a man I was certain was innocent.

Jonah would remain in jail until his trial on Monday, April 3, two weeks away. "At least there's hope for the fire investigation. They'll determine the cause and prove Jonah couldn't have set it." Doc rose to his feet and tugged his hat onto his head. "Unless someone monkeys with that story." Shaking his head again, he wearily ambled away.

Rondo

The remainder of that week was a blur as my thoughts churned in constant turmoil. Dense gray clouds spewed relentless spring rain every single day, bringing the fire investigation temporarily to a halt. News had leaked about the attempted rape charge, and since word-of-mouth spreads faster than any fire, gossip was rampant.

Stoically, I waded through the swirl of excitement over leaving for spring break, a fake smile on my face when warranted. I had borrowed money from Saluda and telephoned home to say I'd be staying on campus for spring break. Gladys had answered and cried in protest until I told her I was working on a special music project, a surprise that I'd share with her later. It wasn't really a lie, since no classes to attend meant more practice time for the competition. But mainly I was determined to take over full care of Jonah's horses while I worked on getting that terrible charge against him cleared.

My first and strongest line of strategy had been momentarily thwarted at the beginning of the week. As soon as Doc had left the stable on Monday, I locked up and headed back to campus at a near run, barely catching Mrs. Long in her office as she gathered her keys to leave. She frowned at my split skirt and cotton blouse, both a bit grungy, but before she could chastise me, I asked where Mary had been housed. "You see, we became so close when I was taking care of her, I'd like to visit. To check on her. And take her some flowers." I smiled, amazed how easily the lies came. Mrs. Long thought it was a lovely idea and wrote down the address. It was on

Valley Street, only a short block from the Martha, so she allowed me to walk there on my own. "Perhaps after you've had a bit of a brushing up, dear," she added sternly.

Within minutes I was ringing the bell at the front door of that address. After I waited for what seemed like an eternity, the door finally inched open and an elderly woman peered out. I introduced myself and asked for Mary, but I learned she'd already gone home to Roanoke for spring break. She would not return until the following week, on either Thursday or Friday; the woman couldn't say for sure which. I thanked her and left, swallowing my consternation that what I desperately needed would be out of my reach for more than a week.

When the weekend rolled around, finally bringing coveted sunshine, the majority of students departed campus, and by Sunday morning the Martha was all but deserted. It was tricky working in a quick trip to the stable before breakfast and church service, still mandatory even during spring break. "I'll come back later to clean up your messes," I promised as I dropped a carrot or apple slice into each feed box. I tried not to look at the empty stalls.

Back at the dining hall, I faced rows of empty tables as we few girls sat nibbling our morning meal. I never thought I would miss the den of babbling voices and clattering dinnerware, but the lack of noise was oddly sad. At the table next to mine sat three remaining Stonewall girls who boarded with us. In my line of sight sat Anna, the girl Ruby had fostered, looking rather forlorn. She was a lot younger than the other two and didn't join in their conversation. For a moment she caught my eye and looked at me with something like fear, although I couldn't imagine why. I decided to befriend her, and caught up with her on the walk to church.

"Anna?" I called from behind her as she ambled alone down the sidewalk. She stopped short but didn't turn around. I came up beside her. "I thought it was you."

"Yes," she replied, then hung her head. I was perplexed, but determined to draw her out.

"I'm Bea. Ruby's next-door neighbor? Your friend Mary stayed with me."

"Oh." I'd tried my most winning smile on her, but it was not returned.

"Let's walk on together. We don't want to be late." She didn't reply but obediently fell into step with me. "I think we're both a little lost without Ruby. She's also my best friend." Anna nodded, but said nothing. "But you must miss Mary, too, the way I miss Ruby." Thinking the mention of her friend's name would be a comfort, I was surprised to see her face redden and her lips purse together in further silence. We'd reached the walkway leading up to the front doors of the Methodist Episcopal church, but when I turned toward it, Anna hung back.

"I've only ever been to a Presbyterian church." She frowned as she stared at the entrance. Its doors were topped with an ornate Gothic style transom, the same as the entrance to Sinking Spring Presbyterian Church down the street. But she regarded it as if it were the gates of hell.

"This church is not so very different, and I'll be here to help you." She locked eyes with me, frozen to her spot. "God knows what you've been through. He'll be just as happy to see you here today." Her wary expression was unwavering, but she allowed me to gently lead her forward. I didn't let go until we were firmly planted on a pew in the sanctuary.

I pondered Anna as I went about mucking stalls that afternoon. Yes, she'd been through a trauma, but to have so much anxiety after two weeks seemed peculiar. She was like a little lost chick, kicked out of her cozy nest too soon. It was clear she needed a friend. But perhaps I needed her, too.

At dinner, I anxiously picked at my food while watching out for Anna. When I saw her enter the dining hall, I moved to a spare table.

"Anna! Let's sit over here, where it's quiet." She gave me a quizzical look but obeyed. I began with small talk, which she mostly answered in monosyllables, but at least I had her engaged.

When she was almost finished eating, I led the conversation in a new direction.

"Anna, did you and Mary ever talk . . . about the night of the fire?" She stopped chewing for a moment, then shook her head. "I know it was scary. Maybe the scariest experience you've ever had." I waited but she said nothing. "Did Mary tell you anything about *her* experience that night?" Anna's fork suddenly fell from her hand, clanging loudly on her plate. She thrust her hands in her lap and began twisting her napkin, so I tried to make my voice as soothing as possible. "The two of you walked over here together after the evacuation. Didn't she say anything?" A small reply came from her lips, whispered too softly for me to hear. I urged her again. "Anna?"

"No!" Her whisper was louder and she shook her head vigorously. "No! She didn't say anything!" Anna sprang from her chair and rushed out of the dining hall, the napkin falling to the floor behind her. I gathered up her dinnerware with mine, wondering why she'd reacted like a spooked horse. Already convinced Mary was lying, I now suspected she had forced Anna into silence. But obviously, I'd overplayed my hand.

Needing an escape from my thoughts, I trekked to the practice room to drown them in music. I had worried how my fingers would hold up to extra work at the stables, but they actually seemed all the stronger for it. As they were the only part of me that wasn't tired, or anxious or fearful, I let them take the lead. Watching them on the keyboard, shaping sounds to surround me in a soothing melodious cocoon, I finally felt at peace. For a few hours, at least.

MONDAY MORNING BEGAN IN DARKNESS TO THE TUNE OF A howling wind. My bedside clock signaled daybreak, but once again clouds and rain were upstaging the sun in a most impudent way. I marched down to breakfast hoping the clouds would wring themselves dry before I ventured out to the stables. The nasty cold morning called for extra fuel, so I shoveled a large helping of eggs and biscuits onto my plate. I lingered at the table willing the rain to stop, but the steady pour stubbornly droned on. Finally, I gave up and plunged in, literally.

Wielding an umbrella would have made me too visible, so my coat and hat were drenched by the time I arrived. Grateful for my boy's clothing, I changed and dried my hair with rubdown towels. Turn-out sessions were out of the question, so I gave each horse extra grooming instead. The hypnotic stroking of the brush helped soothe my nerves from scouring the newspapers each day for the past week. They were frustratingly devoid of information, except that heavy rains had delayed the fire investigation. There was nothing more about Jonah. But Doc knew everybody in town, so I hoped he might discover news the paper wouldn't report. Plus, he'd promised to visit Jonah in jail.

The rain set in for the whole day, making my trip back that afternoon equally soaking, but I wouldn't dare miss meeting Doc at five o'clock for news. I busied myself organizing a tack room that didn't need organizing, while Wesa sat atop a saddle giving himself a thorough tongue bath. Finally, at five fifteen the stable doors rattled and I heard Doc shaking his umbrella and stomping his boots.

"Good Lord! Beatrice, we might have to start building an ark." I had to smile at the same words Granddad loved to say during an all-day downpour. We settled ourselves on the straw bales, my eyes wide with questions.

"No fire investigation report yet, and with this rain pouring again, who knows when it'll get finished." I bit my lip as Doc took out a handkerchief to mop his face and hands. "But folks are really worked up over this attempted rape charge. More incensed about that than the school burning down, it seems." My stomach churned.

"Have you seen him?"

"I went to the county jail a couple of times, but they refused to let me see him. Wouldn't tell me anything, either, and that just didn't set well with me. So, this weekend I went straight to the sheriff's house—he's a friend of mine—and found out Jonah's in the old jail, in the basement of the town hall."

"But why?! I heard they only put rabid dogs there now."

"To keep his location under wraps. For his own good, they say. Public outrage is fierce, people claiming he's dangerous." My outrage was fierce. A man who loved the outdoors like he loved his own soul was shut away in that dark hole in the earth.

"But people don't really know him. He was always a solemn person, mostly stuck to his family. I guess to others he and his wife made an odd couple. Different shades of dark. Then after she was gone, he really shut himself in. Took up more of his Native ways. Folks think he's strange and they're scared of him." Jonah was a stranger in his own town. No wonder he was bitter. "Of course, he pleaded not guilty, but, poor fella, he's so honest. He admitted being in the school and helping folks escape the fire. But people don't want to believe that's why he was there. They just don't want to believe he's a good man."

Doc gave a long, tired sigh while I picked at the straw.

"I don't understand people sometimes," he mused. "I guess that's why I work with animals."

"Smart choice."

Con Disperazione

I felt a kindred spirit with Doc on that note. I knew my business with horses, but Anna was a different matter. She had tried to avoid me after our awkward encounter Sunday evening, so I switched to a subtle approach in hopes of regaining her trust. Having never been in a fire myself, I realized it might play on a person's nerves more than I'd imagined. I sat with her at meals over the next few days, keeping our conversation light, gradually making headway in getting her to open up.

As the week wore on, I settled into a routine of alternating indoor and outdoor work. Each morning was feeding and mucking, then exercising the horses. The spirited Xander and even Copper made the most of their turnouts, but I put the draft horses through their paces on a lunge line; they needed a little encouragement to give their muscles a good workout. I'd then spend the rest of the day at the piano, always stopping in time to head to the stables by five, hoping for news. At the end of our sad conversation on Monday, I pleaded with Doc to use his influence with his commonwealth's attorney friend to seek a delay of the trial. I knew fickle Mother Nature might not let up on the rain for many more days and Jonah needed that fire investigation report ready at his trial. He said he'd try and let me know by Friday.

Every day I hoped to see Doc. Every day he didn't show up I grew more anxious.

By Thursday morning, I awoke sick with worry. But the rain had stopped and the skies were clear, so I hopefully trudged through

The Martha Odyssey

the day's chores, landing back at the stables before five. As the minutes ticked by with no sign of Doc, I abandoned my hope of news and headed directly over to Valley Street with my hope of finding Mary back from spring break. By then, stress-fueled adrenaline had me primed for a confrontation, but once again I was turned away empty-handed. Forcing black thoughts from my mind, I returned to the Martha for dinner, despondent and exasperated.

Seated with Anna, I was the one who was unresponsive for a change, too preoccupied to carry the conversation myself. Anna seemed relieved at the quiet, although I caught her casting inquisitive glances my way. My only consolation was that maybe a little pullback of my attentions might entice her to come to me.

On my way out of the dining hall, I caught sight of a newspaper left on a table near the entrance. It was a repeat of the same stories: little progress in the fire investigation; strong public sentiment against Jonah. I slammed the paper down and stormed out the door, hot tears stinging my eyes.

Without breaking stride, I marched straight to the Student Parlor and parked myself on the piano stool. I launched into a raucous Joplin rag and imagined Ruby dancing behind me, Saluda and Hazel laughing and cheering us on. I don't know how long I'd been playing when I sensed a presence in the room. If Mrs. Long had sent Rena to admonish me, I didn't care. She'd have to pry my hands off the keys with her own brute strength. But when I ended the piece and peered over my shoulder, I saw Anna hovering in the doorway.

"Anna! Come in. Take a seat." She shyly eased into the room and sat on the edge of the settee. Remembering my new tactic, I smiled and kept quiet until she finally spoke.

"I didn't know you played piano. And so well!"

"Thank you."

"I was watching your fingers. They go so fast. It's...it's fascinating."

"Well, that's the nature of most ragtime music. A bright tempo helps people feel good. Cheers them up." I kept smiling, trying to convince myself it had worked for me. "Do you have a favorite piece?"

"Oh. No. I'm not allowed . . . I mean, I've never really heard this kind of music." She lowered her eyes, looking at her hands folded in her lap. But she was responding more freely than ever before and I wanted to keep her talking.

"I guess everyone needs some cheering up these days."

"That's true." She actually looked at me then with a half-smile.

"I was just reading in the newspaper about that man. The blacksmith. How he's in jail, accused of arson. They haven't even finished investigating the cause of the fire, so they don't know yet. And, I mean, if he didn't do it, it's such a shame to punish him. Don't you think?"

"I guess so." She gave a light shrug, her head lowered again. I watched her fingers fiddle with the sash of her dress.

"The paper said some girls claim they saw him in the halls, but . . . he was probably trying to help get people out. Do you think that's possible?"

"Maybe." Her fingers tightened around the sash.

"Did you see him?"

She shook her head and stood abruptly. "I better get back to my room."

"No wait! Not until I've played something for you." My gentle gaze held her until she took her seat again. "A nice, soothing piece." Turning back to the keys, I began Schubert's "Serenade" from his *Swan Song* collection that Liszt had transcribed for piano. I'd heard Hazel sing the beautiful lyrics: a pleading in the night for a lover to come. Recently, I had often taken solace in the lovely piece, and I played it now for myself as much as for Anna. After the soft final chord, I found her snuggled into the corner of the settee, eyes closed with silent tears trickling down her cheeks.

THE "SERENADE" DIDN'T SOOTHE LIKE I'D HOPED. I SLEPT THAT night, but fitfully. Stoically, I tended Friday morning stable chores thinking only of Doc's news yet to come. I then attempted to carry

The Martha Odyssey

out the semblance of a normal day at the Martha despite my apprehension. After a lunch left half eaten, I ventured back toward the practice room, but even thoughts of the piano failed to rouse me from distress. I abandoned my good intentions and instead headed for the company of my furry companions.

I gave a delighted Copper and Xander another turnout while the draft horses were content to munch hay in their stalls. I found more leather to polish, then paced up and down the barn corridor randomly raking up straw. Finally, I climbed to the hay loft where I found Wesa curled in his grassy bed. Seating myself nearby, I stretched back against a stack of soft bundles, closing my eyes and taking in their sweet, tangy aroma. Before long, the tabby padded over and rubbed his head along my shin. He paced back and forth, stopping occasionally to look at me and utter a mournful meow. "He's coming back. Soon. I promise." He settled next to me and I soothed him with gentle strokes, the motions lulling us both to sleep. A couple of hours later, we both startled at Doc's voice from below.

"Beatrice?"

"Up here!" I scrambled toward the ladder and began a fast shimmy down its rungs.

"Sorry I haven't come 'til now. It's still birthing season and I've been up to my eyeballs in vet calls. Holy smokes, you okay there?" I'd nearly lost my footing as I plopped to the ground.

"I'm fine. Just please tell me something good."

The somber look on his face told me he would not.

"Public outcry is getting out of hand. People are riled up, saying the trial won't come swiftly enough. There's no way the judge will agree to delay."

"But the fire report! What if it isn't complete by then?"

"Well, he says surely it will be, but I don't know. What I'm really afraid of is that whatever it says won't make a difference for Jonah's fate. The outrage over the attempted rape charge is so heated, he's already been tried and convicted in the court of public opinion for that. Pinning the fire on him as well is just convenient. People need somebody to blame and they've made Jonah their target." My stomach quailed in anguish. Without a confession from Mary, Jonah's fate was sealed.

"If he's convicted in court, what will happen to him?"

"That'll be the worst tragedy in all of this." He took a moment to heave a deep sigh. "A state prison guard will escort him to Richmond, to die in the electric chair." I sat in horrified silence. I'd heard of these executions, but they always seemed unreal, like something from a bizarre ghost story. An atrocious way to die. Doc hung his head. "What a damn shame."

There were no more words after that. After several long moments, he rose to his feet and reached into his jacket pocket, pulling out a wad of dollar bills that he held out to me. "Here, this is for you. For all the work you've done."

I looked at the bills, mute and dull-eyed. I didn't want money; I'd taken care of the horses out of love. But he was insistent.

"There's a young man needing to work off a vet bill for his family. He'll take over for you before school starts up again next week. He's coming Sunday afternoon about four o'clock. I can't be here then, but told him 'Benjamin' would show him what to do."

He patted my shoulder before leaving with a promise to check on the new stable hand at the first of the week. Before he walked out the door, he turned to me again. "Try to keep your chin up, young lady. All you can do now is pray."

I stared after him as he walked out of sight. Trembling, I quickly stuffed the folded bills in my pocket, secured the stables, and took off for Valley Street at a run. I raced up to the house where Mary lodged, vowing to plant myself on the front steps until she arrived. Long after ringing the doorbell, I kept hammering on the door until the alarmed lady of the house answered and finally asked me inside. She was probably relieved I would no longer be pestering her.

Mary was called into the family's parlor, rather taken aback when she saw me sitting there. I asked to take Mary for a walk and the woman readily obliged, glad to be rid of us both. We made small talk as we strolled down the street, but as soon as we were a block away, I came to my point.

"Look Mary, this isn't a social call and I think you know it."

"I don't know what you mean."

"You do so know. The whole town is talking about it, and an innocent man is in jail."

"How dare you call him innocent. He tried to assault me. I almost lost my virginity."

"You almost lost your life! He was only there helping people get out of a burning building."

"Ha! That's what he says. Who's going to believe a dirty Indian?"

A sudden popping sound jolted us both. Mary stared at me wide-eyed, cupping her hand to a fiery red cheek. Without thinking, I had slapped her soundly across the face. Her astonishment quickly turned to anger and she turned to walk away. I roughly grabbed her arm to hold her in place.

"Look, I don't know why you told such an outrageous story, but you've got to go to the authorities and tell them the truth."

"I've already told them the truth!" Stronger than I expected, she wrenched herself free and stomped back up the street toward the house.

"A man's life is at stake!" I called after her, but she ran all the way until the front door slammed behind her. I stood alone on the street, as alone as I had ever felt.

Exasperated and distraught, I returned to the stables, unlocked the front doors, and stepped into the wide corridor. I stood looking at Xander, and at Copper, then the draft horses. The horses I loved. That Jonah loved. I looked through Xander's window at the forge, where Jonah had toiled and sweated over the fire. Protecting horses' feet and creating beautiful works of art from cold steel. Making hot coffee and sharing food with a bedraggled girl who'd taken refuge in the straw. Healing her, protecting her. Awakening a thrill and a hunger in her that she'd never known before.

Doc had told me all I could do was pray, and I shut my eyes and tried. But instead of comfort, I felt only profound frustration and sat down hard on the straw bales, thrusting my face into my hands. The bulge of folded bills bounced against my thigh and I pulled it from my pocket. For a long while I stared at the money. Then I decided to do far more than just pray.

Tremolo

"You've got to trust me." A warning blast of breath hissed from swollen nostrils. Coal black eyes rimmed in white glared at me as I approached with the folded blanket. I ran one hand over the satiny black pelt, I hoped with a reassuring touch. "If you love him, and I know you do, you've got to trust me." Slowly he accepted my hands and allowed the blanket on his back. Keeping my voice at a low pitch, I continued talking as I followed up with a saddle. He grudgingly cooperated, keeping one eye fixed on me. Once I tightened the girth, he and I both knew the battle was over. The bridle was then no problem, especially with a filled hay bag dangling in front of him. I then headed back toward the Martha under cover of my long-time enemy: darkness.

Reaching the edge of campus, I gave the grounds a thorough survey before slowly crossing to the rough hedgerow at the rear of Litchfield Hall. After coiling my muffler tightly around my head with only a slit for my eyes, my gloved hands parted the prickly branches and I gingerly climbed into their midst. As the brambles quickly flung back into place, I crouched to search for the wooden cellar door Ruby described in her hazing adventure. My hand finally landed on a metal latch and sure enough, its rusty lock gave way. Slowly I heaved the door open, a dank smell of moldering earth rising up to penetrate even my tightly wrapped muffler. Reluctantly, I lowered myself into the gaping hole while pulling the door shut above my head.

As if I'd fallen into a giant inkwell, utter blackness surrounded me. Seized by panic, I fumbled in my pocket for the flashlight, my violent trembling causing it to fall from my grasp. I stifled a cry as it bounced against the hard rock steps and rolled away into the abyss. Breathing in quivering gasps, I felt my way down to the dirt floor and began to crawl. Desperately patting the cold earth, my terror swelled until the flashlight's chilly cylinder finally rolled beneath my fingers. Hungrily I scooped it up with both hands and flipped its switch. A soft circle of light sprang forth, to my frantic soul more beautiful than a glorious sunrise.

I got to my feet, only to bump my head on the hardened earth ceiling. The tunnel was shallower that I'd imagined and my towering height forced me to hunch over. Shining my beam on the ceiling, I saw the tunnel had been hewn out of the raw earth, leaving only rock and dirt, unbraced with wooden beams or metal rods. Trying not to think of the precarious hole I had just entered or the soldiers who had met their death in that forbidding passageway, I began my journey. The tang of the fusty earth stung my nostrils as I searched ahead for the crude wooden planks that sat at my destination.

After what felt like an hour but could only have been minutes, my light landed on the wooden door plugging the end of the tunnel. Navigating the crude steps leading to it, I stepped down and located the turn-button latch. Propping the flashlight between my knees, I worked at the latch to slide it upright, braced my shoulder against the door, and pushed. It sprang open much easier than I'd anticipated and I tumbled into the room, sharp yapping erupting near my head. The flashlight rolled across the floor but gave enough light for me to quickly pull slices of bacon from my pocket and toss them into the dogs' cell. Luckily, there were only two dogs, so each got a substantial treat and quieted instantly. I grabbed up my light and trained it into the other cell, where Jonah's shocked eyes locked with mine.

"Beatrice," he whispered. I put my finger to my lips to shush him. Obviously, no one had been around when Ruby's group came here, but with a human prisoner, I couldn't be sure there wasn't a guard outside. I felt along the walls until I located the cell keys on a peg and headed straight to Jonah's cell door. As I began working a key into the lock, Jonah put his hands through the bars and closed them over mine. In the faint light I saw him frantically shaking his head, but I leaned forward to whisper in his ear.

"You have to trust me," I found myself saying for the second time that night. I then held his eyes with mine, trying to telegraph my entire desperate message with one look. Slowly, he released my hands and watched as I carefully unlocked the door to his miserable prison. As Jonah stepped out, I quickly returned the keys to their peg and carefully turned my light toward the wooden door to the tunnel. We both crawled through and Jonah pulled the door snugly shut and fastened the latch. We climbed the few roughhewn steps and started our cramped trek through the tunnel.

When I determined we were about halfway through, I stopped to listen behind us. All was quiet. Relieved we hadn't been detected, I sat down to catch my breath. Also, Jonah deserved an explanation.

"Thank you for trusting me."

"*I* should thank *you*, but Beatrice—the risk! I'd never want—"

"But you're in serious danger. Do you know what's happening?"

"No one tells me anything. They just bring in food, stare at me, and sneer. I know better than to ask."

"You're facing execution." I told him everything Doc had shared with me. Then I told him Mary's ludicrous story that had led to his arrest. Jonah frowned and shook his head.

"The roof was on fire, so I ran straight to the top floor, and the first door I banged on popped open right away. There was a full moon that night, shining in the window, and I could see a girl kneeling on the bed. But it wasn't me who was clutching her. I saw—"

Suddenly a cracking sound silenced him and a fine mist of jagged pebbles fell to Jonah's shoulder. He shifted away and I trained the flashlight upwards only to find the same gravely debris raining down on my head. We both crawled out of the way just as some rocks the size of baseballs came tumbling down. As they pelted the dirt floor, a thunderous cracking within the rocky ceiling above sent a rip of terror through my gut. "Run!" Jonah cried as he pushed me forward and followed close behind. I lunged ahead with as much speed as my trembling legs could manage, spurred by the deathly pounding of boulders hitting the tunnel floor behind us. My flashlight beam bounced in a chaotic dance along the narrow walls, desperate to find the stairs to the cellar door that led outside. When they finally appeared, I threw myself on them, pulling Jonah with me.

We sat in a quiet daze, letting our breathing steady and listening to the rumbling sounds as they gradually died away. In the eerie silence I directed my light back over our path, finding only a cloud of dust visible in the distance. Decades of heavy traffic on Main Street above had finally taken its toll. No one would traverse the famous Civil War tunnel ever again.

My heart still pounding, I told Jonah what lay beyond the cellar door. He suggested we crawl on our bellies until we reached the pines, an idea I wished I'd thought of before. Taking in ragged breaths, I grabbed fistfuls of the dewy grass and propelled myself forward, braced to hear the threatening yell of someone who had seen us. Finally, we made it to the pine grove and I led Jonah over the path I'd come to know so well.

Once inside the stables, my light found Xander at the opposite end. As we approached, he pricked his ears and gave a soft joyful nicker, then nuzzled Jonah's back while he enjoyed a long hug from his master. I stood back and let them enjoy their reunion as long as I dared.

"We have to get moving, Jonah." He released his hold and turned.

"We?"

"Yes." I explained my plan.

A train would be leaving from the Bristol depot at two a.m. traveling south. We would ride Xander together the fifteen miles to a hidden spot near that depot. Jonah would walk a final mile, then jump a freight car and ride hidden away until it reached the end of its line, in Whittier, North Carolina. I pressed a list of connecting trains into his hands, and prayed he could find them in the dark.

"I remembered you telling me a community of Cherokee people live near there. You'll find them and they'll help you." Suddenly he was hugging me as tightly as he had Xander.

"I haven't known kindness like this since my Schumacher parents."

I clung to him, not wanting the hug to end. But he was in danger every minute he stayed put and I forced myself to break away. I lifted his spare jacket off a wall hook.

"Here, put this on. I've packed my music satchel with some food and a canteen of water. There's one of my skirts and a shirtwaist, for disguise. Just leave some buttons undone and wear the jacket over them with the belt on the outside. There's also a lady's hat and a pair of glasses. And some money."

"Beatrice, I can't take—"

"No, it's fine. It's really from Doc, he paid me for taking care of the horses all this time."

"He's a good man."

"He says the same about you. And you're both right."

We walked Xander out, shutting the stable doors and corral gate behind us. Once safely surrounded by trees, Jonah mounted and helped me up to sit behind him, the satchel slung over my shoulder. I hadn't thought through a travel route, but Jonah knew the forests intimately, the twists and turns of every creek and branch. He knew exactly where to go and pointed out landmarks for me to look for on my return journey. I took note of each, but didn't want to think about that. I simply held on tight, relishing the chance to hold Jonah close and rest my head against his neck.

Xander seemed to understand the urgency of our mission and used his pent-up energy to speed us through the darkness. We made good time, coming to stop in a patch of trees a safe distance from the depot by one o'clock. I slid off the horse's back and tied his reins to a branch while Jonah dismounted. I wanted everything to move in slow motion, every moment preserved for as long as possible. I handed Jonah the satchel, but he set it on the ground and stepped to Xander's head. Placing his forehead against the horse's neck, he stroked the long locks of his mane.

"Czar Alexander. My trusty emperor. Take good care of Beatrice now."

He turned to me then, his image blurred from thick tears flooding my eyes. The possibility I might never see him again nearly rendered me in two. Suddenly his arms were around me and his mouth covered mine. I held him tight, drinking in the kiss like a parched desert traveler desperate for water. Everything we were to each other was spoken in that one kiss.

When it came to an end that neither of us wanted, we slowly, painfully, released each other. Jonah picked up the satchel and looked back to me, but we both knew we were beyond words. He shouldered the bag and began to walk away. I watched, even after the darkness had swallowed him, until the whisper of his footsteps dissolved into lonely silence.

I turned toward Xander and found him looking straight at me. His eyes told me we shared the same heartache. Slowly I untied him and placed my foot in the stirrup. I'd never mounted him alone, and as I swung myself into the saddle I braced for a battle. But he stood quietly like a perfect gentleman, revealing the depth of his loyalty. He would be true to his master's command and take good care of me.

Our journey back to Abingdon was less speedy since I needed to search for landmarks Jonah had pointed out. But Xander seemed to recognize all the right paths before I did and adjusted direction on his own. Slowly I calmed from the adrenaline-fueled efforts of the previous hours, hoping all the while that Jonah was safe on the train. Retracing the events of the night, it suddenly occurred to me that in our mad rush to escape the tunnel Jonah hadn't finished telling me who he'd seen with Mary on the night of the fire. Whoever it was, Mary was desperate to conceal their identity despite the deadly consequences for an innocent man. It was up to me to discover the truth and undo those consequences.

We made it safely back to the stables well before sunrise, both of us bone-tired and grieving our loss. Before I dismounted, I closed my eyes and imagined Jonah reaching into the satchel and finding the tiny cedar horse I had placed there. "Please keep him safe," I whispered. Xander stood perfectly still, honoring the prayer. We were both solemn as I cooled him properly and took extra care with his rubdown; he had more than earned it. I fed and watered all the horses before I left, because once I climbed into my bed, I had no idea when I would rise again.

Staccato

A muffled thumping tickled my ear and I pulled the covers over my head. The thumping grew staccato, no doubt a brazen woodpecker on the windowsill. But I didn't want to leave my warm nest to scare him off. It persisted, coming faster and more intrusive, growing into a loud cracking of jagged rocks that flew at my face. I threw up my arms to shield myself and when I felt nothing, opened my eyes to stare at bright daylight flooding the room.

I scrambled up to answer the insistent knocking on my door.

"April Fools'—I'm back!" Ruby sang and struck a fanciful pose, her arms and legs taking up the entire doorway.

"I thought you were coming back tomorrow?"

"I know, but it got boring at home. And besides, I missed my Honey Bea!" She had walked in and plopped on my bed. "You were still in bed? Who's the sleepyhead now?"

"What time is it?" I asked through a yawn.

"Half-past noon! My, but you've become quite the lady of leisure while I was away."

"Oh, Ruby. You don't know the half of it."

"Get dressed so we can go eat."

"We're too late, lunch is almost over."

"Not here, this place is crazy. Bunches of girls checking back in today. I'll treat you to lunch at Maiden's Drug Store." I looked at her, incredulous. "Don't be so surprised. *I* was a lady of *industry* over break. I'm flush with cash at the moment." She hopped up and scampered out the door. "Meet me downstairs in ten!"

The Martha Odyssey

When we arrived at Maiden's, it was crawling with people. All the tables were full, but we nabbed the last two stools at the counter. While Ruby kept up her usual chatter as we lunched, I surreptitiously listened to bits of conversation around us. News of Jonah's jailbreak was already out with agitated speculation rippling through the crowd. The stories were ridiculous, ranging from drunken jail keepers to Jonah using Indian magic to spirit himself away. I could rescue him from iron bars, but not from the hateful judgments of those hungry for a scapegoat and hell-bent on condemning him. A search party had already been dispatched, and I decided to take Doc's advice after all. I prayed Jonah was tucked safely deep inside a train, or even somewhere in the forests of western North Carolina.

By Sunday afternoon, the Martha hallways were again abuzz with girls laughing, talking, showing off new frocks, or talking about their beaus. I drifted through them in a haze, speaking when necessary, smiling when obliged. Jonah was never far from my thoughts. I could focus only on the fire investigation report that would surely surface the following day, trial or not. It would prove Jonah hadn't started the fire, making it clear he was actually a hero who helped people escape. Mary's story would then be rendered absurd, seen only as simple hysteria in a young girl traumatized by fire. I pinned all my hopes to that premise.

On Monday, I steeled myself to attend classes and duties, my nerves in a bundle waiting for news from court that finally emerged midafternoon. The cause of the Stonewall fire had been determined as faulty wiring, and Jonah's charges of arson were dismissed. Ironically, the cause of Jonah's wagon shed fire was determined as clearly arson; traces of kerosene residue had been found along its foundation and near its vehicles. But as it was unrelated to the Stonewall fire, and Jonah was a fugitive still facing criminal charges, the law had little interest in finding the culprit. I was incensed and bewildered. Taming that fire was the only reason Jonah had seen the Stonewall fire and rushed to help people escape. And he'd been landed in jail for his trouble.

My premise that Mary's story would be discredited had proved false. The attempted rape charge still stood, and now Jonah also faced a possible charge for felony escape. A new trial date was set for April 17, meaning I had only two weeks to get Mary to tell the truth. I would have to double down on my efforts, but for the moment I needed to devote the remainder of the afternoon and evening to another quest.

The date for the music scholarship competition was May 27, only eight weeks away now. Professor Zeisberg had announced a special master class for the next day for those entering the contest, no doubt to check for slacking off during spring break. Although I was no slacker, events of the past few days had gobbled up my time and energy, leaving me with a practice deficit to make up. But I was actually grateful. With the multitude of anxieties pressing on me, escaping into another realm via music was a saving grace more than ever.

THE AIR THICKENED WITH TENSION WHEN VARINA AND I SAW each other at the Tuesday master class. She had returned from spring break sporting a huge engagement ring from Charles, which she made a show of removing and placing on the piano's music shelf before sitting down to play. The pear-shaped diamond sat between two sparkling sapphires that "Charles chose to match my eyes," I heard her tell some girls later, prompting coos of admiration. Still, she was my biggest obstacle, the one I had to defeat. Facing the possibility of never seeing Jonah again, winning the scholarship meant more to me now than ever before.

Many of my hours sequestered in the practice room had been devoted to my competition piece, Chopin's *Polonaise-Fantaisie* opus 61 in A-flat. Still, Professor Zeisberg was not totally pleased with my rendition. "You show marvelous technique with your fingers, but where is your heart? You have to make the instrument sing, convey the warmth and beauty of the piece along with exacting accuracy of notes." He had posed a good question and a compelling challenge. The piece was a fantasy as well as a dance, reflecting Chopin's sense of imagination in the way he explored new ways to blend harmonies and melodies. But that was not where my heart was at the moment. I needed to relax and give over to that creative spirit. It was a struggle.

I watched Varina play, trying to listen beyond her exceptional technique to hear if she made her piece "sing." Her heart, if she had one, was in a different place than mine. She probably believed her engagement to Charles was killing me with jealousy, which of course would give her no end of delight. That thought alone probably spurred her into a spirited performance fueled by her own special brand of spite. Too bad she didn't play a Liszt *Mephisto Waltz*. A devil's dance certainly suited her. But how she achieved her performance wouldn't matter. If it was artistically superior to mine, I would lose.

Accelerando

After that, I needed solace in the form of horses. I also wanted to see how Roy, the new stable hand, was managing the instructions I'd given him on Sunday. Even dressed in boy's clothing, I'd suspected Roy had figured out my gender. Still, he didn't mention it and called me Benjamin.

When I arrived, he seemed to be doing fine but appreciated my offer to exercise the horses. I took one of the draft horses to the front corral and began circling him on the lunge line. Standing in the center, I noticed a large white sheet of paper tacked to the stable door. Slowing the horse to a halt, I stepped closer to read it, then in disbelief jerked it down to read again.

It was an official court notice, declaring the seizure of Jonah's property for delinquent tax payment and giving him twenty-one days to respond. If he did not come forth to make restitution by April 24 at 9:00 a.m., his property would be sold at auction.

My screams of indignation brought Roy rushing from the feed room. The low-pitched voice of my disguise had vanished, replaced by a shrill tone devoid of caution. I crumpled the notice and threw it to the ground, pacing the corral like a caged lioness. Roy picked it up and smoothed the paper, reading with widened eyes.

"Can they do that?" He frowned and scratched his ear.

"There's got to be some mistake. This is not right!" The gentle draft horse looked at me with sad eyes, then shook his head and lowered it to nibble fresh sprouts of grass at the corral's edge. "Is Doc Gilmer coming here today?"

The Martha Odyssey

I had been hoping to take Copper for a ride, but I didn't dare leave the premises until Doc arrived. I ran to meet him at the stable doors, strangling the notice in my hand.

"They can't really do this, can they?" He glanced only briefly at the paper, already knowing what it said.

"Sadly, they can. Jonah's county records show he hasn't paid his taxes for nearly three years. Thinking back, I realized that's about how long it's been since his wife died. Still, the law can be . . ." Doc heaved a sigh and frowned. I knew he had the same thought I had, that this was a ploy to get Jonah to return for trial. Even though he'd been proven innocent of setting the Stonewall fire, public outrage over the attempted rape held fast and people were angry over his escape. I had just wanted Jonah out of danger. To stay alive until there was time to get his name cleared. Now his property might be taken from him.

"Ah, it's a mess," Doc declared, shaking his head. "A mess and a damn shame."

I wondered if Jonah could even know about the impending foreclosure. But Doc had checked with the newspaper office and the story had been shared with every single newspaper within a one-hundred-mile radius of Abingdon. Jonah had a right to know what was happening with his property, but still I didn't want him to return until his name was cleared. Uncovering the truth could resolve all of this, and I was the only one who could make that happen.

WITH EACH PASSING DAY, I HEARD THE CLOCK TICKING LOUDER and louder, my task made more urgent by fear of Jonah's return. They would slap him with the felony escape charge and throw him back in that awful hole with the rabid dogs. Even roaming the woods exposed to the elements was preferable to that.

Every day after classes, I would sneak away from campus and land on Mary's doorstep. The lady of the house would go to fetch her, leaving me on the porch for longer and longer waits, then return to tell me, "Mary says she's under the weather and cannot possibly receive visitors at this time." Heading back to the Martha, I would pass the posters that had sprung up all over town. "Wanted, Dead or Alive" with Jonah's photograph. They sent a chill through me every time I laid eyes on one.

My hunch that Anna knew the truth was still quite vivid, but she eluded me as well. Other Stonewall students housed with us had returned, forming a protective clique that she was clinging to like a barnacle. I needed a clever way to separate her from the herd.

On top of it all, Martha's music students now had an extra obligation heaped upon our already heavy load. The conservatory had been charged with providing all the special music for Easter services at the Methodist Episcopal church, and our professors were determined it would be spectacular. Extra rehearsal time was usurping evening hours on most days, cutting into my available time to approach Mary or Anna.

But the weekend proved equally unsuccessful. Mary went back to Roanoke for an unnecessary (in my opinion) visit, and Anna went home with a classmate. This left me only with time to think, which, while painful, was fortuitous.

I realized I'd been working so hard to get Mary to recant, I hadn't known exactly how to make that happen with the court. Doc seemed to know everyone involved with law enforcement, so I put a hypothetical question to him. He told me the local commonwealth's attorney could hear such a statement in a private meeting, before the trial. Then, in the absence of enough evidence to obtain a conviction, he could announce to the court his decision not to prosecute. This was a relief to hear. Knowing she could speak in private rather than in court was bound to put Mary at ease and convince her to acquiesce.

For the rest of the weekend, I alternated rides on Copper with putting in much-needed practice time for the competition. It seemed ages ago that in those practice rooms I was plagued by an imaginary phantom playing a violin. Now those hauntings were replaced by thoughts of sinister possibilities all too real. Visions of Jonah's face on wanted posters swirled in my head, along with bounty hunters roaming not only southwest Virginia but eastern Tennessee, western North Carolina, and even eastern Kentucky and southern West Virginia. But as long as Jonah eluded capture, I tried to imagine him safe and surrounded by people who cared about him. It took incredible willpower to hang on to that picture and quash all other scenarios. But to survive, and succeed, I would have to.

ON MONDAY I TRIED TO PUT THE WEEKEND'S FRUSTRATION AND anxiety behind me. With renewed determination, I marched back to Mary's temporary home that afternoon, but not only did she refuse to see me, she ordered me to stop coming. The lady of the house seemed embarrassed to deliver that message, and I imagined playing host to a willful, selfish young girl was wearing her down. She had my deepest sympathy.

I doubled down my efforts towards Anna. She still managed to elude me, so by Tuesday I devised a plan to knock on her door at bedtime, when she was compelled to be alone. Tucking away that idea, I attended that evening's Easter music rehearsal, then cloistered myself in a practice room to work on conjuring the heart of my competition piece. But I became totally absorbed in it, stayed longer than anticipated, and didn't make it to Anna's room before light bell. In the dark I crept to her door anyway, but she never answered my knock. Cursing myself, I returned to my room, only to toss and turn the night away.

Wednesday morning, I awoke reeling from frustration at my failures. Nearly out of ideas, I needed to start thinking like Mary but had a hard time getting into her head. She obviously felt no remorse. I didn't know how to deal with someone like that. Or did I?

There was no time to muse further; the agenda for the day was crammed full. With no morning chores at the stables, my load was easier, but I missed that extra time with the horses. By afternoon, I decided the smell of hay and manure was just what I needed to clear my head, so as soon as my last class dismissed, I slipped away.

Watching Copper and Xander revel in their turnouts was a balm to my soul. I longed to frolic with abandon like they did, wondering how long it had been since I had. After they were spent, I tucked them into their stalls and brought a draft horse into the corral to exercise. It occurred to me that I now had more in common with him—plodding heavily along, forced to move forward while tethered to a line, working at someone else's will.

Doc stopped by for a brief check-in and I momentarily brightened, hoping for good news. He laid a gentle hand on my arm. "Not yet, but maybe soon. I heard bounty hunters are going deeper into western North Carolina where there's a Cherokee community. They think he might have taken refuge with his own kind." A fright bolted through me like a shock of electricity. I went rigid in my effort to hide it. Then Doc's face went grim and his eyes darkened. "If he's brought back for trial, though, I'm afraid he's going to need a miracle." He bid us goodbye and shuffled away.

Anxious frustration swelled inside me anew. That miracle depended on me.

It was getting late, so I put away the lunge lines to hurry back to campus. But just outside the tack room door, something unusual caught my eye: hanging on a peg was a rather formal-looking black hat that looked oddly familiar. I plucked it off for a closer look.

"Like my new hat?" Roy grinned as he rounded the corner with a wheelbarrow.

"This is yours?"

"Yup. Found it in the crotch of a maple tree when I was cleaning up the burnt stuff in the old wagon shed. It was all wet and kinda punched in, but I dried it out and brushed it up." He popped it on his head. "I think it makes me look smart!" He gave another quirky grin before handing it back to me. "But I don't wear it while I work, it's too fancy for that."

I turned it over and examined the inner lining. The fine gray silk was water-stained, but some black threaded embroidery was undamaged and distinct. I angled it toward the light and read "C. E. S.," each letter the same size, the original owner's initials.

"Could I borrow this? Just for a couple of days?"

"Ah . . . well, sure! What? You got somebody you want to impress?" He lightly punched me in the arm.

"You might say that."

THERE WAS NO EXTRA REHEARSAL FOR EASTER ON WEDNESDAYS, so after dinner I went to work in the practice room. It should have been a good distraction, but the more I played my competition piece, the more I felt out of sync with it. Any tactic I tried seemed to fall flat. It was obvious the inherent nature of the piece didn't fit what was going on in my soul, and I soon abandoned it in favor of old favorites. Not a disciplined approach to preparing for a competition, but I felt incapable of doing anything else. It was also easier to keep a careful eye on the time.

I left early enough to reach Anna's room while the halls were still lighted, and on the way, I fetched my new prop from my room. Calmly and casually, I strolled to her door, Roy's refurbished hat tucked neatly into a cloth bag looking like poorly bundled knitting. After a couple of attempts at knocking, her neighbor happened by and told me Anna was in the infirmary, and had been since the day before. My heart sank, showing as much on my face, making me immediately guilty. I clumsily offered well wishes, but her suspicious friend said she had no idea when Anna would return. Tired of my efforts being thwarted at every turn, I decided to take to the street with my new piece of ammunition.

Thursday dawned cloudy and drizzly, a light spring rain to green up the grass and refresh the jonquils. I hoped for clear weather by midafternoon, but luck didn't serve me. At four o'clock, under shelter of a sparse umbrella, I stood on the corner of Main and

Pecan Streets in front of the Presbyterian church. Looking east, Main Street took a steep incline up a hill to the courthouse at the top, positioned directly across from the Dagmar Hotel where the Stonewall girls took classes. Court Street crossed Main, flanking both buildings on their east sides, with a statue of a Confederate soldier keeping guard at the intersection. "The Common Foot Soldier," it was called, a man in scruffy clothing wielding a long rifle. Was that what I was? Minus the rifle, of course. My only weapon was in a cloth bag clutched tightly to my chest. Shaking each foot by turns to fend off the wet, I began to wonder if I'd been told the correct time for classes to end. Then suddenly I glimpsed what I was waiting for. The Stonewall girls were unmistakable, resupplied after the fire with old gray uniforms, whether they fit or not. Three umbrellas came bouncing down the street toward me, tilted forward in a futile attempt to keep dry the too-long wool skirts undulating beneath them. They were chatting and laughing in spite of the weather.

When they reached the corner and began to cross Pecan Street, the girl in the middle suddenly halted, jerking the others back so severely they nearly went sprawling. I stared directly into the middle girl's face to see Mary's astonished eyes glaring back at me. Amidst cries of protest, Mary steered the girls into an abrupt right turn and proceeded across Main Street, barely escaping collision with a passing buggy. Clutching them tightly, she forced them to pick up speed as they traveled along Pecan heading for Valley Street. I had to wait for a motor car and a man on horseback to pass before I could follow, and they gained a good fifty feet on me. Putting my long legs into high gear, I was soon trotting along right behind them as the drizzle turned into a downpour.

After a left turn, we were all traveling west on Valley Street in the direction of Mary's home a scant block and a half away. I tried calling her name, but she looked straight ahead, never breaking her stride. I called again and the other girls looked back, curious, then tried to get Mary's attention. She stubbornly ignored them and plowed ahead while holding their arms in a vice grip. When she reached the house, she unceremoniously detached herself and stomped up the steps to the front door. The other girls looked at each other, then back at me, totally perplexed. In the driving rain, I trudged back to the Martha and hunkered in my room, nursing my wounds at being foiled yet again.

MY ERRATIC CONCENTRATION MADE EVERY TASK MORE DIFFIcult, and approaching the piano at Friday's master class felt surreal. I closed my eyes and willed myself to transform the composer's notations into the sounds of his soul. My fingers touched every correct key in the correct time, but a familiar tug of disappointment stirred in my gut. I had not yet made peace with Chopin's *Polonaise-Fantaisie*.

But I was still determined to outwit Mary. That afternoon, I walked all the way to the door of the Dagmar as classes ended, making it impossible for her to avoid me. Then her friends told me she'd left early for a weekend excursion with her host family. I was convinced she was simply trying to hide until the trial was over.

One last hope for the day presented itself when I learned Anna was released from the infirmary. After light bell that evening, I tucked the cloth bag with Roy's refurbished hat under my arm and navigated the darkened hallways to Anna's door. At first, my quiet knocking brought no response, but with insistent muffled rapping, it finally opened a tiny crack. Anna's sleepy eyes peered at me from her thin face, framed by a tangled mass of mousy hair.

"It's Bea, Anna." I pushed open the door and walked in without waiting for an invitation. When I flicked on my flashlight, she quickly closed the door while I quietly took a seat in her vanity chair. Never taking her eyes off me, she slowly walked back to her bed and sat. I removed the hat from my bag.

"Have you seen this? Ever seen anyone wearing it?" Anna fixed her stare on the black Homburg. Her soft brows knitted together and she shook her head. I had fixed my own stare on her face and when she looked up, she instantly turned her eyes away. I got right to the point.

"On the night of the fire, before it started, did Mary have a man in her room?" She turned back with an expression of true surprise. "You know I was with Mary when she told her story to the fire marshal, don't you?" Another surprise that appeared to baffle her.

"No. I didn't know," she stammered.

"But I suspect her story is a lie." She pressed her lips together and stared straight ahead. "And even if Mary is the one who lied to the law, if you know the truth but don't tell it, you are just as much at fault." I was leaning toward her, but she held her gaze straight. "Helping someone to lie is like bearing false witness yourself." Finally, I stood over her. "You would be guilty of the *sin* of lying!" I was counting on her pious belief in the Bible and the Ten Commandments to break her. She only pulled up her knees, wrapped her arms around them, and began to rock on the bed, trembling. Her show of fright told me my suspicions were on target, but without words from her, I was powerless.

There was only one more person I could interrogate.

Con Brio

I slept surprisingly late on Saturday morning, exhausted from the past week. Each day had played out like another verse of a dirge. Rumors and speculation were rampant and ridiculous. Some said the longer Jonah was gone, the more it proved he was guilty. And despite the dismissal of the arson charge, some said proceeds from the auction of his property would go toward making reparations for the burned school. Had the authorities really hoped to lure Jonah back for trial or was the foreclosure simply to placate the public? Regardless, time was running out and my efforts to set things right were falling short at every turn. I felt encased in the bottom of a giant hourglass, its sands spilling rapidly over my head, threatening to bury me alive.

I grabbed a quick lunch and then trekked to the stable with Roy's hat in tow. He asked if its charms had worked for me.

"Well, I'm actually not quite finished with it, but I thought you might want to wear it to church tomorrow. Then could I borrow it again in the afternoon?"

"Oh, sure thing. I'll just leave it hanging right here in its favorite spot."

He lovingly gave it a brushing, then hung it on its revered peg, high above a workman's earthy toil. He was abuzz with news, telling me that every day since the notice, men had come around to look the place over. I knew from Doc that people had always resented Jonah's ownership of that property, a prime spot near the center of town. His inheritance from a white man, despite his being Mr.

Schumacher's legal son. Now the hungry vultures were circling the property to pick at the carcass of Jonah's spoiled livelihood.

I took Copper for a ride away from the stable, and when we reached the Meadows, I gave him his head. He took off at a raging gallop, one that could not be fast enough for me. I closed my eyes and imagined us flying, far, far away. Soaring over trees and mountains and rivers, into the hills of North Carolina. We would land deep in the forest, find Jonah, and hide away forever.

When we returned to the stables, Roy was still hard at work. "I'll be stayin' late today," he said, filling a water bucket. "Got to clean up in the forge. Some high-roller buyer's comin' in tomorrow to see it." My heart clenched at the thought. With Jonah's land and buildings coveted by so many, there would be a string of hopeful buyers preparing competitive offers. I told Roy I'd finish watering the horses so he could get started, and he scurried out to the forge.

I lifted the heavy bucket and headed for the first stall on the far end of the corridor. As water splashed into the trough, I heard overtones of whistling from the front corral. A boisterous, overpowering tune, nothing like Roy's usual whimsies. I stepped from the stall, then stopped short. There was Charles, waltzing into the stables, hands in his pockets and blithely assaulting our ears with his shrill melody.

"What are you doing here?" The sight of his immaculate suit and polished shoes in a barn were always jarring.

"Well, Beatrice. I'm just here to conduct a little business. I see you're still doing the heavy lifting for your boyfriend, even after he flew the coop." He never looked at me, just nonchalantly walked around, peering into stalls and utility rooms. I ignored his nasty remark.

"You already filched what you wanted from here."

"Aw, now don't be like that. I'm looking to buy this place, now that it's so conveniently up for sale. Then you could come work for me." He let loose a snarky laugh.

"It's not for sale. Not yet." I dropped the bucket at the spigot with a loud clang and turned to face him, hands braced firmly on my hips. "You should be afraid to come around here after what you've done."

"I just took what was rightfully mine."

"Just like you took that poor Stonewall girl?" He stopped mid-saunter and swung around to finally look at me.

"What the hell are you talking about?"

"You were seen. In her bed. The night Stonewall burned." I had no proof it was Charles, but I had to test him.

"You've been breathing in horse manure too long, Beatrice. It's done something to your brain."

"That girl sheltered with me at the Martha right after the fire. She told me so herself." My gaze held steady as I lied, but he seemed truly flabbergasted.

"Those Stonewall girls are so tightly reined it's no wonder they end up cultivating gigantic imaginations. And the more they're repressed, the wilder their stories. Why in the world would I waste my time with one of those tight-assed prudes? Marching around in their stiff little military uniforms. Yes, most alluring. More than any healthy red-blooded young man can resist." His head waggled as he spilled sarcasm. Then he laughed out loud. "Why, Beatrice, you've insulted my manhood! This is Charles Sloan you're talking about. Ladies flock to me. And you did, too, remember. Thank God I realized my mistake soon enough." I wanted to shout that the mistake was mine, but held my tongue. "Just rest assured, I never want for female company. There's no reason I would ever go sniffing around that ultra-pious hen house." His arrogance was insufferable. "Ah, Beatrice, you're just jealous your savage boyfriend took a shine to one of those uptight lasses. Even though he did have to take her by force." He threw back his head in a mocking guffaw and I barely held back my rage.

"I know for a fact you were in the vicinity!" I snatched the hat from its peg and thrust it at him. "This was found, in a tree.

Where there used to be a wagon shed." I spoke the last sentence with slow deliberate emphasis and watched his reaction. He took one look at the hat and abruptly stopped laughing; I saw a momentary break in his façade.

"So. You found a hat. Good for you."

"Not just any hat. A black Homburg, custom made."

"Someone has very good taste." He clasped his hands behind his back and began to wander the stable corridor again.

"No one else but you wears such a pompous hat." He continued his slow saunter. "Initials are embroidered in the silk lining." Still, he ignored me. "C. E. S." He stopped and stood still for a moment, then turned on his heel and walked confidently toward me.

"Ah. You don't say." He took the hat and turned it over in his hands.

"It belongs to Charles Edgar Sloan, lost on the night of the literary society debate at the Martha. The same night Stonewall and the wagon shed burned. You were late to the event because you were busy buying kerosene. Then after the dinner you hung around town until midnight, came back, doused the shed, and set a match to it. You were so intent on a quick getaway you didn't realize you'd lost your hat in the process. You didn't dare come snooping around to try and find it." Charles's eyes had intently examined the hat throughout my recital. He fixed a cool gaze on me and spoke with utmost patience.

"Beatrice. I must say, even a Stonewall girl's wild imagination is no match for yours. It's a hat. I rode my motorcycle that night, parked it on the side street, and when I left by way of Water Street, the wind was blowing something fierce. Like it always does in March. The hat blew right off my head and I couldn't find it in the dark. End of story." He popped the Homburg onto his head and gave me a curt smile. "But I'm so glad you found it for me. Thanks." Without a bit of remorse, he began walking away, turning back after a few steps. "It's too bad that wagon shed burned, though. It would've added value to the property. But, like the fire marshal said, you'll never find out how that fire started." He had the audacity to tip his hat before turning to leave, whistling his horrid tune as he walked out the door.

UNABLE TO FACE PEOPLE OR FOOD, I SKIPPED DINNER AND LAY curled up on my bed, fuming. Copious angry tears had drenched my face, then dried into a salty paste. I watched the sun fade, leaving me in a hazy twilight. Suddenly something bumped into my door.

"Hey, in there. It's the Easter Bunny. If you don't open up, I'll have to turn you into a rotten egg." I rolled over as Ruby gently turned the handle and crept inside. She slipped off her shoes and climbed onto the foot of my bed, holding out a little bundle made from a tied-up napkin. "Alms for the poorly." I couldn't help cracking a small smile and sat up, untied the knot and found a roll with a slice of ham and an apple. "I couldn't let you starve. But something big must be up for you to miss a meal."

"Let's just say I now know how a fly feels caught in a spider's web." I bit into the roll and slowly chewed. Ruby waited patiently, her soft clover-petal eyes caressing my face like a loyal spaniel's. I imagined a fluffy tail wagging, gently thumping the counterpane. "I'm mired in a serious conundrum. I try to fight my way out but keep coming up against all kinds of barricades."

I got up and paced the room while I recited the sordid story Mary had told the fire marshal. "But Mary's story is a lie!" Ruby's widened eyes cast a questioning look. "Don't ask me how I know this, it's better if you don't know. But her lie instigated everything that's happened to that blacksmith. And now he could be killed or lose everything." Angry tears rushed my face again. Ruby sensed there was more to my distress than an unfair arrest, but kindly deferred asking. "I've confronted Mary, but she won't budge. When I talk to Anna, she clams up or runs away. But Mary's hiding something, and Anna is covering for her!" I flung myself back on the bed, grabbed the apple and tossed it viciously toward the ceiling. Nabbing it harshly upon its descent, I then tossed it higher and higher as my anger boiled.

Ruby had shifted to the edge of the bed, her legs crossed and her dangling foot swinging. For another minute she sat quietly, the foot swinging faster and faster.

"Then it's time you talked to the two of them together."

Sforzando

By Sunday's dinnertime, I was a bundle of agitation, but Ruby remained cool as a cucumber all through the meal. Afterwards, she strolled me calmly through a labyrinth of hallways until we reached a door tucked into a corner alcove. It was the expression studio costume storage room. I then marveled as she magically produced a key. "You sure are good at getting those," I whispered. "It's easy, I just volunteer to organize it," she winked as the rickety door shuddered open and she ushered me inside. Rows of clothing racks bulged with garments of all kinds, and wall shelves were crammed with crates of accessories that spilled onto a floor cluttered with dozens of shoes. No one had done any organizing for a long, long while.

"There, over behind that dress form. Pull up a stool, crouch down, and wait." Ruby was gone in a flash, closing the door behind her as well as shutting out all light. With no windows, the entire space was drenched black. Desperately I patted the walls for a light switch but found nothing, bringing on a panic. Dropping to the floor I grabbed my knees, fighting back tears. I took several deep breaths and told myself that relative to everything else going on, this wasn't the worst. Then crawling on my hands and knees, I felt my way to the dress form, found a stool, and sat in the dark trying to calm my fluttering heart.

After what seemed like an eternity, I inwardly rejoiced at the sound of a key in the latch. "Come on in, ladies," I heard Ruby say, followed by the chink of a small chain being pulled. To my relief, a sudden dim but warm light from a single hanging bulb spilled over the room. Mary and Anna began murmuring in wonder at the myriad of treasures before their eyes. Ruby took the opportunity to tightly shut the door, then stood firmly against it.

"So much stuff!" Anna whispered a shy exclamation.

"All this was found in the ruins of the fire?" Mary seemed incredulous, but notes of admiration tinged her voice. Ruby remained quiet and let them take it all in. After a short minute, Mary's patience wore thin.

"So, where is my pearl and diamond ring? And Anna's grandmother's shawl? You said they were found in the cleanup after the fire."

"Well, that's just the problem, Mary." Ruby spoke up from her guard post. "The cleanup from the fire isn't finished. Not yet. Is it, Bea?"

That was my cue. Slowly I rose from my stool and appeared from behind the dress form. The girls had turned abruptly when they heard my name, and now they stood face to face with me.

"You again!" Mary spat, then turned to Anna. "Your note said my ring had been found, and to meet here to get it. You didn't say anything about *her* being here."

"My note?" Anna was totally flummoxed. "I didn't send you a note. Ruby just told me to meet her at seven o'clock to get my shawl. I didn't even know you were coming."

Ruby's deep-throated giggle crescendoed from mildly underscoring their argument to a full-throttled laughter. Abashed, both girls stared at her.

"Sorry, girls. I guess I'm just an even better actress than I thought I was." Ruby took a deep cleansing breath and smiled.

"Ruby's not the only actress in this room." I looked pointedly at Mary, not one ounce of mirth in my voice.

"We've been over this. I told nothing but the truth."

"I don't believe you."

"That's your problem."

"Someone was with you that night, and you were seen. Who was it?"

"I already told. That Indian, he tried to rape me!"

"You had a man with you, in your bed—"

"I did not!"

"—and it wasn't rape—"

"—The only man there was that Indian!"

"Bea! Hold on a minute," Ruby's voice cut through our rapid-fire argument. "I think she's right, Bea."

"What?"

Ruby, cool and collected, her back still leaning on the door, gazed at Mary. "She's telling the truth. About the only man there." Mary squinted distrustful eyes at her, but Ruby turned her attention elsewhere. "Isn't that right, Anna? The only man there was the Indian." Anna's eyes grew instantly round, then snapped away from Ruby's gaze as if scorched. "Because what he saw, in Mary's bed . . . was you."

Silence reigned for an awful moment as Ruby's words echoed in our heads.

"That's ridiculous." Mary tossed off a haughty shrug with her reply.

"Is it?" Ruby raised her eyebrows. "It's not that big a leap from rave to lover."

"I don't know what you're talking about."

"It happens. Girls get lonely, away from home. They make a special friend, become close, then closer, and—"

"No." Anna's voice was barely a whisper.

"It's okay, Anna," Ruby soothed. "It's perfectly—"

"I would never do that."

"We understand—"

"It's a sin against God!"

"Not as big a sin as getting an innocent man killed!" I interjected.

"He's not innocent," Mary insisted.

"You're lying and he could die because of it."

"He should die!"

I lunged at Mary and shoved hard, my hands leaving imprints on the front of her gauzy blouse. She stumbled backwards into Ruby, who held her there while I swung around at Anna.

"You've got to tell us the truth, Anna."

"You heard her, she said she didn't do that!" Mary spouted venomously. Ruby pulled a handkerchief from her pocket and stuffed it in Mary's mouth. I kept at Anna, changing tactics.

"Anna, think of what the Bible teaches you. Remember the holy commandments. 'Thou shalt not bear false witness against thy neighbor.' The false words came from Mary's mouth, but if you help her by your silence, you have broken the commandment just the same." Anna didn't speak, but the tempo of her breathing quickened. "Anna, they're hunting for the blacksmith now, and he will be put to death. They may even kill him before they bring him back." Still mute, she dropped her head, her chin touching her heaving chest. "The Bible also says, 'Thou shalt not kill.' If you don't speak up, it will be as if you committed murder! An innocent man's death will be by your hands!!"

"Yes!!!" Anna screamed and fell to her knees. "It was me! In Mary's bed. He saw us . . . that Indian . . . We were afraid he'd tell . . ." The words dribbled out between choking sobs.

Ruby released her grip on Mary, who wrenched the handkerchief from her mouth.

"You fool! You stupid imbecile!" Mary's foot sprang up to Anna's shoulder, sending her sprawling over the floor. The room was silent as we watched the poor girl peel herself up and turn sad, reddened eyes toward Mary.

"How can you say that to me?"

"She's crazy. She's making that up."

"How can you say that?"

"You and your blabbering mouth—I don't want to ever see you again."

Anna groped for Mary's hand. "You said we'd always be together. That we're a matched pair. Like we're just one girl, 'Mary Anna.'"

"Sentimental slop." Mary spoke under her breath while Anna sank back into tears.

I turned my focus to Mary.

"You have to tell the court, Mary."

"Absolutely not."

"You only have to talk to the commonwealth's attorney. Just tell him . . . students are forbidden to be together after lights out and you were afraid of getting in trouble. Maybe that you were burning lots of candles, and didn't want to be blamed for the fire. No one has to say you're a sapphist."

"I'm not a sapphist." Her capacity to lie, even to herself, was boundless.

"You can talk to him alone. No one else will be told."

"No one will be told, period, because I'm not talking."

"And you're young! Only fifteen, they won't punish you. Plus, if you don't, I'll tell your headmistress at Stonewall."

"And you think she'll believe you? You'll just be telling lies about poor girls who lost everything in a tragic fire." She was gloating, actually believing she was impervious to any blame. "Besides, I could tell your Martha headmistress that you had a relationship with the Indian. You must have. How else would you have known what to ask us? Unless you'd spoken with him?"

My mouth went dry as I struggled to keep an intimidating gaze on her. I longed to counter, but my brain went blank. Smirking and triumphant, Mary turned on her heel, swung the door open wide, and marched out. As her marcato steps faded down the hall, a grieving Anna rose from the floor and quietly drifted away in her wake.

"Oh, Bea, Mrs. Long would never believe such a preposterous story." Ruby tried to keep her tone light, but she was vexed. We both knew I could never risk it.

I felt the strands of the spider's web closing around me, squeezing tight. And the tighter they squeezed, the angrier I became. I was pacing furiously in the small room, punching at random dresses on the racks and kicking shoes across the floor.

"I can*not* let her get away with these lies! I have to clear Jo— the blacksmith's name."

Ruby eyed me pointedly, twisting a finger through one of her golden curls. "Well, with a girl like Mary, you've got to beat her at her own game."

I paced a few more strides before stopping abruptly in front of a dress form draped with a fringed shawl.

"You're right!" I turned and grabbed Ruby's arms. "The only way to catch a lying weasel is to set a trap!"

Recapitulation

I wondered if the sunny but breezy Monday morning was a harbinger of how the day would unfold. At a quarter to nine I was trekking east on Main Street with Anna in tow, Ruby linked in on the opposite side. We had blindsided Anna after breakfast, swooping her out a service entrance and tossing a long coat over her uniform while ignoring her questions. We swept her along Water Street until well out of sight of the Martha, then turned up Chinquapin Alley and crossed to Main. Only then did we tell her that Mary was going to court to talk to the commonwealth's attorney. "No!" she cried as her knees buckled, leaving her dangling between us like a pathetic marionette. "Don't worry!" I reassured her. "She won't divulge anything 'intimate,' she'll make up something else. And the testimony will be private, only to the attorney. But you need to be present when she talks." Stunned into silence, she reluctantly got to her feet and came with us without further protest.

She only faltered again near the top of the hill, when the courthouse came into view on our left. It was an imposing red brick structure, three stories high with four colossal white round columns holding a broad corniced roof over its entrance. The double cupolas stacked on its rooftop towered above us, piercing the clouds. Although she'd passed by it each day on her way to classes at the Dagmar Hotel, Anna suddenly balked and stared with fear. Perhaps she envisioned the massive white columns as bars of a jail cell threatening to entrap her.

Gently we led Anna up the steps onto the vast portico and ducked behind one of the columns. I removed my own coat and hat to fasten a special headpiece to my hair and let down the skirt of a large white apron I'd rolled up to my waist. As a dazed Anna watched, I told her Mary was waiting for me to fetch her from class, that when she talked, she wanted me with her as well. I handed my outerwear to Ruby and crossed the street to the Dagmar.

Ruby had remedied my lack of a Stonewall uniform by pilfering a nurse's cap and apron from the costume storage. I didn't possess her acting skills (even if I had become a rather proficient liar), but she told me to assume a stern face and walk confidently like I was supposed to be there. Coupled with my considerable height, the advice worked and no one stopped me in the hallways or on the stairs. Apparently, a "community nurse" was free to roam and peer into classrooms at will, and finally I spotted my prey in a history class.

Taking a deep breath, I walked straight into the room, informed the instructor that Mary needed to come with me, that it had already been cleared by the headmistress. Apparently, everyone respects a uniform, especially a medical one, because the instructor released her into my charge right away. A shocked Mary had never counted on me abruptly showing up in front of an entire class, posing as a nurse no less. Giving her no time to respond, I scooped her up by the arm and led her from the room before she could make a scene.

Thoroughly chagrined, she uttered curses under her breath as we walked the entire length of the hallway. Reaching a window overlooking Main Street, I planted her in front of it and warned her to listen to what I had to say.

"Look out the window, Mary." Across the street, Ruby had carefully placed herself and Anna in a spot visible from a second-floor window of the Dagmar. Our appearance there was Ruby's cue to straighten Anna's hair and take her hands in a comforting manner. "What do you see?"

"I don't see anything but that stupid Confederate soldier statue." Roughly I pulled Mary in front of me and pointed straight at Anna.

"The courthouse steps! Your friend can't live with your lie anymore. She's going inside to tell her story." A little gasp escaped Mary's throat.

"She wouldn't do that. Not in front of people. She's too scared." Mary tried in vain to cover her alarm with bluster.

"She won't talk in public. She'll have a private meeting with the commonwealth's attorney. That's all." A long moment passed while she absorbed the news.

"Well, I have to stop her."

"It's already been arranged." Another lie, but Doc would be there and could arrange it. "The only way to stop her is if you talk to him yourself." Mary swung around to face me with panic and anger, knowing I had her right where I wanted her. She took off down the hall and I followed at a brisk trot. No one seemed to think it strange to see a student running from a nurse, but at the front door I grabbed her arm and held tight as we exited the building.

Ruby had already taken Anna inside the courtroom to keep them apart, and when Mary saw the courthouse steps empty, she rushed me forward like a runaway pony with the bit in its teeth. With a firm grip, I ushered her inside the vestibule, bumping into Doc as I entered. He looked quizzically at my nurse's garb as I leaned in to whisper, "We have our miracle, but I'll need your help." He listened to my request, then slipped through a side door into a hallway. Before Mary could question me, I told her the attorney would be informed that she was here now as Anna's replacement. I struggled to hide it, but my stomach churned with worry until Doc finally reentered the vestibule and motioned for us to follow him.

We were led down the hallway and into a small office where we were seated side by side in two chairs facing the attorney's desk. Doc left and the attorney asked us both to properly identify ourselves before turning to Mary.

"All right, young lady, what do you have to say?"

"Well, sir . . . Oh, um, Your Honor, um—"

"You needn't call me that. I'm just the commonwealth's attorney."

"Oh. Uh, well, uh . . . I am afraid I was mistaken when I gave my account to the fire marshal. About what happened the night of the fire."

"I see. And what was your mistake?"

"Well, I've been having terrible memory problems. Ever since the fire. You see, I was just thrown into such a shock. What with the putrid smell of the smoke, the flames licking at the doorways, threatening our very lives! I was just driven insane with fear."

"And does that have anything to do with Mr. Schumacher?"

"Why, yes. Yes, it does. You see, I was in such a state of traumatic shock, I *thought* I was being chased by the Indian. Mr. Schumacher, I mean. But really it was just that my mind, it was . . . it had gone all haywire on me. He was really . . . just, helping people escape the fire." Mary slowly batted her eyes, trying to look sorrowful and contrite. I suspected the attorney wasn't fooled by this display, but sent up a fervent prayer he would accept her altered story. He fixed her with a hard stare.

"Well, young lady, your mistake certainly stirred up a whole mess of trouble. Causing an innocent man to go to desperate lengths to evade an irrevocable penalty he obviously didn't deserve." The attorney took a deep breath and expelled it fiercely through his nostrils. "How old are you?"

"I'm fifteen. Sir." Mary sat ramrod straight, but a faint tremor flickered in her voice.

The attorney held her in his stare for several more moments, then swiveled his chair to the side and gazed out the window. I didn't dare look at Mary. After a long, uncomfortable minute, he swiveled his chair back to face her.

"Making a false accusation like this is a serious offense. I don't regard it lightly." His stare was relentless as Mary's short, ragged breaths filled the silence. "But fire is a frightful thing. Could scare a child near to death, caught inside one. So, because of your extreme youth, I'll not charge you." Mary no doubt resented being called a child, but couldn't contain an audible sigh of relief. "However, I suggest you call up your daddy and your mommy and tell them to come fetch you, because you might not want to be around when Mr. Schumacher returns to town. As a matter of fact, I also wish I could tell them to turn you over their knee, but I don't have that power. So, you are hereby dismissed, and I don't want to see you in this court ever again."

Mary spoke not another word until we were outside descending the courthouse steps.

"Hmph, I'm not afraid of that Indian. I've got classes to finish and I'll stay in town as long as I like." She strutted across the street with her chin raised, but I could tell she was shaken by the attorney's words. Just as she reached the Dagmar, I held her back.

"Well, just remember: you're lucky your headmistress knows nothing of any of this." I gave her a pointed look that she returned with a reluctant nod before swinging open the door to return to class.

I hurried back and slipped inside the courtroom. As planned, I nodded to Ruby, who led a stupefied Anna out and across the street to the Dagmar, telling her Mary had been allowed to speak without her after all. Ruby had also prepared a story about Anna feeling dizzy that morning, to explain her tardiness to the headmistress. Ironically, it was the closest thing to the truth either of us had said all morning.

I stayed to witness the attorney's announcement because only once I'd heard those words would I believe the nightmare had ended. The wooden pews in the gallery were brimming with spectators, but I found a small spot on the back row. When Jonah Schumacher's name was finally called, heads turned and eyes searched the entire courtroom, ridiculously wondering if he'd slipped in unnoticed. The commonwealth's attorney stepped forward and announced, "Nolle prosequi." His decision not to prosecute. Immediately the gallery erupted in gasps of disbelief and protest, a roar requiring several bold strikes of the gavel to restore order. When the judge calmly asked the reason, the attorney simply stated that presently there was not enough evidence to obtain a conviction. The murmurs of incredulity that rippled through the gallery were ignored. The charges were dismissed. Jonah was free.

Tumultuoso

For the next few days, everything seemed light and easy. I breezed through classes and relished the piano with renewed fervor. All newspapers that had called for Jonah's capture now circulated news of his acquittal. The telegraph office in Whittier, North Carolina, had even been sent a special message, to be taken directly to the Cherokee settlement. In my mind this ensured Jonah would get the good news. Every afternoon I slipped away to the stable, each day certain I would welcome his return.

But as the end of the week approached with no sign of him, a heaviness began to descend on me again. The sun set on Friday evening with no Jonah, his taxes unpaid and the sale of his property looming the following Monday. I thought surely after his mistreatment, he deserved a grace period to allow him time to return before the foreclosure. But the town had already waited three years and needed the money. Roy had worked off his family's debt and there were no longer means to maintain the property. The auction would go forward as scheduled.

Although handled separately, the horses would be auctioned, too, prompting me to worry about who would buy them. The draft horses would get good homes; Doc knew of three reputable farmers planning to bid on them, all able to pay a fair price or more. But with motorized transportation now more popular, the outcome for saddle horses like Xander and Copper was uncertain. As I nursed my heartbreak over their potential destination,

I was suddenly panicked by a horrible thought: Would they be sold on site or be taken to Jockey Alley?

Jonah had told me about the infamous Jockey Alley event that took place every fourth Monday of the month. A slew of disreputable men would gather on Valley Street directly behind the courthouse to carry out their own corrupted brand of horse swapping. Whisky flowed like a river and drunken ruffians held impromptu horse races, spouting profanity and lashing the poor frightened animals without mercy. The terrified horses filled the street with their droppings, then tromped in their own filth, sending up a frightful stench. It was the worst possible fate for a horse, yet this indecency and cruelty went unchecked month after month, year after year. Why was there no public outcry for this?

Borrowing money from Ruby this time, I made a telephone call home on Saturday morning. Little Jenny answered and began chattering right away, but I soon managed to gently ask her to get Papa for me. I sat holding the receiver to my ear, waiting impatiently. But when I heard my father's voice, I suddenly found myself trembling.

"Papa?" I squeaked into the mouthpiece.

"Yes, Bea, it's me. What kind of trouble have you gotten yourself into?"

"Trouble?" My mind went racing. What had Jenny told him? I cleared my throat. "No trouble, Papa. School is going fine."

"So, you're wasting hard-earned money to tell me everything's fine?" The sternness in his voice both intimidated and annoyed me.

"No. I have something to ask you." Sweat trickled between my breasts, soaking the chemise underneath my corset. I'd rehearsed my plea beforehand, but this was a rocky start. In a rush I blurted out the story of the Stonewall fire, testing to see what he knew; Papa didn't read headlines, only farm reports and financial news. As I'd hoped, he was unaware of anything about Jonah or the trial. But he was impatient to know why I'd called.

Under the circumstances, I thought it prudent to amend the story a wee bit. I said only that a poor hardworking blacksmith in town was facing foreclosure and had two beautiful horses to be sold. But if they weren't bought at Monday's sale, they were at risk of being sold to cruel owners at a sham auction, describing it in detail for good measure. "Could you buy them, Papa? Just to keep them safe on our farm until their owner gets back on his feet. Then he'll buy them back." I didn't know how Jonah might do that with all his property taken, but what was one more lie?

"You think I'm in the horse-trading business now, do you?"

"I'm sure it won't be for long. So, Papa, could you? Please?" Aside from attending college, I had never begged for anything, and he knew it. I chewed my lip, listening to the soft crackling of the long-distance connection filling the miles between us.

"All right, then." My shoulders relaxed. "But when I come Monday to get them, I'm bringing you back home, too."

"What?! Why?"

"Well, now, I can't be paying for college and horses both. You've already got a perfectly good horse here at home; if you want more you can just stay home and take care of them!"

I struggled to steady my voice. "Papa, the one thing has nothing to do with the other. You're not being fair!"

"The way I see it, I'm being perfectly fair. You're the one making an outrageous request." He spoke so calmly I wanted to scream. Papa wasn't rich, but money for a couple more horses was not a stretch, despite how he painted himself as barely making it. He was simply stubborn and miserly.

"But the school year's almost over. I *have* to stay and finish." My sisters deserved their chance at college.

"Looks like you've got a hard choice to make, then."

"But there's no reason to have to choose. You can save those horses!" The panic and anger lacing my words only antagonized him.

"I'll be damned if you'll tell me what I can do. You can just stay put and to hell with buying any fool horses!" With a loud click assaulting my ear, he hung up.

Bonny Gable

THE AUCTION WAS AT TEN O'CLOCK AND I FULLY INTENDED TO be there. I had gotten away with a classmate answering role for me when I'd skipped an early class the previous Monday to attend court. However, my ten o'clock class was not overcrowded, making the same trick far riskier. But Ruby couldn't resist a challenge and happily volunteered. Then in the hallway, I ran into Miss Bremer, the art instructor, who stopped me to chat. She asked if I'd heard from Laura Mae, talking at length about her copious talent and how she loved teaching such talented young ladies. I squirmed inside as we spoke, but after what I hoped was a polite interval, begged off to attend my practice hour. I walked away slowly, then after she'd rounded the corner, I scampered out the service entrance and headed toward the stables.

There was no time to trek through the pines, so I stealthily edged over to Water Street and then took off running. I hadn't gone far when I spied Copper in the distance, a deputy sitting astride him trying desperately to hold Xander on a lead. They exited the front corral gate and headed east on Water Street with Xander giving the deputy a full throttle protest, prancing and snorting, the whites of his eyes flashing warning signals. I ran on ahead, stopping square in front of them.

"What are you doing? Where are you going?"

"Don't know if it's any business a yours, lady, but these here horses are headed to Jockey Alley."

"But these are Jonah Schumacher's horses. To be sold at the foreclosure auction."

"Well, I'm just doing what I'm told, by somebody with a right smart more authority than you." The distracted deputy had let the lead go slack and Xander began to sidestep away. He let out a hateful "Woah!" and meant to yank the lead, but I was quicker, grabbing it and jerking it from his hand. "Hey, you! That's court property. You want me to haul you in for horse thievin'?" He was nettled to be bested by a girl. Xander calmed immediately when I stroked his neck.

"Hold on, hold on. Nobody's doing any horse thievin' here." Doc was trotting towards us from the top of Water Street. "Got held up by a calf refusing to make his entry into the world," he huffed and mopped his brow. "I know this young lady, she's no thief. But she's right, these are meant for the foreclosure sale. Where are the two draft horses?"

"Well, that's just it. All four horses were sold, the two grays to Ed Whitley, farmer over in Meadowview. And these two to a Mr. Armstrong, come all the way from Richmond to buy 'em, for his daughter that goes to school here." Richmond. Armstrong. Alarms went off in my head. "But the fella what bought the stables has his own mounts that'll fill all the stalls. Mr. Armstrong said if they couldn't board there, he didn't wanna buy 'em. By then, ever'body was gone, so I'm takin' 'em over to Jockey Alley."

"No!" I lunged for Copper's reins and tried to pry them from the deputy's hands. Doc stepped into the scramble, trying to calm me, when suddenly we heard yelling.

"Hey! Hoh, you fellows up there!"

We all turned toward the voice coming from downhill at the opposite end of the street.

"Hold up there!" it came, louder this time. A man in a rumpled Norfolk jacket and well-worn Boss of the Plains hat lumbered up the hill, looking oddly familiar. When he was within a few feet of us, I was afraid to believe my eyes.

"Granddad!" I tossed Xander's lead to Doc and immediately threw my arms around him.

"Bea?! Well, Lord have mercy," he chuckled, breathing heavily from his climb. "I've found you out in the middle of the street!"

"I can't believe . . ." I pulled back to look at him, then returned to my bear hug. "You're here!"

"Yes, I'm here." He patted my back like he did when I was a little girl. He looked up at the deputy. "I came about some horses.

Been lookin' all over for the big foreclosure sale. Someone told me it was up this way?"

"That sale's done over, and—"

"Well, you're in luck," Doc cut in. "There's these two horses left." Doc's firm grip on Xander's lead prevented any movement; the deputy gave him a sour look.

"Yes, but now I'm takin' 'em to a different sale, on the other side of the hill." The deputy took pleasure in fixing me with a cold glare.

"Well, now I can save you the trouble," Granddad offered. "I came to buy them, so you can sell them right here." I was stunned but smart enough to keep quiet.

"Sorry, sir, but I got my orders. Treasurer's office says they got to be sold today, so I'm takin' 'em to Jockey Alley." No doubt he had a seedy friend anxious to make a quick sale and purloin a cut of the price.

Granddad frowned in concern and glanced at me. The deputy smirked and reached for Xander's lead, but Doc held tight.

"Now hold on, Cecil." Doc addressed the deputy by his first name, which perturbed the man. "These horses were already sold at the stables, but the buyer backed out. There's no reason you can't make that sale again to this gentleman."

"There's every reason. I got my orders from the treasurer's office."

"Well, how about I give you a reason to sell right here. I'm sure your wife would like to know just where you spend your Friday nights. And how much you're on the payroll for, since not all of it gets taken home to her." Lacking a retort to those promises, the deputy now fixed his cold glare on Doc.

"The other buyer was gonna pay one hundred twenty-five dollars. Each. Horse and tack together, that's the deal." The peeved deputy spat the words at Granddad, then looked away. I sucked in a breath as my heart clenched. Those horses were worth every penny, but that was a lot of money.

"I know the stable boy was at that sale," Doc spoke up before Granddad could answer. "If I were to ask him to verify that price, would he say the same?" The deputy looked at Doc through narrowed eyes, then jerked his head in a single nod.

I prepared myself to see Granddad shake his head. Then he astonished me by reaching into his jacket pocket and pulling out a huge roll of cash. In amazement, I watched as he slowly counted out five fifty-dollar bills. He handed them up to the deputy, who made a big show of recounting the money before tucking it into his shirt pocket. He dismounted and grudgingly slapped the reins into Granddad's hands. Those two magnificent animals were safe at last.

Doc demanded a proper receipt, then after the deputy stomped off, he handed me Xander's lead. "If you two will excuse me, I'll follow along and make sure all that cash gets to where it's supposed to be."

I threw my arms around Granddad again, causing him to topple slightly.

"Thank you, thank you! But how did you know?"

"Oh, Granddad has his ways," he chuckled with a big wink.

He could have only gotten the details from Papa, yet there was no mention of my going home. I was amazed that Papa had given in, but too overjoyed to wonder why. We turned the horses around and headed back to the stables.

Roy was just locking up when we got there, but we asked to leave Copper and Xander there until the train journey home that afternoon. He was happy to oblige, since he was coming back with a cage anyway. "The new owner don't know about Wesa, so I'm taking him home with me 'til Jonah gets back. He ought to have something from here." I wondered how easy it would be to catch that cat. But it was a sweet gesture and I wished him luck.

Ballade

"Shew, lordy, what a morning," Granddad declared, mopping his forehead with the faded bandanna he always carried. "Well, I guess today is different from your usual morning routine at Martha Washington College."

I had forgotten all about school and had to hurry to make my eleven o'clock voice lesson duty. Granddad agreed to wait on the front veranda in hopes of having lunch with me. When I finished the lesson, I headed to Mrs. Long's office to beg permission.

"Ah! Miss Damron!" She abruptly stood from her chair, thrusting her fists onto her desktop. "You've just been reported missing from your ten o'clock class this morning. What do you have to say for yourself?" Her robust tenor voice thundered. I froze as her cold gray eyes pierced me, her thick black eyebrows arching into threatening question marks.

"Well, um . . . Mrs. Long. I, uh, after my first class, I started not feeling so well. I think something from breakfast didn't sit right in my stomach. I was afraid I'd be sick right on the hallway floor. And make a big mess, and—"

"You did not report to the infirmary, as per protocol. I checked."

"Oh. Well, no. I forgot to do that. I wasn't thinking, I guess. In my misery. And, I just went back to my room to lie down."

She glared at me sternly before sitting to fill out my demerit slip.

"Hello there, young lady. Is this where I can find the headmistress?" Mrs. Long's head popped up and I swung around to the open door.

"Granddad!"

The Martha Odyssey

"Why, Beatrice, I didn't see you standing there. Just the person I've come to visit. Do you think the young lady behind the desk can direct me to the headmistress's office?" He gave Mrs. Long his most charming smile. Of course, a plaque with "Mrs. Long, Headmistress" was plainly visible just outside the door, but she took the bait. Granddad poured on flattery in spades and I watched, fascinated, as the iceberg I'd faced only minutes ago melted to slush.

He spun her a woeful tale how he traveled constantly for his job and had missed seeing me at Christmas. But he was passing through Abingdon today, the only day he would have to see me for another year. All while making the saddest face. Before I knew what was happening, they were laughing and joking, and she had agreed to Granddad's request.

"You may go out to lunch with your grandfather, but you must attend all of today's remaining classes, after which you are confined to back campus for the rest of the week." With a stern face she thrust the demerit slip into my hand, then turned a smile to Granddad. "I do hope you enjoy your time with your granddaughter. *Most* of the time, she's an exemplary student."

"You are quite the charmer," I teased him once we were out of earshot. He chuckled and put my arm in his, reminding me where I got my knack for making up a story in a tight spot.

We took a small table at Maiden's Drug Store, both famished but talking up a storm as we ate. After missing my spring break visit, I wanted all the news from home. We got back to the Martha with time to spare before my next class, so we settled onto a bench in front of the octagonal fountain on the front lawn. The sun was high and we shed our jackets in the new warmth of April. Soon we were lulled into a near doze by the afternoon heat.

"Your papa doesn't know I'm here." His statement startled me awake.

"But . . . how did you know about the horses?"

"Well, I guess I wasn't supposed to, but you know how your papa gets to talking pretty loud when he's riled. I heard him tell your mama all about your telephone conversation. How he wouldn't buy them if you didn't agree to come home, and how you sassed him back. Then he spouted off, 'but she begged and pleaded to go to that highfalutin school, so she can just stay put and horses be damned!' and stormed out the door."

Papa's words didn't surprise me, but they still stung.

"I know how tenderhearted you are, especially with animals. But I did wonder: why these particular horses, and why right now? I figured there must be a mighty special reason." I was silent, but he sensed something chewing at my brain. "So, I reckon this is about more than just a couple of horses you took a fancy to?"

After all he'd done, he deserved an explanation.

"I know the man they belonged to. I actually know him quite well." I told how I'd discovered the stables by accident, and how it had become my refuge. My home away from home, every creature there becoming family to me, albeit Jonah not quite like a brother. Then Stonewall burned and though he'd acted as a hero, he'd been made a victim.

"Jonah is Cherokee, and false accusations landed on him all too easily." I relayed the entire Mary fiasco, my difficult journey to ferret out the truth, her threat to tell my headmistress about my relationship with him and get me dismissed. "But I was determined to clear Jonah, even if it cost me my place at the college. Then my friend and I tricked Mary into recanting her story." Granddad smiled, always impressed with cleverness to obtain a good end.

"But now he's lost everything, and I was afraid someone cruel might buy his horses. You saw they were almost taken to that horrible horse swapping event. I just want to keep his horses for him until he returns and can buy them back."

Understanding what was at stake, Granddad didn't question why Jonah had fled. He reached for my hand, a touch like a tonic. I gave it a squeeze.

"I've tried to never interfere in your papa's business, or his family. But this time I just felt in my bones that I should. And I was right."

"But Granddad . . . how did you come by that much money?"

Earnings from his farm and my father's had always been combined to provide for our entire family. But he'd been squirreling away money of his own for years from odd jobs he'd done for people, who insisted on paying him a little something. Plus, he'd never touched the money from selling his house years ago when he moved in with us. "Living in a house full of family is riches enough for me, so being frugal is easy. I knew a little extra might come in handy when you children left the nest." He had dipped into his savings to rescue those horses, yet he didn't require anything of me in exchange. I fought to blink back tears but lost the battle.

"Ah, now, no need for snuffles. You'd do the same for your old Granddad. You're no stranger to making sacrifices for others." I clumsily dried my eyes with my sleeves. "It's time you knew where that impulse comes from."

He removed his ancient hat and began slowly fanning himself.

"Once there was a young man restless to see what lay beyond his family's farm nestled in rolling hills near a small mountain town." I tilted my head toward the sun, a child once more, captivated by a story. "He took off traveling alone, picking up work wherever he landed. He was smart, strong, and handy. Never lacked for a job as a lumberjack or carpenter. He lived a happy vagabond life—until something caught his eye. Or rather, someone.

"His travels took him into the mountains of North Carolina, where he picked up work on a logging crew. First day on the job, he went to the mess tent for lunch, and there was a beautiful girl dishing out the stew. When everybody was served, she picked up a fiddle and played tunes all through the meal. Melodies to match her rare beauty. Her long fingers fluttering and her bow flying over the strings. An enchantress, she was. The young fella learned she lived in a Cherokee settlement west of the logging camp and set out to pay her some visits. Each time he came, she regaled him with sweet music. And not just on fiddle, but the dulcimer, the guitar, and mandolin. Any instrument she touched, she could make it sing.

"Well, Cupid's arrow hit him hard and pierced him deep. He left logging and got himself a steady job, over in Asheville, running a hardware store. He married his musical sorceress and took her there to live. They were happy as two foxes curled up in a hollow log, and before too long had a little kit to prove it. A curly-headed girl, their pride and joy. But before the year was out, tragedy struck. A sickness overcame his beloved, stealing the magical music from his world forever. Left the young man and his little princess all alone. Feeling helpless, the young man journeyed home to the family farm where his own mother and father would help him raise the wee babe. 'On one condition,' they said—that no one would ever know she was Cherokee. 'She will have a much better life that way,' they claimed. The young man was heartbroken but wondered if there was some truth to what they said. People had called him 'squaw man' and such, and although that kind of thing never bothered him, it might be hard on a little girl. So, he agreed.

"When the little girl grew up, tall and as beautiful as her mother, a young lad from the neighboring farm took a shine to her. He married her and took her to his farm to start a family. And fruitful they were, having six little kits, four girls and two boys. The oldest girl is tall and beautiful, just like her mother and grandmother. No one knows the secret to that beauty, except the young man who found it in the mountains of North Carolina."

He fell silent and placed his hat back on his head.

As I'd listened to his story, I'd felt a strange sense of déjà vu. Each line delivered in his low melodious voice felt familiar as it landed on my ear; as if I knew it, but hadn't known that I knew it, until now. A whole world opened up inside me, new but not strange, one that felt right.

"You look so much like her, Bea. More even than your mother does."

"Does Mama know?"

"She's the only one who does. Until now. Many a time I've regretted holding back the truth, but I'd promised your great-grandparents. And your mother and father married and had you and Jim before they passed. It seemed too late by then."

"All those stories you told me growing up. 'Our secret stories' you called them. You'd say 'someday you'll need to know these stories.' They were always about the Cherokee."

He nodded silently. We watched a butterfly flit from shrub to shrub, parading its elegantly painted wings in the sunlight.

"Of course, in due time I'll tell each of your siblings. Unless I'm no longer around. Then it'll be up to you."

Adiratamente

Granddad escorted Jonah's horses to Clintwood on the train that afternoon while I dutifully attended classes. But all the while, one last facet to the day's saga burned beneath my skin. After the last class bell sounded, I crept inside Mariah Cooper Hall and parked myself in a secluded spot under the first-floor staircase. When I saw Varina saunter into the hallway, unlock her room and enter, I pounced. She turned to close the door, but I slammed my palm against its hard wooden panel. "A word, Miss Armstrong?" I walked straight in, forcing her to back into the room as I firmly shut the door.

"Your father was in Abingdon today."

Varina's eyes flicked, but she quickly regained her cool demeanor. "So? He has business dealings all over the state."

"But you know why he was here today."

"Well, I'm certain it was something important to—"

"Let's just cut to the chase, Varina. How did you even know about the foreclosure sale? You don't care about local news, and neither does your father. You sent him here, and instructed him to buy those two particular horses. Why?"

A smirky smile sliced her face before she slowly paraded over to her dressing table.

"Oh, Beatrice. Don't you know I have eyes everywhere? Sometimes even my own. Nothing goes on around here without me knowing about it." She preened herself, gazing in her mirror at me as she explained. She had learned of my association with Jonah from Charles. But instead of acting on that information right away, she waited, looking for the best way to utilize it. Finally, the perfect opportunity presented itself the night Stonewall burned and the poor traumatized girls were huddling in Preston Hall. She overheard Mary and Anna crying in a corner, afraid the Indian had seen them together. "I'd seen the blacksmith leaving the fire, so I gave the girls a solution to their problem. I told them the way to ensure he didn't tell on them was simply to tell on him first."

I should have known. Mary's behavior had Varina's stamp all over it. They were two of a kind.

"Your advice nearly got an innocent man put to death. Thank God the charges were dropped." I was careful not to mention Mary had recanted; I'd had to coerce her, but I'd also promised her secrecy.

"Yes, I heard. Too bad he broke out of jail and is nowhere to be found." Varina swung around to face me. "And I know you had a hand in that, even though I can't prove it." She spat the bitter words, hating nothing more than to be thwarted in her machinations.

"Jonah's wagon shed. Did you put Charles up to setting it on fire?"

Her voice immediately acquired a silky-smooth tone. "Why, I don't know a thing about that. But I'm not surprised if somebody tried to put that savage in his place. Hoarding someone else's prize livestock."

"Livestock that Charles nearly—" She wasn't worthy of an explanation, only of my wrath. "You know, Varina, that corn silk hair on your head is a total deceit, because inside your soul is black as tar. You couldn't destroy me by driving me insane, so you set out to destroy everything I love. Do you really have so little faith in your own musical abilities that you have to eliminate any competition?" Stung, flaming spears shot from her eyes. "It's too bad you've wasted all that energy." I flung open the door and stormed from the building, my footsteps an angry cadence echoing behind me.

Elegy

Time. Granddad often talked about time. Saying he'd spent quite a lot of it on this earth, and it had taught him a thing or two. It could be both cruel and kind. We wanted more of it or less of it, depending on what was at stake. Whatever was to befall us would come to pass in due time, the proper time. Sometimes predictable, sometimes not.

As the sun peeked over distant hilltops, turning indigo dawn into amber daylight, I walked along the serpentine paths of the Martha lawn. Golden daffodils trumpeted the significance of the day while fragrance wafting from lilac bushes threatened to lull me listless. But nothing could take the edge off my excitement. It was time. It was the morning of the music scholarship competition.

Later, after a barely nibbled breakfast and a fidgety session at my vanity table while Ruby tamed my hair, I walked alone into Litchfield Hall. The judges were in plain sight seated in the front row, but my eyes held a singular focus: the magnificent Steinway grand piano on the stage. I had come a long way from my first meeting with it, that early September day when my eyes were so dazzled and my fingers itched to touch its fine ivory and ebony keys. Now this would be my day of reckoning, the day my future would be decided.

I sat in silence until my name was called, then with unhurried steps walked onto the stage. I adjusted the bench to accommodate my long legs and seated myself at the keyboard. Then placing my fingers on the opening chords, I whispered, "For you, Jonah, wherever you are," and began to play.

Coda

Da Capo al Fine

MAY 28, 1931

"No, Beatrice. I'm not dead."

We stand facing each other on the Martha's back lawn, the familiar well-traveled path in the fragrant pine grove only a few feet away. I struggle to breathe as time spins out of control. A current, like the rushing waters of the stream where my haunting dreams were once prayed away, sparks to life inside me. He reaches for my hand and that current surges between us, fusing us together as if no time has passed at all.

Occasional silver threads twine through the ebony hair, still long, still braided. Fine creases etched into the rugged bronze face tell a hundred stories. But the same brawny, resilient, compassionate man I'd known all those years ago is here. Meshing with my world as I had gladly meshed with his.

"Jonah."

Several long moments passed as our eyes drank in each other.

"I got news about the college closing, and the reunion. I trusted you'd be here."

Music and nostalgia had brought me back to the Martha, unaware that this astonishing private reunion awaited me. One I had never quite relinquished hope for during all my years away. Now those years collapse and I'm that eighteen-year-old girl again, doting on the man who gradually opens his world and his heart to me. What have our divergent life journeys made of us?

When I first arrived at the Martha's front door, my ambition was singular: music would be my ticket into the world beyond my Appalachian home. Then came the Peabody Conservatory scholarship competition, a windfall that advanced my chances to realize that ambition. No need to settle for Papa's short trip ticket; I could book passage on an expanded grand tour. All I had to do was win.

So, with the naïve confidence of youth, I considered my path carefully mapped out and secure. Certain of my mission, I deemed nothing impossible and regarded risks as mere adventures. Then in a provident turn of events (although I didn't think so at the time), the course of my life veered into an entirely new direction.

Jonah did not return that spring of my freshman year. I felt him lost to me forever, and the music scholarship became a point of hyperfocus. Winning it was my only pathway into a future I could endure, fighting for it all I had left to sustain me. My fire had been stoked by overcoming the obstacles Varina had so wickedly placed in my path. And I was convinced that honesty, good intentions, and hard work always paid off.

I spent every spare minute at the piano. But thoughts and fears about Jonah still at large crept into the practice room with me. Week upon week passed after the court dropped charges, but no trace of him surfaced. "Wanted" posters disappeared and gossip died away, the silence after his acquittal as robust as the uproar over his assumed guilt had been. It was as if he had never existed at all. Yet inside me his presence was as vivid as ever.

Fighting black thoughts, I wrestled intensely with my competition piece. I'd spent countless hours with the *Polonaise-Fantaisie*—digging at its soul, searching for its heart, trying to make it sing. Then one day Jonah's words rang in my ears: "A relationship in balance is peaceful; when balance is disturbed, there's trouble." The emotional demands of the piece and my own emotional state were opposing forces, needing to be brought into balance.

So, six days before the judges were due to arrive from Peabody Conservatory of Music, I put aside the Chopin and took up a Beethoven piece I'd worked on early in the semester. The third movement of his Sonata opus 23 in F Minor, the "Appassionata," was a daunting technical challenge. But if anyone knew angst, it was Beethoven. The sonata's ominous rumbling of rapid sixteenth note runs and driving minor chords were sounds that matched the troubled despondency that consumed me. I could use my grief and longing to feed the passion of the piece. It was a risk, even madness, to make the switch at such a late date. But I'd become accustomed to taking risks, and this one I felt "in my bones," as Granddad would say, was necessary.

I suppose it was foolish. Or maybe it wasn't. Maybe it was exactly what I was meant to do: to unhinge the certainty of my path and chart the course of my future on a new, unimagined route.

When I didn't win the music scholarship, my devastation was complete. With no Jonah and no ticket to a musical career, I took to my bed. But dear Ruby would have none of that. She hauled me from my puddle of self-pity and insisted I write to Franceska Kaspar Lawson, the professional soprano I'd helped accompany back in March. That gamble won me an invitation to Washington, DC, to work as her personal assistant and rehearsal accompanist, and the chance to study with some of her concert pianist colleagues.

With Mrs. Lawson, I entered that wider world I'd always hoped to see. Besides visiting all the wonderful and historic sites in her home city, she took me on her concert tours. With the war raging, travel to Europe was out of the question, but we covered most of the eastern United States. We even stopped in New York City, where I got to see Ruby dancing on a Broadway stage. It was a tiny role in the chorus, but she was proud to be working toward her dream, just like she'd promised. As we toured, I saw sights I'd only read about, tasted new foods, met interesting and accomplished people. Until, after only two years, it all came to a grinding halt.

In the autumn of 1918, the Spanish Flu launched a devastating invasion of Washington, DC, soon to have the whole world engulfed in its pervasive death grip. Mrs. Lawson feared for my safety and packed me off home to Clintwood.

There I began to wear a nurse's uniform for real. Mama was executive chairman of the Red Cross in Dickenson County, and I helped her serve the sick when a terrible flu outbreak hit just after I arrived. Somehow, most likely because of Mama's extremely strict hygiene practices, we both escaped the ravages of the virus. But the disease was particularly harsh on the elderly, and we lost my beloved Granddad. I was devastated to imagine life without him; his absence left a deep, empty hole inside me. But as Granddad had said, time inevitably brings all kinds of changes.

The ambition that had driven me to the Martha's front door altered. I had traveled two glorious years with Mrs. Lawson only to come home and witness people I loved ravaged and taken away by treacherous illness. I began to view my blessings with new gratitude. My restlessness subsided and I longed to cling to the ones I loved, to my home.

But home was not without its own changes. Lillian had enjoyed her one year of college, then promptly married and moved out. Gladys refused college to follow suit. And no one had been able to talk Jim out of enlisting in the army. Most likely, he had tired of farm work and wanted to see some of the world, like I had. But Papa made the best of changed circumstances, the vacated rooms prompting him to turn our spacious home into a boarding house. A move that had a profound impact on my life.

By the time the pandemic subsided in 1920, I was completely content back at home in the mountains. A young graduate from Emory and Henry College had come to teach mathematics at the local high school the year before. Blaine Chester White, or "just B.C.," whom I'd met at the Hermesian reception years before, took a room in Papa's boarding house. We picked right up with our easy banter, and soon decided to chat with each other for the rest of our lives. Along came a son, James Franklin—named for both our grandfathers—whom everyone affectionately calls "Jimmy Frank."

I took up the work of Mrs. Counts, another tragic casualty of the Spanish flu. I teach all piano students within Dickenson County, plus many from surrounding counties and even from next door in Kentucky. B.C. is now the principal of Clintwood High School, where I've instituted music into the curriculum. I play for church and even travel occasionally to perform recitals. I carry on everything Mrs. Counts and Professor Zeisberg taught me.

Now, back at the Martha, I have already crept inside Litchfield Hall to have a practice run on my old friend, the Steinway. I'll be performing at a farewell concert later tonight. I have played many a fine grand piano in the years since my very first master class here, but none ever made the thrilling impression on me that this one had that day. I recall all the fierce battles I've faced in that room. With myself as well as my rivals.

Varina won the piano scholarship. I had to watch her sail off to Peabody, a celebrated Martha graduate covered in accolades, making her professors proud. Saluda won the vocal scholarship, but I was delighted to join in her celebration. Once I was in Washington, we corresponded often about our respective adventures. The following year, she wrote with some news she knew would be particularly interesting to me. Varina surprised everyone that first semester when she married Charles in a lavish Christmas wedding, never to return to the conservatory. That summer, she gave birth to a "premature" baby, settling in Richmond for good.

At home in Clintwood with Mama, during one of our nighttime vigils by a sickbed, I had shared Granddad's story. Knowing my true heritage had completed my roots and grounded me. She agreed it was time to reveal our Cherokee heritage to the whole family, as Granddad had asked. I'd wondered what Papa's reaction would be, but he was only intrigued. Even a little hurt that Granddad or

Mama never told him. He loved my mother beyond measure; nothing could change that. We're proud of who we are, of our history. No longer hidden from anyone.

LONG BEFORE JONAH REACHED THE CHEROKEE SETTLEMENT IN North Carolina, bounty hunters had already come sniffing around. When he arrived dressed in my clothes, the tribe thought it wise to continue the ruse. They distrusted white man's law; they had been betrayed too often. Even when the telegram arrived announcing Jonah Schumacher's acquittal, they chose to disregard it and keep him hidden.

They also kept newspapers hidden, shielding him out of fear he'd be tempted to return. By the time he learned of the foreclosure, it was too late. Not that he had funds to prevent it anyway. His self-imposed isolation in the previous few years had resulted in a severely dwindled income, his grief leaving him powerless to care. The Stonewall fence repair work had given him hope to set his finances right, but then . . .

He was still dressed as a squaw when Doc Gilmer finally traveled to the settlement looking for him in the fall of 1916. When Jonah laid eyes on Doc—finally someone he could trust—he burst from a clutch of women to greet him in a joyous reunion. Doc told him I'd orchestrated the confession that made him a free man. He then asked Doc to bring him to Abingdon, but in secret. Only two forces pulled him back: me and the graves of his family.

Doc inquired after me at the Martha, but they would only say that I'd gone north, pursuing a golden opportunity to expand my musical ambitions. Jonah refused to let Doc try to find me. "You were so young, full of talent and potential, and then you had a chance to realize your dream. You made sacrifices to give me my life. I wanted to do that for you."

Jonah visited his family graves and took cultivars from their blueberry bushes. He planted them in the soil of his new home in North Carolina, joining them with the new family he had found there. The Cherokee way of life brought him comfort, especially once again becoming fluent in the language of his early childhood. It was a rediscovery that took him on an unexpected turn in his journey.

When America joined in the Great War in the spring of 1917, Jonah enlisted in the military. His infantry regiment was sent to aid British troops, where eventually he provided invaluable service as a code talker. When it was discovered that Germans were intercepting telephone communications of the Allied forces, he and other Cherokee soldiers sent and received messages in their native language, which completely foiled the enemy. I smiled to hear the pride in his voice as he told this story.

After the war, he returned to North Carolina and his work as a blacksmith. Still committed to creating practical pieces with beauty. He also married, and now has two young daughters.

"I thought I'd never set foot in Abingdon again. But I wanted to see you, at least once again. And give you this."

Jonah takes my hand and covers my open palm with his. When he removes it, there balanced in the center of my hand is the tiny cedar horse.

I TELL JONAH THE STORY GRANDDAD TOLD ME THE DAY HE'D come to Abingdon for Copper and Xander. Did it have any bearing on what we'd shared? Or had we simply been two souls, lost in our respective darkness, taking comfort in what the other had to give?

We agree that it doesn't matter.

I had ventured out, away from the nest, but eventually circled back home. Jonah's journey, far more complex and riddled with challenges, had also circled him back to his place of origin. His home. Our lives had intersected for a bare moment and were made richer for it. Now we've found each other again, if only for another brief moment.

I turn the little horse in my hands, reflecting on its journey and where else it has yet to travel.

From our seat on the bench, we gaze at the sights surrounding us. The grassy lawn, the pine grove, the majestic Martha. Where this odyssey began, and now was ending. Or moving on to newer chapters. If we dare to open more doors. In due time, we'll know.

Author Notes

The Martha Odyssey is a work of fiction. The inspiration for its protagonist was my grandmother, Beatrice Earle Damron, who graduated from Martha Washington College in 1916 with a degree in piano. The faculty named in the novel were actual faculty at Martha Washington College during the 1915-1916 academic year. With the exception of soprano Franceska Kaspar Lawson and her concert program at the college, all other characters are fictional and the story is all my invention. I incorporated many aspects of local history and legend into the novel, although I have taken liberties with certain details and dates in order to accommodate the fictional narrative.

Acknowledgments

My research for this novel was informed by many books, including *Three Quarters of a Century at Martha Washington College*, by Claude Davis Curtis (1928); *History of Southwest Virginia, 1746-1786; Washington County, 1777-1870*, by Lewis Preston Summers (1903); *History, Myths, and Sacred Formulas of the Cherokees*, by James Mooney (1912). Also, *The Eastern Band of Cherokees 1819-1900*, by John R. Finger (1984), and *Cherokee Americans, The Eastern Band of Cherokees in the Twentieth Century*, by John R. Finger (1991); *Legends, Stories and Ghostly Tales of Abingdon and Washington County, Virginia*, by Donna Akers Warmuth (2005); *Forgotten Tales from Abingdon, Virginia and Holston River Valley*, by Donna G. Akers (2012); *Meet Virginia's Baby: A Pictorial History of Dickenson County, Virginia, from Its Formation in 1880 to 1955*, by Elihu Jasper Sutherland (1955); and *In the Company of Educated Women*, by Barbara Miller Solomon (1985). I am also indebted to the wonderful Historical Society of Washington County, Virginia, for their extensive collection of newspaper archives, recorded lectures, college yearbooks, and maps.

To capture details of Beatrice's life and immediate world at the college I drew upon my grandmother's personal diary, *My Senior Year*, a journal with college photographs in which she meticulously recorded activities and collected memories from classmates during her final year at the school. I also studied the college yearbook, *The Cameo* 1915-1916, in which I found extensive narratives written by the students.

My research was further advanced by scholarly journal articles: *A Note on Cherokee Theological Concepts*, by Alan Kilpatrick in American Indian Quarterly (Summer 1995); *Kill the Indian,*

Save the Man, by Jane Yu, Pennsylvania Center for the Book (Spring 2009); *Going to Water: A Cherokee Ritual in its Contemporary Context*, by Barbara Reimensnyder Duncan, Journal of the Appalachian Studies Association (1993); *Red: Racism and the American Indian*, by Bethany Berger, Faculty Articles and Papers, University of Connecticut (2009); *A Sketch of the Early History of Southwestern Virginia*, by Ralph M. Brown, William and Mary Quarterly, (October 1937).

I was also able to tread the very halls and grounds Beatrice walked as a student. The college campus still thrives today as The Martha Washington Inn & Spa.

Many helpful souls were willing to share their expertise with me, playing a role in bringing this novel to life. I offer my deepest gratitude:

To my better half, William Gable, for his first-hand knowledge of artistic blacksmithing, as well as his undying moral and literary support during this journey.

To my brother, Scott White, for details of our family history.

To John Gifford for his extensive expert advice on legal matters included in the storyline. Any missteps that may have worked their way into the narrative are my own.

To Rana Duncan and Cindy Honeycutt, fabulous and extremely beneficial first readers.

To Rhonda Kindig for her Greek translations as well as encouragement.

To Skye Lloyd for her diligent work as my editor.

To my publishing team at Luminare Press—Patricia Marshall, Kim Harper-Kennedy, Kristen Brack, Rosemary Camozzi, Sallie Vandagrift, and Caitlin McCrum—for helping me bring my story into the world.

For guiding me through my own journey in music, I offer many thanks to my former piano instructors: Virginia Counts, C.C. Loomis, and Kenneth Huber.

BONNY GABLE's love of storytelling is fueled by her career as a college theater professor, a performer and a playwright. She is an arts journalist and a member of Dramatists Guild of America. She lives in historic Abingdon, Virginia, with her husband and two Burmese cats, Nellie Bly and Murphy Brown.

WWW.BONNYGABLE.COM

www.ingramcontent.com/pod-product-compliance
Lightning Source LLC
LaVergne TN
LVHW041656060526
838201LV00043B/453